MARS ONE

CHARLOTTE ROBINSON

bantam

TRANSWORLD PUBLISHERS

UK | USA | Canada | Ireland | Australia
India | New Zealand | South Africa

Transworld is part of the Penguin Random House group of companies
whose addresses can be found at global.penguinrandomhouse.com.

Penguin Random House UK, One Embassy Gardens, 8 Viaduct Gardens, London SW11 7BW

penguin.co.uk

First published in Great Britain in 2026 by Bantam
an imprint of Transworld Publishers

001

Copyright © Charlotte Robinson 2026

The moral right of the author has been asserted.

This book is a work of fiction and, except in the case of historical fact, any
resemblance to actual persons, living or dead, is purely coincidental.

Every effort has been made to obtain the necessary permissions with
reference to copyright material, both illustrative and quoted. We apologize
for any omissions in this respect and will be pleased to make the
appropriate acknowledgements in any future edition.

Penguin Random House values and supports copyright.
Copyright fuels creativity, encourages diverse voices, promotes freedom
of expression and supports a vibrant culture. Thank you for purchasing
an authorized edition of this book and for respecting intellectual property
laws by not reproducing, scanning or distributing any part of it by any
means without permission. You are supporting authors and enabling
Penguin Random House to continue to publish books for everyone.
No part of this book may be used or reproduced in any manner for the
purpose of training artificial intelligence technologies or systems. In accordance
with Article 4(3) of the DSM Directive 2019/790, Penguin Random House
expressly reserves this work from the text and data mining exception.

Typeset in 12/15.5pt Sabon MT Pro by Falcon Oast Graphic Art Ltd.
Printed and bound in Great Britain by Clays Ltd, Elcograf S.p.A.

The authorized representative in the EEA is Penguin Random House
Ireland, Morrison Chambers, 32 Nassau Street, Dublin D02 YH68

A CIP catalogue record for this book is available from the British Library.

ISBNs:
9780857507341 (cased)
9780857507358 (tpb)

MARS ONE

To my mum, my dad, and James.
They always believed.

A PALE BLUE SPHERE HANGS IN THE DARKNESS. A SMALL blip on an infinite canvas of black. If you really concentrate, you can just about make out the shapes of the continents, the swirl of an atmosphere, but no indication of life.

A white-gloved hand reaches out and places the blue dot between its chunky thumb and index – a whole world between its fingers. Alyssa smirks. The crew have been doing this trick for weeks, every time they do a spacewalk, like a bunch of tourists by the Washington Monument. Of course, the first few times, they had to use both arms. But this is the first time it can be encompassed by just one hand.

'All right, Rutherford, enough with the photo ops, you've got maintenance to run,' Alyssa mumbles to herself.

As if he heard her, the hand drifts off-screen and Rutherford's helmet camera pans across to the first set of guide rails outside the airlock. One inch at a time, he makes his way across the bulk of the spaceship, humming tunelessly as he goes. There's no way he heard her. Even if Alyssa had been pressing her communication button, it would have taken sixty-seven seconds for her voice to reach him. Radio signals take a while to travel nearly twenty million kilometres.

Alyssa leans away from her console and takes a swig of Coke as Mission Control chirrups around her. A huge screen on the wall displays Rutherford's point of view, along with a data feed of the ship's velocity, distance, pitch, roll and yaw.

It's day forty-two of the first crewed mission to Mars, and Alyssa Wright is bored.

Of course, it's a privilege to be a part of the greatest exploration mission humanity has ever undertaken. Of course, she takes her job as Capsule Communicator very seriously. Of course, she would do anything for the welfare and safety of the crew. But FUCK, she wishes it were her clambering over the *Mayflower* right now. Instead, she's a shadow on the ground, watching her comrades soar.

'EVA 1 to Control,' Rutherford's steady voice rings out, from sixty-seven seconds ago. 'I'm moving out towards the first array of panels now. First look, everything's as expected. And the view is pretty awesome, too.'

Alyssa clicks her mic on.

'Copy that, EVA 1. Proceed. And stop rubbing it in.' She glances at the monitors. Rutherford's heart rate is climbing, but that's to be expected; spacewalking is like rock climbing and weightlifting all at once, while the most uncomfortable outfit ever designed by humanity rubs your skin raw. In return, though, Rutherford gets the bragging rights for the deepest spacewalk ever achieved. For now, at least. The one next week will be even further away from Mother Earth, and they are only a quarter of the way to Mars.

'Hey, Control.' Alyssa's attention snaps back to the screen. He's breaking comms protocol. Something must be wrong. She glances up at the clock, so painfully aware that whatever the problem is, it has already happened.

'Can you have a word with welfare when we're done?' Rutherford continues. 'They keep updating the goddamn video library and putting the final episodes of *Game of Thrones* at the top of the home screen, so I keep seeing spoilers. It's really grinding my gears.'

Others chuckle around her and she suppresses a smile as she clicks the comms mic on again.

'Serves you right for being about fifteen years behind everyone else, Sam. But yes, I'll speak to them. And quit talking about your viewing habits, you know this whole thing is live on NASA's streams.'

The calm sounds of Mission Control tick along as Alyssa waits for Rutherford's reply. The distance the *Mayflower* has travelled rolling up, and up, and up.

Two minutes and sixteen seconds later, his reply crackles through the room.

'Even spacemen need to be entertained, Control.'

Alyssa is about to click her mic back on to reply when something silently shoots across the back of the screen. Almost instantly, warnings and alarms start sounding within Control.

'Woah!' cries Sam, his helmet jerking around to face a part of the ship that was previously off-screen. Debris is flying everywhere.

'Control! What's going on?'

But this all happened over a minute ago. Control are clueless.

Alyssa looks on in horror as a small plastic pouch floats across the screen. It's just one of thousands of shapes flying around above Sam, but she can't take her eyes off it. She can barely hear the raised voices of her colleagues around her as they try to get a grip on the situation.

'*Mayflower*, this is EVA 1.' Rutherford tries his intercom, his voice betraying his desperation to speak to his crewmates inside the ship. 'Temi, Dave, what's going on? Are you OK?'

It's chilli sauce. It's a packet of chilli sauce. Spinning. Over and over. Alyssa recognizes the branding. It's a crew favourite. Microgravity gives you a permanent head-cold, and spicy food is pretty much the only thing you can taste after a while, so there are hundreds of chilli sauce sachets stored on the *Mayflower* – enough for a three-hundred-day mission – all packed away in the crew's communal hub. *Inside* the communal hub. So what's it doing floating out in the vacuum of space?

'Hello? Anyone?' There's real panic in Sam's voice now and Alyssa feels her training kick in.

'I'm here. Listen to me.' She glances over to another console, where her colleagues are muttering to each other and furiously tapping at keys. One of them gives her a brief shake of the head, and her fists clench.

'You need to get back to the airlock. You hear me? We need to get you back inside.'

The silence is excruciating. As each second clicks by, Alyssa and her colleagues watch Sam turn this way and that, trying to see the origin of the debris.

He looks so alone.

The alarms inside Control have been silenced now, but the room is still bathed in an ominous red as warning lights continue to pulse.

Alyssa can tell the instant her message reaches him. His head snaps and he turns towards the direction of the airlock.

'What's going on with the others?'

Alyssa closes her eyes and pinches her nose. She just hopes that by the time her response reaches him, they've figured this out.

'We're doing everything we can, Sam. There's been a breach. The rest of the crew are probably sealed off and going through the boldface, OK? Let's not give them more to worry about. Let's get you back inside.'

Thankfully, before her message has finished hurtling across the solar system, Sam turns away from the stream of debris and begins to make his way back the way he came, doing breathing exercises to reduce his oxygen consumption rate. He's doing everything by the book. Breathing in. Breathing out.

'That's great,' Alyssa encourages over the comms. 'Your heart rate is decreasing. Great job. Oxygen supply at seventy-five per cent, you've got plenty of time.'

Despite the chasm of time and space between them, Alyssa talks steadily, counting down the distance to the airlock, her eyes flitting between Sam's helmet cam and the rest of her team. But their expressions remain grim.

Frank, the chief of the flight control division, appears behind her. He places his hand on her shoulder and she clicks off her mic, keeping her eyes trained on Sam's slow progress. But of course, this is all in the past. Sam may well be at the airlock by now.

Frank's voice is soft as he leans down to her ear. 'Catastrophic failure of the ship's hull. Multiple ruptures. Complete loss of pressure within the communal hub and on the flight deck.'

Alyssa can barely bring herself to ask, but she must. 'And the crew?'

Hand over hand, Sam continues onwards. Breathing in. Breathing out.

'He's the only one left.'

Breathing in. Breathing out.

PART ONE

FOUR YEARS LATER

MARS ONE CREW TO BE ANNOUNCED

USA Today
By Samantha Stuart
January 3 2031

In two days' time, the world will know the names of the astronauts who will be launched into space as part of the most ambitious and controversial expedition in human history.

The Mars One project confirmed today that their first episode will air 21:00 EST this Sunday, January 5 in the USA, with simultaneous broadcasts around the globe.

A privatized one-way colonization mission to Mars, Mars One is the brainchild of Finnish billionaire Lars Anders, who first announced his ambitions to put people on the red planet twenty years ago.

Since its founding, both the Mars One mission and Anders himself have endured criticism from space agencies, politicians and activists around the world, with many questioning the safety of the project and some parties even pressing legal charges against the company. But what is perhaps the most contentious issue surrounding the mission is that of its funding, which has been raised, in part, through the creation of a reality television series that will document every moment of the lives of the six as-yet-unnamed astronauts onboard. The first episode of *Mars One* has been billed as a chance to 'meet the brave pioneers' who will be the first human beings to set foot on Mars, in just over six months' time.

The timing of this mission has also come under scrutiny, following on from the four-year anniversary of the *Mayflower* disaster. NASA's first crewed expedition to Mars, the Mayflower Mission, ended tragically when the ship suffered a catastrophic failure while Mission Specialist Sam Rutherford was conducting an EVA (Extravehicular Activity). All five astronauts inside the *Mayflower* were killed instantly when a cluster of micro-meteoroids ruptured the ship's hull, and Mission Specialist Rutherford was confirmed dead just three minutes later as he tried to re-enter the *Mayflower*'s airlock. It remains the worst accident in the history of the American space program.

Regardless of the political tensions surrounding their mission, let us hope that Mars One has learned from NASA's mistakes.

Jia

I DON'T HAVE TIME FOR THIS.

Another roadblock for another pointless climate protest. You'd think that they'd have given up by now. Hong Kong is free no longer. Even with parts of the city underwater and the rest of the world burning, you can't present your political opinions on the streets – those days are long gone. They disappeared almost as soon as my parents arrived in this city. Everyone knows the situation now. Two girls from my first-year accountancy class went to a democracy protest in our first semester. They never came back.

Mom freaked out, terrified that I'd throw my life away on activism, just like them. As if I would—

I jump back as a police truck pulls up in front of me. Officers swarm down the street to my right. I swerve left, head down, eyes low.

I really don't have time for this.

At least I got my paper in on time. Three minutes before the deadline. And now, I'm going to be late getting home, which means I'll be late getting to work, which means I'll be late seeing Mom. I might even miss visiting hours. It's always tight on a Friday.

Kai better have picked up my uniform from the laundromat. One job. That's all I've asked of him. Otherwise I'll have to wear yesterday's coffee-stained shirt.

Smack.

Next second, I'm down on the floor. My right knee feels like it's about to explode and my palms burn. I look up just in time to see feet running away, police storming after them. I cower, terrified they'll trample me, but they part around me at the last moment.

Gasping, I push myself back up. Anyone else would be embarrassed, but I'm clumsy. I'm used to falling over, and I'm also used to people laughing at the fat girl on the floor.

I assess the damage with a grimace. My tights are ripped. The contents of my purse – lip balm, ID, tissues, face masks – are strewn on the ground. As is an abandoned sign. As I crouch down to scrabble for my belongings, it stares up at me – a picture of Earth on fire, and a red planet crossed out with the words: THERE IS NO PLANET B. END MARS ONE MISSION.

These people. Terra Revolution, they call themselves. So concerned with the planet, yet they'll plough straight through a person in the blink of an eye.

I feel the heat of someone's gaze on me, and glance around. Another group of police has just arrived and some of their eyes are flitting between me and the sign. Heart pounding, I kick it in dismissal and vaguely shake my head, keeping my eyeline squarely on the sidewalk as I hurry off down the street, dreading the feeling of a hand on my shoulder.

Nothing to do with me, I think. *This is not my fight.*

As predicted, I get home late. My manager will insist I stay longer to make up the time.

The latch on the front door of our building is still broken, but the lift is working again, at least. I type another message to the super as I bounce on my heels on the ride up.

Kai better have grabbed my uniform. I'll be so angry if he's been locked into some coding trance the whole afternoon and not moved. No real job, hardly makes the rent – the least he can do is run some errands. His computers could pay for several months of Mom's fees, maybe even a whole year of our food and energy bills, too. I could do what other girls in my class do: sit and *drink* coffee all day long instead of serving it.

'Kai?' I yell, as I barrel through the door, head straight for the kettle and pull out some instant noodles. No answer, but that's not unusual. I glance around, and my heart sinks. The place is incredibly tidy – just how he likes it when he goes into one of his deep dives.

'Kai! Did you get my uniform? I need to leave in five minutes.'

As I wait for the kettle, I slip into my room. My filthy uniform from yesterday is right there on the bed. And there's no fresh laundry next to it. Of course he forgot. I snatch up the stained top.

'Kai!' I shout, tearing down the hall to where the door to his room stands ajar. 'What the hell? I asked you to do one thing for me and—'

All the air escapes me as I push his door open.

The place has been turned upside down. Glass smashed, his mattress thrown against the wall. His computers are all gone.

And there on the desk is a smear of red. The unmistakable shine of blood.

I scream, then scream louder as a ginger streak zooms out from under the bed and out through the door.

It's Orion. Kai's stupid cat.

I turn and rush after him.

And now I see it: specks of blood, leading out of Kai's room and to the front door.

'Orion!' I cry as the cat pelts towards the living room, his paws stained red.

Hissing and wailing, he jumps up at the window that leads out onto the fire escape. It's never open – this city is too polluted. He claws at it. Unable to get out, he throws himself onto the kitchen worktop. I scream more as noodles and cups and bowls go flying.

I have to stop him. I have to find Kai.

What the fuck is happening?

I slip past Orion and yank open the window. I shrink back as the acrid air hits me and before I can even think, Orion is out of there, his tail disappearing into the fading light.

I feel a twinge of alarm, but it quickly subsides. He's Kai's cat, not mine. I never wanted him. And I've got bigger problems right now.

I run back to Kai's room, muttering his name over and over. I fumble for my phone and dial his number. It goes straight to voicemail. I try again. And again. Nothing.

I run to the front door, which I only now realize had been unlocked when I came in. When he's coding, Kai always locks everything. He has his headphones on, doesn't want to be disturbed.

I shuffle down the outer hall, calling his name, not sure what I'm looking for. Is that blood, by the stairwell? Did he take the stairs?

'What's going on?' someone barks. I don't know who. I don't care. I look down. Why do I still have my stained work uniform in my hand? I turn back to our apartment as I dial and press my phone to my ear.

'999. What's your emergency?' I peer into Kai's room again. His absence weighs down the air like lead. The metal tang of his blood stings my nostrils – or am I imagining it? I feel sick.

'Hello?'

'Sorry. Yes. Police.' The voice that comes out of me doesn't sound like my own. It's like I'm a million miles away. So small. So detached from the nightmare in front of me. 'My brother. He's missing.'

Alyssa

'SO.' THE JOURNALIST SITS FORWARD IN HER CHAIR, SMILING at me innocently. 'How does it feel, as a female astronaut, to be commander of such a groundbreaking mission?'

The first thing I want to say is that I'm not an astronaut. I know the press release introduces me as a former NASA astronaut who was then headhunted by Mars One blah blah blah. All that is true except for the excruciating, soul-incinerating detail that I have never flown in space. These days, NASA call you an astronaut as soon as you're picked out of the application pool, but if you're like me and have a military background, you only get that badge when you fly higher than fifty miles above this Godforsaken planet. And I haven't done that yet.

I was going to, though.

I was on my way.

Before all this, I was biding my time, playing the NASA game. Smiling, waving, kissing babies – well, kissing ass. All the while fighting the hot-headedness my father always hated.

I wasn't good at it, but I was getting there. I even volunteered to run CAPCOM on the mission I'd been passed over for, hoping it would push me even a little closer to that dream assignment.

Until that day.

Because the reality is, the *Mayflower* destroyed more than six people's lives when it depressurized twenty million kilometres from Earth. It broke me in more ways than I could imagine. And it annihilated any chances I had of reaching space.

I know. I know that sounds callous, but everyone who has ever signed up to be an astronaut at NASA is unified by one thing: we are all selfish overachievers who want nothing more than to get into space as quickly as possible. Of course, that is not what I said when I first sat down for my psych assessment all those years ago. But it's true. And I have to live with that.

I have to live with a lot of things . . .

I didn't realize just how much of a selfish asshole I am until the memorial service. As we placed wreaths for our fellow astronauts, I saw the years clicking by in my mind and realized that even in the most optimistic scenario, with operations still shut down, it would be many years before any of the pre-scheduled missions would possibly fly. I wasn't old – at thirty-one, I was one of the youngest mission specialists in the program – but despite my best efforts, I wasn't assigned to anything yet. And another shot at Mars? That would be out of the question.

So I was devastated. Devastated at the loss of six lives, astounded that I had witnessed it, and overwhelmed with grief for my own career. I went to bed that night cursing whatever it was that had failed the *Mayflower* and woke the next morning bitterly ashamed of what my ambition had made me become.

Ambition. My mom was always told it's such a dirty word for a woman. And yet I have tonnes of it. I have so much of the damn thing I don't know what to do with it. So, in the aftermath of the *Mayflower* disaster, as the world mourned and questioned whether the cost of spaceflight – both financial and human – was really worth it, as Congress began to defund the space program and presidential commissions tore the agency to shreds, I finally answered an email that had been lingering in my personal inbox: *I'm interested. When can we meet?*

No, I'm not an astronaut yet. But I'm going to be.

I can't say any of that to this journo, though. So instead, I simply say: 'I'm not an astronaut yet. I have a lot to be getting on with, so if we could move this along, that would be great.'

*

Anders pauses the clip on his screen after that and laughs at me for a long time. I sit there and take it in dignified silence. His office is minimalist and softly lit. Through the window, the light is fading as the sun sets. The plains of Kazakhstan stretch ever onwards and I'm reminded how far away from home we all are. Eventually, his laughter peters out.

'You know, I take some pride in the fact that I'm the one who brought out this side in you, Wright. Before me, you really were a walking, talking piece of NASA merchandise.'

'Thank you for rescuing me,' I retort.

'You're welcome.' He grins. 'But I think you shouldn't be so honest when you're next interviewed. They can barely use any of the footage they shot with you. But then again, you probably knew that all along.'

I scowl at him. It had gone wrong from the start. From the model space shuttle they placed on my desk to the pile of books I would never read – one was an undergraduate introduction to astrophysics, for God's sake – to a photo of my family, it felt like I was walking onto a television set rather than into my own office.

'Fine. I'll do it again, but they can't make my office look like a pre-school teacher's classroom this time. And no questions about my family.'

Anders glances down at the piece of rock he's holding, smooth and shiny from years of being tossed up and down in his heavy hands. It's a moon rock, a gift from his father many years ago.

'Fine, but you wear your M1 uniform,' he says, gesturing to the screen. 'You look like a hobo.'

I follow his eyes to the screen. I'm in my Mars One T-shirt, but the logo is covered by an old NASA sweatshirt from my training class, emblazoned with a cockroach. All the rookies who passed out of Johnson Space Center in 2024 had one. They affectionately nicknamed our class the Roaches, for our ability to survive the budget cuts that year – although the sweatshirt has seen better days. My cartoon roach has a big old oil stain on it.

I'm wearing it now, in fact. I zip it up with pride and shove my hands in its well-worn pockets.

'Sure,' I say through gritted teeth.

Anders observes me thoughtfully, setting his moon rock down on the table, like a judge's gavel.

'Good.' Case closed. He stretches and brushes his hands through his short blonde hair. He's in pretty good shape for a man in middle age. Some of the crew joke that it's because he wants to pass the physical for one of the later missions. But I know Lars Anders: so long as he has a colony on Mars to support, he won't ever leave this planet.

I stand up. 'Are you done with me?'

He appraises me. 'Why are you here, Wright?'

My forehead creases into a frown. 'Because you asked to speak to me.'

'Come on.' He pushes away from his desk and moves towards me. 'You know what I mean. Your crew fly in tomorrow, but why are you here tonight?'

I hate it when he does this: examines me like I'm some anomaly. A curiosity from another world. Like that damn rock.

'Two weeks out from a one-way mission, about to be quarantined, why are you here? Don't you have anywhere else in the world to be? Anyone else to be with?'

I look him straight in the eye and tell him what he already knows: 'No.'

He gives a half-hearted laugh and shakes his head. 'OK.' He opens the door and ushers me out, just as his beleaguered assistant, Gwynne, enters with a ream of paperwork and smiles at me.

'Well, fuck off, then. Enjoy your last night of freedom.'

I swing past my office – now thankfully back to its original state – to pick up some reports. The whole complex is eerily quiet. The calm before the storm.

There are, however, many people still working. Thankfully,

Kajal in Legal is one of them. I find her at her desk, glasses on and surrounded by paperwork and sticky notes.

'Hello,' she says, in her crisp British accent, eyes fixed on her screen.

'Hey.' I sit down in one of the vacant chairs next to her. 'Here to pick up my last will and testament.'

She laughs and finally looks at me. I smile at her.

'You don't have to look so happy about it.' She turns and rifles through her filing drawers. Out comes a brown envelope bearing my name.

'There's also your Power of Attorney for you to sign. You'll need a witness. And if there's anything you want to change, let me know. There's still time.'

I take the envelope and slot it into my bag. 'I won't need to change anything. Thank you.'

'You're more than welcome.' She looks tired. Her glasses have left a mark on the bridge of her nose, and she has three coffee mugs on her desk. She cocks her head to the side. 'Look, do you want to grab a drink? I don't have to get back for Neha for a bit, she's on a playdate.' But instantly I can tell she wishes she hadn't said anything, because she knows what's about to come.

'Kajal, I'm sorry, I'd—'

'You'd love to, but you have shit-tonnes to do,' she finishes for me, her expression annoyingly sympathetic. 'You don't have to be alone, you know.'

'I know.' We both sit in silence for a moment.

I get up and gesture at her brimming desk. 'Thanks. For everything.'

'I'll see you tomorrow.'

I walk away and kick myself. After everything Kajal has done for me, all I give her is cynicism and insincerity. Then I have a thought, the perfect way to show my appreciation. I turn back.

'You can tell Neha she has a quarter of a pound.'

'Huh?'

'My PPK.' She looks blankly at me. 'My personal preference

kit. Neha can send something to Mars in it. But only if it weighs less than a quarter of a pound!'

Kajal stands up, stunned. 'Really?'

'Why the hell not?'

Back at the sparse accommodation block we've appropriated from the former Russian Space Federation, I crack open a full-fat Coke and take out my will. I grab a pen and flick to the tabs that show me where to sign, before remembering I need a witness. I mutter a curse.

I'll have to ask one of the team tomorrow.

Tomorrow.

I turn my attention to the other paperwork I've brought with me. It's the reams of notes I've made over the course of four years. I could be reading simulation schedules, checklists, weather reports. But by now, I know everything. The boldface – the important bits of the manuals – is etched on the very inside of my skull. That stuff is easy. It's the human stuff I need to work on. Up there, my crew will be a surrogate for the whole of humanity. I'm about to spend the rest of my life with these five people. And how long that life lasts depends on all of us working together as one team. So, like a serial killer, I've written up everything I've learned about them during our years of training, from their favourite films to their family's medical histories. Their darkest fears, their wildest dreams, and the little glimpses of vulnerability I've seen in the quietest of moments. Anything that will help me understand and know them like I understand and know the machine that's going to be launching us across the solar system.

As I'm starting, I glance out of my grubby window at the glimmer of the Milky Way above the horizon, the courtyard out front bathed in starlight. An idea hits me.

I strip my bed down to the bare mattress and chuck the files onto it, then start to roll it up. It's cheap and thin, and rolls easily. People around here have got better things to spend time and money on than our bedding. I drag my giant cigar of a mattress out of my room and into the deathly quiet corridor. Before I lock up, I grab some extra provisions, loading up my sweatshirt pockets.

I haul the mattress and its contents up the stairwell and push out onto the roof, where the stars are astoundingly bright. I drag everything into a clear area, roll out the mattress, scoop up my files and finally sit down. It's a warm night; a dry breeze blows across my face, fluttering the corners of my papers. From several miles away where our launchpad glows under floodlights comes the low hum of generators and the faint clanking of metalwork. Our rocket and spacecraft aren't up there yet, but preparations are well underway for launch in just over a couple of weeks' time. My pulse quickens at the thought of it. I can almost hear the hiss of the propellant coolant, the beeping of a countdown clock.

But not yet. Not just yet.

I pull my gaze away from the launchpad and lie back. There's a reason why the Soviet Union claimed this land from Kazakhstan seventy years ago for their space agency. Midway between the equator and the North Pole, surrounded by miles of plains, with barely any human settlements nearby, it's the perfect gateway to the cosmos. All of which is stretched out above me. Towards the western horizon, Saturn is one of the brightest bodies in the sky. And to the south, just above Gagarin's Start – the very first place a human being left the planet – waiting ever so patiently, is Mars herself.

After a while, I sit up on my elbows and open my next can of Coke, the cool droplets of condensation dripping down my hand. The sound of the ring pull clicking and hissing open echoes across the roof. I'm going to miss Coke. After a gulp, I open up a packet of Reese's Pieces and pop one into my mouth. I'll miss them, too. Picking up my files, I turn onto my front, like a beachgoer trying to bronze their back.

Right now, in the dark of night, the light of five thousand suns is just enough to read by.

Jia

THE POLICE DUST FOR PRINTS AND TAKE PICTURES. TO them it's routine, mundane. They don't seem to understand that it's anything but for me. I hover over them, telling them what Kai had been wearing that morning, who his friends are, who they should check in with, and they just roll their eyes.

They tell me they can't rule out him just leaving, as there was no sign of a break-in, there's no other prints and the blood was 'minimal'. It's madness. My brother is odd, infuriating, selfish, but he would never leave like this. I tell them this over and over again. The block's front-door CCTV shows nothing, and the service entrance around the back hasn't had coverage for ages.

I call into work. I don't call Mom. Or college. I'm not due in class over the weekend and there's no point with Mom until I know more.

I stay home.

Next day, four new officers arrive. They're not in uniform, but they carry ID and badges and hold themselves in a completely different way. These men don't look at me dismissively; they nod and seem sympathetic. As soon as they enter the apartment, they are all over it. They ask me to stay on the couch as they search through everything, even my room. I wince, picturing them wrinkling their noses at my dirty underwear on the floor, my week-old cups of tea. One officer asks me to run through everything again, apologizing for the inconvenience, explaining that they believe me and they're going to do everything they can to help find Kai.

Even though I've done nothing wrong, my hands sweat. I try to tell them everything I can, but unease creeps through me. I know who these men are: National Security officers. My heart palpitates as they start to pack things into brown boxes and envelopes. They're practically clearing out Kai's room. Then they move to my room. They take my laptop. I ask why, but the officers just calmly say it's 'potential evidence'. It seems they're taking everything that's digital. Anything at all that has data on it. Kai's enormous DVD collection is scooped up and packed away. His games console too.

'Anything that is not useful to the investigation will be returned,' they say.

Why don't I believe them?

Then they run through our family history. When did we leave mainland China? When did our father die? Where is our mother now? My school, my studies. They even ask about the cat. I explain that he hasn't come back since I realized Kai was missing and the officer seems satisfied.

I think of Kai's coding and how he was always so private. Suddenly I don't feel like I know him. What the hell has he been doing in that room all those years?

But strangely, that is the one question the officers never seem to ask.

After many hours, they leave, but not before telling me that that I must stay home for the foreseeable future. Just in case Kai returns or anything else happens that might help the investigation. I'm told to call them if anything comes to mind or seems unusual. Otherwise, they'll be in touch.

As soon as they're gone, I crumble. I'm a mess – shaking, weeping. I move through the silent apartment. Everything is clean now. His room is almost empty, the blood gone. Even my room has been tidied, my soiled clothes placed in the overflowing laundry bin. My bed made.

I try his phone once more. Still not even a dial tone.

Something shifts in the other room.

My stomach drops and I throw myself out into the hall, expecting to see Kai making himself a coffee in the kitchen, looking at me with a baffled expression and asking why I'm in such a state.

'Dì dì?'

But Kai isn't there. Instead, standing frozen on the kitchen counter, is Orion. He looks at me, his big green eyes wide. His encrusted food bowl is in the sink. That's clearly what he was after.

I didn't realize I'd left the window open this entire time.

We stare at each other, both of us stuck to the spot. His ginger fur is ruffled, but other than that he looks fine.

He blinks at me and I feel a sudden rush of anger. This stupid thing witnessed whatever happened and can't tell me what he saw. Useless. Pathetic. This damn cat that was the only thing that Kai ever cared about. Not me. Not Mom. Just his computers and this waste-of-space cat.

Before I know it, my slipper is in my hand and I'm launching it at Orion.

It misses, but sends him flying back out the window again without a backwards glance.

Good riddance, I think.

But then I realize I'm alone again.

I head back to my room and crawl into bed.

A knock on the door breaks through my sleep. It's loud. Insistent. Like they've been going for some time.

I get up quickly, pulse racing. It could be the police. They could have news.

But it's just a delivery guy.

'Li Jia?'

I nod, and he thrusts a small package into my hands, before heading back down the hall.

I shut the door, a little dazed, trying to remember what I ordered. Books for school?

Then I jump out of my skin as something brushes up against my legs.

Orion. Purring and making a *chirrup* sound at me. He looks up at me and slowly blinks, weaving in and out of my legs.

He must be hungry. I feel a wave of guilt. Kai would kill me.

I sigh, step over Orion and move to the kitchen. I find a bowl and some cat food, and shove it down on the floor. Orion is on it like a shot, purring as he wolfs down the chunks of meat.

I turn my attention back to the package. Just my name and address printed, no supplier. I throw myself down on the couch.

Inside is a solitary plain disc.

I turn the package over, double check everything. But there's no delivery note, no label.

I'm on the edge of the couch now. The disc is white on one side, shiny on the other. A CD? A DVD? Who uses those any more?

I look up at the empty TV console opposite me. Kai. He always said that if you love a film, you should buy it. The streamers will collapse one day, films will disappear, blah blah blah.

My pulse quickens and my eyes shift to the NS officer's card on the coffee table. This is definitely unusual. But what the hell do I say if I ring? Best to try it first, see if there's anything on it.

Orion appears, looking over the brim of the couch cushion at me, licking his lips. He jumps up onto the couch and sits next to me. After turning on the spot for a bit, he curls up. He's never done this before. He sits on Kai, sure, but he's always so skittish around me.

His presence feels strangely reassuring.

As the disc is sucked into the TV, I settle myself right on the edge of the couch. Orion eyes me half-heartedly.

At first, the screen is blank.

The player whirrs.

And then it's him. Kai. Smiling. In his room.

My breath catches in my throat.

'Heyyy jiě jie.' Orion's head snaps up at the sound of his master's voice. 'If you're watching this then I haven't checked into my online server in a couple of days, and that's triggered a delivery I organized a while back. Basically, something is fucked.'

He looks so happy. How can he look so happy?

'This is so crazy, like something out of a film. OK. So, you always say I never take anything seriously. Well, let's just say something's changed recently. I've started working on something new and . . . I've decided to take a few precautions, and this is one of them. So, if you're watching this, I'm gone, but I have a plan, and you have to trust me.' He leans into the screen conspiratorially.

'I know you're gonna want to know more, but I can't tell you in case someone else sees this.' His smile breaks a little, and I see a flicker of concern in his eyes, but then it's gone. 'God,' he laughs, 'I'm going to look like such an idiot if this is never needed.'

Somehow my hand has moved onto Orion's back. I can feel his warmth. His little heartbeat.

'Anyway, hopefully, I'm just lying low and I've been able to wipe my set-up myself.' I glance towards his bare room. 'But just in case the worst has happened, I need you to do some things for me. So watch *everything* on this disc very carefully and follow my instructions. First, I need you to destroy the hard drives of my computer. I took pictures of everything you need to get rid of. They're behind the toilet cistern. Get a drill and make lots of little holes in them. Even you can manage that.'

My snort makes Orion jump.

'Second, I need you to look after the cat for me, OK? I know you love him very much and he holds such precious memories for us both.'

I look down at Orion, snatching my hand away like he's a hot stove. He knows I hate the cat. What the hell is he—?

'And third, try not to worry. Like I said, I have a plan, and as long as you follow my instructions, everything will be fine. So relax! Watch a film. I've actually ripped one onto this disc, that I thought you should see. You know – the film I watched over and over for like five months after Dad? You said you hated it. But I think if you watch it again, you'll get it.'

'He's gone mad,' I whisper to no one.

'Anyway.' He picks up a pad of paper and reads from it. 'I have some friends who can help – I just need you to get a message to them, then get the hell away from it all. In the meantime, stay calm, destroy my hard drives, look after the cat, watch the film,' he winks as he puts his notepad down. 'And Jia, unless I say so . . . Don't. Talk. To. Anyone. Especially the police. Be careful who you trust, OK? And even then . . . well, just be smart. Which I know you are, if you try . . . And give Mom my love.'

And then he leans forward and the screen goes blank.

I sit for a while, staring. Orion sits too. Both of us waiting for my idiot brother to come back on and really tell us what the hell is happening.

But he doesn't.

So I scream and throw a pillow at the screen instead.

Alyssa

WHEN MY ALARM GOES OFF, MY BRAIN CLINGS TO THE LAST moments of REM, where I can still hear Sam Rutherford's breathing. In and out, in and out. Totally alone. A constellation of debris spinning about him . . .

As I jerk to consciousness, my heart races and I push down that sickening feeling of helplessness that has been creeping back into my dreams recently.

After a quick shower, I throw my training overalls on and dash to the cafeteria to gulp down some cereal. For the next two weeks I'm going to try and cram every kind of food in my mouth that is not possible in micro-g. Lumps of sugary goodness floating in milk is one of them.

Next is my interview reshoot. As soon as I'd said yes to Anders, it appeared in my schedule, squatting between the actually important things. Thankfully, when I arrive, they haven't messed with my office. The only thing that is still lurking is the family photo on my desk. I wait for one of the producers to come in before pointedly shutting it in one of my drawers. She doesn't say anything and we get down to business. I give them their soundbites and do the usual 'honoured and proud' spiel.

At the end of it all, the producer comes over to me, looking sincere. 'Thank you so much, Commander Wright, we know you're really busy and we appreciate the time you're giving us.'

'No problem,' I lie. I'm good at that. She physically relaxes and

I feel a stab of guilt – God, do these people think I'm a nightmare? Then I remember: they're making a television show in which the main thrill is going to be whether I live or die. And now I don't feel so guilty after all.

'We're going to have just enough time to edit this together for the launch tomorrow night.'

I frown, confused, then it hits me: *their* launch and *our* launch are very different things.

We've done most of our training over the last few months here in Baikonur, so my crew are familiar with the whole set-up. But now we have the press and TV crew to appease, as well as family. Once everyone arrives today, we're doing a tour of the facilities. It's useful to do a tour of the various departments as a group so that everyone working on the mission can remember that it's real human beings who will all die if they don't do their jobs well enough. Anders calls it a mortality march.

When I turn up at the airstrip, Anders is already there, in his uniform of a dark polo and jeans. He's in a passionate discussion with George Abbey, one of the executive producers and owners of Valdivian, our television overlords. Dressed in chinos and what looks like a very expensive designer linen shirt, he is the complete opposite of Anders. Their two personal assistants buzz around nervously.

'Wright!' Anders shouts, and I flinch. Gwynne grimaces at me as I approach. Abbey has headphones around his neck that he clearly thinks make him look important. A couple of his crew members stand around looking bored, cameras pointing to the ground.

'Commander,' Anders says. He's smiling, but lines of tension crater his brow. 'Please tell George why we can't switch the dorm cameras on until tomorrow.'

'Lars, we don't need to do this now—' Abbey's British accent is cold, harsh.

'Mr Abbey, sir.' I turn to Abbey and try to give him my politest smile.

'George, please call me George.'

I try not to gag.

'*George*. My crew are about to go into two weeks' quarantine. They're going to say goodbye to their friends and family and they need some space to be able to talk freely and bond as a crew again.'

'Before they take part in the most ambitious exploration mission in history,' Anders adds in his signature grandiose style.

'No one understands that more than me,' Abbey places an insincere hand on his heart, 'but this is a must for Valdivian. All our surveys and algorithms point to audiences wanting real, raw, human moments—'

'And you'll get that. But we agreed we decide when the observation cameras start rolling. Once they start, they don't stop.' I find myself shifting uncomfortably at the thought of this, but Anders continues: 'So until tomorrow, only stock shots. Wides. Formal shit.'

Abbey's jaw tightens.

'Sir,' I say. 'All I'm asking, on behalf of my crew, is that you give us one more night. You have the rest of our lives. You can give us that, surely?'

Abbey stares back at me. His eyes are cold, calculating, like he's planning his next move. But then a plane's engine roars.

'Ah!' Anders laughs and puts his arm round Abbey's shoulder, turning him towards the runway. 'Saved by the T-38!'

Abbey's production crew scramble to get the cameras rolling as the small jet comes into view. I step out of the way, feeling unsettled. When Anders sold the television rights to Valdivian to finance the mission, we all knew what that meant. Most of us had shrugged it off – there'd been live camera feeds for years on the space station and NASA had always recorded essential moments during missions. But it was only when I moved into the accommodation block a couple of weeks back and saw the newly installed cameras in every corner that it truly hit me: Big Brother will be watching – and he's keen to get started now.

The opening of the cockpit breaks me from my reverie. I wave at the man emerging, taking off his mask and harness. The cameras catch him waving back. Professor Sébastien Brun, our botanist, is here.

Sébastien was one of the first citizen applicants to sign up and his CV is second to none. Raised just outside of Paris, France, he's been obsessed with plants from an early age. His parents had a copy of Verne's *From the Earth to the Moon* in their library and that sparked in him a love of science fiction as a teenager. Soon, the likes of H. G. Wells and Arthur C. Clarke showed him that his love of plants and his love of planets could be married together. So he studied astrobotany. And in between that, he took part in ultra-marathons across the world. A lot of people find Brun intimidating. I respect him.

After posing for some pictures, Brun shakes hands with Anders and Abbey and then beelines for me. As he gives me his usual kiss-on-both-cheeks greeting, I'm very aware of the cameras. He stands back and looks me over.

'You look well.' His French accent is subtle, his English is perfect.

'So do you. Welcome back.'

'It's good to be back. Clémence could tell I was counting down the hours. You did the right thing, staying here.'

'Is she not coming today?'

'She has a peer review. She'll be here for the launch, but we've said our goodbyes. We are not sentimental.'

During our years of training together, I've noticed that Sébastien and his wife, who is also a scientist, have an unusual relationship. They seem more like business partners than anything else. Sébastien has never shown any qualms about leaving her behind, and rumour has it that she has just signed a book deal with a global publisher.

Before I can say anything else, Brun is whisked away for his interview with the TV crew. Anders joins me as I watch him go.

'I didn't think there'd be anyone else as keen as you, Wright, but looks like you have some competition.' He looks at his watch. 'Forty-five minutes until the rest of them arrive. Shall we grab a coffee and go through tonight's agenda?'

Gwynne raises her head from her cell phone and marches over to us. 'Rubio's not on the flight.' She grimaces, and my stomach sinks.

'What do you mean?'

'He didn't arrive at the airport this morning. No way to get in contact with him. The charter had to leave without him. He checked out of his hotel but hasn't been seen since.'

Anders swears in Finnish. I don't blame him. If Rubio doesn't make it to Baikonur tonight, he can't quarantine, and if he can't quarantine we'll have to sub someone in, and that could cause delays. Not to mention what this means for the show, the press . . .

Anders composes himself. 'Do the producers know?' Gwynne shakes her head. 'Good. We tell them Rubio has a personal issue that he is dealing with. He will be joining us later. In the meantime, let's get some people out looking for him. Tell them to check any bullshit cultural landmark. He's an artist. He'll be doing something ridiculous like soaking up the beauty of the fucking moment.' He turns and marches towards the terminal building.

A huge breath escapes me. Just when I thought we were getting somewhere.

'Thanks, Gwynne.' I try to smile at her. Then we hear a final bark from Anders.

'And check the bars.'

Shit.

I spend the next thirty minutes going through the ramifications of Rubio's tardiness with Gwynne. Lucky bastard is going to miss the mortality march. My phone rings. I assume it's him, so I pick up without even looking.

'Alyssa?'

'Mom?' My stomach flips when I hear her voice. It sounds strangely small and weak. Gwynne gestures towards the hangar behind us. Dazed, I head over to it, relieved to have a rare moment of space for this conversation.

'Hold on a sec, I just need to get somewhere quieter . . .' I dip into the shade of the hangar, where the shadows of dormant jets lurk. Some sad-looking sandwiches are strewn on a table by the door for the production crew.

'We got your papers from your lawyer today.' So that is why she is calling. I don't know why I ever thought otherwise.

'Good.'

'You're giving him power of attorney?' I can hear the judgement from ten thousand kilometres away.

'Yes.'

Silence on the end of the line.

'It made the most sense. He'll know everything that's going on and can make the best judgement call if something happens. He has the mission in his best interests.'

'Right,' she says. And then leaves me hanging. I open up one of the sandwiches. Salami on rye. The meat is drying up, the lettuce limp. It's the least appetising thing I've ever seen. Still, I take a bite.

'Did you have anything else you want to say?' I ask through my mouthful. It makes me sound casual, which is good.

'You go into quarantine tonight, don't you?'

'Yep.' I don't know what's more dry, the sandwich or this conversation. 'Just two more weeks. Waiting on the crew arrival now.'

'Before you leave, your father wanted to ask you . . .' She pauses. He must be there with her. 'Alyssa, your father wants the Purple Heart back.'

I stop chewing.

'He wants you to send it back as soon as possible. Please.'

A stunned pause.

'Can you put him on the phone?'

There's an uncomfortable silence. I know the lie before she even says it.

'No, Alyssa. He's not here.'

'Mom, I know he is. Please. I need to speak to him.'

Another pause, shorter this time.

'You know I can't do that. Now . . . just tell me you'll send it back. It's his father's medal.'

'I know what it is, Mom.' Pressure builds behind my eyes. I'm feeling hot. Fuck. Outside, through the glare, people are gathering for the next jet.

'We will cover the costs of the shipment,' she almost whispers. I bark out a laugh, try to take a deep breath. I can't be dealing with this right now.

'No. It's fine. I'll pay. If this is what he really wants.'

She releases her breath. 'Thank you.'

'Well, then. I need to go. Great talking to you, Mom.' I go to hang up.

'Alyssa!' she blurts, almost like a yelp.

The phone flies back to my ear.

'Yeah?' Another long pause.

'Make sure . . .' she finally says, 'make sure you send it tracked.'

I don't know what to say. So I click off.

My nose is running, and I sniff a little. The sound of a jet approaching says I need to get back out there. I stare hard at the half-eaten sandwich in my hand, with its shitty filling. It's the breadcrumbs. Sandwiches are a no-go in space because bread's not robust enough and the last thing you want is the damn thing breaking up and floating around, getting in all your instruments and buttons. Gemini 3 learned that the hard way.

I head out into the baking sunshine, towards the runway again, throwing the sandwich into the garbage on my way out.

The TV production crew are getting themselves in a frenzy. Not only are three more crew members arriving, but also their loved ones. For the people on that plane, this is going to be one of the most difficult days of their lives. Families find it hard to say goodbye for ever. Apart from mine, apparently.

First to emerge is the warm and reassuring smile of Dr Ruth Okeowo, our crew physician. In her early fifties, she's our eldest crew member, and British Nigerian. She looks great in her mission overalls, and she's had a haircut, short and practical – a woman after my own heart. She waves energetically as her brother and two twenty-something nieces emerge behind her.

As Okeowo reaches the ground and strides over to shake Anders' and Abbey's hands, our flight engineer and leading robotics expert, Lee Dong-hyun, steps out, blinking, into the sunlight. His parents follow swiftly behind.

Last, but by no means least, Dr Heather Morin emerges. I breathe a sigh of relief when I see her smiling, looking cool as anything with her Ray-Bans on and her hair blowing in the desert wind. She holds a hand up in greeting and then turns to check on those behind her. At her encouragement, two awkward teenagers and their dad step onto the stairs. Morin's family. She is the only mother on our team. The TV crew zoom in, panting with excitement.

Anders opens his arms wide and gives Morin and her husband the biggest handshake of all, followed by the kids. Abbey smiles at them all politely; I can practically see the dollar signs in his eyes. I approach the group and hug the crew members and their families one by one. This is something NASA would never have allowed. It would have been all formal ceremony and handshakes, but this is my mission, these are my crew, my family now, and I'm going to hug them. Plus, I read once that physical contact is important for bonding.

I greet Dr Morin last of all.

'You should've gone home,' she chastises me in my ear. Then she takes my shoulders and appraises me. I smile reassuringly, trying not to think of the phone call I just had.

'I'm fine.' Before I can ask how she is, she's re-introducing me to her kids, Maggie and Ben, and her husband, Max. Maggie looks excited, if a little uncomfortable with all the attention. Ben is sullen, while Max looks like he's about to sit through a tooth extraction.

'My God, Ben, is that what maple syrup does to a guy?' The

whole family laugh at my shitty joke, except Ben. He just shrugs. So he's going for moody teenager. I try the husband next.

'Great to see you, Max. I'm really looking forward to us introducing you to some fellow math nerds down in coding.'

'Heather has been singing the praises of the team you've got out here. It'll be great to see what she feels so passionate about,' Max replies, automaton-like. You don't have to be a psychologist like Morin to know what's going on beneath his surface. This is a man whose wife is leaving him, not for another man, but for another planet. And he has to grin and bear it.

'OK!' I clap my hands together. 'Anders, shall we begin the tour?'

'Let the mortality march begin!' Anders booms, and launches straight into one of his monologues about the facility.

As we file off towards the vans, Okeowo falls into step with me.

'Any news on Rubio, Commander?' she murmurs. Always so respectful, so measured.

I try to sound reassuring. 'We're working on it.'

Jia

I WATCH KAI'S MESSAGE OVER AND OVER, BUT EVERY TIME it just confuses me more and I have to hit pause on his shit-eating grin. What message does he want me to pass on? And who to?

I call the super, but the CCTV didn't catch the delivery guy coming into the building. He must have used the service entrance and stairs. I don't touch the card from the officers. Kai's words ring in my head: *don't trust the police.* If you can't trust the police, you definitely can't trust National Security.

Eventually, I do as he says. I look for the pictures in the toilet cistern, but there's nothing there. The officers must have taken them in those brown envelopes.

Beneath the fear, anger bubbles away. Mom and Dad's precious son, the one they doted on and sacrificed everything for – who was never grateful in the first place, never even went to see his own mother these past couple of years – of course he was up to something illegal. Of course he would get himself, and therefore both of us, into trouble. How could I not see this coming?

As I search the apartment, Orion finds a home for himself on Kai's bed. I've shut the window now, so there's nowhere for him to go. A prisoner, like me.

Eventually, I find myself opening up the top cupboard in the kitchen and grabbing a bottle of red wine. I pour out a whole tumbler and glug it down. It doesn't help the ever-present panic, but it silences my grumbling stomach. The television screen stares at me, silent, so I resort to the only thing left to me. The one other clue my joker of a brother has given me.

I hit play again and allow the disc to continue.

After a couple of minutes of black screen, a studio logo appears, and I recognize the opening bars of music instantly as credits roll on a starry sky, declaring the film to be *Men in Black*.

I sigh. In those months after Dad died, Kai holed up in his room and played this over and over again. To the point where Mom threw the disc away, just to force him to come out into the rest of the apartment.

I've never liked sci-fi. None of it is real. It's all so overblown, about things no normal person could ever relate to. Kai used to say it's because I have no imagination.

Perhaps he's right. I cannot begin to imagine why the hell he has sent me this.

I slump down onto the couch, wine bottle and glass in hand.

About twenty minutes in, Orion appears around the corner and slowly approaches. Once again, he jumps up onto the couch. Tentative at first, he watches me. But once he's convinced I'm not going to throw anything at him this time, he curls his paws up beneath him and closes his eyes.

I watch him for a while, his ginger fur lit by the fluorescent glow of the screen. It's dark outside. I've lost all sense of time now.

He suddenly stirs when the dog on screen barks, and then the cat in the movie yowls. His eyes flick to the screen and his body tenses. A smile tugs at my lips for the first time since Kai disappeared. I follow his line of sight.

The woman Will Smith has been flirting with is stroking the cat on screen as it purrs.

'*Boy when you want attention . . .*' The woman tugs at a collar around the cat's neck. '*Orion, that's a pretty name.*'

I freeze.

I lean forward and grab the remote off the coffee table. On

screen, the film zooms in on the cat's collar. A swirl of dark and light.

I hit some buttons. The film jumps back. When I get to the bit where the actors are talking to a pug, I hit play.

'*Rosenberg said something about a galaxy on Orion's belt.*'

They shake the pug for a bit – it's a ridiculous scene, but I watch avidly.

'*The galaxy is here,*' the dog tells them.

'*The galaxy is hundreds of millions of stars and planets. How's it here?*' Will Smith demands.

I think I've stopped breathing. But something is forming in the back of my mind.

'*You humans, when you gonna learn that size doesn't matter. Just 'cos something's important doesn't mean it's not very very small . . . like the size of a marble or a jewel.*'

I skip forward again, and the cat doesn't like it. He crouches low, glaring at the screen. But I don't care. The love interest is back, and she's looking at the fictional cat's collar with the orb on it. I never realized before . . . but he's also a ginger cat . . .

'*Orion, that's a pretty name.*'

And then I hit the remote again and the film skips. Back. And back.

I jump as I find what I'm looking for. Jab at the remote. The film plays again. An alien is dying, but manages to gasp out the phrase:

'*To prevent war, the galaxy is on Orion's belt.*'

I stop it there.

I turn to Kai's Orion, sat blinking slowly at me on the couch. Oblivious to the crazy thoughts running through my mind.

I dart to the kitchen, find the cat food and pour a whole packet into his bowl, which he pounces on as soon as it hits the floor.

As I watch him chomp down, the lines play in my head.

That's the clue. That's the key to the whole movie. The thing Will Smith is looking for is on Orion's belt. But not the belt. The collar.

Orion is so distracted by the food that he lets me bend down and touch his collar. It's simple. Green, with a small disc tag on it. I try to turn it, but Orion flinches.

'Shhh,' I soothe, giving him a stroke, and he purrs. I move the collar more gently and take the disc in my hands.

Weirdly, the tag doesn't have Orion's name on. All it has are the words 'If lost, call:' on one side, and the name and number of the veterinary surgery he's registered at on the other.

I let go and stand back, letting him eat his fill until he looks up and around at me, licking his lips. Purring like an idiot.

If lost . . .

I am being ridiculous. It's just as far-fetched as talking pugs and little aliens. But I have an awful feeling I'm right . . .

Alyssa

THE FAMILIES ARE AWE-STRUCK WHEN WE SHOW THEM THE scope and scale of the campus.

One room I'm keen to move through quickly is programming. There's a reason why no space films focus on these heroes. A group of (mostly) guys staring at lines of computer code on a screen is not sexy. Anders, however, clearly disagrees.

'A rocket's greatest enemy is gravity,' he begins. 'That's the thing we have to beat if we want to escape this planet. Now, we all know, the heavier something is, the more energy we need to move it. So, every kilogram we take with us has to be worth it. Some supplies and the crew habitats have already been sent up to Mars. But within this spacecraft, we have to make everything that keeps our crew safe as light as possible. But guess what is weightless?'

The production team and some of the families look a bit bored. My fellow candidates and I keep our interested faces plastered on.

'Software!' He gestures grandly at the room, oblivious to his audience's indifference. 'So, instead of getting a lot of bulky hardware to do the heavy lifting, our software does it all—'

'YOU CAN'T BE HERE, SIR!'

Our heads whip around to see a couple of burly security guards trying to block someone from entering the room. Gwynne is there in a flash. She grabs hold of one of the security men and tries to shield what is happening from view. But two of the handheld cameras are already pointing towards the fracas.

'On the Space Shuttle program,' Anders continues valiantly, 'NASA had two teams of hundreds of programmers working separately on their code. It got them down to an impressive 0.11 bugs in every thousand lines. Trust me, that is impressive. Software such as—'

Then a voice I know well breaks through.

A voice heavy with liquor.

'I'm fucking supposed to be here. Gwynne! Tell them, darling! It's ludicrous!'

The chaos finally spills into the room, and the ruddy face of Rubio Lindroos appears. A security guard has him in a headlock but he's not a small man and he bucks, throwing all his weight to one side. The two figures go flying into the workspace of a very flustered coder, who has had to rapidly move his wheelchair out of the way.

Rubio and the security guard crash into his desk and drawers. Paperwork, mugs and personal effects fly everywhere. Rubio has broken free of the headlock and lies, eyes wide, gaping out at the rest of the room. The security guard staggers to his feet, panting.

All of us are frozen to the spot.

Gwynne darts over to the guard and whispers furiously in his ear, then both of them rush to help Rubio to his feet.

I turn to look at Anders and see the flash of devastation on his face as he stares at his best friend and biggest liability. Luckily, no one else sees it; they're all too busy gawking at Rubio. Then, quicker than lightning, the beaming smile is back.

'Rubio!' he cries, opening his arms and breaking the awkward silence. 'There's always one who is late to the party. So glad you could join us!'

Rubio sways a little as he's righted. A middle-aged man dressed in jeans and a crumpled shirt, he looks nothing like our sixth and final crew member should. He hesitates. Even through the fug of the liquor, he can clearly tell that he's upset Anders. Then he rushes over and embraces him in a bear hug, the unmistakable stench of whiskey trailing in his wake. Abbey murmurs into the ear of a nearby cameraman, and I know he's intent on capturing every excruciating minute. Across the group, Morin watches everything like a hawk.

Eventually, Anders pulls back from the embrace. Rubio is now quiet, sheepish. The two old friends acknowledge each other's sadness.

'I'm sorry I'm late, Lars,' Rubio breathes.

And with that, my team sweeps into action.

Okeowo does the same as I, heading over to Rubio. She holds him straight, making it look like a greeting, but I know she's also doing a damage assessment on him. On the other side of the room, Morin and Lee gracefully gather the families, herding them all over to one of the rolling cameras, blocking its view of Rubio.

Elsewhere, Brun strides up to Anders. 'Software, Anders, you were saying?'

Anders blinks for a moment, but then cottons on and turns back to the camera that is still lingering on Rubio, to whom Gwynne is now subtly handing a bottle of water.

'Yes . . . NASA's teams . . . well . . . here's the cinch, it cost them $500 million doing so . . .' Anders ploughs on. 'That's the problem with national space programs: no efficiency, no flexibility. For Mars One, we searched the world for the best coders, innovators. We don't need multiple teams; we have the best brains on the planet, all in this room.'

BANG.

Everyone stops again and looks over at the source of the sound. The flustered coder is attempting to put his workspace back together but his top drawer has been damaged in the fray and he can't keep it shut. He puts up his hand in apology, grimacing. Poor guy.

Anders barely misses a beat. 'So, as I was saying,' he raises his voice, and everyone turns back to him. 'This means that our code is showing only 0.06 errors per thousand lines. "But what does this all mean?" I hear you ask.' Anders gives Morin's son a friendly punch on the shoulder. 'It means your mother and her crewmates are flying in the safest, most technologically advanced vehicle created by humankind. So, how about a round of applause for our coders?' Everyone claps obediently. Even a chastened Rubio plays along.

'Now, on to the main assembly floor.'

As the camera crew gather a few more shots of the coding room, and Abbey beadily watches Rubio fall into step with the rest of the crew, I hang back and take a route through the room that passes the flustered coder's desk. Good-looking, muscular, well-dressed, he's completely the odd one out in this den of insular nerds. While all the other desks are littered with junk food packets and seem to be developing their own ecosystem, his is full of personality: a picture of a football team, a succulent, a stylish coffee mug. I squat to pick up the rest of his scattered paperwork, and nod as I hand it to him. He looks startled, but nods back.

As I move to leave, I notice the Colts horseshoe on his desk has been left the wrong way up, and right it.

'Careful,' I say. 'All your luck will fall out.' He stares at me. Surprised, I guess, that the commander of the prime crew is actually talking to him. His colleagues are agape. I smile at him. 'Thank you for keeping us safe.'

'You're welcome,' he replies. His voice is pleasant: strong and confident.

'And I'm sorry for the disruption.'

He simply smiles at that, and then turns back to his monitor. Back to work. I take one last look at the room of coders, then follow the circus out the door. As I leave, there's another BANG as he tries to get his drawer to shut again.

I flinch, wishing to God that was the only damage caused this evening.

Jia

FIRST THING MONDAY MORNING, I LEAVE SOME CAT TREATS in the middle of the living room floor. It does the trick. As soon as Orion is on them, I grab him and drop him in the pet carrier.

He gives a guttural howl, but I don't care. I need to get out of this place now, while I still have the courage. I grab my keys, my purse and dart out into the hallway. I take the stairs to avoid the CCTV.

I can feel Orion's weight shifting from side to side in the cage, and hear his wails as I move as quickly as I can through the streets. The carrier is unwieldy, and I apologize to passers-by as I bump them with it.

Luckily, the vet surgery is not far and I'm not too much of a sweaty mess by the time I make it through the door. A kind older woman smiles at me from behind the reception desk.

'Good morning. Name, please?'

'Li Jia . . . but I, er, I haven't got . . . I'm looking for Erica? She said she'd see me.'

The woman gestures to the seats and disappears behind a door.

Deep in the bowels of the surgery, another cat howls, and I realize that Orion has gone silent for the first time since leaving the house. I place the carrier on the seat next to me and peer in. He's staring out, wild-eyed, his little chest heaving.

'Not a fan of this place, I take it?' I whisper.

I don't blame him. But this is all I have.

I'd recognized the vet surgery on Orion's collar. It's where Kai's friend from college, Erica, works. So I called ahead earlier this morning to ask if she could see me. She's a veterinary nurse. I've never met her, but she was the one who had told Kai about Orion in the first place. One mention of an unwanted litter of kittens and then boom, there he was in our living room. No discussion with me. But that's Kai.

The door behind reception opens and the older lady is joined by a pretty young woman in blue scrubs.

'Jia?' she asks, smiling. This must be Erica. She's stunning. I pull on my frumpy top.

'Err yes,' I jump up and awkwardly offer my hand.

Erica politely follows my lead. But then she frowns, concern flitting over her face. Her perfectly winged eyeliner is a stark black against her skin. I shift uncomfortably, suddenly aware that I've not showered in days. Not changed my clothes. Heat suffuses my cheeks.

She moves closer to me. 'How are you?'

'Well, I could be better.'

'Yeah, I heard. I haven't spoken to O-Cat, or anything. I mean, I don't know where he—'

O-Cat. Eugh. That ridiculous name Kai calls himself on the internet.

'I know,' I cut in. 'I'm not here about Kai – well, not entirely. I'm sorry but I need your help with something.' She moves back a little, suddenly looking nervous – clearly she's heard the police are involved – but then I gesture to the carrier and she relaxes.

'Is something wrong with Orion?' She bends down to the carrier.

'No. Well, I don't know.' As Erica puts her fingers through the cage door and coos, I feel very aware of everyone around us.

'Is there somewhere we can talk?' I mutter.

She studies me, staying low. 'Do you need him to see a vet?'

'No. I just really want to talk to you.'

Erica looks at me, then at her watch, before straightening up. 'I can give you five minutes.'

I nod, and follow her down a hallway to a small consulting room. She slides the door shut, takes the carrier from me and places it on the table.

'Let's let the little guy out,' she says. She strokes and shushes him as she lifts him out and begins checking him over. She looks into his eyes, checks his teeth and feels his stomach. Then she takes a stethoscope from a drawer and feels for his heartbeat.

'A little fast, but I think we're a bit scared,' she murmurs. She could be talking about me. I laugh nervously.

She stows away the stethoscope before turning back to me, absent-mindedly stroking Orion, who has now settled.

'Jia, are you OK?'

'Err, yeah. I mean, no. But . . .' I shrug. Why can't I speak properly? *Just get it out. Ask for her help. Tell her.*

'Look, I'm so sorry about your brother. I heard you called round to a few of our old college friends. It's awful. But as I said, I really don't know any—'

'Kai sent me a message after he left saying that he has a plan and that I have to follow his instructions, but I don't understand what they are and I can't work all of them out, except this one thing about his cat and a message and I'm really worried about him so you have to help me.'

There. I said it. So fast, I'm not sure she even registered any of it. But it's out there.

Erica closes her eyes, rubs her temples. Orion rolls onto his back, purring for her attention.

'Shit,' she finally says, then moves over to the door and turns the lock, before gesturing for me to continue.

A few minutes later, Erica is feeding cat treats to Orion as I finish my story.

She eyes me warily. 'You genuinely think that the message he sent you, the movie, the collar, all of that is meant to lead you to me? With your brother's pet cat?' We both look at Orion. He slow-blinks.

Hearing it from her makes it sound even less likely. Then it all hits me: my fear for Kai, my confusion, my anger at him, my frustration, my exhaustion. My adrenaline must have finally run out and despite my efforts to quell them, tears start to well.

'I know it's crazy. But he's gone and I have no clue what happened and all I have is his damn cat. And in the film, the answer to everything is on the cat's collar. *Orion's* collar. But there's nothing on *this* Orion's collar except the words *if lost* and the details for this place. And then I thought, what if the friend he wants me to get a message to is you?'

Erica shakes her head. 'I have no idea about any of this.'

'I'm just trying to do what he said,' I plead.

Erica looks at me for a moment, then pushes herself off the table to some drawers behind. From one of them, she pulls a small handheld device with a tiny screen.

'Hold him still,' she says, and I do as I'm told while she waves the device over Orion's neck. It beeps, and she looks at it.

'Shit,' she says. She waves it again.

Another beep.

'What is it?' I ask.

'His microchip should be registering, but I'm getting an error code. Hold on.'

She rummages again in another drawer and pulls out a larger device. She plugs it into the computer behind her and pulls up a new window on the screen.

'This should work.'

Again, she waves this new device over his neck, eyes locked on the computer screen. This time, lines and lines of incomprehensible code appear. It stops about halfway down the screen.

'Woah,' Erica balks. She puts the device down on the table and feels Orion's neck, pinching at something. Her eyes widen.

'What?' I ask.

'His microchip,' she says, standing back. With neither of us holding him, Orion jumps off the table to explore again. 'It should have a fifteen-digit number on it, but look . . .' She gestures to the screen.

'That's a lot more than fifteen digits.'

'Yeah.' She half laughs. 'And feeling that thing, it's a lot bigger than it should be.' She shakes her head. 'I think . . . I think there's some data hidden on it.'

I don't know how it's possible, but both relief and dread fill me instantly. I'm not going mad. Kai did mean for me to bring Orion here. There is something hidden in him. But what the hell does it mean?

Clearly thinking the same, Erica taps at the keyboard and a printer starts whirring.

'They asked about the cat,' I say, quietly.

'Who?' Erica says, staring at the printout.

'The guys from National Security.'

Erica's head snaps up.

'National Security?'

Ah. Yes. Somehow, I hadn't mentioned their involvement. I avoid her accusatory look.

'Jia! You're only telling me this now?!' She jumps up and pulls down the blinds on the only window. She braces herself there for a moment.

'They asked about a lot of things,' I offer, pathetically.

'The NS, seriously?'

'I'm sorry. I just didn't know who to talk to, and Kai's message . . . I was right. Now we just have to work out what that says and maybe—'

'There is no "*we*" here, Jia. I only did this because I wanted to help—'

There's an ear-splitting bang and the lights go out.

It feels like we're in some nightmarish horror film. Especially when I hear screams from the reception.

'Please! Officer, we know nothing.'

'Get on the ground, now!'

Dogs bark, a bird screeches. A woman screams again, and men yell even more aggressively.

'Li Jia?' My name echoes down the corridor and my stomach flips. 'Li Jia?!'

'Go!' Erica urges.

'But I haven't done anything wrong.' My voice shakes.

'They won't care. Don't let them catch you!'

Instinct takes over and I run for the emergency exit. I slam the bar and bright sunlight streams in. I shield my eyes and stumble out into the day – and then I remember. The cat.

I can hear doors being kicked in. The room we're in is at the end of the hall, but I haven't got long. I dart back inside, flailing around uselessly, but then something darts between my legs and straight out the emergency exit. The cat's gone without me.

The door bursts open and the first thing I see is the barrel of a gun.

'Get down on the ground!'

Do police wear masks? Who are these—

But before I complete the thought, the door slams into them again and Erica emerges from behind it, screaming. She grabs my arm and yanks me towards the fire exit. I turn and run with her as the men yell behind us, the door banging open once more.

Outside, we find ourselves in an alley. I have no idea where I am, but Erica does, so I just follow her. Behind some hazardous-waste bins I see Orion backed up into a corner, hissing. Erica expertly grabs him by the scruff of the neck and thrusts him to my chest as we dart around a corner. His claws dig into my flesh and he squirms to get out of my hold. But I can't lose him. Kai will never forgive me – and I have to find out what's on his microchip.

Erica is still running and I follow, panting and wheezing. God, she's fast.

We turn another corner and see the main street up ahead. It's busy. People are running behind us, yelling. No gunshots, though – yet.

We burst out onto the street, and just when I think I'm about to pass out, Erica gestures to me to slow down. Keeping my head low, I move with the crowd, just behind her, and it's clear her strategy is to try to blend in. My heart feels like it's about to explode, with both exertion and fear.

People stare at me as I clutch Orion in my arms. He's still squirming, trying to get over my shoulder. I pull him down lower so no one can see him from behind, and hush him urgently.

Erica moves quickly, parting the crowds ahead, checking behind her to make sure I'm there. I keep expecting a hand to land on my shoulder and pull me back, but it doesn't. It takes everything within me not to look behind me.

There's a bus up ahead. It's about to leave, the last person getting on board, so we run for it. Erica jumps on first then turns to hold out her hand to me. I make it just in time. The driver rolls his eyes as I leap on, wheezing. The eye roll turns into confusion as he sees the cat in my arms. My face stings, so presumably I have a few scratches on my cheeks, too. I smile at him and try to style it out, but I feel myself wither. The other passengers give us a wide berth and miraculously a seat opens up by the window. Erica claims it and allows me to sit down.

Orion seems to have calmed down now that I'm not running. He stays very still in my arms. I try to slow my breathing, bring it down to a normal level, aware of all the eyes on me. I risk a glance out of the window and see a couple of men weaving through the crowd. They're searching, scarves that could easily be used as masks around their necks. They don't see us as the bus pulls away.

Erica sighs, staring out at the city streaming past. Then she turns back to me. 'I think I know where we can go,' she says, low.

'What do you mean?'

'You said your brother told you he has "some friends" who can help? Well, I know someone who might be able to work with that code. And I also don't think they'll be too fussed about the feds.'

I gesture for her to get closer, and she leans in. Her hair smells of coconut. 'Who are we going to see?'

'O-Cat's girlfriend,' she says simply, sitting back up and looking at the bus map as I blink in utter astonishment.

Alyssa

'WHAT THE FUCK, LARS?' I BURST OUT.

He rubs his eyes. His office is dim in the dying light of the Kazakh steppe.

'NASA used to do it all the time. It'll be good for the crew. Keep you busy.'

It sounds almost as if he's trying to convince himself. He picks up his rock off his desk and tosses it between his hands.

'We're reworking the schedule. Cameramen with diving credentials are being flown in. Obviously, they won't have been quarantined, but they'll be in full diving gear. Hermetically sealed. Not a problem.' He can't even bring himself to look at me any more. 'The timing is going to be tricky. We're trying to ease you into the launch hours, but—'

'Would you stop with the fucking moon rock?' I snap.

He sets it down on his desk with a thump. 'OK, Wright, say your piece. Let's get it out so we can start working through the problem.'

'It shouldn't even be a problem, Lars. We shouldn't even have to consider a live LAS simulation right now. We're twelve days out from launch! We need more time in the flight sim. We need more time to mentally prepare for what is ahead. A tank sim is pointless. We've run it to death and it's the least likely scenario that we are going to face. We need to focus on what happens when we get *off* the planet.'

Lars nods along like a nodding fucking dog.

'No one knows the likelihood of a launch abort more than I do. But that tank simulation is the only vaguely interesting thing to watch.'

'They signed up for a real space mission, and that means watching us do real training. That means sitting with us for six hours while we practise undocking, adjusting course trajectories and purging the goddamn waste pipes. Not seeing us launched at high speed into a swimming pool and scrambling to get out of a tin can just because it feels more like an action movie.'

He throws his hands up in the air. 'What do you want me to say?'

'Say no! You said the interests of the mission would always come first. You never said a fucking TV crew would derail our training.'

Anders gives a huge sigh. Then he pushes back from his desk and heads over to the massive wall-mounted television. He picks up the remote and puts it on, before slumping into his couch. The news is on. They're talking about the DOW-Jones and an upcoming summit. I fold my arms and wait for his point.

'Look,' he gestures to the news channel, his voice unusually quiet, resigned.

I shrug.

'Look at the news,' he continues. 'Nothing. Our first episode went out last night announcing you all to the world and there's no coverage. The ratings came in this morning. Fourteen per cent of the world watched the moon landing in 1969. Twenty per cent watched a Pakistan versus India cricket match two years ago. More people watched that cricket match than our first episode – we barely reached four per cent. Even with Rubio's little . . . indiscretion.'

'We always knew fewer people would watch that than the actual launch. No one watches those things live any more,' I say.

'The networks are nervous. Yes, we accounted for a bigger

pick-up for the launch, but the size of audience is not justifying what we're charging for the advertising slots so—'

'I don't care if they're making money. We have to focus on the mission and the crew. They'll be watching by the time we make it to Mars. Besides, you're the damn billionaire – you can cover us until then, surely.'

Lars snorts and shakes his head. 'Alyssa, I'm sorry, but you just don't get it. Yes, your rocket is ready, your hab is already up there, your fuel is being chilled as we speak. But even my fortune is not enough. Your next resupply relies on the money we get from the networks. I can get you to Mars, but it's ratings that are going to keep you there. Keep you alive. If we do something that looks scary, people will watch. If we get the ratings up before the launch, that will give them more confidence. And I can keep signing cheques.'

I stand, stunned.

Of course, I knew Anders had entered into a difficult agreement with Abbey and the production company. But I'd naively ignored the niggling suspicion I had, deep in the back of my mind, that he'd sold our souls to the devil. That we would end up being held hostage.

I join him on the couch. We stare absent-mindedly at the news for a while.

'Lars, I can't stand by and watch things fall apart again.'

I feel his eyes on my face. He reaches out and places his hand on mine. I don't pull away, but I keep my eyes pinned straight ahead. Afraid of what will happen if I look at him.

'Alyssa,' he says, softly. 'There was nothing you could have done.'

'I know,' I reply, even though we both know I don't.

'This time is different,' he says. 'You'll be there. This is your mission. Your crew.'

'I'm just trying to protect them,' I reply.

'As am I,' Anders says. He pulls his hand away and looks back to the TV screen. 'And one death-defying stunt might just do the job.'

Jia

AFTER A VERY UNCOMFORTABLE JOURNEY ACROSS THE city – which thankfully does not involve any more armed pursuits – Erica brings me to a small, anonymous office block. From the outside, it looks like the sort of place you would go to hire a cheap lawyer or accountant, but as soon as we walk in the place is ablaze with colour, anger and passion. The hallway walls are covered with a riot of posters and signs, all overlapping and demanding attention:

> REBEL FOR LIFE.
> LOVE. RAGE. REBELLION.
> ECOCIDE.
> ONE FUTURE. ONE PLANET.

As we move further into the building, Erica leading the way, we pass by an old doorless office. Inside, a number of teenagers sit on stained sofas, staring at laptops and tablets, BBC World Service playing on a solar-powered radio. They pay no attention as we walk past.

Erica takes us up the narrow stairs to the first floor and gingerly approaches an office door with a broken window that's been boarded up with old cardboard boxes. She knocks awkwardly, Orion in her arms.

'Come in!' sings a voice from inside, in English.

Erica gestures for me to open the door and we move into a wide room that was clearly once an open-plan workspace but has now been filled with hundreds of boxes. Placards and signs lean up against the wall. But the owner of the voice is nowhere to be seen.

'Hello?' says Erica, still in English, looking as confused as I am.

'Hi.' A head and shoulders pop up from behind a stack of boxes. As we move closer, a young woman with spiky short hair is revealed sitting on a cot bed, a sheet over her legs and only a crop top on.

'Erica! What are you doing here?' She stands up, stretching. She has a lithe, toned body and no pants on, just her underwear. Erica looks away as the woman shrugs on a huge T-shirt that has seen better days. She slips her feet into some sandals and moves over to the desk by the window. ''Cos I know you weren't out there this morning at the protest.' She has a strange accent – American, but with the odd lilt here and there. It's the hallmark of an international-school education. She gestures for us to join her as she taps away on her phone.

'I was working,' Erica says stiffly.

'You always were a square, even at college,' the woman says, not looking up. 'What's with the cat?'

'Can I put him down?' Erica asks.

'Sure. Can't guarantee we'll find him again, though.' Erica takes the risk and Orion pads away, under some boxes.

Erica slumps down in a chair in front of the desk as the woman sends something on her phone and then logs on to her laptop. I can't imagine Kai with someone so confident and . . . well, cool. Finally, she glances up at me as I perch down on one of the seats next to Erica.

'And you are?' she asks, typing.

Erica steps in. 'Agnes, this is Jia.' She pauses. 'O's sister.'

Agnes stops typing. 'Oh. Hey.' She smiles.

'I didn't know he had a girlfriend,' I blurt.

She laughs. 'He doesn't. We're just close.' She goes back to typing. 'Besides, we've not seen each other in a while. He's busy, I'm busy. We've had two protests this week, and twenty-five arrests.'

Her phone buzzes. She looks at the number and silences it.

'Kai's missing,' I say.

She stops again and her smug smile drops. 'Really?' She looks to Erica for confirmation, who nods, grim-looking. 'How long?'

'Three days.'

'OK.' Her face is suddenly serious. She wheels her desk chair out. 'Do you guys have phones?'

Erica pulls hers out of her pocket and I do the same. Agnes grabs a box from under her desk, opens it and puts her own phone in it, before gesturing for us to do the same. We drop our phones in and Agnes shuts the lid.

'Faraday box. Blocks all EMF signals,' Agnes says, as if it's completely normal, placing the box to the side. 'So tell me what happened.'

I can't seem to speak.

'Jia?' Erica prompts. I turn to her. She's looking at me expectantly. But I hear Kai's words all over again.

'Babe,' Agnes jumps in. 'If you're worried about talking, I'm a pro-democracy, anti-capitalist environmental activist in Hong Kong. Whatever you tell me will go right to the bottom of the list of shit I shouldn't know or be doing. Your secrets are safe with me.'

And so I tell her about the day Kai disappeared, I describe his video message.

'And his stuff was gone, and there was blood?'

'Yes.'

Agnes looks to Erica.

Then I explain how I called the police.

'You called the police?' she sits back, surprised. Another glance at Erica. My fists tighten. I'm so done with people treating me like an idiot.

'Yes, why wouldn't I? My brother is missing.'

She laughs and shakes her head.

'So you clearly don't know what your brother does? For work?'

'He's a coder,' I say, irritation edging my voice. 'Software and stuff.'

Agnes snorts, and Erica laughs.

'And stuff?' Agnes echoes. 'The "and stuff" is probably why you're here with us instead of at some trendy coffee shop on a Tantan date right now.'

So that's what she and Kai have in common. They're both condescending. I glare at her.

Sensing the tension, Erica steps in. 'O did a few legitimate coding jobs on the side, yes. He would spend a minimum amount of time on startup apps and shit like that. But his real money-maker was a bit more . . . romantic, I guess. He was a bounty hunter. A cyber Boba Fett, if you will.'

'A what?'

'Come on. *Star Wars*?' Erica looks at Agnes, stunned, then back at me.

I blink at her, my face blank.

'Are you sure you and O are related?'

I give her a tight-lipped smile. 'I don't watch that stuff. But of course, I know what a bounty hunter is. Kai barely left the apartment, though. How on earth was he out searching for bounty?'

Agnes leans back in her chair casually. 'You shop online, you date online – you don't think you can bounty hunt online? Say you're Microsoft, or maybe even the government, and you're about to launch new software or an app or website or whatever. There's over forty million lines of code in some of those things and one single error, one tiny bug, could bring the whole thing down and lose you a shit tonne of money. So, if a certain individual, like your brother, gets his hands on that code and then comes back to you saying, "Excuse me, but this error here means your whole system is compromised," then you, as Microsoft, say, "OK, please don't tell anyone, we'll fix this and here's a bunch of money for you to stay quiet about it."'

I think on this for a second. 'So it's hacking. And extortion.

He hacks and extorts organizations.' Oh God, no wonder people are after him.

Agnes gestures *ta-da* with her hands, but Erica grimaces. 'Not necessarily,' Erica says, giving Agnes a reproachful look. 'It's a service. Some people even invite you to do it. It's an insurance policy, I guess.'

Agnes scoffs.

'Fine.' I try to ignore Agnes. 'And were all his targets people who "invited" him? Because those men earlier didn't look like they were friendly co-workers.'

Erica looks sheepish.

'You can't sugar-coat it, Erica. We both know that O is in on some dodgy shit,' Agnes chimes in.

There's a bleak silence.

'Right,' Agnes says eventually. 'You two came to me for a reason. And now time is clearly of the essence. So, what do you need from me?'

I look to Erica, who thrusts her hand into the pocket of her scrubs and pulls out a crumpled piece of paper: the printout of the code from Orion's microchip.

She places it in front of Agnes. 'We need to know what this says.'

Agnes's eyes light up. 'OK, now we're talking.'

As she works, Erica quietly tells me how Agnes is more than just a protestor. She is the empress of protesting. First, she was part of Extinction Rebellion when she was just a tween. Then, when that petered out and the democracy protests began to really kick off, she joined that movement. Now that everyone has either been extradited or accepted that Hong Kong is screwed, she's gone back to trying to save the entire planet, rather than just her own country. When she isn't trying to organize rallies and convince politicians to listen to her, she's bailing out her fellow protestors who've been arrested.

'But how can she afford to bail out so many people?' I whisper to Erica as she teases Orion with a piece of string among the chaos of boxes.

'She's loaded,' she replies simply. I glance back at Agnes in her tatty T-shirt and shabby surroundings.

'How loaded?'

'Really loaded,' Agnes calls out, not even looking up. I blush. 'This office block, if you hadn't already noticed, is full of crap. It's not all ours. This used to be my grandfather's company's. He's a hoarder. We use it as a place to gather and organize ourselves. It's more discreet than their newer offices.'

'Where are they?'

'Central Plaza.'

Holy shit.

'Like, where the Bank of China and Sing Mobile are?' My voice comes out in a squeak.

Erica grins. 'Hey, Agnes,' she calls across the room, 'what's your surname?'

'Sing,' Agnes replies, nonchalantly.

I gape at her.

'Yeah, my uncles do a lot to keep my name out of the papers. I'm the black sheep of the family.' Then she launches into the air. 'Fuck yes!' She turns to us. 'I have something.'

'Told you she could help,' Erica says, weaving through the office detritus to Agnes's desk.

'You're a hacker, like Kai?' I ask.

Agnes laughs.

'He's much more sophisticated than me, I just code.' There's a new hint of affection in her voice. 'He's like Rain Man. He tried to teach me, but I was too slow. That's why they pay him the big bucks.'

I frown. 'Kai never has money. I always have to cover him for rent.'

'Oh, hun,' she says, so condescending it makes me wince. 'He does have money. He just never spends it that way.'

Before I can say anything, she turns back to her screen and

points to a few lines of numbers and symbols that make absolutely no sense to me.

'So, it's software code,' says Erica as she leans in and looks at the screen.

'Yep,' Agnes says. 'Only a very small section of something much bigger. There is definitely more code hidden inside the microchip itself, but the only data that presents itself to a reader is here. But without context, though, I won't be able to tell you what the hell any of it means.'

Frustrated, I turn to look at Orion, who's planted himself in another box nearby. The midday sun is pouring in through the dirty windows and bakes his fur.

'However . . . I *can* see that the code was updated on the chip last Thursday.' She looks at me.

'That's the last night he was at home.'

She nods and looks back at the screen. 'He must have had his set-up ping this wirelessly to Orion's microchip. Maybe as a daily backup. I'm guessing this is what he's been working on the last few months.' We sit in silence for a while.

'And?' I ask.

'Well,' she holds her hands up. 'It's a "clue" as to what he was up to, for sure. But instead of it being a map to pirate treasure, where X marks the spot, we have, like, a postage stamp square with perhaps one squiggly line leading off it to God-knows where.'

I take a deep, calming breath.

'Can't you take that code and stick it in Google or something? Surely you can find a match and then we might know what he's been working on, or what might have happened?'

Agnes snorts. 'It doesn't work like that. Firstly, this is ten lines. Do you know how much code is even in one of your apps on your phone? They have, like, a hundred thousand lines. Each. This is like trying to work out what building you're looking at by just one brick.'

'Then why leave me the brick?!'

'I don't know!' Her voice leaps up an octave. It's strangely satisfying to know she's frustrated, too. 'Your brother doesn't really make much sense at the best of times, Jia. He barely told me what he was up to and I was sleeping with him. Which was fine by me. I don't care.' But the edge to her voice suggests that maybe she does . . .

'What if there's a clue within the clue?' Erica pipes up.

'What?' Agnes's brow crinkles.

'Like, thinking through that brick thing. What if it's like Lego?'

'Erica,' Agnes wearily sighs. 'It was a simile.'

'Yeah, but on Lego, on the bumpy bits that connect to the other bits, there's the Lego logo, right—'

Agnes almost launches herself at her screen. 'Erica, you're a genius!' She frantically clicks, looking back at the code again.

'Not really,' Erica says, but she looks pleased.

'Will someone please tell me what's going on?'

'A signature in the code,' explains Agnes, her voice feverish. 'A lot of programmers, and a lot of hackers, put a signature somewhere in their work. It can be for practical reasons – just like the way old mapmakers used to purposely put an error in so they knew if someone copied them or whatever. Software companies do the same thing. But a lot of programmers are also egotistical dicks, so they just do it for the glory. Your brother was the same, that's why we call him O-Cat.' She hits the keyboard and then grabs a pen and starts circling things on the battered piece of paper Erica brought.

'So, if these ten lines contain a signature, it could lead us to the programmer, the programmer could lead us to whatever this code is for and that—'

'Could lead us to whoever Kai was working for, or whoever he is running from,' I finish for her.

'Exactly! Right. This part repeats a couple of times. I thought it was a command or a reference back to something within the program. *However* . . .'

She's back typing again. Erica goes to say something, but Agnes holds up her hand to tell her to shut it, and she obeys.

After what feels like an age, she cackles, pushes herself back from the desk, and turns to us.

'He's called Frybread.'

Erica and I glance at each other, puzzled. 'What?'

Agnes points at the circled parts of the code. 'Erica was right. The code does have a signature. That must have been why O chose this part of it to be seen by the reader.'

I struggle to share her enthusiasm. 'But why Frybread? And how does that even help us?'

'I just checked on some forums. This coder was previously known for a couple of significant patches on Microsoft software a few years back. He used to seed in the same signature back then. The signature itself is the coordinates for a restaurant somewhere in the US. The Frybread name comes from what's tagged at the end of the signature: the number twelve. The coordinates are pretty clear, but the number twelve . . . well. You have to Google the restaurant itself . . .'

She turns her screen round to face us, where a dated-looking website is loaded. A banner declares the name of the restaurant as Blue Bird. She clicks on the menu and scrolls down, and I finally get what she's doing. The dishes on the menu are numbered for ease of takeaway ordering, and in at number twelve is Frybread.

'Frybread!' Agnes declares happily.

Erica gasps. 'So now we know who this guy is, let's get in touch with him and find out what he knows.'

'How do you know it's a he?' I turn to Erica.

She shrugs back. 'He plasters his signature all over his code. That's gotta be a guy.'

Agnes turns her screen back to face her. 'That's where we hit a problem, young Erica.' She sits back in her chair. 'All we know is his signature and his nickname. He's actually been off the radar for a few years. The only reason one of the guys on the forum knew him is because he'd been working on the same bug five years ago and this guy beat him to it.'

My heart sinks. Just when it seems like we're getting somewhere, we run into a brick wall again. I put my head in my hands and breathe out.

'You OK, hun?' Agnes asks. It's the first time I've felt her soften since we arrived.

I pull my head back up. 'Yeah. I just don't know what to do right now.'

Agnes nods. Then we both realize that Erica is shifting uncomfortably, glancing at her watch.

'I'm sorry, Erica,' Agnes says. 'Do you have somewhere more important you need to be?'

Erica blushes. 'No, it's just . . .' Her eyes dart to her watch again. 'I should have been home from work two hours ago, and if I don't call my mom then *she* will call the police.'

'Good thinking.' Agnes gestures to the box where our phones are being kept. 'Make it quick.'

Erica darts for the box. 'Sorry.' She gets up and moves towards the door. 'One sec.'

Agnes turns back to me. 'I can put some feelers out and ask questions. You never know, someone might know who this guy is. But in the meantime . . . I don't know what else we can do,' Agnes says, defeat creeping into her voice.

'Thank you,' I reply. Then Erica's voice breaks through everything.

'What?!'

Both Agnes and I look over at Erica. She crashes back into the office from the corridor.

'Who did they say they were?' She glares at me, and my stomach sinks.

'OK. How long ago was this?' A beat. 'Fine. Mom, I don't want you to freak out, but could you grab some of your stuff and go and stay at Aunty's for a while?' Another beat. Agnes crosses the office to shut the door again.

'I don't know what's going on, but I don't want you to be alone in the apartment right now. I can't come back yet.' Agnes draws the blinds and moves back to her desk. I can't stop watching Erica.

Her usually calm, smiling face is twisted with concern, and I know it's all my fault.

'Great, thank you. I love you too. Stay safe. Bye.' She hangs up and throws her phone onto a chair.

'What the fuck, Jia?!' she erupts. I shrink back from the heat of her fury.

'Woah! Let's keep our voices down,' says Agnes soothingly.

'They were at my mom's house, Jia.'

'Who's they?' Agnes asks, moving between me and Erica.

'They said they were police, looking for me, but she thinks they were NS. They also asked if my mom knew a Jia.' She practically spits out my name.

'Calm down,' Agnes says slowly. 'You ran with Jia. You helped her escape. They're simply trying to track her down. They'll be doing that with anyone who might know where she is.'

I can't look away from Erica's panic-stricken face. 'I'm so sorry. I don't . . .' I tail off; nothing I could say would make this better.

Erica growls and turns away, clearly trying to calm herself down by pacing.

Agnes frowns. 'Depending on who exactly these people are, it probably won't take them too long to work out where you travelled to. Especially if they're with the government.' She sighs and stands. 'Which means you two need to move. They won't be able to tell exactly what building you were in, but I have a feeling they'll be watching the streets for you.' She stretches and then heads over to her bed. Orion, who had settled on her blanket, springs up as she searches through her belongings. She finds a purse and claps Erica on the shoulder.

'Come on, fugitives. You've fucked up my evening plans. Let's get you the hell out of my office. I have somewhere you can go.' She heads to the door but Erica stays rooted to the spot. 'Unless you want to risk going alone or you want to talk to the feds . . .'

Her question hangs in the air.

Finally, Erica looks up at me, no longer furious, just resigned. My stomach churns.

'No. I'm coming. We're all in this now.'

'Great!' Agnes exclaims, overly cheery. 'O-Cat would be thrilled we're all getting along so nicely. Jia, grab your pussy.'

Alyssa

THE LAS, OR LAUNCH ABORT SYSTEM, IS PRETTY SELF-explanatory. If something goes wrong during launch, it's the system that should help us abort, escape from the rocket and land safely back down on Earth. If their rocket had had one, the crew of the *Challenger* would have, almost certainly, survived.

The training simulation is all about us trying to survive in a theoretical water crash landing. There's no water on Mars – well, at least, there are no oceans – so this is purely an exercise for if we fail to get off this planet – something that is highly unlikely. So of course, it makes total sense to disrupt our entire pre-launch schedule to practise in front of a whole damn camera crew.

It's 6 a.m. in Baikonur, 8 p.m. central time. Prime time. We're all wearing mock-ups of our pressure suits – the ones we'll be wearing on launch day. They're not as bulky as what NASA used to send people up in, but they're certainly by no means light or easy to manoeuvre. This exercise envisions what would happen in a worst-case scenario i.e. if we didn't have our helmets on, so our heads look tiny compared to the rest of our bodies. A pathetic crash helmet protects our skulls in an attempt to minimize the chances of concussion. Any slight injury at this point in the training would put the entire mission in jeopardy, so they make an allowance for this. Of course, if we were to crack our heads open in a real LA, we'd be completely fucked.

People say that as an astronaut, you have to be fearless, but that's bullshit. Fear is a response that has been genetically programmed into us. Fear is necessary for survival. But what an astronaut has to do is take that fear and use it to motivate you. Rather than your typical response to something scary, such as panic, you have to instead think about what comes next.

Okeowo is quiet. She has been the last day or so. She isn't the strongest in water. During our years of training, she has changed herself to have a different fundamental response to being rapidly submerged underwater in a confined space. She no longer focuses on what is happening, but how she reacts to it. Time and time again, she has followed the steps to the point where they're instinctive now. But her fear is still there – and it's there in the lines of her face right now. I'm relieved that we don't have heart monitors on us for this sim; she would hate for the world to know how her body is responding.

Finally, we get the signal that we should head out. This training takes place in a vast hangar with a giant swimming pool – yet another training facility repurposed from the former Soviet Union, who left a lot behind in their exodus to a new spaceport on home soil.

Suspended above the pool is a looming grey cone. This is our capsule, the part of the *Argo* that will separate from the main section and the rocket boosters if everything goes wrong on launch day. It will hurtle, three times faster than the speed of sound, up and away from the *Argo*, before heading back to Earth.

However, in spaceflight, things don't always go to plan, and a relatively soft landing on solid ground may turn into a hard crash landing in water. To make matters worse, the shape and weighting of the capsule (plus the fact that there'd probably be waves – the ocean has a lot of those) would mean that the capsule is most likely to flip once it inevitably makes impact, and start taking on water. So our mock-up capsule also has various levers and pulleys attached to it. They're going to fire us into the water, then flip it. We've all been assured it will make great TV.

As we come out on the poolside, a cameraman tailing us, my

eyes squint against the glare. The production crew have hoisted huge halogen bars up around the capsule, and it looks as though they've even added more lighting under the water. I guess they don't want to miss one moment of us nearly drowning.

Some of the crew and other members of the press are up in a viewing gallery on the far side of the pool. We've been instructed to wave at them as we walk out, and as commander I'm first. I try to give a polite smile as I hold my arm up in greeting to the gawping faces. When I used to visit the zoo as a kid, the keepers would tell us not to use flash photography. No such concerns here.

In the pool are several training marshals in full scuba gear. They're there in case anything goes wrong and to assess whether we follow the steps properly. We're used to seeing their smooth rubber bodies floating around. But this time, they're not the only ones. Three other divers are in there – the specialist camera operators Anders mentioned. They're above the water right now, floating. Waiting. I wonder what they would normally be doing.

Protocol snaps me back as I get the call for us to enter the capsule. They never bothered to fill it with all the electrics and equipment; it's just a rudimentary set-up of our seats and harnesses.

Lee and I are in first, up front, as commander and flight engineer. Okeowo is behind and slightly to the right of me. I hear her take a deep breath as she slides into the seat and straps herself in. Rubio is next to her, with Morin and Brun on the opposite side of the capsule.

Rubio tries to break the tension for Okeowo, exaggeratedly breathing in. 'Oh, this harness is a little tighter than it was last—'

'Eyes up, team,' Lee says stiffly. I glance across at him, wondering at his tone, and then I see it. In the corner, to the left of him, another camera has been mounted to our capsule. How do I keep missing these damn things? Did they put it out of my eyeline on purpose? We've had cameras in here before; we'd all watched our performances on the first few rounds to see how we could improve. This camera is a lot larger, though. They want to see this in all its Ultra HD glory.

Rubio falls silent again. We've not spoken about it, but we all seem to have silently agreed to keep up an air of complete professionalism in front of the cameras. We don't want to show an inch of weakness.

Once we're all secure, the deep voice of our chief technician booms out of the public address system. 'Crew. Prime for LAS Egress test.'

'Showtime,' Rubio whispers from behind.

The pistons and pulley motors fire up around us. My heart pounds and I take two slow, deep breaths to steady it. I eye the porthole nearest me, my exit, and place my left hand on the centre of my harness. My right hand goes against the metal wall, to the right of the porthole seal.

'Brace for impact,' the voice booms. 'Brace. Brace. Brace.'

A whirr and a click. And then my stomach rises as we drop, at great speed, towards the surface of the pool.

The brief feeling of weightlessness is snatched from us as we slam into the water. The impact goes all the way up my spine and the harness strains against my shoulders. I grit my teeth, and one of the others grunts. Then there's a clunk and we're jerked violently to the right, and the water starts gushing in as our whole world turns.

Two quick breaths, then a deep third as the cold water slams into my cheek. We keep rolling until we're fully upside down. But the bubbles and turbulence of the water make it hard to see.

Not that I need to. Once I feel the capsule stop turning, I take my hand off the wall and press the central buckle of my harness. I shrug my right shoulder out of the straps. My left one, too. Bubbles stream from my nose. I'm counting. Not sure why, but it always helps.

The world is muffled. I hear exaggerated swirls and eddies through my ear drums and clicks and clunks as my crewmates do the same as me.

I spot the porthole again and reach out for the escape handle near its rim. My hand finds it first time. I grasp it firmly and jerk it down. A burst of air sounds as the porthole glass is fired away from the body of the capsule. Other similar bursts boom around me.

Just outside the porthole, I glimpse a black shadow. A marshal, watching closely.

As soon as the window is clear of the capsule. I grab for the hole and pull myself through. I find my feet on the edge of the porthole, stretch out my arms, hands together, and push away from the capsule.

As I move horizontally outwards, I feel the slight pull of the capsule sinking behind me. I turn and face up to the bright lights of the surface and kick my way to them.

My head breaks through and I gulp for air through my tight throat.

I instinctively look around at the four blue helmets bursting to the surface, on the other side of the pool.

There should be five. There should be another near me. I wait for what feels like an age.

'Wright!' Rubio yells from the other side of the pool. And then I realize: Okeowo.

I take another huge gulp of air and roll downwards with all my might, back into the water.

Below, I see the capsule. Flippers. A cameraman holding his camera as a blue helmet flails by the porthole I just exited from.

Okeowo's porthole hasn't been blown. She's tried to come through mine instead. And she's stuck.

I claw down towards the capsule. A marshal is also surging towards her, his oxygen tank leaving a trail of bubbles. He gets there before I do, grabs the camera that's perilously close to Okeowo and shoves it, and its operator, out of the way.

I reach Okeowo. She's panicking. Her leg is caught in the trailing straps of my harness. The more she flails, the more it twists. Precious air bubbles escape from her mouth as she tries to pull the straps away from her leg.

I grab the capsule and pull myself down to her. I take hold of her arm, and her terrified face snaps round. Her wide eyes lock with mine. Air. She needs air.

I raise my two fingers to my eyes and point to her left, where the marshal is holding out his mouthpiece. Her gaze follows mine, and she lets go of her leg and reaches for it. She clears out the mouthpiece, as we're trained to do, and takes her first gulp. I turn my attention to her leg.

Manoeuvring myself halfway through the porthole, I hook my foot under one of the capsule's metal bars to steady myself, just as I would on a spacewalk. I methodically unwind the straps around her leg. With her leg now still, it's simple to free it. As I pull, I feel the presence of the cameraman moving back in again somewhere above me. As soon as the strap is out of the way, I tap Okeowo's leg. She releases the marshal's mouthpiece and kicks away from the capsule, heading to the surface.

I turn to follow.

CLUNK.

The capsule jerks. It's moving again. There's a sharp lurch on my foot and a pop, then excruciating pain surges up my body. My arms flail as the world turns downwards. I try to kick away from the capsule, but only one leg is working. The other just burns. I scream and water hits the back of my throat. I can't see. Can't breathe. Can't move.

Shadows churn in front of me. Flippers swirl water into my face. I reach out to grab them.

I see a lens. A cold, dark lens.

Then black.

Jia

IT'S BEEN A WEEK SINCE KAI DISAPPEARED, AND WE'RE NO closer to discovering what happened to him.

Instead, we've spent the last four days in what Agnes is calling 'the safe house' but is actually one of the most expensive pieces of real estate in the whole of Hong Kong. A mansion on the edge of the bay, looking out over the city's skyline.

'Whatever you do, do not use a phone,' was the first thing she said to us when she moved us in.

'Where the hell are we?' Erica gawped.

'Grandfather's old weekend retreat. Lots of security. Plus, my uncle and his neighbours are friendly with the chief exec. His goons don't come round here.'

The house is built around a massive living space, with floor-to-ceiling glass windows looking out on the view. Agnes has filled the place with hundreds of plants. It's like a mini rainforest, with plush designer seating that you can sink into. I think of my and Kai's tiny apartment in the building we can hardly afford. Two worlds so completely apart.

We spent the next two days waiting for Agnes to arrive with news and supplies. First, she brought clothes. Not ours – there's no way she can go to our apartments – but some casual stuff she's had picked up for us. Initially I was alarmed by this – I'm not as skinny as Erica and Agnes, nor am I as trendy – but Agnes managed to pick out the right sizes for me and the clothes weren't too outrageous. Erica looked effortlessly gorgeous in her new denim jumpsuit. The veterinary scrubs hadn't done her justice. I blushed and turned away when she noticed me looking. Cat food came next, and Agnes told us she was tapping up all of her contacts to try and track down Frybread. In the meantime, Agnes assured Erica that her mom was safe and staying with her sister. How she knew this, we don't know.

Erica was a lot less frosty with me after that.

I understand, of course I do. Here we are, staring out across Discovery Bay day in, day out. All of Hong Kong's beauty laid out before us. But despite the glorious view, I can't stop thinking about my mom either.

It started with little things. Mom's condition. She'd lose her train of thought, or buy dishwashing detergent thinking it was fabric softener. She forgot my birthday, then said she'd been confused about the date. This went on for a few months, and then I caught her swearing under her breath. Our mom never swore.

In the end, it was Kai who bit the bullet and told her she should go to the doctor. At first, awful as it sounds, I hoped it was a brain tumour. I'd seen a story on Instagram about how a woman's memory had deteriorated and her personality had seemed to shift, and then they found a giant tumour pressing against her brain that they were able to operate on, and then she'd recovered and gone on to start a wig-making business for other cancer survivors.

I wish it had been that.

But it wasn't.

It was like the tests opened the floodgates. After her diagnosis, she deteriorated quickly. Kai refused to accept it. He was adamant there was a way to get our mom back, to retrieve the person she once was. In the end, he didn't even help me arrange her move to the home. He didn't speak to me for weeks after.

So then it was up to me to visit all the time, to make sure she settled in. I was left with sorting the paperwork, the power of attorney. I stayed on at school. I knew that's what she wanted, and it was what I was supposed to do. Become an accountant. Get a good job. Find someone. Start a family. Be respectable. Sensible.

Kai, on the other hand, spent all his time at his computer or with his stupid cat. The cat I'm now dragging around Hong Kong while armed men beat down doors searching for us.

When I find him, he's going to be so damn sorry. And I'm going to drag him to go and see Mom, whether he wants to or not. In the meantime, I need to find a way to get in touch with her, or at least the home. Make sure she's not worried, that they haven't hurt her . . .

On our fourth day in hiding, I find Erica sitting on one of the couches, looking out at the vista, stroking a dozing Orion. He seems to like her and has no problem falling asleep on her lap. He's still wary around me.

'Hey,' she says, her voice warm.

'Hey,' I reply, and sit on the other end of the couch. Restless, I pull out a drawer within the teak coffee table in front of us. It's full of leaflets. The first stack demands 'PEACE!' and explains how militarism is a big cause of climate destruction and violence against children. I stare at the picture on it: a small child, crying, being handed through a barbed wire fence by a woman, also crying. There's so much love and grief in the woman's eyes as she gives her child over to anonymous hands, smoke and rubble behind her. I quickly put that stack aside and pick up the last bunch right at the bottom of the drawer. Stuck together, they have the headline: 'EARTH BEFORE MARS – DEFUND NASA'S MAYFLOWER'. These are old – *Mayflower* was a few years ago. The doomed silhouette of it is crossed out, and inside is a ream of arguments for what NASA's budget could be better used for. I sit back and marvel at the relic.

Erica continues to scratch Orion behind his ear. He stretches his head up to get a better angle.

'Hey, what have you told your work?' I ask.

She shrugs. 'The raid probably shut the place down. And

whoever is after you has probably ensured I don't have a job there any more. So, what the hell?'

I watch her, feeling so bad that she's stuck here with me, sucked into all this.

Erica shifts under my gaze, picks up the discarded leaflet.

'Mars,' she declares, in a big voice. 'You would not catch me going up there.'

'I don't know,' I find myself saying as I stare out of the windows. The city has a haze of smog around it. 'Why not?'

'You'd travel millions of miles just to bounce around on a dusty desert?'

'Well, listen to Agnes and her friends. The world is fucked. Not like anything can be done about it. And besides, it's not like I'd have much to miss down here.'

Erica shakes her head. 'I don't believe that.'

My face flushes with annoyance. 'You don't know me,' I snap.

She doesn't pull back like I thought she would, doesn't look offended by my sudden snipe. 'You've got O.'

I snort. 'A brother I barely speak to and who I didn't even know had a girlfriend, let alone a career as a cybercriminal? He'd never even notice I was gone.'

'I don't know what O would be like,' she concedes. 'But I think you'd miss him. You're here, after all.'

I open my mouth to give a scathing retort, but can't think of one, so I shut it.

'You know,' Erica says, shifting both her position and the subject. 'I've been thinking about this thing in Orion's neck.' She gestures to the cat, who turns onto his back for a better belly rub.

'And?' I say, then instantly regret how snappy I sound. Erica carries on regardless.

'A couple of months back, O asked me for the numbers of some vets, but he said he wanted someone discreet, who would take cash. He sounded pretty stressed.'

Orion's contented purrs are now rumbling through the couch cushions.

'I thought he was just being eccentric, so I gave him the number of this trainee vet and thought nothing of it. But . . . this,' her hands move over the back of Orion's neck. 'It's too big to be a generic microchip, but it's small for a wireless device.'

'OK,' I reply, not sure where she's going with this.

'To store, receive and then transmit data, it needs energy, but I think it's too small to have its own power source. I think Orion is the energy.'

'What do you mean?'

'Bioelectricity. All living beings make tonnes of it. And there's loads of research into harvesting it and using it for medical devices. I think even Agnes's uncles have some kind of subsidiary company trialling this kind of stuff. What if Kai paid a guy to put a chip in Orion that ran off of his own bioelectricity? No need for a big chunky battery, and it's guaranteed to keep running.'

'I suppose that make sense. Unless . . .' I look down at the creature purring next to Erica, the thing Kai seemed to love more than anything else in the world.

'Unless Orion dies. If I'm right, it's a dead man's switch. Or, in this case, a dead cat's switch. Whoever wants to get hold of that code has to keep your brother's precious cat alive.'

'And that's why he was so adamant in that message that I look after him.'

'Precisely. I think your brother took a job, but he started to worry that it would put him in danger somehow. So, as a precaution, he decided to hide clues as to what he was up to, maybe even who he was working for.'

It sounds like something Kai would have thought of after watching too many sci-fi movies.

'The switch also means we can't just take it out,' Erica continues. 'If we remove it from Orion, without a seamless transition to another power source, then our only clue from O will be gone.'

'So he's forcing me to care for his pet?'

'Or he trusts you with Orion, and his secrets, more than anyone else?'

I let out a grunt of frustration. 'But what am I supposed to do with them?' I cry, throwing my hands in the air.

As if on cue, Agnes barges in. 'Good, you're both here.' She's agitated, on edge. This is not the Agnes I've come to know, and I'm instantly terrified. Erica can clearly sense it too. She stands up suddenly, sending a startled Orion flying.

Agnes storms over to the couch and thrusts a phone into Erica's hands, gesturing for me to come over.

'It broke earlier today. It's even being picked up internationally.'

Erica's eyes go wide, her mouth making a perfect 'o'.

'What?' I ask, taking the phone from Erica's hands.

My stomach drops.

FINANCE STUDENT WANTED IN CONNECTION WITH BROTHER'S DISAPPEARANCE

My eyes fly across the lines, snagging on certain awful phrases.

. . . treating the incident as a suspected murder.

Li Jia . . . missing for seven days . . . last seen fleeing her apartment.

. . . refused to cooperate.

But one part feels like a gut punch. The part where they warn people not to approach me because I have—

'A history of mental illness?' I croak. Looking up at Erica, I see nothing but sympathy in her eyes. 'I had counselling, after Dad . . . and Mom. School counselling!'

Agnes snatches the phone away from me.

'Jia, we've got to get you out of the country,' she says, simply.

'What?' I cry.

'Seriously?' Erica echoes.

'Come on, you both know what this means. The police, the press. The government are involved, and I can't hide you for ever.'

I feel everything I've eaten that day rising within me. The room is suddenly stiflingly hot. How can this be happening?

Apparently unaware of my meltdown, Agnes ploughs on. 'Jia, I have a proposition for you. No one seems to know who this Frybread is, or how to contact him. He's been dark for too long. And the longer you're here, the more dangerous it is. For all of us.'

Erica shifts nervously next to me, and that familiar wave of guilt hits me again.

'So, what do we know? We know that Frybread is somehow connected to this restaurant in the US. Right now, this Frybread is the only lead we have, and the only person who might be able to tell us what this code is all about and maybe even what the hell O was up to. So . . .'

'Just say it, Agnes,' Erica says, her voice strained.

Agnes sighs. 'So, Jia, I think you should go there. To the US, with Orion, and track this guy down. I've got you a ride.'

'With who?' Erica barks.

'Some friends of mine at Sea Saviour. They're heading to California,' says Agnes.

'Environmental pirates?!' Erica splutters.

Agnes smiles and drops down into an armchair. Orion is there in a flash, jumping onto her lap and nuzzling into her.

'Yep.'

'She's a wanted fugitive and you're sending her out to sea with *more* wanted fugitives?' Erica's tone takes me by surprise. There's care there, there's worry.

'Who better to hide her? Calm down, Erica. This is more of a recon mission. They're tracking plastics, that sort of thing. No hot pursuits. At least, nothing planned.'

Erica rolls her eyes and moves to the kitchen. There's a rustling. Orion instantly thinks Erica is feeding him, so he jumps down from Agnes and follows her, tail high.

'How long would it take?' I ask, as Erica opens cupboards behind me.

'I'm not sure,' Agnes replies, more serious now. 'They estimate about forty days, but if their priorities shift it could be longer. But don't worry, you'll have plenty to keep you occupied. No one is a passenger on their ships – you'll have to work for your bunk. The time will fly by. Then once you hit land, you can grab transport on to Indiana.'

'Forty days,' I cry. 'Are you joking? Kai's been gone for a week, and you want me to take over a month to sail to America? Anything could have happened to him by then!'

'Better forty days than for ever – because that's what we're looking at if you don't get out now. You can't save him if you're in jail.'

'Agnes,' Erica cries from behind me. 'This is insane. You can't expect her to—'

'Even before this shit,' Agnes gestures at her phone, 'I was trying to find a way to get Jia out of here. And that's *hard*. She can't go anywhere near the mainland. And everyone is terrified of getting tied up in extradition laws these days, so our pool of potential helpers is tiny. We need people who are willing to turn a blind eye. People who are already on the edge of the law.'

'What about a fake passport? Surely we could get hold of one. I could fly out. And when I find Kai, we could pay you back.'

Agnes lets out a huge breath. 'With the facial recognition they have at the terminals these days?' She shakes her head. 'I know forty days is a long time, but we have to get you out now. Otherwise, it won't just be Kai who goes missing. You, me, Erica – if we're arrested, they'll make us all drop off the face of the Earth.'

There it is. The truth.

We're all totally fucked, thanks to my little brother.

'Kai left you Orion, he left you clues. I genuinely believe he wanted us to help you. Hell, he probably thought all you'd need to do is give us this code and I could fix the rest. And I really wish I could. But they're not just after him any more.' Agnes's eyes bore into me. 'You have to get out of here, Jia. And you have to find Frybread.'

'OK,' I say, my mind whirring. 'I've . . . I've never been on a boat before.' If I'm honest, the thought of it terrifies me. I'm not a strong swimmer, and I get seasick just sitting on a swing. Plus, it's a long time to be stuck on a ship for, with people like Agnes. I'm nothing like her and her friends . . .

'It's a ship,' Agnes automatically corrects me. 'And think of this as a baptism of fire. You'll take to it in no time. You'll have to go vegan, though – no meat on this trip. Although, I'm not sure what we'll do about him.' Agnes throws her head towards Orion. 'We'll have to smuggle in some cat food. That should be interesting.'

'Are you sure this is a good idea?' Erica is back, potato chips in hand. She eats when she's anxious, although you'd never know from looking at her.

'Well, do you have any others?' Agnes asks, overly sweet.
Silence.

Agnes leans forward. 'I wouldn't be suggesting this if I didn't think it was necessary. Right now, this is our only option.'

I look between their faces, one creased in worry, one full of fire.

Agnes takes my hand. 'I know this is a big decision, but they leave in five days. You have until then to decide.'

With that, she turns on her heel and leaves.

As I spoon cat food into a bowl for Orion, who chirrups in anticipation, Erica watches me from across the kitchen.

'So they're terrorists,' I say.

'Ecoterrorists,' Erica replies. I place the bowl down and Orion leaps on it. 'They're sort of the guys that Greenpeace kicked out for being too hardcore. They'll do anything for the planet.'

'Makes sense that Agnes knows them, then.' I sip at a cup of tea, leaning back against the counter. 'Where does she keep going? She's never here for more than a few hours. She never seems to sleep!'

'I think she's got a lot going on. With Mars One and the wildfires and the crazy weather systems hitting Europe right now,' Erica says with a sigh. 'It sort of all feels like it's coming to a head, you know? There's so much to be angry about, to draw attention to.'

'Do you think she's . . .' I don't know why, but I lower my voice a little. Orion's ears shift, like he's listening in too. 'Do you think she's with Terra Revolution?'

Erica laughs. I've not seen her do that for a while. It's nice.

She hoists herself onto the counter and swings her legs. 'Nah. They're far too extreme, even for Agnes. She wouldn't blow shit up. She's just pissed off, as we all should be, really. You know, I always had a reason not to go to her rallies or protests or whatever. But now . . . I sort of want to.'

Orion finishes his food and rubs up against my legs. I don't move away as I would have before.

'Isn't it all too late now anyway?' I say, quietly. 'If the world is burning and flooding, and that spaceship is about to launch, what can anyone do? People glue themselves to buildings and the companies don't do anything. Even Agnes with all her influence, her cash, and passion? It doesn't work. There's nothing that can be done.'

Erica is quiet for a moment. Watching me, like she's staring straight into my soul. Then she says, 'Is that how you feel about your brother?'

Her eyes are so sad, so sympathetic. They're impossible to look away from. And then I feel it, building up inside of me. All the feelings I've buried. The fear, the anger. The sadness. It's like she's drawing them out of me. Opening me up. I feel tears on my cheeks. For a moment, Erica looks surprised. Then she jumps down off the counter and rushes to embrace me. It feels like relief.

'I'm sorry,' Erica says into my hair.

I sense Orion settling on the floor next to us.

'No, I'm sorry,' I cry. 'I'm sorry I dragged you and your mom into this. I'm sorry you're stuck here. And I'm stuck here. And I'm sorry I have no idea where my stupid brother is, or what the hell he's got himself into. Of course I don't want to just give up on him, of course I don't want to believe there's nothing that can be done. But all I have is his cat and a scrap of code and now I'm being told to head off on a damn ship halfway round the world on what feels like a pure hunch and leave my mom behind . . . and . . . I'm scared. I don't think I can do it.'

Erica squeezes me more and rubs my back. I don't think I could stand up without her right now. We stay like that for a while, the sun fading behind us. Then Erica gives me a final squeeze and breaks away. She makes us both a fresh tea, guides me to the couch and sits next to me, Orion between us. I reach out and stroke him. He doesn't flinch, so I do it a couple more times.

Erica looks at the two of us. 'You don't have many friends, do you?'

'What do you mean?' I say sharply.

'No one who cries like that does it regularly. That felt like it was long overdue. And I can't imagine Kai is much of an emotional support. Am I right?'

I shift awkwardly. 'I have friends on my course. I study with them. And go for drinks, or whatever . . .'

We stay silent long enough for Orion to settle again and close his eyes.

'I'll be your friend,' Erica says softly, over the sound of Orion's purrs. And as she takes my hand and we stare out at the Hong Kong skyline, I finally accept that I have to get on that ship. But there's something I need to do first.

Alyssa

I OPEN MY EYES AND BLINK A FEW TIMES AGAINST THE light. It must be those damn TV lights. But then I realize I'm not lying on the tiled poolside. I'm somewhere soft. As things come into focus, I feel sheets underneath, a blanket lying over me. I see clean, white walls and ceiling tiles.

They've taken me to medical.

Shit.

I do a quick assessment of my situation. My throat and chest are sore. That must be from water inhalation and where they cleared my airways. Maybe even chest compressions.

I ball my fingers into a fist and release them a few times. Apart from a strange tingling, all is good. I shift focus to my legs. The left one feels sore, but I can bend it at the knee. Right one is numb.

Then I remember the pop.

I slowly look down my body to find my right leg raised, and my lower leg and ankle dressed. In my arm is a drip. I look to my left. Out the window, it's green. But Baikonur is not green. It's dusty. Dry.

So, I'm not in Baikonur any more.

Fuck.

A groan. It takes a moment to realize it's coming from me. It sounded pathetic, and I give myself a mental shake. *Come on, Alyssa. Sort yourself out.* I try to sit up, but my head feels impossibly heavy and dots form in my vision, so I grope around down by my side and find a lead with a remote attached to it. I mash some of the buttons.

As expected, it brings someone into the room. A woman. She's pleased to see me awake and says something in Russian. I know a little Russian, but my mind feels sluggish and I can't make out what she says. She smiles sympathetically and switches to English as she approaches my bed and looks at some machines out of my sightline.

'Hello, Commander Wright. I'm so glad to see you awake.'

I'm not glad, because I don't know this woman. She's not part of our medical team. She's not been in quarantine with us for the last week. So, I'm obviously no longer in quarantine.

All the breath in me surges out through my red-raw throat.

I'm off the crew.

I must have blacked out again, because it's suddenly dark in the room. A low, warm light comes from a lamp by the side of my bed. And sat in one of the chairs by the window is a familiar shape.

'Hello, Anders.' God, my voice is croaky.

'Hello,' he replies, his voice stifled by the mask over his nose and mouth. He's wearing disposable gloves and he holds his knee, which is crossed over his other leg. How long has he been here? 'How are you feeling?'

I try to laugh, but it comes out more like a cough. My chest stabs with pain. 'Like shit.'

Anders' eyes crease up in a smile beneath his mask. He uncrosses his legs and sits forward, but he can't come nearer. He's already breaking protocol by even being this close.

'You don't need to be here, you know,' I tell him, finding my voice again. 'It's obvious what you've come here to say.'

'I know,' he replies simply. He stares down at his gloves.

'How's Okeowo?'

'Very upset about what happened.'

I try to shake my head. 'It's not her fault.'

He regards me a moment, and I let the silence sit between us. I don't have the energy to fill it.

'Okeowo did not blow her porthole,' he begins eventually, as though reading from a report. 'After releasing her harness, she became aware of a camera operator moving close to the capsule and feared that blowing it would injure him. With no way to communicate to him, she chose to instead egress through your porthole. She proceeded to move through the capsule, where her foot became entangled in your harness. You know what happened next. The force dislocated your ankle and I am told caused a trimalleolar fracture of the joint. You began taking on water and you blacked out. Our marshals freed you from the capsule and brought you poolside, where you received resuscitation. You were taken to the medical centre, where the extent of your injuries became apparent and you were transferred, by air, here. To Astana.'

Astana, the Kazakh capital. Outside, there's the muffled sounds of a hospital ward. People talking, a brief burst of laughter.

'How long ago?'

'Two days.'

I turn to look at him. 'L-minus-seven.'

He nods. 'L-minus-seven.'

They are going to launch without me. I knew that. But somehow, Anders' nod feels like a kick in my already pummelled chest.

I stare at him, and he doesn't shy away. He keeps his gaze steady. My eyes well again. Every ounce of my energy drains away.

'Collins will do a great job as commander.' My voice sounds small, weak.

That's when he finally looks away, shifting uncomfortably in his chair. Perhaps he thinks I can't take talking about my replacement. Maybe he's right. I don't push it. All our backups have been waiting for something like this to happen. Collins is an ex-military pilot. He knows how the game works. He'll take my place respectfully.

My place.

I can't think about that. Not yet.

'How were the ratings?'

'What?' Anders looks confused.

'Their precious ratings.' I cough again. 'How were they?'

Anders barks out a laugh, shaking his head. 'You really want to know?'

I lick my dry lips and give a little nod.

He scoffs again. 'Through the roof, Alyssa. Through the fucking roof.' He stands, but with nowhere really to go he paces back and forth in his little corner of the room. 'Millions of the fuckers,' he continues. 'All of them, watching you and Okeowo, again and again. It's . . .' I don't think I've ever seen him lost for words.

'Well. He got a very good shot,' I mumble. I see a flash of that lens coming towards me, my heartbeat rising. Anders stops and stares at me again, all humour gone from him now. The look in his eyes – pity? sadness? – is unbearable. I turn away.

'He was blocking her on purpose. That cameraman.' I croak. 'They wanted drama and they got it. And how come the capsule moved again? That's never happened before.'

He gathers his jacket and phone from the small side table as I speak, then moves round to my side of the room, still keeping his distance. He hovers by the door.

'They're giving it another day for the swelling to go down, then you're having an operation to pin the fracture.' He gestures out to where the ward must be. 'We've had someone flown in from Germany.' His gloved hand hovers over the door handle. 'I'll let you rest.' He opens the door and turns to leave. But then he stops again and looks back at me.

'I'm sorry, Alyssa.'

I swallow a gulp of air that seems to rush up from within me.

'Me too,' I whisper.

Jia

'YOU'RE INSANE.'

I carry on packing the suitcase full of cat food as Erica stands over me.

'I'd expect this of Agnes, but you?' she continues. 'You're more sensible than this.'

I stand up, trying to muster my strength.

'I have to do this, Erica. I'd have thought you'd understand.' I move over to the other bags piled up in the corner. I've seen how much it hurts her, not talking to her mom.

'This has nothing to do with me, Jia.' Her beautiful face is contorted with fury. 'You need to drop this and get straight on the ship.'

I know deep down that she's right, but I can't just leave.

Erica sees this in my eyes.

'For fuck's sake, Jia. We've been holed up here for days trying to keep you safe. And now, just as we've finally managed to find a way to get you out of here, you want to risk it all?'

'Agnes and I have a plan. It's going to work.'

'You know they'll be waiting for you,' Erica snaps. 'They'll have people looking out for your face and they'll pounce as soon as you show it.'

'I know,' I reply, hoping my voice doesn't betray my terror, 'which is why I won't show my face. I'll be on a ship before they even realize it was me.'

Erica throws her hands and walks away from the table, her body vibrating with frustration. Any connection there was between us feels like a distant memory. Now she looks at me like I'm ruining her life – which I guess I kind of am.

'Will I see you, at the dock?' I call out to her.

'Will you make it?' Erica retorts, before slamming the door of her bedroom. I wince as the noise reverberates through me.

Agnes shakes her head and smiles a sad smile. She lifts up one of the bags and heads to the door.

'You ready?'

I nod.

Mom has been at the same facility since she left home two years ago. It's pricey, but I wanted to assuage some of my guilt by putting her in the best possible place we could afford. For now, at least. I'm all too aware of how quickly dad's life insurance payout is dwindling.

The Shing Mun Centre for Positive Ageing overlooks the river that gives it its name, although now the view is somewhat blocked by flood defences. Agnes drops me off, with a large portfolio case tucked under my arm. Before I head towards the centre, I put on a face mask and make sure that my hat is pulled down low over my brow, which should conceal me from any CCTV cameras.

At the staff entrance, I hit the intercom buzzer with my elbow and pretend I am trying to push paper back into my portfolio, so as not to look up towards the cameras. A chirpy voice rings out.

'Can I help you?'

I experience a moment of terror. *Oh God. I can't do this.* But I have to.

'Oh, erm, hello. I'm Miss Ko. I'm, err, here to cover Miss Chen's calligraphy class. She's not well.' Yesterday, Agnes used some of her connections to send a fake email from the teacher's account. Meanwhile, poor Miss Chen thinks the centre has been shut down due to norovirus . . .

'Oh yes, you're on the list.' The door buzzes. 'I'll send someone to show you to the rec room.'

'No!' I trill, trying not to sound panicked. 'I've been here before. I'm sure you have lots to be getting on with. I'll find my way.'

There's a moment of excruciating silence, then: 'Great. Just grab someone if you need anything.'

Relief makes me light-headed as I bundle through the door. I make sure to turn sideways to get through with my portfolio, facing the right-hand wall, avoiding the CCTV that's dotted throughout the building.

Two floors up, I hover by my mother's door. I need to get inside as soon as possible, but for some reason I can't bring myself to knock. I close my eyes, take a deep breath, knock softly and slip in, shutting it behind me just as I hear a nurse emerge into the hallway.

'Who's there?' A sharp voice calls out from further into the room. As silently as possible, I put my portfolio down and take off my hat.

'Ma? It's Jia.'

'I don't know a Jia.'

Things like that used to hit me hard, but now I'm almost used to it. I steel myself as I move further in, past her en suite and out into the wider part of her room. It's fairly dated. A tired cream on the walls and mismatched furniture with clashing floral cushions and drapes. But it's clean and some fake, bright flowers sit in a vase by the TV, which is on but muted. Mom is sitting by the window, looking out on the green hills that rise up behind the building.

As I move closer to her, I hear her muttering under her breath. 'Really pissed off. Shit day. Such a shit day.' Then she looks at me suspiciously. 'What do you want?'

'I'm here to see you, Ma,' I say softly and sit down on the side of the bed, near her chair. 'How are you?'

'Fine, thank you,' she says politely, as if to a stranger.

'What have you been up to?' I go to hold her hand, but she pulls it away from me.

'Nothing much. I'm glad I'm going home tomorrow. I shan't be coming back to this hotel again.'

'You aren't going home tomorrow, Ma. This is where you live now, remember?'

She ignores this and her mantra begins again. 'Awful. Shit. Really pissed off, I am.'

'Ma, I need to tell you something.'

When she turns to me, it's like a switch has been flicked. She seems more lucid. Warm, even. She takes my hand.

'What is it, my dear?' She smiles for the first time since I entered the room. This glimpse of who she used to be upsets me more than anything. I blink hard against the sting in the back of my eyes.

'I'm afraid I won't be coming to visit for a while. I might be going away for a bit.'

She nods. 'Are you going on holiday?'

'Yes,' I say slowly, 'sort of. Kai's gone somewhere and I need to find him and bring him back.'

She smiles again. 'He's always been such a good boy.'

'Not always, Ma.'

She pats my hand. 'I hope you have a lovely holiday.'

'Thanks.' I pull away and begin to rifle through my pockets, finding some change. 'I'm going to leave some money in your top drawer. If you need more snacks, you ask the nurses politely and they'll get it for you, OK?'

'I won't need anything, dear. I'm going home tomorrow. I've booked a table for dinner tonight with my husband.' She's looking wistfully back out of the window again now. 'I think we'll have steak.'

'That sounds lovely,' I humour her. Time is ticking. I need to get going but I want to try and get through to her somehow. Just enough to make her realize who I am, now, before I get on that ship. I crouch down in front of her, placing my hands on her knees. She looks surprised.

'Now, Ma,' I say, more firmly. 'There might be a time where you will worry about where I am. And I'm sorry, but I want you to try and remember what I'm saying right now. I promise I will come back and see you.'

I realize then that I am being too intense, but it's too late – I've triggered something. She looks worried suddenly and pulls her hand back. She avoids my gaze and looks around the room erratically.

'Err. My shower, it's not working. Will you look at it?'

I stare at her a moment, trying to discern if what I've said has sunk in. I hope it has. But I have no way of telling. I sigh.

'Sure.' I slowly rise up and head to her en suite. I turn on the faucet and run my hands under the stream. Just as the temperature begins to turn from tepid to warm, I hear a shrill squeal.

'. . . someone in my room. Help me!'

Shit. I drop the showerhead and rush back in to find my mom on her bed, trembling, the room's telephone glued to her ear.

'Ma, it's me. Put it down.'

'Help!' she shouts down the phone, then drops it. She moves as far back on the bed as she can, terrified of me. Her eyes are wide with panic, her chest heaving. Tears run down my cheeks as I watch her claw at the sheets.

I have to go. They'll be coming.

'Ma.' I move towards her but a frightened yelp erupts from her and I freeze. There's nothing I can do any more. I begin to back away.

'Remember what I said, OK? I love you, and I'm coming back.'

'Get out!' she screams. 'Fucking get out!' She's screeching now, throwing her whole body into it. I run to the door, tear it open and glance down the corridor to see if anyone's coming, but the tears are making everything blurry.

Mom is still screaming behind me, and I hear distant echoes of footsteps charging up the stairs. I head away from them and duck into the nearest open door. Just as I squeeze through it, I hear feet hammering down the corridor and rushing into my mom's room.

'Shhh, it's OK. We're here. Everything is fine.' It hurts like a physical pain that they are able to bring her a comfort that I can't.

Her yelps begin to quieten. 'Mei. Oh, thank God it's you, Mei,' she stammers. I can't take this any more. I pull open the door to escape, but then another set of footsteps comes down the hall towards us. I dart back, leaving the door open a crack.

A gruff male voice speaks. 'What's going on here?'

I hear a low, soft mumble of a reply from one of the nurses. Then:

'Mrs Li, who was in your room?'

Mom's voice raises again. Whoever this man is, his blunt way of speaking is clearly causing her anxiety again. 'I don't know!' she wails.

More shushing noises as they calm her again.

'Officer, please—' the nurse says, but the man talks over her.

'Mrs Li, you must cooperate. Who was in your room? Are these their things?'

He is obviously referring to my portfolio. I curse myself for not grabbing it. If they fingerprint it, they'll definitely know I was here.

'Mrs Li!' I have to hold myself back from tearing open the door and running right in there. How dare he talk to her like this?

'Was your daughter here? Jia?' I freeze.

There's a silence.

'Was it your daughter?'

A mumble.

'What?' He sounds like he's spitting.

'I don't have a daughter!' The words ring out loud, clear and defiant. I haven't heard her voice that strong in months. 'I have no idea what you are talking about. Now leave me alone.'

It hurts to hear her say it, even though I know she can't help it. I slump against the wall and slide down to a squat. My nose is running now – I'm an absolute state. I try to mop it with my sleeve. Next door, I hear more mumbling. And then the man is storming out, his strides purposeful, back down the corridor. The door to the stairs bangs behind him.

My mom is sobbing now. I can't stay any longer. I can't listen to her cry. I force myself up, try to compose myself and open the door a crack, looking out onto the corridor again. All is quiet.

I dash out and decide to take the other set of stairs and make it down and into the entrance hall. A security guard stands by the door, scanning the faces of people coming and going. Fear grips me. I've never seen a guard here before; he must be looking for me.

He hasn't seen me yet, so I bolt through a door marked THE ROSENBERG SUITE. As I duck into the room, I realize it's the centre's new sensory suite, mercifully empty. At least for a moment . . .

'Excuse me?' A gruff voice breaks the silence. I turn and see the security guard.

A scream leaps out of me. I spin and spot the window out to the car park, which is open.

'Miss, I'm going to have to ask you to—'

I don't wait around to hear what he wants. I dash to the window, throw one leg over the sill, then the other. Next moment, I'm ducking under the window frame and rolling out and down into a bush. I land with a thud and all the air leaves me in a grunt.

I lie for a moment, stunned, then scrabble onto my front and push myself up. I throw myself through the bush, branches scratching across my skin as I tear through the foliage and out onto the drive.

Several passers-by stop and look at me like I'm a madwoman. But I don't care. I start running, willing my legs to pump harder. There's yelling behind me, but I force myself to ignore it. I keep my eyes on the main road. I'm supposed to meet Agnes a block away, so it's harder to track us. But then a car beeps to the left of me. I ignore it, but it beeps again. I turn and see a black car with someone frantically waving both arms at me. Agnes!

I swerve. She revs her engine and yells, 'Come on!'

There's a small fence between us. I push harder and leap over it, hoping to God my toes don't get caught, but then the ground rushes up to meet me and I'm over. I scrabble for the passenger door and dive in.

'Go!' I scream. Agnes needs no encouragement – she's already shooting off, turning the corner and heading towards the car park exit.

'Close the door!' she cries. I grab the handle and pull it to, just as she zooms out of the hospital car park and onto the main street. The pink building fades behind us in the rear window. A few figures watch us, some rushing to get into cars, but we're gone.

I'm exhausted, my breath heaving. I hold my head in my hands as I try to recover. All I can hear is the rush of blood in my ears and the thrum of the engine. Agnes carries on driving.

'That went well,' she says.

I hug my knees close to me as I stare down at Orion sitting in the footwell of Agnes's car. He jerks suddenly and stares at the floor. My watch has caught some of the afternoon light, creating a little bright spot that he's now mesmerized by. I move my wrist a little, and he wiggles his bottom and pounces on it, utterly bewildered when it doesn't end up in his paws. Stupid creature.

'You and that cat have a lot more in common than you think,' Agnes says, making me jump. The light disappears from the floor. Orion looks up, bereft.

'What do you mean?' I ask, straightening up.

'You know. Both chasing after something, but no idea what it is.'

'I don't really feel up to big philosophical discussions right now. Besides, I know what I'm after: my brother. Someone you don't seem that worried about.'

Agnes flicks the indicator and joins a busy road. 'How do you know what I'm worried about?' She smiles at me.

All the emotions from the day flare up in a fiery ball inside of me. 'You know, you and *him* have a lot more in common than you think,' I snap.

She raises an eyebrow as she pulls up behind another car. The traffic is piling up and I feel a dart of anxiety.

'He's exactly the same, never bothered by anything. Always telling me I worry about the wrong things. Laughing at me when I get stressed out. It's so easy for him. He doesn't have to worry about anything because he never takes responsibility for anything.

All he cares about is himself – and now it's up to me to clean up his mess!'

She doesn't rise to my anger, and I'm left feeling like an idiot as the silence grows between us. Orion has given up on the light and moves on to licking himself.

'I understand why you went today,' she says, soft, sympathetic. I snort, but she continues. 'O explained how hard this all is on you.'

My head snaps up and I give a bitter laugh. 'Did he? Well, I've no idea how he knew that given that he never used to even talk about it, or come with me to see Mom, or ever be even mildly bothered by any of it.'

'Maybe that's what he was like with *you*.'

'What the fuck do you know?' I almost shout. 'You didn't even know he was missing until I turned up. You make out like you and he were super close, but I never even knew you existed! I'm his sister! I've known him his whole life. You've known him for, what, five minutes, and you think you know him more than me? He's a genius, sure. Obsessive. Immature. Weirdly in love with his cat. Anyone can tell you that. But did you know how he used to be scared of balloons, or that he once needed stitches because he stabbed himself in the cheek with a fork? Or that when Dad died, he didn't shed a single tear? Or when we had to put Mom in the home, he didn't even show up. And that whenever I said *Mom would really like to see you* or *I would really like some company today*, he would just say *maybe next time* and leave me to do everything all by myself?' Hot tears are streaming down my cheeks now. My nails make indents in my palms as I clench my hands.

'And you know what the irony of it all is? Everything was for him! We came here, for him! Dad held down two jobs. For him! I did everything that was expected of me, but it was always him they thought about. And now? As Dad's money dries up, I'm the one taking all the extra hours of work to pay for Mom's care while he's doing – what? Chasing code on the internet and earning shit tonnes of money and throwing it away on more computers? Elaborate fucking microchips and expensive cat food? And when he gets into trouble, it's left to me again to clear up his mess. So, yeah, today was hard, thanks. Because I went to see my mom, maybe for the last time, and she didn't remember me, she remembered him, even though he's the reason she's going to be left all alone in that place now.'

By the end, I'm breathing hard, chest heaving.

Someone honks in the distance. The car edges forward.

From the footwell, Orion gazes up at me, seemingly confused as to what all the fuss is about.

'Even Orion,' I say, quiet now. 'Even the thing he seemed to love so much, he was self-absorbed enough to use. To put in danger. He never thinks past his own needs. So fucking selfish.'

Agnes is dead still, looking at me in the gridlocked traffic. Then she pulls her phone out of her back pocket. She types quickly, brings something up on the screen and places it on the arm rest next to me. She turns back to the road.

Feeling like an idiot, I pick it up. It's the website for my mom's home – a page about their facilities. NEW: THE ROSENBERG SENSORY SUITE. The suite I hid in. I put the phone back down and look at her.

'Why are you showing me this?'

'I think you know,' she says simply.

'Rosenberg?'

'Yeah.'

And that's when I understand why I took note of the suite's name, even as I was running for my life.

'Rosenberg is the name of the owner of the cat in *Men in Black*. It's Kai, isn't it? Rosenberg is Kai.'

Seemingly satisfied that I've calmed down, or at least been stunned into submission, Agnes takes her phone back.

'He donated the money for the room under a false name. He does that a lot because he's worried the government will get suspicious if he suddenly starts writing huge cheques. He also donates a load to this place.' She pulls up another website and shows me a research charity for dementia.

'There's a couple more institutes he gives to as well. O is quite the philanthropist. He's probably one of the single biggest donors to Alzheimer's and dementia research in the city.' She laughs to herself. 'He never would give anything to any of my causes. Said that was my domain. He had his own battle to fight.'

I look up at Agnes, stunned.

'I wish he'd told you himself,' Agnes says softly. 'I don't know why he didn't. Maybe to protect you?'

The tears start welling up again. Luckily, the cars in front start moving and Agnes moves her eyes back to the road.

'It probably doesn't make up for him not being there. But he does care. And no, I don't know him like you do, but I do know he only does things with intention. Like Orion's code. Everything is hidden for a reason; it all has a purpose.'

'I have to find Frybread,' I whisper. 'I have to find Kai.'

'You do,' she nods. 'And you will.'

A weight lands on my lap. A soft furry thing, kneading at my thighs, as the road ahead finally clears.

Alyssa

L-MINUS-THREE DAYS AND I AM FINALLY BEING LET OUT OF the hospital. Lars has even sent a helicopter to come and pick me up, although the destination is, as yet, undecided. He left me a voicemail overnight and told me that there was a job open for me, if I'm interested. The crew will need a number of CAPCOMs to communicate with them throughout the next few months from Mission Control, and a friendly voice like mine may help keep their spirits up when things get tough. On the other hand, he understands that this is 'difficult' for me and I may just want to cut my losses, get some distance from everything.

I laughed when I first played the voicemail back. 'Take a break,' he says, like I'm the sort of person who would just be able to rest up on a beach somewhere in the Caribbean and get over the fact that my life's dream has been snatched away from me. And that's not even taking into account the fact that I'm in a ten-tonne cast, unable to even wash myself properly without having to stick a goddamn condom over my useless lump of a leg.

But, as the morning dose of painkillers kicks in, I begin to wonder if I can bear to go back there. That was supposed to be my ship, my crew, my mission, but now I'll be a glorified observer, relegated to the sidelines of history.

But more importantly, I'll be impotent.

Again.

The memory of it brings me out in a cold sweat. I force the nausea back down.

Since the accident, my dreams have been full of haunting images and sounds. Gasping breaths, soul-crunching pops, chilli sauce spinning in the darkness, the sensation of screaming silently into a void . . .

The nurse comes in to check on me. Have I got everything I need? The transfer should be here soon. The moment of my decision is edging nearer. Going back is the right thing to do; it's my duty to help my crew complete their mission in any way I possibly can. But what if it's also the very thing that will destroy me?

Integrity first. Service before self. Excellence in all we do.

The Air Force's core values, and therefore my father's. He is many things, but one thing everyone agrees on: he is a man of his word. Which is why, the day he told me that he would never forgive me, or speak to me again, I truly believed him.

The first betrayal of my father was my distraction by college. In his eyes, my path had already been set. It ran in my blood. My grandfather had been in the military. A poor kid from Illinois, with no job prospects, the army seemed like the only option for him.

It was 1967. Kennedy was long dead, the Civil Rights Movement was tearing itself apart, and more bombs were raining down on Vietnam than had been dropped in the whole of World War Two. They needed more feet on the ground and my grandfather, Matthew Wright, signed up. Conceived during a rare break back home, my father was born three months after young Matthew died. In late 1969, he chose to throw himself on a grenade to save his fellow soldiers, leaving behind a grieving family, a pregnant girlfriend and, later, a twenty-mile section of State Route 93 near his hometown that was named in his honour: a mile for every year of his very short life.

And a medal.

The thing my father treasured most when he was growing up. It was inevitable, then, that my father also felt a calling to serve his country as soon as he was old enough.

He made it into the Air Force and steadily earned his stripes. As he would regularly remind my mom and me, it was the Air Force and, in turn, the United States of America that put food on the table, clothes on our backs and a roof over our heads.

But NASA was forged in the fires of the US's armoury. In fact, it was founded on my grandfather's ninth birthday in 1958 to fight in the very same ideological war that he threw his body on a grenade for. And so, to my father, NASA was more than acceptable. It was perfect. What could be more American than the space agency that won the race to the Moon? My position as an astronaut was folded into the family myth. He showed his approbation by gifting my grandfather's medal to me. Finally, I was worthy of the Wright name. I bathed in the warmth of my father's pride. My time at NASA was four happy years of fulfilment and pride for both of us.

I will never forget the moment I told my father everything was changing. I can still smell the filtered coffee and sugary biscuits sitting next to the steaming mugs on the table. The sombre ticking of my grandmother's clock on the fireplace. My mom's nails were a very pale pink. I remember so precisely her sharp intake of breath and his bulging eyes when I said the words:

'I'm leaving NASA.'

'What?' my mom gasped.

'To go where?' he asked.

His voice was strong, confident, as though he already knew the answer: that I had finally taken all his hints and returned to the Air Force. I remember feeling sorry for him.

'I'm going to go to Mars.'

My mother leaned away from us and began praying, clutching her chest. It was only a couple of months after the *Mayflower*, and I'd seen her watch that footage on repeat.

Of course, she didn't know how much it haunted me, too.

She was lost to us now, in her own spiralling panic. It was just me and my dad. He narrowed his eyes at me.

'I don't understand,' he said slowly.

'I'm leaving NASA and joining a private colonization mission. To Mars.'

'A private mission.'

I nodded, taking a deep, calming breath. I was annoyed with myself for being so scared.

'They're based in California now but they're moving soon to Baikonur in Kazakhstan. A mission date is set. I'm going to be commanding the first one.'

His eyes never left me once, his expression still and impenetrable.

'And it's a one-way mission. I won't be coming back.'

My mom wailed and clutched at my father's back, as he stared at me. She clawed at him, snot and tears streaming down her face. 'Bill. Tell her no. No!'

I'd never seen her act like that before. It was like I was dying. Like I had told her I had a terminal illness. But I was focused entirely on my father, waiting to see what he would do. I think even the clock stopped ticking, as the universe waited with me.

After a moment, he began to nod. Subtly at first and then more defined. Like he was making a decision. He raised a hand and put it over my mom's, half-heartedly tapping it as she continued to weep into his shirt. I braced myself as he finally opened his mouth to speak.

'All right,' he said, his voice low and deep.

I watched as he gently disentangled himself from my mother's clutches. He stood up slowly, his old joints clicking at the knees, and walked past me, across the living room, towards the front door. He scooped up his keys from the hall table, slid his feet into some sandals and, without a glance backwards, opened the front door and left.

I had nothing left to do but push myself up from my armchair and sit next to my mother, who wrapped her arms around me. Her whole body heaving with sobs.

Later that evening, my mom had washed her face and was cooking up a frenzy. The kitchen table looked like it was about to collapse with the number of dishes on it, but my dad's seat was empty. A dutiful daughter, I ate a little of everything, making the right noises. The radio was on loud and she was humming to it, out of tune, even when she didn't know the songs.

Every now and then, a car's lights would slide across the room and I could see her watching to see if they turned into our drive. When the radio began reading the ten o'clock news bulletin, I clanked down my knife and fork. In a few quick strides, I was at the front door and fishing my car keys out of my pocket. My SUV rental was parked up on the side of the road. I hopped in and fired up the engine, hit the gas and headed off into the night.

I tried the cemetery first – where my grandma is buried – but when I got to the gates, there was no car parked up. Dad wasn't there. I headed back into town. It was a weeknight, so the main street was quiet. I slowed as I passed my dad's favourite bar but I couldn't see his Buick anywhere, so I decided to head home. He was most likely driving around in silence.

Then I caught the number plate of his car in the corner of my eye, parked outside of Old Mike's garage. The two of them had met soon after my parents moved back here in their retirement, and he and Dad would sometimes get together on the weekend and do up old trucks and engines.

I pulled up on the other side of the road and steeled myself to go in. The lights were on in the workshop. At least with Mike around, my dad would probably come home quietly, and I could deal with his wrath in private. I locked up the car and jogged over to the half-open shutters, ducking under and into the warm glow inside. Hearing a low mumble of voices coming from the back office, I moved through the workshop and down the dark hall leading to the office. Messy piles of boxes were stacked all along the length of the hall, so I had to weave my way towards the voices and the low lamplight seeping through the grimy glass of the office door.

When I reached the end of the hall, I leaned round yet another pile of dusty boxes and looked through the gap in the door. Dad was on Mike's saggy leather sofa. I could see the back of his head moving gently as he spoke. Next to him sat Mike's bulk, his weather-worn face watching my dad with a concerned expression.

I raised my fist to knock, but froze at a sound I'd never heard before. My dad's shoulders were shrugging, his head bowed, sobs racking him. Mike's big arm wrapped around my dad's back and held him. Dad closed his eyes, his head resting on Mike's shoulder. Then they both pulled back, and Mike's rough mechanic's hand slid up my dad's back and round to his face. He cupped his chin and pulled his head up, and he slowly leaned in to kiss his cheek. Then his other hand rose up to hold my father's face and drew his lips to his. My father's sobs were silenced, and his arms wrapped around Mike as the two of them came together in a loving embrace.

BOOM.

I had knocked a box to the floor with an almighty sound. I gasped, looked back to see both Mike and my dad staring at me through the door, wide-eyed. We stared at each other for a long time. Then Mike pulled back, looking down. My father scrambled up off the sofa and darted out of sight. My stomach felt like it was doing somersaults as I turned and strode down the hall, back to the light of the workshop. I had to get to my car. I had to go.

From behind me, I heard voices again, but I had no idea what they were saying, until I heard Mike's voice call out.

'Alyss—!' But he was silenced.

I ducked under the shutters, my eyes once again struggling to adjust to the night. I was shivering.

As my car came to life, music blasted from the speakers and jolted me back to attention. I punched the sound off and sat in the stunned silence. A few seconds later, the workshop door flew open and my father stormed out. He got straight into his car and pulled away with a screech.

A minute later, I swung my car around and followed, wondering what the hell I was going home to.

I tried to figure out what to say to him when we got back. I'd get him on his own, that was for certain. I had no idea how much my mom knew, and she was already fragile from earlier. I'd find a way to speak to him alone and say . . . what? I'd tell him that it was all right. That this was a good thing. But was it? As I sped through the streets, I couldn't help but feel angry. My life had felt like one big test, of my integrity, my strength. But this whole time he'd been lying to us, keeping up some bullshit pretence. I winced at all the times I'd heard him say derogatory things about anyone who was different. How could he have hated who he was so much? And once again that selfish beast within me came to the surface: if Mom discovered this, along with the fact that I was leaving this planet and never coming back, it would kill her. Why did I have to find this out now, when I already had enough to deal with?

By the time I got home, I'd decided my priority was to make sure my dad was OK, to reassure him that what I had just seen was not the end of his world. That I loved him.

I needn't have worried, though. I must have only been a couple of minutes behind him, but as I made it through the front door I could hear the door of my parents' bedroom slam shut. I took the stairs two at a time to follow him, but Mom was standing guard in the hall, in her nightdress.

'Not tonight, honey,' she said softly, her eyes still puffy from earlier. 'Leave him. We can talk in the morning.'

She looked tired and suddenly very old. Grief-stricken.

I retreated back to my room. It wasn't a childhood bedroom, but my mom had ensured there was a single bed, with a big, soft comforter, a desk and a small wardrobe ready in the event of me coming to stay.

I kept the shades open and climbed into bed. It wasn't the right time of year to see Mars, and the window was facing the wrong way anyway. But I could just about see the moon, so I looked out at it as I waited for sleep to come, comforted by the fact that soon I wouldn't have to worry about any of this. Soon, I'd be looking at the other side of that cragged disc, and watching this place and everyone in it receding far into the distance.

By the time I woke, showered and dressed next morning, they were already in the kitchen, bacon sizzling on the stove, my father reading the paper at the table.

'You're going today,' he said, without looking up. I couldn't tell if this was a question or a command.

'Yes. I have a lot to tie up before I finish.'

He sniffed loudly. I sat down at the table opposite him and my mom produced a plate of bacon and eggs from nowhere.

'Thanks,' I said. She waved her hand in acknowledgement before turning back to her stove.

I didn't pick up my knife and fork. Instead, I shifted in my seat a little, building up the courage to say, 'Dad? I'd really like to talk to you.'

My mom froze. Dad finally looked at me over the rim of his reading glasses. I widened my eyes, trying to communicate everything he wasn't allowing me to say.

He slowly put down the paper, smoothing invisible creases out of it along the table before adjusting the position of his coffee mug.

'There is nothing to say.' His voice was like steel. My mom had turned around now. She was hovering, teasing a towel between her fingers.

I sighed. 'Dad, I can't leave until—'

'Enough!' His baritone voice bounced off my mom's pots and pans and rang round the kitchen. He squeezed his eyes shut and took a deep breath. When he opened them again, they were full of fury.

'We have nothing to speak about. Ever again. You want to go to Mars? You want to break your mother's heart? Fine. Go.' I felt myself recoil at his words. My mom darted forward to reach out to him, but he held up his hand and she stopped, her eyes bouncing between the two of us.

'You can go now.' He dragged his eyes back down to the paper in front of him, assuming an overly casual position.

I felt sick. My legs shook as I tried to stand. I found myself heading upstairs, picking up my overnight bag and softly closing my bedroom door behind me. As I came back down the stairs, concentrating hard on every step, my mom stood twitching in the hall. Alone.

I reached the bottom of the stairs, the front door looming in front of me. Dust motes floated in the sun that streamed through the window. Tears rolled silently down her face. Her whole body shook as it struggled to hold itself together.

'Mom?' It jolted out of me. So childlike, so scared. Her arms darted up and around me and she enveloped me in the strongest embrace I've ever felt. I returned the squeeze, my hands clasping around her. I still remember how she felt; her bra cutting deep into her back beneath her blouse and the nodules of her spine below her skin. She inhaled my scent as she buried her nose in my chest, and I did the same as my chin rested on her forehead. Bacon grease, grapefruit-scented soap, fabric softener and lavender. Home.

And then I did what my father told me to. I pulled away from my mom, told her I loved her, and left.

A sharp rap on the door of my hospital room breaks through my painful memories. My ride is here. Will I leave Baikonur and Mars One behind me? Or try to build a new life for myself?

Integrity first. Service before self. Excellence in all we do.

I already know my choice.

Jia

I'VE LIVED MOST OF MY LIFE IN HONG KONG, A CITY ALMOST entirely surrounded by water, but I've never been to a dock, let alone on a ship.

The first thing that hits me as I get out of the car is the smell. Rotting fish and sewage. The second is that there's no ship. Not even a dock. Just a small speedboat at a pier.

'Sea Saviour have a running tab with this pier. They can't come into dock, so they moor up offshore and tender everything. If they're in and out in under a couple of hours, the owners look the other way. If the port authority realizes they're here, they're in real trouble. So, time is of the essence.' Agnes gestures back to the car, and I take the hint. We both retrieve my measly belongings: a large rucksack full of warm, layered, practical clothing; the suitcase full of dried cat food; and Orion, looking intrigued in the bubble of the cat backpack that Agnes purchased for him.

'I knew it,' Agnes laughs behind me. I turn and see Erica, leaning against a wall, still pissed. But she's here.

'Go on,' Agnes nudges, taking Orion from me.

I approach sheepishly. 'You made it, then.'

'So did you,' she replies, still frosty.

We both stand there, awkward.

'Thank you,' is all I can manage.

Erica sniffs and I follow her eyeline towards the bay, and the ship that's going to smuggle me out of the country.

I wish she was coming with me.

'You can do this, Jia,' she says, her voice soft now. I turn back to her and all trace of anger has dissolved away. Instead, she's smiling sadly.

Before I can talk myself out of it, I throw my arms around her and we're hugging. The solidity of her body makes me aware of just how close I am to falling apart.

'I'm sorry,' I say into her sweet-smelling sweater.

She pulls back to look at my face, and once again I'm struck by just how beautiful she is.

'Stop apologizing, Jia. None of this is your fault.' And for the briefest of moments, it looks like she's going to say more. But something behind her eyes closes, and she gives me a gentle shove. 'Now, go find your brother. He's the one who's going to need to do some grovelling.'

I try to laugh, to show I appreciate everything she's doing right now, everything she's done. And how much I'll miss her, even though it's only been a matter of days.

'It's time,' Agnes's voice sounds from behind.

I step back, give Erica the most pathetic of waves, shoulder Orion, and turn away.

Agnes has already introduced herself to a man on the boat, who nods curtly and holds out a hand as I half jump, half fall onboard. Before I can even sit down, the whole thing surges, and we're away, speeding out to sea, Erica shrinking away with every second.

Within just a few minutes, a ship is looming in front of me, great white shark teeth snarling on its bow. The entire vessel is painted in the greys and blues of navy camouflage, with the ship's name inscribed on the side just above the ship's 'jaws': *DOLLY*.

I feel incredibly small sat next to it. The words 'ANTI-POACHING' painted on its side are as tall as me, and the whole thing is a hive of activity. Another RIB bobs beside it, as mechanisms lift seemingly endless stacks of crates. Agnes smiles and throws her arm around my shoulder, giving me a reassuring squeeze.

As we're thrust onto a makeshift gangplank, my legs shaking like jelly, I get a lot of strange stares. Kai used to tease me that I look like a middle-aged mom-of-two. I try to not let it get to me, but compared to the crew of the *Dolly*, I know I look square. Even in their uniform Sea Saviour T-shirts, they look edgy, confident, full of purpose. I suddenly feel very young and fat.

Agnes asks someone for First Officer Penny.

'On the bridge,' they clip, giving me a confused frown. I try to smile.

'Penny and I go way back. I knew her in her navy days, before she transitioned,' Agnes explains in a low voice as she leads the way. 'She owes me a favour, so I've cashed it in. She's going to look after you, but you have to do as she says. OK? Trust her.'

Compared to the chaos of the deck, the bridge is orderly and peaceful, with panoramic views of the bay. Agnes knocks on the open door to get the attention of a figure sat poring over some paperwork. The woman turns to face us and when she sees Agnes, she smiles.

'Hey!' A broad American accent greets us, and she embraces Agnes in a huge hug.

'Hi!' Agnes squeezes back then pulls away and gestures to me.

'Penny, this is Jia. Jia, Penny.'

Penny shakes my hand. She's tanned, tall, her long hair elegantly pulled back in a ponytail that pokes through the back of her baseball cap.

'So you're our stowaway,' she says, looking me up and down. 'Never been on a ship before?'

'No,' I say, apologetically.

'You'll get used to it soon enough.'

Agnes pulls out an envelope stuffed full of cash and thrusts it out to Penny.

'For the trouble.'

Penny eyes it. 'You don't have to do that. She'll earn her keep.'

'I want to. It's a donation. Upgrade your water cannons, or whatever.'

Penny doesn't need more convincing. 'It's your money,' she shrugs, pocketing it.

'Where's the captain?' Agnes asks, peering around.

'Below, with the chief engineer. But he knows nothing. He's in a bad enough mood as it is. He hates the science missions.'

Penny's expression grows serious as she turns to me. 'I'm the only one who knows why you're really here, Jia. This is to protect the rest of the crew. We all know not to ask any questions on this ship, so don't go giving them any information that might endanger them. You're simply hitching a ride with us to California.'

I nod. I'd rather not tell anyone else I'm a wanted fugitive, anyway.

'And how about the other guest?' Agnes says, cryptically. For a moment I'm confused, and then it clicks. I shrug my backpack off and turn it to face Penny, who bends down and looks at it, bemused.

'Ah yes, our resident carnivore,' she says, grinning at Orion, who gives her an admonishing look through his bubble. 'It's gonna raise some eyebrows, but we're all animal lovers on this ship. Just keep him out of the way. You clean up after him, you feed him. We've got enough to worry about.'

A bell rings somewhere deep in the ship. Penny strides to the door and yells, 'Mike!' She and Agnes have a lot in common; neither of them would be out of place on a battlefield.

A white guy with a ponytail and a lip piercing sticks his head through the door.

'Yeah?' he asks, out of breath.

'This is Jia, your bunkmate and galley hand. Get her down and settled.'

Mike turns his beady eyes towards me, and disappointment is clear. 'Seriously?' he asks. He sounds Australian.

'Seriously,' Penny replies firmly and then turns back to her work. Mike pulls a face, before gesturing for me to follow him.

'Come on, then,' he sighs, and bangs the door back open again.

'Well, I better get out of the way.' Agnes heads out behind Mike onto the deck once more, with me in tow.

I look down the ship to see Mike storming off ahead of me. I know I have to follow, but I feel nauseous at the thought of Agnes leaving me. I grab her arm.

'Agnes—'

'Don't worry, Jia.' She grabs both my hands and squeezes them tight. 'You got this.' As she pulls away, I look down and spot a small retro-style cell phone in my hand. 'We can check in with each other, when you get signal. Erica insisted. She's grown pretty fond of you.' She winks, and I blush. 'Now, go find Kai for me. I'm beginning to miss him and it's weird.' And then she skips towards the gangplank and down onto the speedboat, with a quick backwards wave as she dodges someone loading more crates.

I gape after her. After all we've been through, she's gone, just like that?

'Oi!' screams Mike from the other end of the boat. 'Get a move on!'

'We both sleep in here?' I squeak, staring at the bunk beds pinned between the walls, stacked tight on top of one another.

'Yep. I'm on top. Now, get rid of your shit and meet me in the galley,' Mike barks, then leaves me to get acquainted with my new home.

I can see why he's taken the top bunk. There's a small window set just above the mattress that gives you an extra alcove of storage, which is well worth the climb into bed. Mike's already made himself at home – there are a couple of small bags up there, a book, a razor.

It's only then that it hits me that this is a unisex bunk. I'll be sleeping beneath a man for over a month. I don't know why, but it freaks me out. Especially when I see the bathroom door directly next to me and how close the tiny toilet is to where our pillows are.

Orion gives an annoyed miaow, and I start. I'd forgotten about him. Suddenly, the room feels even smaller. I shuffle in further and slide the door behind me, then let him out of the pack. He launches himself out and onto the bottom bunk, sniffing around tentatively.

'I have to go,' I say as I fill up his food bowl and then the kitty litter tray. There's no other place for it than the shower tray. Orion sniffs at it as I shuffle to the door and slide it open behind me. Orion pads straight for the gap, but I block his path.

'Stay!' I hiss, backing out into the corridor and sliding the door shut on him.

I head past the stairs and into what is obviously the crew quarters, and it proves easy to find the mess. It's big, compared to the cabin I just left, with three dark-wood tables and plenty of chairs. To the side is a long set of worktops and cupboards with heat lamps mounted above a counter, and racks of condiments above. At the end of the room is what looks like a bar. But the most striking thing is the far wall, painted along its whole length with a mural of undulating swirls of blue and green, fish, whales and other sea creatures. The imagery sweeps all the way through the next doorway, and I follow it, entranced, until I reach an industrial-looking kitchen.

Mike is in the process of loading up the fridges with fruit and vegetables. There's not a single animal product in sight. I swallow hard, my stomach already growling.

Mike looks me up and down again. I can already sense what he thinks: another lazy, meat-eating land-lover. He's right.

He turns and heaves up a huge crate of potatoes then slams down a peeler. 'Over two dozen vegans on this ship. Hope you're good at peeling.' He doesn't even wait for my reply before turning back to the fridges.

The *Dolly*'s engines whirr into life. In what feels like seconds, the skyline of the city is already sliding away from us. I put my hands on the counter and push myself as close to the window as I can, trying to get one last glimpse of home.

One last glimpse of the place where I last saw Kai. Where I last saw Mom. Where everything was normal.

But it's gone.

I return to the potatoes. How far did Agnes say this journey was? Something like eleven thousand kilometres? Forty days. Who knows where Kai is, what state he might be in by then. I close my eyes, hoping, praying, that he's safe, that he can hold out for another few weeks.

That no one finds me before I find him.

Then the sounds of the waves join the cacophony of the engine. The floor beneath me starts shifting, bobbing.

My stomach begins to churn.

'Peel!' Mike growls from behind me, making me jump.

Swallowing down the urge to vomit, I get to work.

This is going to be a very long trip.

Alyssa

THE HELICOPTER DOESN'T TAKE ME TO THE MARS ONE COMplex. Instead, we go to Baikonur itself. Only mission crew, Lars and those in the Green Zone for quarantine are staying on site; everyone else is stationed in this old Soviet town, fifteen minutes down the road. It doesn't surprise me that this is where they bring me, but it hurts. It's another sign that I am no longer part of the inner circle. I crane my neck to see my old accommodation block through the window, but I can't. I throw my head back against the seat, hard.

After landing in a sad-looking park, I'm driven the short distance to a block of green low-rise apartments, facing a square that is mostly occupied by a rusting plinth, where a former Soviet rocket used to sit. The Russians took it back when they left this place, so it's empty, now. Like me.

Reluctantly, I allow myself to be wheeled into the foyer, where Gwynne is waiting for me. I breathe out when I see her. Her presence is comforting, despite the fact that she's wearing a mask over her nose and mouth. Her eyes smile at me.

'It's wonderful to have you with us again, Alyssa.'

The man wheeling my chair leaves me in the middle of the foyer and heads out. Another man enters with my tiny bag containing my medication and what little bits were brought to me during my brief hospital stay.

'Thank you,' says Gwynne. 'I'll take that.' And then we're alone again.

'Where's Anders?' I ask, looking around. The foyer is clean, tidy, but drab.

'I'm afraid he's busy, but I'm here to get you settled and fill you in.' She says this breezily, but I can tell the casual facade is an effort. 'Are you OK to . . .' She gestures at the chair.

'Yes.' I grab the bars on the wheels and thrust myself forward. I'm not used to manoeuvring myself around, but I'm already fed up of being moved by others. I'll be getting up on crutches as soon as possible.

'Great. Come with me. We've got you on the ground floor.'

I follow her down the corridor, wondering who else I'll be sharing this building with.

'This is one of our quieter blocks,' she calls over her shoulder, like she read my mind. 'Mostly legal. Kajal's upstairs. I'm sure she'd love to see you when you're ready.' She stops by a door and waits for me to catch up before handing me a key. 'After you.'

The smell of fresh linen and lilies hits me as we enter the apartment. We come straight into a lounge-diner area, with a simple but modern kitchen in the corner. Directly in front of us are patio doors that lead out to a small veranda. It's bigger and comfier than my room back at the cosmodrome, and will be the most permanent-looking home I've had in years. I hate it.

'I've made sure you've got some bits in the fridge, and some toiletries. I took the liberty of getting your clothes and other things boxed up. You'll find them in the bedroom.' She heads over to the couch and places the overnight bag down, adjusting a pile of papers next to it.

'Thanks,' I mutter, instantly wheeling myself over to the left-hand wall and grabbing the television remote that sits under the big screen. I turn it on and begin to flick through.

'Anders got the lilies flown in.' She turns. 'I thought we could go through some of this paperwork and catch you up on a few things.'

'Sure. I just want to see what's going on.'

She moves over to me and hovers nervously. 'The livestream isn't up yet.'

'I know, but the dedicated channel should still be—' And there it is. The Mars One channel is broadcasting, clearly airing a repeat of an earlier interview with the whole crew. But it can't be, because who is that tall blonde woman? My stomach lurches.

'Who the fuck is that?' I almost yell, surprising even myself. Gwynne jumps and tries to stand in front of the TV screen.

'Alyssa, why don't we—'

I try to lean around her to see my crew, but Gwynne grabs my chair and wheels me round to face the other way, before darting back to maintain social distancing.

'Alyssa!' Her voice is raised. It's never raised. 'We need to talk, OK? There's been some changes we didn't anticipate.'

My mind is racing, my eyeballs practically popping out of my skull.

'Where's Collins?'

'He's not on the crew.'

'So who is?' I cringe internally at how high-pitched my voice is. Gwynne switches off the TV behind me and gestures for me to move to the sofa. I wheel over to her and slide onto it, and she pours us both a glass of water from a bottle in the fridge before taking a seat herself. Every second she takes is excruciating. The blankness of the television looms.

'Her name is Anastasia Petrova. She's British-Russian and she was not part of our original backup crew,' Gwynne begins, choosing each word with care. 'Soon as you were injured, we notified Collins and sent a car to transport him from the second quarantine facility. But before he arrived, as you were being airlifted to the hospital, Anders was pulled into an urgent meeting by Abbey, which included dial-ins from the other Valdivian execs.' She looks uncomfortable now. 'Alyssa, I don't know what was said in that meeting – Anders won't tell me. But when he came out, I was ordered to have Collins turned back. Dr Morin was to be made commander and a flight was being arranged from the UK with a new mission specialist. Someone who had been in the wider training pool for future missions and whom, it turns out, Valdivian had put in a quarantine facility of their own just outside of London a week before. They have their own backup crew, it would seem.'

Gwynne pauses, leaving room for me to say something. But there is only silence. She twists her hands together before pushing on. 'She's not a pilot like Collins. In fact, she has no military history. She's a computer scientist who has been working on programming geological models. She has a PhD, and she's been training for nearly three years. She was in the second wave of candidates after you, from the European search – someone we were considering for the third or fourth crewed missions. She's not a complete novice. But . . . well, she's obviously not what we were expecting.'

She watches my face carefully. I don't know if it's the fact that everything over the last week has been just one disastrous realization after another, or the meds I'm on, but I'm suddenly feeling strangely calm. Confused and shocked, but also composed.

'So, Anders didn't want to tell me himself?'

Gwynne stands and begins to unpack my overnight bag.

'He's got a lot on. And I wanted to make sure you found everything OK.'

I don't bother replying. Instead, I watch through the window as a stray feather skitters along the ground in the breeze. Behind me, Gwynne turns on the kitchen tap and washes her hands. Always following the rules.

'Does it hurt?' she asks quietly. I turn back to look at her. Is she talking about my leg, or everything else?

'Yes,' I reply to both, my voice cracking.

'I'm sorry.'

A silence hangs between us, and I clear my throat.

'Thank you, Gwynne. I know I don't show it, but this is . . .' I wave at the soulless hole they've stuck me in. 'This is great.' I smile with my lips, but can't make it reach my eyes. 'Tell Anders and the crew that I'll be there for them on launch day.' I swallow hard. 'All of them.'

Gwynne gives me a sad smile, and a brisk nod. Back in business mode.

'Great. Let's catch up tomorrow. We have some rundowns to go through before the big day. I'll get the flight director to give you a shout.'

'Wonderful.'

She turns and gives me a final smile on the way out, and then she's gone, her purposeful strides retreating down the hallway. As soon as they fade, I lunge for the TV remote that she's left on the kitchen counter. I have to see my crew. See that face again—

I crash to the floor. I grab for the coffee table, but it doesn't stop me. There's a smash and a cascade of water from the lily vase. I've somehow forgotten about my goddamn leg. I stare at the plaster around it and smash my fist into it, like a toddler having a tantrum.

I growl and push myself up with my arms. At least they're still functioning. I manage to limp over to the counter and seize the remote, pressing the 'on' button before I'm even facing the TV.

The Mars One channel appears again. The interview is over, and presenters are now talking over footage of the crew waving goodbye as they head back through the door of the briefing room. I don't blink. I don't think I'm even breathing.

Everything within me is locked on her. The stranger. The imposter. Blonde and beautiful. She's tall, poised, and moves in confident strides. She hangs back to let Okeowo move in front of her. As she waits, she looks back to camera and the journalists, her hair moving softly away from her eyes. Why is it so impractically long? Does she not know about Judy Resnik, whose hair got caught in a camera on a shuttle mission? The presenters' faces suddenly appear on screen.

'With only a few days until launch, let's take a look at what some of you are talking about on social media!' A grinning woman exclaims.

Her male colleague takes over. 'Stacy from Oregon tweets "*Ana sounds like a great addition to the team! #AmazingAna*". Thanks, Stacy. In fact, our new astronaut is getting a lot of attention online, particularly from some of our male viewers. Clearly Brad, from

Tennessee, is a huge fan. He posted *"Ana is hot. #AILF".'* He chuckles. 'I won't even try to explain that hashtag, Rachel!'

'Well, Brad, you'll be seeing plenty more of Ana and the rest of the crew soon. Don't forget, our daily episodes are on at nine central every night until the launch. After that, you'll be able to see a livestream of the entire mission right here, twenty-four hours a day, seven days a week. For now, here's a recap of all we know about our latest intrepid explorer, the beautiful Ana Petrova . . .'

Her face fills up the screen and I just can't take it any more. My head is about to explode with the lunacy of it all. It's unbelievable. It's crazy. It's a fucking joke! A scream erupts right from the pit of my stomach, reverberates up through my chest, burning the back of my throat. I heft the remote across the room with all my might and it collides with the cheap TV screen, which shatters in a pattern of jagged concentric lines that expand outwards, flooding the display with a dark blue that blocks out almost the whole picture. Only a glimpse of her golden hair remains.

I stop. I breathe. The scream has drained me. I hobble on my one good leg and my cast, down the hall to the bedroom.

A couple of boxes are lined up on the far side of the room. I swear profusely as I fling myself around the bed and stub my protruding toes on the corner of it. The pain tingles all the way up my encased limb, but right at the top of the first box, I see my prize: my laptop. I throw myself back onto the bed and open it up, praying that Gwynne has made sure the Wi-Fi is set up . . .

Yes.

I open up a browser and type: 'Anastasia Petrova'.

I pause, breathing hard. As soon as I hit enter, I know I'm going to fall straight down the rabbit hole and into something I won't be able to control. But somewhere deep down in my cold, hard gut, I know this isn't right. As soon as I saw her perfect face on that screen, I knew she wasn't meant to be there. A secret backup crew? Does Lars really think I'll just sit back and take this bullshit? What was it Anders had said before my accident? *If we get the ratings up, I can keep signing cheques.* This is all Abbey's doing.

No way have I been replaced by a supermodel Russian because she is best for the crew; best for the mission. But I am going to find out who she really is.

With a shaking hand, I hit enter.

Before I know it, dawn is breaking and, after barely any sleep, I'm up and out of the apartment. I refuse to be in the chair today. I've got crutches and am grateful for my upper body strength. As my car moves through the circles of security, I notice the buzz and activity have picked up. We're L-minus-two. Everyone has a job to do. Except me.

The main building looms up ahead, and over to the right is my old accommodation block. I glance at my watch. It's early. My crew are probably just finishing the morning briefing then heading down to the surgery for tests. I wonder if they're running simulations today. Normally, they'd have the launch procedures down by now and this would be a chance for a bit of R and R before the big day, but with a new team member . . . I rub my eyes, hoping no one can see the dark rings around them. The telltale sign of my obsessive hours staring at screens, researching *her*.

The car pulls up outside headquarters and the driver heads round to open the door for me as I fumble to get out. I give him a nod as I take my first tentative steps away.

Inside, an old man sits calmly waiting for me, his legs crossed and a folder placed in his lap. He stands as I enter; it looks as though he has the weight of the world on his shoulders. The deep lines around his eyes crease as he smiles at me. My shoulders relax, just a little.

'Commander Wright.' He extends a liver-marked hand.

'Bob.' I'm thrilled to see him, but hesitate.

'Don't worry, we're in the same bubble. We can touch.' I rest my crutches against the wall and hop over to clasp his hands. They're soft and warm. He's the first person I've touched in a long time, and my hand lingers a little longer than necessary.

'It's so good to see you,' I say, taking a seat opposite him. Bob

Kelly is my only fellow NASA defector here. Our flight controller, he'd been working in Houston for years before I joined the space program and has clocked up more hours in Mission Control than most astronauts have in sims. He even worked under the legendary Gene Kranz during the shuttle era. When he left NASA, just before the *Mayflower* disaster, we all assumed he had retired. You can imagine my surprise when I arrived at Baikonur four years ago, haunted and guilt-ridden, to find the old man here, teaching these rookies how to set up a mission control. Anders had received a lot of ridicule for hiring Bob – what good was an old man in a high-pressured, fast-moving environment? But we candidates felt safe knowing there was at least one person on the ground who knew what the fuck they were doing.

'Likewise,' he says in his southern drawl. 'You had us all worried.'

'Well, I survived,' I reply feebly.

'Yes, but there's more to life than simply surviving.' He studies me as he relaxes back in his chair.

I shift my gaze from his. He's one of the few people I opened up to when I first got here, after the *Mayflower*. One of the few who knows the full story.

'This is going to be tough on them,' he states. My crew.

'I know.'

He sighs. 'But I believe having you as CAPCOM is sure as hell going to make them feel more at ease.' He hands me the folder from his lap. It's weighty. 'You may not be with them in the capsule, but you'll be with them in their minds. And you know more than anyone how important that is. Especially when things go—'

'I'll do my best to help them in any way,' I say quickly. I can't talk about it. Won't. Not when this mission is falling apart, too.

'I know you will.' He gestures at the folder. 'That there is a rundown of our latest schedules and what will be expected of you. I imagine you'll already know most of it. What you might not be used to is the "shooting memo".' He says these last words with more than a hint of disdain. I look at him quizzically. 'All

CAPCOM transmissions will be broadcast live on air. There's a number of guidelines you'll need to follow whenever you're communicating with the crew.'

I find the memo and scan through it.

I need to *be aware of language, discourage crew use of obscenities, avoid needless use of jargon and acronyms, use official brand names of equipment onboard* . . . 'What the hell is this?' I say to Bob. 'Surely my priority is clear communication with the crew and their welfare, not—'

'This is precisely why I'm glad to have you with us, Wright. We're the only NASA vets here. The more people who realize this thing ain't no damn infomercial, the better.'

'Has Anders seen this? He needs to tell them where to stick it.'

Bob pushes himself up again. He's still tall and I find myself craning up at his ancient, craggy face. He shakes his head sadly.

'Anders is seeing a lot of things. But he ain't saying nothing.' He moves towards the door and gestures for me to follow. I shove the folder under my armpit and loop my arms into my crutches.

'Come on,' he drawls. 'I'm sure there's a lot of folks who want to see you.'

The rest of the morning is a blur of briefings and reintroductions. I find myself comforted by the tsunami of information that's thrown at me. It feels great to fill my head with numbers and procedures again, and to force out the other dark thoughts that have been plaguing me.

I've worked with a lot of these guys for the last few years, but I somehow feel like a stranger again. When I enter a room, they smile and nod and say how great it is to see me, but they don't meet my eye. And when they're done briefing me, they rush out as quickly as possible. I try and convince myself that some of this is because of the complications around quarantine bubbles. But even those who aren't wearing regulation face masks seem to have their barriers up with me. I catch a few of them darting their eyes towards my plastered leg and looking away again.

By lunchtime, both my leg and my head are throbbing. It doesn't help that I've been herded around by Bob for the entire time. I get the sense that he's been charged by Gwynne to look after me, but he's a busy man and when we sit down in the cafeteria to eat, he's glancing at his phone and looking concerned. Despite it being busy, no one else chooses to sit near us. It feels like those days at NASA after I announced I was leaving.

I twirl my spaghetti around my fork – I wonder if this is possible in microgravity. But then something kicks my gut and I thrust the fork down with force.

'I'm a big girl, Bob. You can leave me here and go do your thing.'

He glances up at me sheepishly, then back down at his phone.

'Well, there are a few things I could do with taking a look at.'

'Go,' I urge him, although he still looks torn. 'I'll take your dessert as payment.' I pluck the chocolate pudding from his tray, smiling in what I hope is a reassuring way.

'Fine,' he grumbles. 'But if you need anything, you call me?'

'Promise.'

He scoops up his coffee as he stands and makes his way down the table. Then he pauses for a moment.

'If Gwynne doesn't have anything planned for you this afternoon, I hear the sims were pretty intense this morning, so the crew are taking a break.' He looks shifty. 'If you want to say hi, or whatever.'

'Sure,' I reply, and it comes out high-pitched. 'Thank you. I might.'

A tray slaps down opposite and its owner – a young, bulky guy with light brown skin, glasses and thick black hair – smiles at me. My face shows that I have no idea who he is, because he reaches his hand across the table. 'Hi. I'm Jacob Kindred.'

I look at him warily, but shake his hand. 'Alyssa Wright.'

'I know.' He picks up his fork and starts shovelling spaghetti into his mouth. I watch him for a moment, then glance around to see if I'm missing something. But the rest of my table is still as deserted as it was before.

'Sorry, do I know you?' I try to ask politely, but it comes out harsh.

He's finishing a mouthful, and sort of wobbles his head around. 'Mmm...' He swallows and grabs his water bottle. 'We met briefly, on your tour. You helped clean up my desk?' He takes a swig of his drink, and it dawns on me: the flustered coder. Although not so flustered now.

'Now you remember.' He smiles warmly. It's still hard to believe this guy is a software nerd. He looks more like he should have been captain of a football team.

'Colts,' I blurt out. 'You support the Colts.'

'Sadly, I do.' He carries on scooping food into his mouth.

Now that my initial surprise and confusion is gone, annoyance kicks in. He didn't even ask if I wanted company. I put up my hands.

'Look, I'm sorry. I was just having lunch and was kinda happy by myself, so I'm just gonna...' I make a move to leave.

'Everyone's avoiding you, right? Acting all weird?' I freeze. He hasn't even looked up from his plate. A strand of spaghetti dangles from his lips and he dips his head to catch it.

'I'm sorry?'

'It's peak lunchtime and you're sitting at an otherwise empty table. No one's looking at you. And even when they're with you, they want to get away.' I can't tell if that's a question or if it's a statement. I sit back down again, and he takes that as a sign to keep going. 'I'm sorry.' He grimaces. 'So that's why I sat with you.'

I snort. 'And what makes you think you have any idea what I'm going through?'

He shrugs. 'Same thing happened to me. People don't cope with grief well. They're not sure how to handle it. Makes them nervous, I think.'

'Grief?'

'Yeah, you know. Loss. You lost something huge, and now people don't know how to act around you. They feel awkward and embarrassed, so they avoid you. It's pretty shitty, but they can't help it.' Somehow, he's already finished his spaghetti. He glances at my tray.

'Hey, you have two desserts. Can I have one?' And then he just takes it and pops it open. I stare at him as he chows down. What he just said, in such a casual way, has hit me fully in the chest.

I glance around us, but as he said, no one is watching. This place feels so large, so busy. I tense up, my palms clammy.

'Actually.' God, why did my voice have to croak like that? I clear my throat and try again. 'Actually, I'm fine. Thank you.'

He looks at me a moment, then smiles out of the corner of his mouth. 'OK,' he scoffs.

My nostrils flare. 'People aren't being "shitty", they're just busy. In case you hadn't realized, we're about to send a mission to Mars. I know it's hard to conceive of when you spend your entire day jumbling around a load of zeros and ones, but some of us don't have time to just sit around chatting.'

Jacob raises his eyebrows and licks his spoon. If he weren't so damn irritating, he would be handsome.

'Fine.' He places the spoon down and looks directly at me. I shift uncomfortably under his gaze. 'All I'm saying is, when you're fed up with being avoided, I'm around. I won't ignore you.'

I can only gape at him, and his face flickers with amusement. Luckily, I spot Kajal out of the corner of my eye, sandwich in hand. I scramble to get my backpack on and my arms in the crutches. Jacob watches in silence, still looking amused. Just as I manage to get my act together, he gestures at my remaining pudding.

'May I?' he asks.

'Fuck you,' I growl, then curse myself. Is that really the best I can do? But Jacob leans over to retrieve his prize, unfazed. I push off in pursuit of Kajal, feeling Jacob's eyes on my back.

'Kajal!' She's still motoring towards the exit. 'Kajal!' I call out, louder this time. How can she not hear me? Luckily, a guy is reversing through the fire doors with a delivery and she has to stop to let him past. I manage to catch up with her.

'Kajal, hey!'

Finally, she looks up and blushes. 'Wow, Alyssa. Hi!' She sort of shuffles, like she wants to hug me, but isn't sure. Then she gives in and wraps one arm around me. As she pulls away, she looks at my leg, and then back at me, guilty. 'I didn't know you were back.'

'First day.'

'Great.' We're standing right in the doorway, so people have to move between and around us.

'I'm so sorry,' Kajal says, her face sombre, 'about what happened. It's so unfair.'

'Tell me about it.'

'Neha was so upset too.'

I slip my arm out of one of my crutches and try to swing my backpack off my shoulder. 'Hold on, I've got her book . . .'

'No!' Kajal grabs my arm and stops me. She looks at her watch. 'We can do this another time. Keep it, there's no rush. I ordered her another one anyway.' She begins to back away. 'I'm so sorry, I'm in such a rush.'

I watch her retreat, my backpack hanging awkwardly.

'Let's catch up soon, yeah? Let me know where you're staying.' She grabs the door handle.

'Actually, I'm in your—' But she's gone before I can finish.

The lunch crowd ebbs and flows around me as I struggle to swing the backpack on my shoulders again. I can still feel the weight of Jacob's gaze, but refuse to give him the satisfaction of meeting it. I force my head back up, and hobble as confidently as possible out of the room.

The press side of the briefing room feels all wrong.

Beyond the glass, the crew side taunts me. I try to distract myself with Neha's book. It's what she chose to put in my PPK, to take to Mars: *The Little Prince* by Antoine de Saint-Exupéry. The spine is cracked and the pages feel heavy with memories, a well-loved tome.

I've never read it before, and my eyes keep bouncing back over the same sentences about bad seeds sleeping in secrecy and bad plants spreading until a planet bursts. It reminds me of the ominous feeling that lingers over me every time I wake up. The room spins, and I close my eyes. Take a breath.

There's a click across the room, and my head snaps up to see the door on the other side of the glass swinging open. My stomach drops at the sight of the person emerging through it.

Ana Petrova.

She's wearing a pleasant, neutral smile and brushes her hair from her eyes, looking out onto my side of the glass. When our eyes lock, she stops and for a brief moment, the smile drops.

'Oh, I'm so sorry,' she says. Her accent betrays her boarding school education, which I've learnt from my obsessive googling. Russian born, a lovechild to an oligarch who fell out of favour and fled to London, she's been living there since she was four. 'I was told I had a press interview.' She looks over the rest of the chairs around me.

'I guess there was a mix-up.' I keep my voice as level as possible. I very deliberately named only *my* crew when talking to the team about this visit. Why is she here?

'Actually . . .' She steps down from the stage and moves towards the glass. 'I was hoping to introduce myself. I'm Ana,' she smiles warmly and places her hand on the glass as greeting. Does she want me to go up to the glass and do the same? I stay rooted to the spot.

She laughs.

'Sorry.' And removes her hand from the glass self-consciously. 'Not sure how to greet someone while stuck in a fishbowl.'

Finally, I raise my hand. 'Alyssa.'

'I wish we'd met in different circumstances. I'm so sorry about what happened.' She sounds like she means it, but there's the teeniest of flickers in her eyes towards the cameras mounted above her. She smiles, her chiselled cheeks blushing. 'I've got so much to live up to.'

It's only now that I remember my own times in this briefing room. Backstage, just before you head out of the door, there's a live feed of who's on the other side of the glass, so you can prepare yourself.

Ana, you sneaky little bitch.

I snap the book closed and move towards the glass to see her face more clearly. She looks pleased that I'm engaging with her. If she wants a good scene for the cameras, I'll give her one.

'It *is* a shame we've not met before.' I try my best to put a warm smile on my face too. 'Especially as we worked so closely with the other members of the backup crew. I don't even remember you from candidate selection.'

'There were, what, over three hundred thousand applicants?' she replies. 'And there was always more than just one backup crew,' she shrugs, so casual. 'I guess they had several fail-safes in place and they didn't want to risk leaks or contamination or whatever. I was in a completely different pool and never thought I'd end up here.' She gestures around her. 'I'm so grateful.' Her sincerity is sickening. I don't believe a word of it.

Now that I'm close to the glass, I look her up and down. Her body is toned and she's very slim.

'It takes a lot to get here, doesn't it?'

She nods. 'Oh yes.'

'What centre did you go to at first?'

'The one in London. I flew to Anders' old offices in Pasadena for the second round. Then we did our isolation training in Mauna Loa. I think we arrived there a week or so after you and Heather left.' Annoyingly, her story adds up. Although they'd never mentioned that another team were coming into HI-SEAS after us. But why would they?

'Those first few tests are intense, right?' The effort to sound friendly is almost painful.

'Completely. The dexterity one was so tough. But somehow, I managed each task first time,' she laughs.

'How about the claustrophobia test?'

'The one with the dark box? Yes, so strange. I managed it though. I nearly fell asleep at one point. I think I did pretty well, timewise. Although I don't think I beat you!'

'No one did,' I say, trying not to sound bitter. Then, an idea occurs to me. 'What about that question they asked on the psych test, about whether you would obey an order to hurt someone?' I ask, trying to keep my tone casual.

'Yeah, that was interesting. I mean, I answered it in the best way I could . . .'

My breath catches in my throat. She's lying. That question never existed in any of our psychological tests. I've caught her out. It's just as I thought: she didn't go through the same selection process as us. My mind whirrs. How is she here? Who placed her here? And most importantly, why?

Something in my face must warn her that she's made a mistake, because she suddenly looks a bit flustered. Her eyes flick again to the cameras.

'How are you feeling, Alyssa?' A wave of faux concern passes over her face. 'I can't imagine what Tuesday will feel like for you.'

I grit my teeth. She's trying to unsettle me. I choose my words carefully. 'Of course, I'm disappointed. But I'll be there on the day, and I'm grateful I can still serve *my* crew. I'll be watching everything.' *I'll be watching you.*

'I know we'll all feel so much better for it,' she almost whispers.

Another click and the door to her left swings open again, and I almost fall backwards with relief at the sight of Rubio. Ana smiles broadly.

'I better go. It was an honour to meet you, Alyssa.'

'Good luck, Ms Petrova,' I say coldly.

Rubio steps aside to let Ana pass. The door closes behind her, and he lets out a long breath.

'Wow,' he laughs, then exaggerates a shiver. 'It's frosty in here.' He moves over to the glass. 'I am so pleased to see you, Commander.'

'Not any more,' I grimace.

'Always,' he replies quietly. I'm relieved to see he looks well. His skin is bright, and his eyes are clear. I wonder what I must look like. My leg is starting to ache again, and I shift my weight a little.

'Where are the others?'

'Not sure. Do you want me to go and try and find them?'

'No!' I blurt, jumping forward. 'I know how stressful these last days are. It's just great to see one of you.'

He nods kindly and looks at my plastered leg. 'How is it?'

'It hurts. But not as much as being left behind.'

Rubio looks up at the cameras. 'Why don't we head outside? I need some fresh air and we could find somewhere to sit, hmm?'

We meet on the ridge west of the accommodation block. The desert swoops downwards from here, out towards the launchpad, giving a spectacular view. It takes me a while to limp out to the bench on my crutches. By the time I join him, Rubio has placed himself in a chair a few yards away from it. We still have to maintain distance to keep up the quarantine.

As I sit down, I realize why he's moved us out here. The only cameras are mounted way back on the walls of the accommodation block. We'll have some time until the shoot crew scramble handhelds to this spot. Rubio fiddles with his microphone – something all the crew have to wear now that we're live. He's placing it right on the very edge of his collar, which is flapping in the wind.

'We miss you, Alyssa.'

'I miss you guys, too. I'm so sorry I let you down.' I find myself staring ahead at the Nova rocket, now in place on the launchpad. Even from this far away, the scale of it is astounding. More than 320 feet tall, it towers over the entire landscape. It's wide, too, with two booster rockets nestled either side. And squatting on top is the *Argo*.

It feels as though the whole thing is pulling me towards it. Calling to me. I clench my fists.

'You didn't let us down. Okeowo is so upset. She blames herself, which we all tell her is nonsense. It's no one's fault.'

'It is someone's fault,' I growl.

He gives me a piercing look. 'You blame the camera crew?'

'Okeowo never would have had to egress through my frame if—'

'If is a big word.' He sighs. 'There's nothing we can do now.'

He's right, of course. But the thought of it all still makes me shake with anger.

'What's the book you were reading?' he asks.

'Oh. It's just something I promised to take up in my PPK, for Kajal's daughter.'

I think about Neha, how excited she must have been when Kajal told her that a little piece of her life would be shot up in the rocket in front of me and end up on an alien planet. Her little marker to the universe, proof of her existence.

I sniff and take a shaky breath. 'Another promise I've failed to keep,' I say.

Rubio nods slowly, as though coming to a decision. 'I'll take it.'

'Take what?'

'The book. I haven't filled my PPK yet.'

'Rubio,' I turn to him, 'you really don't have—'

'I insist.' He's staring out at the rocket now. 'I want you to keep your promise. Besides, we'll all need extra reading material, and a children's book is more on Brun's level.'

I feel a huge surge of warmth towards him, and shuffle a little closer.

'You should send something up yourself,' he says, turning towards me.

I can't help but laugh at this.

'So you guys heading off with all my hopes and dreams isn't enough?'

My laugh dies instantly. That's the first time I've said something like that out loud. It takes everything I've got not to scream.

Rubio smiles sadly. 'A part of you belongs on that planet, far more than me, or anyone else.'

A growl of grief erupts from me. I turn away. I don't want to show this much. He can't see it. No one can.

'We're taking Anders' moon rock.'

I whip round to look at him again. 'Really?'

'Really. He asked us the other night, and Ana volunteered.'

I can't quite conceal my eye roll.

'She's been very respectful. Very . . . studious,' Rubio says.

'How are the sims going? I heard they're tricky.'

Rubio pauses, clearly trying to find the right words. 'She's very aware of the catching up she needs to do.'

God, he sounds as if he's doing a freaking press conference. What was the point in dragging me out here if he's going to toe the party line like a brainwashed zombie?

'Catching up?' It bursts out of me before I can stop it. 'You of all people must see it, Rubio. The cameras start rolling, but the ratings are low, then I get injured *because* of the damn cameras, and then they bring her in? A Russian Barbie? Who the fuck is she? It's a stunt, a trick. Hell, she could even be a Russian spy for all we know. Something is going on, you must see it!'

He winces. There's such pity on his face it's sickening.

'Alyssa, you know this isn't you, don't you?'

'What the hell do you mean?'

'You've lost your dream. You've lost everything you've worked for your entire life, and there's nothing anyone can say except "I'm so sorry". But you can't let it destroy who you are. You can't let it turn you into something you're not.'

I recoil from the truth in his words, but he ploughs on.

'You were our commander, Alyssa. I saw you handle fifteen-hour simulations, never getting your numbers wrong. I watched you suture up an artery in the middle of an Antarctic snowstorm. Everything you did was composed, logical, reasoned. And now? Spending your nights watching the same footage of your accident on repeat? Researching Ana – even emailing her schools to check her records? Ranting about what sounds very much like the beginnings of a conspiracy theory? This isn't you.'

I jump up from the bench, stung.

'How did you . . .? Are you spying on me?'

He stands up too, trying to calm me, but the gulfing distance between us only grows.

'No, Alyssa. It's aftercare. I'm worried about you. We all are.' As he says this, a goddamn trio of shoot crew turn up with a handheld and a furry microphone. They're keeping their distance for now – maybe they can see the daggers I'm staring at them. I move as close to Rubio as I can get without compromising his quarantine. And then a terrible thought occurs to me: maybe I should. I could bring him down with me. We could be grounded together . . .

He looks wary as I approach – perhaps he can see the wild thoughts in my eyes. But I stop, just in time, and try to appear calm and sane. What was it Anders said to me once when explaining Rubio's importance? *We have to have someone there to tell the story.* Rubio must launch. But I cannot let them go without a warning.

If I keep my voice low enough, they still won't be able to hear me. 'Maybe you should spend more time worrying about what is really happening with the mission.'

There's that pitying look from him again. From a guy who was once going to let me lead him across the damn solar system.

'Just take some time, Alyssa. Talk to someone. Leave me that book, and something of your own, and I'll pick it all up when it's been UV'd. Not everything has to be ruined by this.'

My throat tightens, my eyes burn.

He's wrong.

But I can't make him see it.

Impotent, again.

I grab my bag and my crutches and begin to move away, painfully aware of the camera lens following me as I leave him there, standing on the edge of everything.

Rubio

I REALLY WANT A DRINK.

But I settle for my oils instead. I'm a photographer by trade, but I dabble in other media: oils, charcoal, sometimes even words.

So, at T-minus-eighteen hours, I am standing on the roof of our sleeping quarters working on my last oil painting on Earth: the distant Gagarin's Start, an industrial insert in an otherwise barren landscape. It feels like the past and the future all rolled into one. I'm losing the light though, so I focus on the shadows created by the metallic struts that open up to the sky, like a mechanical flower.

What would oil painting be like in zero-gravity? Sorry, MICRO-gravity – Alyssa would have corrected me on that. I'll probably stick to photography and sketches for the six-month voyage. Much cleaner, more accurate. More truthful.

I smile to myself, thinking of what Alyssa calls me: their artist in residence. She's right, really. I will be there to observe and document and inspire. The TV crew will be focused on us and our drama. It is purely entertainment, a constructed reality that will fuel our ship. But I will be there to look outward, to show what it is all for. I'll be capturing the human truth of starting a home on a new planet.

I pause and take a sip of one of the Cokes Alyssa left behind. Our captain. Our commander. Her wings truly clipped.

The sweet bubbles hit the back of my tongue and I sigh as I put the can down. The truth is that I yearn for something that burns my throat rather than tingles it, centring me in a way that nothing else can. I grimace. It's been nearly two weeks since my last drink. I turn back to Gagarin's Start and focus on the sky, trying to block out the look of disappointment on Lars's face from that night. I throw my paintbrush down and clench my trembling fists. The worst thing is, deep down I don't even regret it. I wish I could. But a part of me – perhaps the only tiny part of me that really is focused on truth above all else – is glad I had one last night. The awareness shames me more than anything else. I'm so weak. This is why I shouldn't be going to Mars. But it's also why I must. There's nothing left on this planet for me but a sultry haze and an early grave.

It's after sunset now, and the whole of the steppe is cast in a serene blue light. It's that moment just before darkness descends, when the warmth of the sun's gaze still lingers in the earth, and the earliest stars and planets emerge.

But in the distance, there's a spot of perfectly white light. Our launchpad, lit up by thousands of artificial suns. The Nova rocket looms large, piercing the sky; the *Argo* perched atop, its wings of solar arrays folded, patiently waiting. Soft tendrils of vapour dance around it, evidence of the coolant systems keeping the roar of reaction and ignition at bay, for now. She's like a racehorse, breathing hard in the gates, steam billowing from her nostrils, every sinew of muscle poised. The enormity of the whole thing is breathtaking.

'My God!' someone gasps behind me. Lars. He's come up the fire escape, I imagine to avoid Abbey's cameras.

The desert wind blows a gentle breeze through his hair and for the briefest moment, I see a younger Lars Anders – when his hair was longer, the lines around his eyes shorter. He was always so very handsome.

'Hyvää iltaa,' I welcome him.

'Hei,' he replies. Stopping just the right distance from me for quarantine.

'How are you feeling about tomorrow?' he asks in English, and I frown. The distance between us seems to grow larger.

'Fine,' I say. 'Could do with something to calm the nerves, though,' I laugh. The English syllables feel cold, rough against my tongue.

Lars doesn't laugh back. Just stares at me, cutting right into me the way only he can.

'Look,' I say, stepping forward. Lars takes a step back. 'I'm sorry,' I say. And I really mean it. 'It was stupid. A moment of weakness. But it will not happen again. I'm not the man I was, Lars. And besides,' I smile at him, 'there will be no temptation now, huh?'

But my old friend does not smile. Instead, he glances at my easel, then looks out towards the Nova and moves over to the edge of the roof, his hand in his pocket again, reaching for the rock that I know is not there any more. That now rests in Ana's PPK.

'Lars,' I start, 'I'm worried about Alyssa. I can't help but think we're asking too much of her to stay here, and witness someone take her place. Someone who . . . well . . . isn't who we expected.'

Silence.

'To be honest,' I push on, 'a lot of this isn't really what we expected. Valdivian. Abbey. The cameras. Ana. It's . . .' For once, I am stuck for words. 'It's a lot,' I end feebly.

He stands in silence. He has always done this: let me fill the gaps. Bare my soul to him.

'Do you trust me?' he asks, finally turning to me. His blue eyes look so sad.

'I agreed to do this because you made me believe there was something more I could give. You said this would give me a purpose again.'

He sighs. 'Do you believe me if I say, I think all this,' he gestures outwards and below him, 'is the only way we can make this thing work?'

I watch a number of trucks and cars making their way back and forth to the launchpad. A camera truck loading.

'I don't doubt it,' I finally respond.

Lars nods and turns back to the launchpad. 'If you can find a price for the future of humanity, Rubio, I believe I have paid it.'

'I hope it is worth the cost,' I say, in our native tongue.

'Me too, Rubio. Me too.'

After watching the Nova together for a few more minutes, and witnessing the descent of the night, he wishes me luck and departs.

I leave the painting as is. It can dry in the desert night air, unfinished. I am done.

Lars and I first crossed paths when I was just nineteen. My father was a miner, a very masculine man, who could not understand why his son seemed to spend all his time reading, writing, and painting. As soon as I was able to start working, I moved to Helsinki, and lived what I thought was a bohemian lifestyle with a number of like-minded gentlemen. Finally, I no longer had to hide the homoerotic art of Tom of Finland from the innocent eyes of my sheltered parents. I could be whoever I wanted to be. I painted and wrote and tried to show the truth in everything, often making the world look and sound even uglier than it was. Looking back, I was a pretentious asshole. But I was just trying to find myself in those heady late-nineties years, when the world was so full of itself, and we thought we had conquered history.

One winter, when visiting my parents, I went out in the middle of the night and tried to capture the snow-laden forest landscape and the sky above it. It was that piece that found its way, as part of an exchange program, to a gallery in New York, where the newly made millionaire Lars Anders was looking to invest.

It was a shitty investment at the time. Rubio Lindroos was an unknown Finnish art student. But something about the picture spoke to Lars, and he bought it. And he sent me an email, introducing himself, asking me about the picture. I was in awe of this person who was showing such an interest in my work. I replied. He responded. And it continued.

Everything about that relationship was exciting. He was my first patron – a wealthy one, too. I soon found a picture of him in *Hesari*, alongside the title 'LARS ANDERS – THE FINNISH BILL GATES?' He was handsome. He wanted to see more of my work, and was thrilled when I sent him a photograph of the newly occupied International Space Station as seen from Kintulammi. He introduced me to an old colleague who was working with curators at the BMA and other New York galleries. My work began to sell.

I was enamoured, entranced. While his days, and nights, were filled with business meetings and conference calls, engineering issues and data crashes, Anders' emails and letters to me were filled with such a strength of emotion. There was a childlike purity to the way he experienced the world, experienced art. And when, in 2002, he finally invited me to meet him, I felt an exhilaration such as I'd never felt before.

We met in New York, where he introduced me to dealers and curators and patrons. He was even more handsome in person. Older than me, yes, but the man I had written to for years was finally there in front of me, and everything about him lived up to expectations.

At the end of my first day, he invited me up to his hotel suite in the Plaza to look at some images he'd purchased from the Hubble. I had fantasized about being alone with him for so long. My friends back in Helsinki had teased me about the 'daddy' I had in the States. How he would only disappoint. But I knew that everything that had happened to me over the last three years had been leading to this.

I was so nervous that as soon as he pulled out the images and spread them out in front of us, I turned and kissed him.

And he pulled away, surprise in his eyes.

He shifted away from me, ever so gently, the whole time never breaking my gaze. I felt my face flush with humiliation, with panic. But he just kept looking at me, with a kindly fascination. As if his mind was processing the new information.

I think I tried to speak, but Lars smiled and said, 'Do not worry. Let's just look at these images. I think you'll find the colours remarkable.'

He was absolutely right.

His friendship with me didn't change after that. Mine with him did, though. He still contacted me often, relaying his thoughts, asking for my opinions. But I didn't reply as quickly as before. It was an act of self-preservation. I did, however, move to the US in pursuit of my career, reassured that Lars was now on the West Coast, while I remained firmly on the East. But my career never quite developed into what I hoped.

After Lars sold his company and began to devote himself to Mars, I never found my purpose like he seemed to. Don't get me wrong, I got by on my work. Had a few pieces of writing published. My photography was used for commercial purposes. I fell in love again, and out of it, several times. I drank – a lot. Lars even paid for a stint of treatment for me, when my mother passed away.

I outgrew the person I was who had fallen for him, but it's never possible to completely erase love, and he clearly never wanted our relationship to end, either. I began to see him in a more objective light. I laughed when I read of his attempts to woo politicians into allowing him access to their space programs. I began to call out his tempestuous nature; how his extreme highs and lows had more of an effect on others than he realized.

But I truly believe he is a genius of our time, who feels the pain of our collective humanity. Long before he approached me about Mars One, I knew that people would be talking about him in future epochs, much like they talk about Einstein, or Leonardo da Vinci. He too seemed to have this sense of unwavering self-belief. As the twenty-first century developed, he would lament to me that the brightest and richest minds on this planet were more interested in getting people to click on ads, than changing humanity.

Then, in 2023, he approached me about Mars One, and asked me to be the first-hand witness; the scribe of humanity's next chapter. Me: a washed-up, underachieving artist? A single, middle-aged recovering alcoholic, with barely a legacy?

As he pointed out to me, the second thing Neil Armstrong did, after he landed on the moon, was turn on the camera – to make sure all of humanity bore witness. That was to be my purpose.

How can anyone say no to that?

Alyssa

WE'RE DOWN TO T-MINUS NOW: LESS THAN TWENTY-FOUR hours until the launch. Tonight is the crew's last goodbye.

Just as we used to at NASA, on the eve of the launch, families and loved ones will assemble outside, near the launchpad, across a gulf of around seven metres, and wave goodbye to the crew. It will be both glorious and heartbreaking. Where it will differ, however, is that this goodbye is for ever. I can only imagine how traumatic this evening will be for Dr Morin. I hope Abbey and the rest of the TV crew allow them some moments of peace, but something within me knows they won't. Not for the first time am I relieved there's a strict ban on alcohol within the accommodation block. It would have been impossible for Rubio to resist, tonight.

I zip up my bag and use the crutches to pull myself up. On the coffee table is a note of apology, not to Anders, but to Bob and the CAPCOM who will be rushed in to replace me tomorrow.

Because I'm leaving.

I can't do this.

I can't be useless on the sidelines. Not again.

I want to send a message to each one of the crew privately, but for that I'll need to use my personal phone. When I first looked at it after the accident, an overwhelming anxiety washed over me. Well over two hundred messages and counting had flooded in, along with missed calls and so many voicemails that my phone had stopped recording them. The first one indicated what most of the rest were going to be: requests for interviews. I ignored them all. Gwynne made sure that everyone within the mission knew to no longer use my personal number, but instead the private one given to me by Mars One. Since then, I haven't turned my personal phone on.

But I am well aware of where this substitute phone has come from, and I can't bring myself to trust that the messages I send to my crew will be read by their eyes only. Which is why I'm sitting, staring at my old phone on the coffee table. Now is my last chance to speak with them privately. After this, it will only ever be through official channels and after just a few hours, there will also be the delay caused by the physical distance between us. Once on Mars, there could be up to a forty-minute gap between receiving a signal, and then sending one back again. The world could end in brimstone and fire, and my crew wouldn't know for another twenty minutes that they were the last six human beings in existence.

I force myself to pick up the phone and turn it on. I squint my eyes against its light, blinding in the dimness of my apartment. As soon as it hits the home screen, the vibrations start. Notification after notification. I put it down and make myself a coffee, watching it writhing as I cradle my mug. It needs several minutes to receive everything and compose itself.

Ignoring every blue dot and number on the screen, I pull my pad of paper towards me, navigate to each name of my crew and type out their message. I wrote them down before attempting to send them so that I could spend as little time as possible on this damn thing.

As I move to each crew member, I read the messages they sent after the incident. Brun sent a signature short but polite 'get well'. There are a number from Okeowo, firstly apologizing, and then some motivational quotes, along with a picture of the crew – without Ana. Lee's is a heartfelt paragraph about how sorry he is to no longer have me as their commander. Morin's start with updates about where the crew are at in their preparations, but end just a couple of days ago with a message of thanks for everything I've done for them; she has clearly been hoping to help me move through some sort of grieving process. Rubio is the only one who has remained silent throughout the last week, with the exception of one message from a couple of hours ago that squats above my text box as I go to type my farewell to him:

I still have space in my PPK.

My eyes shift to the kitchen counter, where Neha's copy of *The Little Prince* sits. I haven't spoke to Kajal since our brief meeting in the cafeteria. That coder was right: people are shitty with grief.

It would need to be fogged with decontaminant before being given to Rubio. Would it make it in time before the PPKs were loaded into the capsule?

I hobble over to it — I'm getting better at manoeuvring with the cast on, although it's starting to itch like crazy — and open it up on the page it finds most natural. It's the illustration of the Little Prince on Asteroid B-612. He stands alone on a tiny, rocky world, with volcanoes and the stars all around him and I'm reminded of what he says at the end of the book: stars and lights in the sky mean different things to different people, but that the narrator should be soothed by the fact that he has a friend among them.

Another vibration breaks through the silence and my phone lights up once more. Sighing, I take the book back to the couch with me and go to reply to Rubio, but the new notification takes my breath away. A message from my mom.

Before I can fully process it, another one bursts in. My thumb moves to dismiss it and head straight to Rubio's thread, but my finger hovers over her name. I swallow hard, and tap. The ellipses are flashing at the bottom of the screen: she's typing. I wait for a moment, my heart pounding, stuck in suspense. But no new message appears, so I look up at the previous two:

We haven't received your grandfather's medal yet.
Please send confirmation of postage and we will track it.

I don't know why I'm surprised. I haven't posted the medal. It's in a Jiffy bag in my case, but I can't seem to bring myself to take it to dispatch. I stare down at the ellipses still looming at the bottom of the screen, flushed with anger. What else can she have to say after that? Then her message pops into existence.

I'm sorry.

Two short words. She was typing for so long, but that's all I get. What else had she been trying to say, before she fell on them? I guess I'll never know.

I feel a sudden, fizzing energy within me. I drop the phone down and shuffle back towards my case, unzipping it. As I reach for the bright yellow Jiffy glowing on top of my clothes in the moonlight, there's a blinding flash through the window. I freeze like a deer in headlights. By turning on my phone, have I somehow alerted the press to where I'm staying? Are they lurking out in my shitty yard, desperate for a shot of the sad, abandoned astronaut?

Another flash, less bright. I pull back the shades and peer out. Nothing but darkness. No shadows lurking. I look up at the sky and see the ominous clouds swooping overhead and moving out towards the desert steppe. Lightning rolls across the sky and another fork shoots out towards the ground with an almighty flash. It's beautiful, epic. I watch for a while longer, before dropping the shades and turning back to the coffee table.

Lightning storms are never good before a launch.

I can see it now, in my mind: the Nova rocket on the launchpad, lit up by the electrostatic discharge around it. And in the accommodation block, the crew feeling every wave of sound pulsate through them as the heavens roar.

They must be terrified. Another rumble of thunder vibrates through me.

How can I leave them to face it all alone?

I pick up my letter to Bob, weighing it in my hand. I shuffle over to the wastepaper basket and let it fall.

I grab a jacket, my keys and the Jiffy bag.

With the growl of thunder reverberating around me, I head to my apartment door and scoop up *The Little Prince* too, leaving my phone behind. Its home screen tells me we're approaching ten o'clock. T-minus-fifteen hours. I hope there's enough time.

Rubio

CAN'T SLEEP. CAN'T STOP SHAKING. IT'S NOT WITHDRAWAL – it's been too long since my last drink. Too long.

Can't lie here just waiting for dawn to come.

I switch the light on and blink in the sudden brightness. The lightning has stopped, which is a relief, but static still crackles in the air. You can prepare for everything, except the weather.

I take a piss, sitting, my head in my hands. The only way to stop the swaying. When I get up to wash my hands, a bloodshot, varicose-veined creature stares back in the mirror. Skin sapped of all colour in the fluorescent lights. Move on. Don't look.

Back in the room, my hands find a sketchpad and a charcoal pencil and begin to shade the feeling of the lightning storm. Imagining what the steppe must have looked like an hour or so ago: a straight dark horizon with ominous clouds hanging above it.

Once the sketch is finished, I find my lighter and set the corner alight. The paper curls as it burns. I move into the bathroom, and drop it in the sink, watching as the murky landscape turns to cinder. Charcoal to charcoal.

Now no one will be able to read into it like an ink-blot test when I'm gone.

A soft knock on the door turns my head, and I open it and peer out.

There's no one there, but on the floor directly in front of me lies a small package. I pick it up and turn it over. A sealing sticker on it states: DECONTAMINATED: 00:17.

I retreat into my room and close the door, then open the package. A book – *The Little Prince* – and a note:

Stay safe. A.

There's something else as well, heavy in my hand. Wrapped in its own blue silk, a gold five-pointed star, encircled by a wreath and suspended from a golden eagle, perched atop a bar inscribed 'VALOR'. On the other side, the name 'PFC MATTHEW WRIGHT'. He died in Vietnam in 1969.

It's still cold from the decontaminating process, but warmth floods through me. Despite her concern and grief, Alyssa listened. Perhaps there is hope for her yet.

Gently placing both objects on my desk, I steal a glance at my watch. Three in the morning. Just in time. PPKs are to be collected at six thirty for loading. My kit is waiting by the door. I weigh it in my hands, which are now feeling a little more steady. I search for the remaining paperback in the kit. I'll have to rely entirely on e-books up there, so that both these precious items can take their rightful place among the stars.

Alyssa

'THIS IS GOING TO BE TIGHT,' BOB GRUMBLES.

He's standing behind me reading the latest meteorological report as the rest of Mission Control buzzes around us. It's like a scene from *Apollo 13*, but with more women, no smoking, and fewer white people. All excellent developments. I'm sitting at the position labelled 'CAPCOM'. Beside, below and behind me are dozens of other members of crew, monitoring everything from Rubio's heart rate to the temperature of the fuel storage tanks (low and low . . . for the moment).

Right up in front of us are giant screens reeling off information, along with visuals of the launchpad, the inside of the *Argo* and, of course, the Mars One Channel livestream, which is also being watched by billions around the world – at least, that's what both Anders and Abbey hope. I don't care. I'm focused on the diagram in the top left of the twenty-foot feed: our mission trajectory. It's a basic line drawing of three different circles: the Sun, the Earth and Mars. A small zero showing the distance travelled so far waits patiently for its time to start ticking over.

My throat catches.

Here I am again.

Phantom alarms begin ringing in my head. Panic rises within me. The sound of rattling, gasping last breaths—

'We've lost an hour. The window is closing faster than we anticipated,' Bob says sharply, wrenching me back into the room.

'Fucking lightning.' He drops the report down for me to see.

I shake my head, forcing everything back down within me.

Not now. Not this time.

I lock my eyes onto the weather report. Last night's storm has abated, but there's still a lot of electrical discharge in the air and there's a high chance of lightning within a ten-mile radius of the launchpad later this afternoon. Our launch window has gone from eleven hours to seven.

I glance up at the live feed showing the dieticians serving up breakfast to my crew. *The* crew. I have to stop thinking of them as mine. Rubio is the only one drinking coffee – he's going to regret that later. Morin is filing her nails with an emery board. I flick the channel my headset is tuned to over to the public live feed. A bubbly voice commentates over the crew footage.

'. . . and it looks like Commander Morin is giving herself a last-minute manicure. She probably wants to look her best for the launch, especially as her loving family are—'

I mute the thing as fast as I can. Goddamn imbeciles. Last-minute manicure my ass. Some of the early spacewalkers ripped off their nails on the inside of their pressure-suit gloves. Morin is making sure hers aren't too long before suit-up. I hope they notice Lee take the file after her and do the same thing. Female spaceflight has come a long way, but some things will never change.

Bob is still hovering beside me, frowning at some other report now.

'It's fine,' I try to reassure him. 'Half-hour pre-launch briefing, then down to suit-up. Then it's four hours until launch. Gives you a couple of hours to spare past our original launch time. You've had tighter than that.'

He harrumphs and moves off.

The live feed goes back to the studio as the crew return to their rooms to put on their urine collection devices and coveralls. One final moment of privacy on this planet. There's just over two hours until crew ingress. I shuffle my checklists and take a sip of my own coffee. I guess I should be grateful that I'm not wearing the giant nappy that was reserved for me today. But truth is, I'd give everything to be climbing into that chafing son of a bitch right now.

A heavy hand lands on my shoulder and I spin to find Abbey, a radio and 'cans' around his neck like he's a Hollywood director and we're nothing but his extras.

'Ms. Wright,' he says, smoothly. 'Can I have a word?'

He leads me into an empty meeting room. The remnants of a meteorological briefing are on the whiteboard behind him, maps and weather patterns stretching out over the steppe. He stands. I try to match him, but my cast is still heavy and I have to relent and sit down in one of the chairs. I stare up into his smug face. He waits for a strange amount of time, but I hold his gaze. He glances behind me, into the corner of the room, and I turn to follow him. The camera mounted on the wall is blinking steadily. And then it isn't any more. I turn back to him and his beady eyes look triumphant.

'I really need to thank you,' he drawls. 'Your accident was the best thing to happen to this show.'

I fold my arms, determined not to bite.

'The ratings skyrocketed, if you'll pardon the pun. Drama is good for us.' He pauses. I keep my face neutral. 'Of course, it must be so difficult for you, to be grounded like this. But wasn't it you who said that the mission must always come first?'

He pulls out the chair next to me, slides into it and leans into me conspiratorially.

'You seem to be forgetting that recently.'

'I don't know what you mean.'

'You've always seen the mission and our TV show as two separate entities. But that's never been the case.' He helps himself to the jug in the centre of the table. 'This coffee . . .' He smells it as he pours. 'Nestlé paid us thousands to feature. This sugar . . .' He plops a cube into his cup, 'paid for with our optioning fee. The milk, the mug, this room, the electricity, this whole godforsaken compound, is propped up by the revenue from my show, my production company. I own this place far more than Anders ever will. This mission is the show. And you've been trying to meddle with that.'

'I haven't "meddled" with anything.'

'So you haven't been encouraging your old crewmates to swear during private conversations? To sing the songs of well-known artists who have protested against Mars One and would never allow use of their music in our broadcasts?'

I fight to quell the rage rising within me. 'And you haven't been violating the terms of our contracts by spying on personal phone conversations?'

He raises his hands. 'Hey, I've a lot invested here. It's not just cameras I've got keeping an eye on this. And you're not the only one with connections among the crew.'

I can't help it. 'Ana,' I growl.

He laughs. God, I hate him.

'You're a little obsessed with her, aren't you?' He sips his coffee. 'You think she's a mole? My puppet, whom I planted?'

I say nothing.

'And so what if she is?' He smiles, delighting in my rage.

'You're playing with people's lives, Abbey. It's not some cast you can just switch in and out. It's space exploration. Every member of that crew is critical to the mission.'

'And as I said, the mission is the show. If you want the resupply missions to fly, if you want the oxygen to keep flowing, you need to do what is best for this mission and Stop. Interfering. With my TV show. You understand me?'

His leg comes into contact with my cast and he leans in heavily. Pain shoots up my leg and into my spine as he grins at me. He hears my breath catch in my throat – then leans back and away. He pushes the mug away from him and stands up, buttoning up his jacket.

'Remember, Wright, I can paint the heroes of this tale, and I can also paint the villains. You're not leaving this planet any more.

There's no escape.' He strides towards the door and swings it open then turns back to me.

'Good luck today. So many will be watching. I expect you'll be a diligent and discreet CAPCOM in the months to come.' And he's gone.

I look back up at the camera in the corner of the room, and just like magic, its beady red light starts blinking again.

Rubio

CHECK. CHECK. CHECK. THE FITTERS RUN THROUGH THEIR lists and we sit at our stations like school children waiting for our mothers to put on our shoes, our coats, our scarves. We're all quiet, the fitters doing most of the talking.

'The biggest protests were definitely in France. You could hardly see the Arc de Triomphe, it was engulfed in flames,' says one of the men attending Okeowo.

'It's not Terra Revolution who set the fires though,' comments a British woman checking Lee's glove.

'Their slogan is *our home is on fire*!' says Okeowo's fitter. 'And it certainly was last night. Did you see the footage from LA? The sky was red again.'

'Those are wildfires,' Brun interjects, calmly.

'I know, but last night it felt like the world *was* on fire.'

An awkward silence hangs over us. The fitters shoot each other uneasy glances, clearly worried they've gone too far. Most of the ground crew have been treading on eggshells around us for days. Like we're on death row.

A small voice breaks through the silence. 'Do you think they will protest here?' Ana. We're all shaking, but she's shaking so much it must be perceptible to the cameras around us. She's sitting in the chair that would have been Alyssa's.

'No way,' the American fitter working on her helmet reassures her kindly. 'This used to be the Soviets' top-secret Cold War base and we've got a billionaire boss. The security around here is like nothing you've ever seen before.'

'They're a huge movement though, maybe even millions, and they did say they'd do everything in their power to stop this,' Okeowo's fitter speculates, but the next fitter along nudges him to stop.

'It is impressive. The scale,' Brun says, almost to himself. Forever the scientist, always balanced.

The American puts himself in front of Ana and grasps her shoulders. 'There is nothing to worry about. It's just noise. Besides, Terra Revolution?' He snorts. 'You guys are *saving* humanity, their beef shouldn't be with you.'

'Their mission isn't to save humanity, it's to save the planet,' Brun corrects him.

'Are we done?' Morin asks the fitter by her side, refusing to be drawn into the argument.

'All good to go.'

'OK, team. Let's get ready for walk out.' She's up and flexing, reminding herself how the suit feels, and we all follow slowly. It's heavy, this all-in-one life-support system.

'Remember, mics will be back up for Anders,' she says. Dr Morin has pored over the call sheet and shooting schedule for today. She knows when they have special guests and livestreams going off to other places around the world, and we can speak more freely.

As if on cue, Anders enters on the other side of our Perspex wall, mask on. He strides across the room and takes his spot. I'm relieved to see there's a bounce in his step. Whatever demons he is battling behind the scenes, nothing can dampen his enthusiasm today. His wild, eccentric dream is about to be fulfilled. He's sending humans to Mars.

He's followed by several members of camera crew, press and ground support, all in PPE. Like a true man of the stage, Anders waits until all are in place and his audience is waiting in silent anticipation before he starts.

'My friends,' he begins. 'I am looking at the first explorers of another planet and I could not be prouder, or more honoured. But you are not the only space travellers among us. Our very planet is soaring around a sun, which is hurtling through a galaxy, which is surging across the universe. We are all, every single one of us, space travellers. So you see, this is our destiny. The great scientist Konstantin Tsiolkovsky famously said, "Earth is the cradle of humanity, but one cannot live in a cradle for ever." That statement has never been more relevant. Our home world sits on a knife's edge, teetering on the brink of mass extinction. And the only way of guaranteeing our continued existence, is venturing beyond it. As you launch today, know that you have the power of eight and a half billion souls behind you. You are the seed from which the next branch of humanity will grow. It is as natural as life itself. And that is what you will be taking to your new home: life. So, thank you. There is no greater mission than this. No greater sacrifice. I, and the rest of humanity, wish you luck, happiness, and long and fulfilling lives – on Mars.'

A flurry of clicks and flashes goes off as Anders comes to the end of his speech. *Mars.* Believe it or not, that is the first time today someone has said that word to us. Everything up to this moment has been steps, procedures, checklists. Our aim is to launch. It feels strange to be reminded of our ultimate destination.

I turn at the sound of a sniff to the left of me. Ana is holding back tears, her beautiful eyes shining. Some of the cameras move away from Anders and focus on her. My eyes latch on to Ruth's, and there's a hint of disapproval on her face. If the cameras weren't around, I'm sure she'd be rolling her eyes. Dr Morin raises her eyebrows at me and turns back to Anders. I know what she wants me to do and, holding back an eye roll myself, I reach out a hand and grasp Ana reassuringly on the shoulder. More clicks and camera flashes, capturing this moment of what I suppose must look like solidarity. Ana smiles shyly and places her hand over mine, nodding at me. Why does it feel like I'm in some Hollywood movie? I hope to God Alyssa doesn't watch this.

Dr Morin speaks for us. 'Thank you, Anders. We're honoured to be part of this historic mission. On behalf of the rest of the crew and myself, I want to thank the thousands of people who have made today possible. We're just the passengers. I also want to pay special homage to those whom we have lost in our pursuit of the stars, and to those who we leave behind. We're taking all these people with us, in our memories and in our hearts.'

At the end of Morin's speech, my hand drops down to my side.

'Well said,' Anders nods. 'Shall we?' He gestures to the door at the other end of the room, but then stops. 'Oh, wait!' he says, pulling out his phone.

Light laughter erupts around the room and the formality of the moment shatters as everyone realizes what he wants. All the crew shuffle together a little more, and we hover a moment as Anders turns his back to us and clicks his phone's camera to take a selfie. Dozens of other cameras flash around us.

'Thanks, guys,' he says, turning back round to face us. Of course, we can't shake hands, but Anders turns to shake hands with one of the technicians and we, the crew, do the same on our side. Brun, Morin and Lee give me sharp, confident shakes. Their eyes look determined, focused. Okeowo gives me a wry smile. I shake Ana's last. I can't read her face. The shiny, watery eyes are gone, and a beautiful smile is there, but there's no warmth in it and her grip feels light when I seize her hand.

'Good luck!' Anders cries, and everyone who filed in with him follows him out.

As soon as the entourage is gone, leaving just one handheld camera, our technicians spring into action. Our fitters and ingress crew, in black jumpsuits, gloves and masks, reach for our packs and umbilical cords stored beside our stations. They attach the hoses to the right leg of our suits, 'locking and loading' us, and hand over the briefcase-like packs that contain our oxygen and coolant. Once we all have the thumbs up, we turn and face the exit. The ground crew have stencilled the words AD ASTRA above the doorway, the same words that used to adorn the exit at the equivalent suit-up room in NASA's Kennedy Space Center. But not too long ago, some smart-ass crossed out 'astra' and wrote 'MARS'. I wonder if the TV cameras will frame that out, or keep it in.

Morin shuffles behind me, moving along the line to check everyone is OK. Even in the bulk of the suit, I can tell her shoulders are tense. She's about to see her family for the last time.

'Right,' she says, over her shoulder as she takes up first position. 'Let's do this.'

A wall of noise hits us as we step out into the dazzling light of day. We only have a matter of minutes left to experience a real atmosphere on our skin, so I try to focus on the feeling of warm wind on my face. Once we're inside the *Argo*, we'll never feel that again. But what could be a beautiful moment is punctured by the yells of press, well-wishers and loved ones all clambering to see us emerge.

Instinctively, I wave. The minivan that will taxi us to the launchpad sits at the end of what feels like a very long walkway through the crowds. Press shout questions at us from every angle. Camera flashes blind us, despite the sun shining above.

'Mom!' A screech breaks through the crowd and a hand comes over one of the barriers. It's Maggie, Dr Morin's daughter. Next to her is Ben, her brother, and behind them in a protective, bear-like stance, braced against the throng of press and other well-wishers, is Max, her husband. Morin's wave falters. She steps a little closer to them. Maggie's hand strains outwards, and then she seems to remember that she can't touch her mother and she grasps the metal barrier instead.

'Mom!' she repeats. My heart aches for her.

One of Abbey's cameramen swoops in to focus on the family, while another scuttles to capture Morin's reaction. The rest of the crew fan out and spot their own loved ones elsewhere in the crowd, trying to give them the privacy they deserve, but will not be allowed to have. There's no one here for me, so I hover in the centre.

After what feels like an eternity waving like a goon, our ingress team usher us towards the minivan. I take the lead. If one of us starts moving towards it, then they might let those like Dr Morin and Lee have just a little longer to say goodbye. Without warning, though, Morin marches past me and is the first into the vehicle. The rest of us follow, our suits making us look clumsy, but the van's been modified to accommodate our bulk. Brun is the last one in, and the doors slide shut.

Through the windows, the crowds shuffle and shift. Some ground crew remove a rope and the crowd parts like the Red Sea, and the loved ones we were just waving to emerge. We're sealed in now, so they can approach the van. Maggie bursts through first and runs straight up to the window. She sees Okeowo, me, and then her eyes find Dr Morin and we can all see that she's crying. She grabs her brother and pulls him next to her. Max stays back, just watching as his children place their hands up to their mother's window. For the first time, I can see love in his eyes. And pain. Morin reaches up both gloved hands and places them on the pane of glass up against her children's.

'I love you,' I see Maggie say, but I can't hear her. I avert my eyes.

'I love you too, sweetie,' Dr Morin says, breathless. 'You too, Ben. I love you both so much.'

My leg is jostling up and down. Surely, we have to move now, we have to go. This is too much for them. It's cruel.

'Look after one another,' Dr Morin says. Articulating every syllable. And then we feel the electric motor kick in and the wheels start to turn. I look up just in time to see Ben pull his sister back as she attempts to jog alongside the moving window.

'Mommy!' Even over the crowd and through the glass we can hear that. Morin takes a big, shaky breath and looks away from the receding crowd. Okeowo reaches over and touches her knee, smiling sadly. Morin responds with a tight-lipped nod, before placing her hand on top of Okeowo's and closing her eyes.

Alyssa

T-MINUS-TWO HOURS.

The Quindar tones beep.

'Mars One, *Argo*, comm check,' I say, loud and clear.

'Copy Alyssa,' Morin's voice responds. 'How you doing down there?' She sounds confident and calm.

I press the PTT button again. 'Great down here, *Argo*. Ready to launch a spaceship.' I glance up at the images on the screen. They're all strapped in.

As they cycle through the other comm checks, I look over the team one by one, checking their facial expressions, how they're sitting. I wouldn't have been able to do this were I inside. I would have been in Morin's chair, at the front. Now, I can see everything, including our team mascot: a green alien from *Toy Story*, stuck to the wall just behind Okeowo's head. Lee is a huge Pixar fan. He looks stoic, seated next to Morin.

Bob gives me a thumbs up. I'm back into action.

'Mars One, *Argo*, that completes the comm checks. Ready for seat rotation.'

'Copy.' Morin rolls her arms to the suit technicians, who take their signal to stand back, out of the hatch. Once they're clear, the crew's seats rotate back thirty-five degrees so they are facing upwards, towards the stars.

There's some more chatter on the channels before the announcement rings out: we're ready for hatch close. The tiny slither of daylight in the left-hand corner of one of my screens is snuffed out. It feels unreal, like one of the many simulations we've all sat through. I push the PTT button again.

'Mars One, *Argo*, latch is closed. T-minus-one hour, fifty minutes. How you guys doing in there?'

'*Argo*, Mars One,' Morin responds. 'We're feeling good.'

'We wish you were with us, Wright,' Lee speaks out suddenly. My heart jumps. Morin's eyes flick over to Lee – he wasn't supposed to say that. I'm very aware of the entire Mission Control team looking at me, and the billions of people watching at home. I take a deep breath and my hand shakes as it hits the PTT button.

'Me too, guys. But you're in very safe hands.' Ana sits blinking in her seat, her luscious lips in an unusually thin line. 'Touch Mars for me.'

'We will,' Morin says solemnly.

'Mars One, *Argo*, this is the FD,' Bob breaks through on the COMs and begins to give an update on the weather. They don't really need to know this stuff, but I can tell he's purposely trying to give me a reprieve. I check the time. They don't need me for a while. It's just a waiting game now until the crew access arm retreats in an hour's time. I gesture to the guy next to me that I need more coffee. I slowly gather myself and my crutches, hooking my empty flask around one of the handles, and make my way out of the room as quietly as possible.

When I head back to Control, I can tell instantly that something has changed. Anders is in the midst of a heated discussion with Bob. Abbey and his cronies stand close by, filming it all. Several people I don't know are rushing in and out of the room.

Anders gestures for me to join them. I realize this is the first time I've been in close contact with him since the hospital. Up until today, we've been in different quarantine bubbles. At least, that was his excuse.

'What's wrong?' I ask as I swing myself over to him.

'Protestors,' growls Bob. Anders turns to us, full of nervous tension. His hand drifts to his pocket for his moon rock, but of course it's not there.

'At the perimeter?'

'Yes and no.' Anders grimaces. 'Our security teams have already broken up a few people. But now a group have started a fire to the south.'

Bob snorts. 'Not very green of them.'

'Well, the fire is just a distraction.' Anders sighs.

'From . . .?'

'Drones,' Bob barks.

I gasp.

'They're too small for our radars to pick up, but some of our spotters have seen them hovering around the perimeter.' Bob begins to pace. 'Our launch window was already tight without all this—'

'I thought this was supposed to be a no-fly zone,' I cut in.

'We have a three-mile radius flight restriction constantly, but we have a temporary flight restriction expansion today agreed with the Kazakh government.'

'Ha!' Bob barks out a laugh. 'If we could buy ourselves in here, I'm sure as hell others can too.'

Anders grabs Bob's arm. 'Be careful,' he mutters, glancing at a boom mic operator, stretching closer towards us. He clearly doesn't want the world knowing just how much money he's slipped into the pockets of Kazakhstani politicians to get access to this place. Bob shrugs him off and readjusts his sleeves. He looks annoyed, but lowers his voice.

'I say we shoot the bastards out of the sky.'

Anders rubs his face. 'This isn't NASA. We're a private company – we can't just shoot shit.'

'Fine,' Bob snaps. 'See what happens when one of those fuckers hits our heat shield. Hell, what if one of the damn things has a bomb on it?' His voice is loud again and other members of ground control are trying to pretend they can't hear him. He throws his arm to the big screen showing the shot of the launchpad. 'There's over one million pounds of rocket fuel sitting on that pad!' Spit flies out of his mouth.

Anders darts right up so they're nose to nose. 'And that's precisely why we can't have ammunition flying around,' he hisses.

I can almost hear Abbey orgasming with glee at this shitshow, and I can't stand it. 'Let's take this down a notch,' I say, pushing them apart. All three of us take a step back. Anders glares at Bob, who gives it straight back. I shift my weight from my cast leg.

'They're Terra Revolution, right?'

Anders nods.

'Then they're environmentalists, not terrorists. There won't be any bombs. We round them up, get the drones down and launch before the window closes. I'll let the crew know.' But my stomach drops as Bob's face shifts from anger to astonishment, his eyes fixed over my shoulder. Anders and I turn to look at the screen too.

It's the drones. But now they're well inside the perimeter. And there's hundreds, maybe even thousands of them. Hovering behind the Nova rocket on its launchpad. At first they look like a faint black cloud, but they're getting larger every second as they cross the distance towards the launchpad. Like a plague of locusts.

Rubio

GOD, I NEED A PISS. I SHOULDN'T HAVE HAD THAT COFFEE. When they asked what condom size I wanted for my urine collection device all those months ago, I did what every man would do and insisted I needed a large. But now I'm not so sure. What if it leaks? I'll go down in history as the man who pissed himself on the way to Mars. I resolve to hold on as long as possible.

'The chatter's gone quiet,' says Dr Morin, tapping at the screen in front of her. 'Something's going on.'

We've been sitting in the capsule for just over a half hour now. T-minus-one hour, twenty-five minutes. The next big milestone – the crew access arm retreating – isn't due for another forty-five minutes. I crane my neck as much as my suit, helmet and harness allow. There's a small window down to my left, but from this angle, I can't see much.

'Everything looking OK?' Okeowo asks. She and I are furthest away from the driver's seat.

'Fine,' says Lee. 'All configurations have happened. Checks are going through. Vehicle interactions looking good.'

'Could be the weather,' Brun says. 'That lightning last night didn't help us.'

The Quindar tones sound.

'Mars One, *Argo*, this is Alyssa.' Her voice rings out around the capsule. Heather clicks in reply.

'Hey, Alyssa. How's it going?'

Is it me, or is she taking longer to answer than she should?

'*Argo*, we have an update on the weather, handing over to our weather officer now.'

I tune out. No matter what the update, nothing can be done. If we can't launch, we can't launch. I turn my attention back to my bladder, telling myself that it has the ability to expand, that the urge to urinate is all in my head.

The weather officer rings off, leaving silence.

'Hey, Rubio, how's that cup of coffee feeling?' Brun calls out. How did he know?

I grimace. 'It's making its presence known.' A few chuckles sound, although none from Ana's direction.

'You'll be the first of us to test out the UCDs,' laughs Brun. 'Let us know how it goes.'

'Darling,' says Okeowo. 'I'm an old woman. I tested mine as soon as they cinched in my harness.'

My body contracts with laughter and the pressure on my bladder worsens. 'Please, everyone. No more. I can't take it.'

'Let me guess,' Okeowo says. 'You asked for large, didn't you?'

Brun guffaws and I hear a little snigger from Lee.

I grin back at her. 'Of course.'

Brun gives me a thumbs up. 'Well, good luck, big boy!'

Diagonally from me, Dr Morin shakes her head. 'I know something's not right. We haven't heard from Bob in a while.'

'Why not ask?' Ana's voice sounds strangely small.

'They won't tell us unless we have to know,' Lee snaps. He's been extra harsh with her the past two days. Tension hangs in the air. The countdown clock in the centre of the display screen ticks through the microseconds. Even when that clock strikes zero, and even when we do finally lift off, I'll still have an hour or so before we can move around the capsule and get out of these suits. I'm going to have to do it. I feel the moment of release all the way through me, and close my eyes, waiting for the spread of warmth across my crotch to confirm my leak. But it doesn't happen. I sigh with relief as my bladder empties. At least that's one issue out of the way.

I open my eyes again.

'Ask Alyssa,' I reply to Lee, belatedly. 'She'll tell us what is going on.'

Morin breathes in, and then out. We can all hear her thinking. And then she hits the COMs.

'*Argo*, Mars One, this is Commander Morin. Alyssa, can you fill us in on what's going on down there?'

Alyssa

I'M BACK AT MY STATION, BOB STANDING BY MY SHOULDER, and Morin's question hangs in the air. I look up at him and he shakes his head. The drones are holding steady, circling the rocket, but not getting any closer than two hundred metres. They're just above the nose of the *Argo* so the crew won't be able to see them. Yet.

I punch my button.

'Mars One, *Argo*. All systems are looking good. There's just a couple of concerns about . . . about the safety parameters.'

'Are you talking about the weather?' Morin fires back instantly. Bob shakes his head at me once more. I grit my teeth.

'It's a concern, yes. Stand by for more information, *Argo*.' I click off and turn back to Bob.

'Come on, Bob. We have to tell them. If we stop the countdown, they'll know something's up. Hell, they clearly already do. They're the only people in the world who don't know what's going on.'

'You heard Anders: we wait and see if security can clear them.' He looks dubious, but he stands firm. 'There's no point alarming the crew unless it becomes critical. We have forty minutes until the access arm retracts. If we can't retract, we tell them.'

'They're not children, Bob. They're going to find out about this eventually and when they do, they'll lose all trust in us.'

'Alyssa, this is my call. Please, sit down.'

I hadn't even realized I'd stood up.

'Bob, please. I can't lie to my crew.'

'They are not your crew!' he whispers. He doesn't look angry, just urgent and sympathetic. And that hurts more. 'This is not your mission any more, Wright. They are not your friends. They need to be managed. I stuck my neck out for you. I thought you would keep a level head. Now, please, stay calm and help us make sure they do the same.'

He moves away as Anders comes back into the room. The two of them talk rapidly. I turn back to the screen. The swarm of drones swerve to avoid each other as they hover. They're a mix of different models and shapes – a motley army, some with the Terra Revolution logo painted on in various colours.

I feel a surge of frustration. All this technology, all this time, all this hope, and it could all be destroyed by a few idiots with remote controls. We're not the ones they should be fighting. What about the governments that are still letting industry pump greenhouse gases into the atmosphere? What about the companies ploughing their way through the Amazon a hundred trees at a time? We're trying to find a solution to humanity's existential crisis. How can they not see that?

My eyes flick to the livestream feed next to the main screen. It's obvious the TV presenters are loving it. They're talking about heat cameras, security dogs, manhunts. I can only imagine what this means for ratings. It makes my blood boil. All I can think about now is Abbey's smug face as he poured that coffee earlier. *Drama is good for us.*

Something clicks in my head, and then I can't unthink it.

Is this him? Could a group of hundreds of protestors with drones really coordinate this and infiltrate our airspace all by themselves?

Drama is good for us.

The live Mars One feed clicks to the screensaver they put up for us while they're running the commercial breaks. A captive audience of billions. It's like a hundred Superbowls all rolled into one. Imagine if the Superbowl got cancelled, though, and then they got to run another one a few days later . . .

I look back to the feed of the crew. They're sitting completely unawares, strapped to a rocket that could blow at any minute. Rubio shifts awkwardly in his seat. Conspiracy theories. That's what he said the other day. Am I being paranoid? But then my injured leg throbs again. I remember the pain from Abbey leaning into it, sneering at me.

Drama is good for us.

I punch the PTT.

'Mars One, *Argo*, this is Alyssa.'

'We hear you, Alyssa.'

I glance over at Anders and Bob. Both are looking at me, eyes wide.

'Multiple civilian drones have infiltrated our airspace and are purposely causing obstruction.' Bob strides towards me from across the room, and I speak quicker. 'Security teams are working to find the operators, but we may need to pause the countdown if they cannot be cleared before access arm retraction.'

'Copy that,' Morin says, clipped. 'Is there danger of collision?'

I look back up at the screen. If they wanted to hit the Nova or the *Argo*, they would have done it by now.

'No, Commander,' I reply, more confident than I feel. 'It seems like they're trying to impede launch. Stand by for more information.'

Bob is by my side now. I remove my headset and raise my hands.

'I'm sorry, Bob, but it was the right thing—'

He throws down a tablet, showing a heat map of our perimeter, dots of yellow and red on a sea of green and blue. 'Security have pinpointed some groups they suspect to be the operators. Ground teams are moving in now. We're pausing the clock until they're cleared.'

I didn't realize I was holding my breath until that moment. I let it all out in a wave of relief. Bob still looks furious. He lowers his head close to mine.

'This doesn't excuse what you just did, Alyssa,' he says, low and fast. 'You and I are the only people in this place who have any idea of what the fuck we're doing.' He looks around the room, trying to hide his contempt. 'And if we don't hold this shit together, the crew is fucked. Understand me?'

I nod.

'We're on the same team, Alyssa. Please act like it.' He gives me one more blistering look before retreating back to his own station and holding his headset up to his ear.

'Mars One, *Argo*, this is the FD. We're holding the countdown at T-minus-one hour, thirteen minutes and twenty-three seconds. Stand by for more information.'

The clock in front of all of us freezes.

I burst into the male toilets to find Anders leaning over the sink, his head hanging low. He doesn't even look up at the noise.

'You've been avoiding me,' I say.

'The Kazakh security forces have arrested over a hundred people and all the drones are grounded. Shouldn't take long now.' He smiles, but his eyes aren't in it.

'Anders, what is happening today, shouldn't be happening.'

He looks up at me, surprised.

I take a deep breath, ignoring the voice shouting in my own head to shut the hell up. 'I think you should delay the launch. We need to stop this now, before it's too late.'

He considers me for a moment, his face blank, and then he pushes himself up. 'What are you talking about?' His voice is quiet.

'You're a smart man, Anders. I just don't think you want to admit that you're seeing it, too.' He doesn't reply, so I push on. 'You said it yourself: the TV show has far more control than it should. That we're dependent on them and the money they bring in. But it's more than that. They insisted on the LAS sim. Me getting injured? It was a fucking cameraman who did that. And then they pull Ana out of a hat, risking everyone's lives by putting in someone who is quite clearly a publicity stunt. And then today, these protestors – how did they get past all our security?' I'm level with Anders now, staring him down as he just blinks.

'You know he threatened me?'

Anders balks.

'Yeah,' I half laugh. 'This morning, before Terra Revolution turned up. He told me to do what he says or else. And he pretty much admitted to Ana being his plant. His puppet. His words, not mine. "*Drama is good for us.*" That is actually what he said.'

Anders sighs and runs his hand through his hair. 'Alyssa,' he says slowly.

'No, Anders. We've been here before. The night before the LAS sim, I told you it was a bad idea, and I was right! And I know I am right again this time. This has to stop. We can't go ahead. Drama may be good for a TV show, but it is NOT good for a fucking space mission.'

'What would you have me do?' he asks, louder now.

'Delay! The orbital launch window is two months. Push it back. Tell Abbey and the other producers to back off. Millions have seen what we're capable of today. We can find more funding. Who knows, maybe even some international space agencies will want to partner with us now. I know that's what you always wanted. And in the meantime, we can sort the crew out and investigate what has been happening around here.'

'Push it back until the very end of the launch window?'

'Yes!'

He looks at my cast. 'Until that thing is off your leg?' he asks quietly, eyebrows raised.

I frown and look down. I keep forgetting the cast is there. Until I have to move again.

'What?' I say, looking back up at him. 'No. I mean, yes, I guess that . . . but that's not what I'm saying!'

But my cheeks are hot, because he's right. That thought did cross my mind once, back in the hospital. If only they could just delay . . .

'Alyssa.' He moves away from me again, like he can't stand to look at me. 'Even if that cast comes off your leg, you can't go up there. You'll have muscle wastage, not to mention the metal rods. You may never be cleared to—'

'This isn't about me!' I cry.

'Isn't it?' he yells, snapping back round to face me, his cheeks bright red, his hands in fists. I've never seen him like this. 'This rampage isn't about your concerns for the mission. It's because of YOU. You've lost your dream. You've lost control. And now you're taking it out on everyone around you. Well,' he laughs bitterly, 'I know quite a bit about losing control. This planet you're so desperate to get off? It's run by money. If you have the money, you have the power. Right now, I don't have the money. But the science is working. We're about to send people off this fucking planet and double our entire species' chance of survival. And I will do anything to ensure that happens. Even if I have to play along with their stupid games. Even if another person gets to take your seat. This is bigger than you, than George Abbey, than me. It's bigger than all of us.'

He breathes heavily, running his hand through his hair. 'So you have a decision to make. Either toe the line, play along, and accept your place on the sidelines. Or leave.'

I stare at him, dumbstruck.

'I . . .' I stammer. 'I – don't know what to say.'

'It's much better that you say nothing at all,' he says, and storms out of the bathroom.

Rubio

IT TAKES FORTY-FIVE MINUTES TO CLEAR THE AIRSPACE around the launchpad.

And once again the clock in front of us starts counting down.

'Mars One, *Argo*. It is T-minus-thirty-five minutes. Commencing propellant loading of the Nova rocket.'

There's a click somewhere deep below us, and a resonating buzz surges through the ship and our bodies. Tonnes of rocket fuel are now surging beneath us. We're literally sitting on top of a bomb.

Next to me, Ana's leg jitters and it's everything I can do not to reach out and grab her knee to still it. Instead, I check my outer suit pockets for a sick bag. Apparently, many astronauts experience an extreme form of motion sickness when they first hit microgravity, and vomit floating around space is not pleasant.

In my left leg pocket, my hand finds something that is not a sick bag. I frown. There shouldn't be anything in that pocket. It's hard. Solid. I move my bulky glove around its shape as subtly as possible, and a chill runs through me. My heart races. Damn it. I'm wired up. They'll see this.

'Hey, Rubio,' calls out Brun. 'What are you fidgeting around for? Did that UCD finally leak?'

I pull my hand out of my pocket.

'Just checking for sick bags,' I reply, hoping no one can hear the shock in my voice.

'Good shout,' Okeowo says, and rummages through her own pockets. I'm left to my own devices again.

My left leg twitches. Now that I know what rests upon it, it feels heavy as lead.

A flask. In my fucking suit pocket.

My mind races. Did someone put it there as a joke? No. A joke would be an empty one, but this is heavy. Full. I can't get rid of it. We're a half hour from launch, and no one would believe I didn't put it there myself. Not after what happened two weeks ago. I struggle to run through the events before walk out. At suit-up, I didn't notice anything unusual. There was no point where it felt like something was slipped into my pockets. Someone put it in there before I even walked through the door? Or maybe as we were strapping in? And what the fuck does it matter how it got there? The point is, it's in there now, and it's coming to Mars with me. My heart feels like it's going to burst through my chest. I can only hope the doctors monitoring my vitals think it's the nerves. Who would do this to me? I'm so hot all of a sudden.

Maybe it's filled with water. A little last-minute tease from my fellow crewmates. Brun probably did it. As soon as we're launched and on our way, he'll ask me if I have something to drink and that will be the end of the joke.

But what if it isn't water? What if someone has slipped me something because they think I need it? Do they think I'm that weak? Am I that weak? One final salute to the man I was. I'm supposed to be leaving him behind. And yet here I am, with a fucking flask down my trousers.

It's now only twenty minutes until launch. Where has the time gone?

I'll have to get rid of it. But there are cameras everywhere. So I'll have to do it the only place we have privacy: the toilet. I'll have to find a way to make the suction function work. But what happens if ethanol goes into the septic tank? It's only supposed to take urine. Would I potentially be endangering everyone by putting something so flammable into a system that wasn't built for it? Funnily enough, we weren't taught that shit.

Or.

Or I could just drink it. Slowly. A tiny amount each day over a number of weeks. My body would break it down. Absorb it. Excrete it through my sweat glands. Tiny, imperceptible amounts that our ship's biological systems could more easily deal with. It would be the ultimate test of my willpower. Proof that I am a different person now. That I can take tiny sips and control myself. It could be a reward for when things go well. A small, warm reassurance when something doesn't. It could be my transition. And when it's gone, it's gone. Just an empty flask as a reminder of what I have accomplished, and what I no longer need. I can bury it in the Martian soil and it will lie there for eternity, sunken into an alien world, never to be seen, never to be thought of, ever again.

I look around at my crewmates. Surely, they're all carrying their own secrets, their own demons, to another world. None of us are perfect. We're human, and that is the point. We're taking everything with us: our hope, our science, our courage, our faith – but also our histories, our fears, our flaws. And anyway, we're almost on our way. I have plenty of time to think about what to do with this demon in my pocket. I'll worry about the flask another day.

For now, I just need to get through the launch.

Alyssa

T-MINUS-FIVE MINUTES, AND FUELLING ON THE FIRST- AND second-stage rockets is complete. Plumes of white jet out from the Nova on the big screen as the liquid oxygen loads.

'*Argo* has transitioned to figure for terminal count,' an engineer.

'Strong back retreat commenced,' answers Bob, standing at his station, eyes flicking from one data set to another. Anders and Abbey stand at the back of the room, one man a living shadow, the other's eyes glued to the Mars One TV channel feed.

I look back at my display and change the feeds to show the inside of *Argo*. There the six of them are, waiting for their moment. Sitting in that fine balance of fear and excitement; joy and dread. Every hour of briefings, every minute of training, every excruciating second of simulations has been leading to this. My whole body aches with the desire to be sitting in that twinkling instant with them. The marrow in my bones yearns for it.

A laugh breaks out across the room. Of course, it's Abbey, smugness emanating from him. He was boasting earlier that Pepsi paid eight million dollars for their advertising slot today. Less than four minutes out from one of the greatest risks six souls have ever taken, and the rest of humanity is being force-fed images of carbonated drinks. While these brave people strive to further our species, you can do your bit by buying, consuming everything in sight. A serpent eating its own tail.

He must feel my eyes burning into him because he turns and

smirks at me, arching one of his eyebrows, goading me. *Well? What can you do now?*

'AFTS Final set-up started.' Which means it's T-minus-three minutes, thirty. I snap back to my screen. Morin stretches her hand open and closed. Lee taps around the screen in rapt concentration.

'*Argo* has transitioned to terminal count and is on internal power,' confirms our chief engineer. I clear my throat and hit my PTT.

'Mars One, *Argo*, you are T-minus-three minutes. All systems nominal.'

'Copy, Mars One.' Morin's voice is strong and steady. Her hand reaches to her helmet.

'Visors closed, team,' she says.

Like a troop of dancers, the crew simultaneously raise their arms and do as she commands. Morin reaches across the cockpit to shake Lee's hand.

'Good luck everybody,' she says. A smile drifts across her face. 'Let's do it like we've trained. Eyes on.'

'Eyes on,' nods Lee.

Behind him, Ana moves slightly. She's mumbling under her breath. I turn her mic right up in my ear, but still I can't hear what she's saying. Okeowo gives her an uncertain glance out of the corner of her eye. Rubio leans forward, frowning with confusion. Whatever it is, it's clearly unnerving them all.

T-minus-two minutes. Her mumbling gets louder.

She's speaking Russian and somewhere in the back of my NASA-trained brain, my mind translates for me. '*O God, cleanse me, a sinner, for I have never done anything good . . .*'

Fucking hell, she's praying. My eyes dart up to the main screen, where the TV feed is streaming. Within moments, the TV producers have scrambled a translation. The caption runs along the screen as she continues to mumble.

'*Deliver me from the Evil one, and may Thy will be in me, that I may open my unworthy lips . . .*'

Shit. None of my crew speak Russian, thankfully. But by the dismayed looks on the faces of Rubio and Brun, they've guessed. Try sitting on a bomb about to explode at any minute, with someone desperately muttering what sounds very much like the last rites. It's enough to throw anyone off. Clearly, Morin agrees.

'Petrova,' she calls sharply.

Ana's mouth clamps shut. On the main screen, the TV producers zoom in on her. Her eyes are wide, her pupils dilated, a watery sheen clearly visible through her visor. Give that woman an Oscar.

'Propellant fills are complete,' an engineer confirms, snapping me away from the drama in front of me. T-minus-one minute, thirty seconds on my countdown.

I glance over at Anders, who has moved off to the side, still seemingly trying to hide in the shadows. His right hand is massaging his temple as he looks down from the screens in front of us. Even he can't bear to watch. Abbey, on the other hand, is leaning over the desk in front of him, his eyes, almost as wide as Ana's, glued to the livestream. Lapping it up. Something tells me they won't be cutting to a commercial for a while.

My screen flashes: T-minus-one minute. I punch the PTT once again.

'Mars One, *Argo*. Nova is in start-up and *Argo* is in countdown.'

I see the red light over on Bob's console: the Flight Termination System. If all goes wrong, if the Launch Abort System fails, and the rocket looks as though it's about to hurtle out of control, Bob is ready to blast Nova, *Argo* – and the crew – out of the sky. Instant incineration.

'Flight Termination System is armed for launch.'

My own heart is racing now, beating far quicker than the seconds streaming past. Ana's closed her eyes again, but thankfully she remains silent. Rubio's hands are in fists on the arms of his chair. Okeowo breathes deep. Brun forces his shoulders back. Lee tenderly adjusts the alien attached to the wall. Morin taps at the screen then tugs at her straps. The TV feed has cut to a shot of the bleachers on the roof of our complex, where the families sit.

They zoom in on Maggie. She looks nauseous as she shields her eyes from the sun, looking out towards the launchpad, and the mother she cannot see.

T-minus-forty-nine seconds. My colleagues around me read out: *Good for launch. Good for launch. Good for launch.*

A beat of silence hangs in the air. Six fragile human bodies. Sitting on top of a bomb. Cameras all around. I see Morin, in the seat that is mine.

Bob clears his throat loudly. I shake my head and punch the PTT. T-minus-forty seconds.

'Mars One, *Argo*. You are . . .' I take a gulp of air. 'You are go for launch.' I release the button and pull back, placing my hands on my legs. I can't trust them not to shake.

Morin clicks her button.

'*Argo*, Mars One, we're go for launch.'

A ripple of excitement runs through the engineers and crew. Bile hits the back of my throat.

'T-minus-thirty seconds,' says Bob, firm and low.

The crew place their hands on the arms of their chairs. Bracing themselves.

Huge digits fill the screen of the TV feed, as they show a shot of the launchpad, the Nova pointing up to the heavens. One remaining plume of white gas shoots outwards, giving a faint hiss.

I've never seen seconds move so fast.

'Stage One tanks pressing for flight.'

'T-minus-fifteen seconds.'

I can't think. Can't blink. I just stare at the images in front of me. My crew. My spaceship.

The huge water faucets at the base of the pad let rip, flooding the basin underneath it with water.

A call out of TEN, the final countdown sounds out over our systems.

NINE.

EIGHT.

I no longer watch the crew. Just the rocket.

SEVEN.

SIX.

This can't be real. This can't be happening.

FIVE.

FOUR.

Everything has built to this?

THREE.

TWO.

ONE.

A surging white mushroom cloud billows out from the side of the pad.

ZERO.

IGNITION AND LIFT OFF OF THE NOVA AND CREW *ARGO*. MARS ONE HAS LAUNCHED.

Red, white and orange blossoms at the bottom of the Nova, and the support structures fall away as it slides upwards with apparent ease.

My dreams, my future, slipping away with it.

Rubio

AT ZERO, THERE'S NO DOUBT THAT WE HAVE LEFT THE Earth for ever. I imagine the hold-down bolts blowing as I'm slapped with over seven thousand kilonewtons of thrust. Everything within and around me vibrates violently. It's side to side. Not up and down. I wasn't expecting that.

The noise is thunderous. Overwhelming. My chest feels heavy as lead. I take short, sharp breaths as I'm squashed into my seat. I can't move my head, but I can just about make out the colours streaming past the window below me. White, and just a hint of orange. The liquid in my eyeballs vibrates as they bounce off the inside of my sockets.

The simulator was nothing on this.

'Propulsion is nominal,' the comms reassure us. This is nominal?

Just when I feel I'll go mad with the vibrations, another voice calls out: 'Throttle down ready for Max Q.'

Oh, shit. We're not even at Max Q?

With the throttle down, it only gets worse. The vibrations surge even more and the very fibres of the ship groan under the stress. The largest amount of aerodynamic pressure is being exerted on the ship as we rattle around inside it. Everything flexes. Should it be bending like that? My straps strain to hold me in place. It feels like the pressure is cutting through the many layers and digging deep down into my flesh. The screens in front of Lee and Morin flash: 2.3 G. I struggle to even keep my eyelids open.

The screens tell us the engines are now throttled right back to stop our rocket from tearing itself apart. As we punch through the sound barrier, everything is hit with an almighty shock. The *Argo* and Nova scream, and I scream with them.

Suddenly, the metal screaming stops.

'Throttle up,' crackles over the comms. As the vibrations lessen, the thrust increases and my stomach jolts. Our Nova's engines roar back up to full power. Our speed flies past fifteen thousand kilometres per hour. We're already fifteen kilometres up.

Moments later, the vibrations ease up entirely as the boosters separate away from the Nova. When the first stage of the Nova shuts down, the main engine cuts off. Within seconds, the main bulk of the huge beast that has brought us all this way simply falls away into the darkness of space. Now, it's just the second stage of the Nova powering us to the right altitude, so we can begin to catch up to Mars.

We're on our way.

Alyssa

I WATCH THEM CLICK PAST 80.4672 KILOMETRES WITH A dull sigh. That number is significant to nobody else but me. It's exactly fifty miles. Morin and her crew are now astronauts in the eyes of the US military. Golden Air Force pins all round. Not that they'll be getting them.

We're getting close to the moment when Nova's second-stage engine will cut off and *Argo* will officially be en route to Mars.

I'm numb now. There's only so much dismay and devastation you can feel before your brain has to switch to some other plane, where you just go through the motions.

Trajectory nudge me, and I obligingly hit my PTT.

'Mars One, *Argo*. We have you on a nominal trajectory.'

'Copy,' replies Morin.

'Stand by for SECO and second stage separation.'

'Copy that. Mars One, we're ready to let this go.'

I turn back to Bob, who nods and smiles at the chief engineer. Once again, our eyes are on the clock and the screens as we wait.

'*Argo*, Mars One. SECO,' confirms Lee from the *Argo*, as the light of the engine blinks out. He lets out a bark of laughter. 'Perfect.'

There'll be silence and stillness in the *Argo* now. And hardly any Gs at all. I close my eyes and try to imagine what that must feel like. The eternal stillness and silence of space.

Something I'll never know.

Whoops and cheers sound around me, and in the *Argo* itself. As the second stage of the rocket falls away, all the tension of the day falls off everyone here in a massive wave. Engineers hug each other, high fives and air punches abound. It's just like the space movies. I'm the only one sitting down, watching it unfold in front of me, as though from the outside.

I breathe out once more and turn back to my console.

'Mars One, *Argo*, this is CAPCOM,' I call out. The feed shows that the crew have finished their own celebrations and are already readying themselves for the next stage.

'Hearing you loud and clear, CAPCOM.'

'All systems nominal. Trajectory nominal.' A checklist floats past one of the camera feeds. 'Confirming a successful insertion into orbit. You're free to move about and get ready for solar panel deployment.'

'Copy that, Mars One,' replies Morin. She's looking serious again. 'And thank you,' she says heavily, staring down the nearest camera lens, so her eyes lock with mine thousands of kilometres below. It hits me right in the stomach.

I don't reply, just watch as the crew take off their gloves, their helmets, and unstrap themselves from their seats. Lee detaches the alien mascot from the wall and sends it spinning over their heads, laughing in such a boyish way – I've never seen him look so young. Rubio bats it over towards Okeowo. Brun launches himself straight up from his seat, slamming into the ceiling in amazement, his helmet and gloves spinning out.

Ana has managed to take her gloves and helmet off, and now her beautiful blonde locks are floating up around her head like some sort of ethereal halo. Both Morin and Okeowo have short, cropped hair. Sensible hair. Ana struggles to get her straps off and Okeowo floats over to her. You'd never guess that she's not been in micro-g before. She helps release Ana from her harnesses, mother-like. Ana nods her thanks and pushes herself out of her seat, as her crewmates begin to wiggle out of their spacesuits, revealing their more comfortable overalls below.

Brun looks a little queasy as he shakes himself out of his trousers. All of a sudden, a look of panic flashes over his face. Kicking off from the wall nearest him, he flies to the back of the cockpit, obviously heading for a sick bag. The idiot must not have packed one in his suit. In his rush, he bashes through Ana, who is sent spinning and hits her left side hard against Okeowo's chair.

'Careful!' Morin calls after him, stowing her suit away under her seat. He answers her with a retch into a bag. Small drops of yellow chyme escape out of the top and hover in the air around his face.

'Jesus,' Rubio scrunches up his face as he too begins to wrestle his suit into submission.

'You OK, Petrova?' Morin asks.

'Fine,' she says quietly. She's righted herself and is feeling around in her left leg pocket for something. Has Brun's vomit made her weak stomach churn? She looks so lost. Space adaptation sickness can hit anyone. My stomach fizzes with shame even as I will her to fall victim to it.

But no, her perfect fingers pull out something palm-sized and round from her pocket. Surely that can't be what I think it—

With a click, it opens, and an infinite number of particles float up into the air. It's a fucking face powder. The internal mirror is cracked, unable to show the wide-eyed look of surprise and panic on its owner's face. Ana jerks her hand to try and shut the case, but that only makes it worse and another cloud of powder erupts into the microgravity.

'Jesus Christ!' barks Okeowo.

'Fuck!' yells Bob, choking on his coffee back here on Earth. 'What the fuck is she doing?!'

I sit, my mouth agape as the powder spreads.

'Ana!' cries Morin as she turns to see what's happened.

Lee swears loudly in Korean.

There's a reason why you don't eat bread in space, or have anything else that crumbles. Fine crumbs, powder, anything like that can get into tiny gaps in the ship's systems. Buttons and other mechanics, yes, but also the filtration system. The very air you breathe is precious. You only carry so much, ready to be recycled again and again. The system can scrub for CO_2 easily enough, and dust to a certain amount, but everything is calculated to a fine degree. There are no margins for error in space.

Morin and the rest of the team know this, too.

'Lee!' she cries out. 'The fire blanket. Hurry.'

Before she's even finished this command, he's already heading to where it's stored. Morin dives back down to her seat, taking out the water pouch stored underneath it.

'Alyssa!' Bob calls out my name. I turn to face him – I hadn't realized I was on my feet. 'Talk to them!'

I turn back to the screen and go to hit the PTT, but before I do, Morin grabs the space blanket from Lee and squeezes some water onto it, which forms into balls. She spreads the blanket wide in her arms and pushes herself towards Ana and the billowing cloud almost obscuring her. Ana retreats back, staring at the mess in shock.

Morin swoops the blanket over the cloud and encompasses it, managing to capture nearly all of it. Lee is there in a moment, helping to wrangle the blanket and condense it down, ensuring that the powder hits the balls of water inside the blanket to make a paste, which is much easier to deal with in micro-g.

As quickly as it started, the crisis is over.

There's a collective sigh of relief around me. I hear Bob growl at someone, 'Find out who let her take that fucking thing up there and if she's got anything else we should know about.'

Back on the *Argo*, Morin takes a breath and turns to face Ana, who looks mortified.

'What were you thinking?' she demands.

'I'm – I'm sorry,' Ana stumbles. 'It was pressed and—'

'Well, it isn't any more,' snaps Lee, giving Ana the filthiest look. The rest of the crew hang awkwardly.

I wait for the cool, harsh words that I know Morin is about to give Ana. How mistakes like that could be the difference between life and death. *Do it*, I urge Morin. *Tell her.*

Instead, Morin just pinches her nose and then looks up again at Ana, the doe in headlights. 'Get rid of it. Then get out of your suit. Get ready for solar deployment.'

That's it? Barely minutes after SECO and into orbital insertion, she compromises the entire *Argo* cockpit and that's it?! I watch, stunned, as Morin moves away from Ana and Ana sheepishly wraps the little box in a sick bag.

One of only three women on the most ambitious journey ever undertaken by the human race, and the first thing she does is pull out a compact? My hands are in my hair, my brain racing. I look back up at her, and I swear I see the tiniest tug of a smile on her lips.

'Alyssa?' Bob growls in warning.

I slowly pull my eyes up to meet his, hoping that I see my anger reflected back in him. Surely. But instead of anger, I see concern. He's looking at me like I'm the problem.

'Bob?' I ask, my voice shaking.

'Alyssa,' he says. 'It's fine. It's dealt with. Just calm down.'

My eyes feel like they're about to pop out of my head.

'Dealt with?' My voice shakes. The other engineers and ground control members turn to look at us. 'You think this is fucking dealt with?' I hiss. 'Look at her!' I throw my hands to the screen. Something inside tells me to stop, but another part – a rawer, hotter, more powerful part – urges me to let rip. 'She's supposed to be an astronaut. Not a fucking airhead!' Spittle flies from my mouth and the cameras turn to me. I don't care. Let them see. Let them all see. And let Anders see me most of all.

'Come on, Alyssa.' Bob raises his hands and leaves his station, approaching me warily like a police negotiator. 'Let's go outside.'

'No,' I snap.

'Please?' Bob almost begs.

'You know as well as I do that this isn't right. No one who should ever get near that spaceship can be anywhere near that stupid. Can't you see? Can't you all see? A fucking powder compact? Give me a break!' Abbey mutters to one of his camera crew, and they move in for a closer shot. 'Yeah, I see you.' I point at him. 'I fucking see you. And I see her, too. Bring your camera closer, I don't care! Bob, you know this is bullshit. We have to stop this.'

For once in his life, Bob looks like he has no idea what to do. I turn to Anders, frozen by the door.

'Lars!' I call out to him. 'You said it yourself: we're not in control here. This can't go on. They're going to kill someone!'

Bob finally gathers his senses and goes to grab my arm.

'Please,' he whispers, 'just come with me.'

But the Control alarms are ringing in my ears again, along with the panicked breaths of someone who knows that this is it, this is the end. That silence and death awaits them. Deep, ragged breaths.

Are those mine? Or a memory?

I pull away from him and hobble back, my cast taking me by surprise again. It's suddenly clear to me that no one will listen. No one has the guts to say it. This mission is fucked. Don't they understand how dangerous this is? How everything can be lost in an instant?

Dammit to hell if I'm going to let my crew carry on in this nightmare without saying something. This time, I can do something. This time, I can save them. For the first time in a while, a sense of calm and clarity of purpose washes over me.

I dive to the PTT and pick up my headset.

'Mars One, *Argo*.'

Bob lunges for me, but I thrash out and hit him square in the face. Gasps break out around us, but I'm already back at my monitor.

'Mars One, *Argo*, this is Alyssa. Do not trust her. I repeat. Do not trust Petrova. She's a plant. A mole. You need to demand a return to Earth.' I glimpse the panic in all of their faces, but my eyes zone in on Ana, who is struck motionless, floating in fear.

'I repeat. This mission is compromised. You must return to Earth—' But several strong pairs of hands have grasped me and are pulling me back from my console. My headset is ripped from my hands. My legs collapse beneath me and I hit the floor hard. I think I scream. Two burly men haul me by my armpits and drag me to the nearest fire exit. My face is wet. Am I crying? I must be mad. My colleagues stare at me as I'm dragged away and their looks confirm it.

I look back up at the big screen. At my crew floating helplessly, stunned, not knowing what the hell to do as my message rocks them to their core. Just as they've left everything and everyone behind.

Oh God. What have I done?

My eyes search for Anders. Beyond the chaos, the cameras crowding me, I see him. He looks like he's crying too.

'Lars!' I call out, but my voice feels small, more breath and anguish than anything. The fire doors slam as the security men thrust me through them.

'Lars!' I cry. But I can't see him any more. All I see is flashing, and cameras, and on the big screen, the diminishing light of the *Argo*, heading out into space. And then the doors shut hard.

Rubio

WE SIMPLY GO THROUGH THE MOTIONS AFTER THAT, exactly as planned. One checklist after another, we ready the *Argo* for our six-month-long voyage. We deploy the solar panels and open up the rest of the ship, moving our lives into the depths of the crew quarters. We power up the life support, check that all supplies, kits and rations are stored correctly and that nothing has shifted in the launch.

The fire blanket and the compact confiscated from Ana are jettisoned out into space behind us. She's quiet, does as she's told and barely speaks for the next few hours.

No one mentions Alyssa at all. A new CAPCOM comes over the system and chirpily informs us that all systems are nominal. He helps us through our checklists and congratulates us on every milestone achieved.

We slowly acclimatize to the micro-g, some of us more quickly than others. Dr Morin insists we eat something. I grab some sort of paste in a tube and gulp it down. There are no celebratory toasts at the table. Ana takes out Anders' moon rock from her PPK and sticks a little tab of Velcro to it, before placing it down on the central table of the crew hab. We stare at it a while and I think of him, left behind. Wondering what more chaos lies ahead.

One by one, we head to our bunks to grab a bit of sleep before the next telemetry adjustment. It feels like a weird dream. Or a very realistic simulation. My bunk is nothing more than a tiny, curtained-off area, with a small amount of storage for my clothes and meagre belongings. My PPK is Velcroed to the wall, and there are straps to secure my sleeping sack so I don't drift away down the ship.

I open up my PPK. There he is, *The Little Prince*, his sad illustration and a wilting flower gazing up at me. And beside it, Alyssa's grandfather's medal. I daren't get it out for the cameras to see; I don't want them to start talking about her again on the commentary. Assuming they've even stopped.

She truly sounded like a madwoman. Like a more evolved level of crazy than when I last spoke to her. Is that what happens when people snap? Alyssa has always seemed so unflappable. So sure of herself and her purpose. But then her purpose was stolen from her.

And as for Ana – is she really a spy? A plant? I am annoyed at her, certainly. Not only did she risk all our lives with that powder, she also set the feminist cause back a few decades at least. Honestly, what was she thinking? As if all that hair weren't bad enough, now she really is singling herself out. And yet, would a spy really be that stupid?

Suppose, just for a moment, that Alyssa isn't crazy. What if she is right, and someone is messing with us? It would make sense, I suppose. We've all seen reality television before; we all know how producers like to meddle. How drama is key. But this is a space mission. This is our lives. They wouldn't risk them for a few extra ratings, would they?

Of course they would, you naive old fool, I chastise myself as I wriggle into my sleeping sack. I'm exhausted, delirious. Few other humans have ever experienced the pressure we just endured. Sleep is the key. Sleep will help all this make much more sense.

And that's when I remember.

The flask.

I transferred it from my suit trouser pocket to my sock when I changed. And now I can feel it, jammed up against my ankle. I can't bring it out or the cameras will see.

My shaking hands find the tethers to hold me in my bunk. I tighten them and make sure they're holding fast, then float in the darkness. My crewmates shift around me, attempting to settle into their home for the next six months, and I have a sudden urge to tell them everything.

And yet, something holds me back. The fear that they won't believe me. That they'll think I've crumbled yet again, and brought this on myself.

Whoever put that flask in my pocket knew I would be afraid to speak. Afraid of what it might look like.

So someone really is playing a game with us. With me. It's clear who Alyssa thinks I should suspect, but I can't bring myself to believe that, not just yet. It makes more sense for it to have been someone I've just left behind for ever.

I have embarked on a journey that will take me away from everyone and everything I have ever known, with five other people who will be my only company for the foreseeable future. If we can't trust each other, who the hell can we trust?

Alyssa

I HARDLY HAVE ANYTHING TO PACK. JUST SOME CLOTHES, a few books. Everything else is related to the mission, and I've been told I must leave all that behind.

They took my phone and laptop. Worried I'll compromise security, I guess. I don't want anyone to contact me, anyway.

Two men stand guard at the open door of my apartment. I've been told to wait for someone from the legal team to come and see me. In the meantime, they're arranging a flight for me. Wherever I want to go, and then that's it.

No. That's not true. They've also given me a referral to a shrink. It's already in the trash.

The television stares at me, blank-faced. I can't bear to put it on.

There's some murmuring outside in the corridor followed by a soft knock and I jump up, ready to meet my fate, but it's not anyone from legal. It's the coder, with an almost empty box on his lap. *Jacob*, the deep recesses of my brain remind me.

He smiles. 'Hey.'

'Hey,' I say, *what the hell are you doing here?* clear in my tone.

'I've been allowed to bring you your personals from your office.' He offers the box up to me. A stapler – that's definitely not mine. A pot plant, also not mine. And some snacks. OK, yes, they're mine.

He winks. I blink in confusion.

'Need any help packing?' he says cheerily, moving into the room and looking around at the two bags I've got closed up and ready to go.

'No, thanks,' I say.

'Fancy some air, then?'

'I don't know if that's allowed.'

He cocks his head to one side and then rolls back out into the corridor. I notice for the first time that his chair doesn't have any handles at the back. This guy will only move under his own steam.

'Hey, fellas,' he approaches the men. 'Do you mind if Lyss and I –' *Lyss?* Who the hell does he think he is? – 'head out for some fresh air for a bit?'

I stick my head out of the door to see their reactions. They look at each other, unsure what to do. Jacob steps up his charm offensive.

'She's not under arrest or anything, right? We'll just go sit in that park out there. No big deal. You guys can get a bit of fresh air, too. It's a beautiful night. Maybe we'll see the rocket!'

The men look at each other again, then back at me. My face must look as confused as theirs, so one of them just nods at Jacob.

'Fine,' they reply. 'But she has to stay within sight.'

'No problem at all.' He turns back to me. 'You got a jacket?'

We make our way across the street to the park in the centre of the apartment complex. I can sense the eyes of the guys behind us, but our leisurely pace seems to set them at ease. One even lights up a cigarette.

There's not much foliage in the park, just some dusty flowerbeds and a few benches all facing the rusting plinths in the centre. Most of the lamps are blown out, creating an eerie glow and a huge shadow where the Soviet rocket once stood.

Jacob is silent as he leads us to one of the benches, our backs to my watchers. He turns and parks up next to the bench with an exaggerated sigh and thrusts his hands in his jacket pockets against the chill of the night. I join him on the bench, leaving plenty of space between us.

He rolls his head back and peers up at the sky, which reveals more of its stars as our eyes adjust.

'We won't be able to see the *Argo*. The Earth will have already rotated round, so—'

'I know,' he cuts me off. 'But they don't, do they?' he says, gesturing behind us. Then he looks at me with those eyes that feel like they're burrowing deep into my soul, even in the darkness of the night.

'So. How are you?'

I snort. He's asked this so casually, like we're life-long friends heading out for a coffee.

'You're asking me how I am, when you saw me commit career suicide in front of a worldwide audience of a billion people?'

'The figures are coming in and they think it's actually over three billion. Rumour has it, Abbey came in his pants when he heard. I think you even gave them a spike.'

I turn away in disgust at the thought. Is that what he planned all along? Surely not – even I never thought I could snap like that.

'But that's why I'm asking you how you are. I bet no one has done that yet. So. How are you?'

I stare at the rusting plinths and the shadowy vacuum of space they stand beneath. They seem to yearn for the weight they once bore.

He's right. No one has asked me. And since the burning humiliation of being dragged from that room and the sick feeling in my stomach as they drove me away from campus, how have I felt?

'I feel . . . empty.' He lets me sit in the silence as I search for the words to explain. 'I feel like I'm suddenly aware of all the endless space within me. All those huge gaps between the nuclei and the electrons. Between the atoms. Endless nothing. What felt substantial yesterday, what felt so solid, now feels so . . . nothing. Just empty.'

He breathes out heavily. 'That's a lot,' he acknowledges.

Someone's dog barks somewhere and the noise bounces off the Soviet concrete architecture.

'So. What are you going to do now?'

This guy. His questions make it all sound so simple.

'I have no idea.'

'You gonna go back home and stay with your folks?'

I laugh, and it too bounces off the walls. I push myself up and limp towards the plinths in the centre of the park.

Jacob comes up beside me.

'So that's a no, then.'

'I don't have a home, Jacob.' My voice wobbles. 'I've lived here for the past few years. And now I'm supposed to be on the *Argo*. I'm not supposed to be on this planet any more. I was leaving Earth, and everyone on it, for ever. I was commanding a mission to Mars. I was going to be the first woman, the first human, to set foot on another planet. I was going to be a moment, for the rest of time. And now . . .' I shrug.

'Now you're here,' he says quietly.

'Now I'm here.'

Jacob spins away from me and heads towards one of the plinths. He places his hands on it – it's just about waist height – and pushes himself up in one swift, easy movement. He sits, his chair recoiling back a little with the force of his movement.

'You have to go somewhere,' he says, then gestures to the plinth a few feet away from him. I roll my eyes, but find myself walking towards it and mimicking him.

'If you want,' he begins casually, 'I have somewhere you can stay.'

I turn to look at him. He's leaning back on his arms, staring at the stars again.

'What?' I ask.

'I have somewhere you can stay,' he repeats. 'Until you work out what's next.'

'I barely know you. Why would you do that?'

'I dunno. You helped me the other week. Now, I want to help you.' He turns back to the stars. 'It's my mawmaw's old house. No one's using it. I'm here.'

I think for a moment.

'Indiana?'

He looks at me, amused, his head tilted to one side.

'Yeah, how'd you know?'

'Colts.'

'Ah, yes,' he says. 'You know, there's more to me than football, and coding.'

I look at him for a moment, his perfectly honed muscles flexing under his jacket. His well-defined jaw lit by the faint glow of the lights.

'Why would I want to go to Indiana?'

'Exactly.' He grins. For a moment the stillness inside me stirs. 'No connections whatsoever there. It's perfect. You can lie low there. These guys won't want you attracting attention, and I'm sure you don't want to be hounded. I won't even charge you rent. It's yours until I'm finished here.'

'And how long will that be?'

He shrugs.

'Until I'm bored.'

'Well, that's reassuringly specific.'

'What other options do you have?' he asks.

'Valid point.'

We sit in silence and I too feel my eyes drawn up to the sky above us. More stars emerge every moment, but I'm thinking about how much the Earth's atmosphere is hiding from us.

'You're going to need to redefine yourself,' Jacob says out of nowhere. 'Work out who you are now. There's more to you than Mars One.'

I scoff. 'You know nothing about me.'

'Maybe . . . But trust me, I know,' he says, firm. He looks at me now. 'Like, how do you introduce yourself?'

'What are you talking about?'

'Go on,' he insists, sitting up a little straighter. 'How would you introduce yourself, if you didn't know me.'

I don't reply.

'Come on!'

'I'd say . . .' I throw my hands up. 'I'm Alyssa Wright, I'm the commander of Mars One. I *was* the commander of Mars One,' I correct myself. The past tense still feels odd in my mouth.

'Exactly,' Jacob says, triumphant. 'If you'd asked me the same question when I was twenty, do you know what I would have said?'

'"I'm Jacob and I'm inappropriately familiar with everyone"?'

'Close, but no.' He smiles. 'I used to say, "I'm Jake and I'm a quarterback." "I'm Jake *and* I'm a quarterback" – I'd put it right up there with my name.' He looks down, back towards his chair. 'But then I fractured my T10 vertebra and I had to see myself as something else.'

I cast around for something to say. Jacob seems to know there's nothing, so he ploughs on.

'And now,' he looks back up again, smiling. 'Now I'm Jake, a guy who loves the colour blue and stodgy food, who has the habit of biting his nails, who likes to code – who is pretty damn good at it, actually – and loves chicken wings, has shitty taste in football teams, and wants to help you.' Once again, he looks up to the stars and the moonlight catches on his extraordinary face. 'You know,' he continues. 'You mentioned atoms earlier . . . Well, there are more of them inside of you than stars in the universe. So what do they all add up to? I'm pretty sure it's more than just Mars One.'

Up ahead, my guards shift at the approach of a car. Must be the legal rep come to read me my last rites.

'I should go.' Jacob's not smiling any more, and I suddenly wonder if he really was given permission to come and see me. He pulls his chair back towards him and drops onto it, then reaches into his pocket and pulls out a wallet, and a small card. He thrusts it out to me.

'You probably shouldn't contact me directly – I don't think they'd like that,' he says, as I too move off the plinth. 'But if you do fancy taking me up on my offer, head here. My friends will give you a key to my place. And they won't tell anyone you're there.' He pushes it forward again, urging me to take it. So I do.

'Thanks,' I mumble, shoving it in my jacket pocket. The car has pulled up at the apartment block and a figure is getting out, talking to the guards.

'I'm sorry, Lyss,' Jacob says, already backing away from me. 'I would have liked to have seen your moment. But maybe there'll be another one.'

I doubt it, but I can't say that to him. So I bark back instead, 'It's Alyssa.'

He just smiles. 'Good luck. And don't worry. I'll look out for your crew.' He raises his hand in a wave, then turns, hunching up against the cold breeze, and moves out towards the other end of the park. I run my finger over the dog-eared corner of the card he's given me, then readjust my crutches and swing myself back to the apartment block. I was right – the legal rep has arrived. My stomach flips at the look of pity on Kajal's face.

'Alyssa, hi,' she says, in a low voice.

'Hey.'

We stand opposite each other, awkward.

'Well. Shall we?' she says, gesturing towards the door with her bag rammed full of papers.

I sigh. 'Sure.'

A couple of hours later, Kajal is packing away her files while my minders silently watch. NDA'd up to the eyeballs, with a large sum of money due in my account in two weeks, and my last will and testament to be shredded, I've been cut-off, paid, and silenced. Never to contact or work for Anders or Mars One again. I wonder if it was an act of cruelty or kindness that they sent Kajal. She's barely said anything that wasn't strictly necessary.

When everything is wrapped up, she looks at me as though undecided, pulling at her ponytail. Clearly, she has something else she wants to say. She sits back down opposite me.

'Alyssa . . .' She shifts uncomfortably. 'I don't know where you want to go, but . . . we've had a call. From your mother.'

Ah. I sigh and sit back. My mother is the last person I want to speak about, or to, right now.

'She's concerned about you. They both are. So we maybe thought, perhaps that's where you'd like—'

'No.' It comes out of me without even thinking.

'They're worried about—'

'No.' I stand up. 'I'm not going there. Now, I'm ready to go.'

Kajal stands and shoots a worried glance over at the security guards. She reaches for my arm, but I pull away.

'Alyssa—'

'No, Kajal. As far as they're concerned, I've still left this planet, OK? Don't worry about me. I have somewhere I can go.'

'Really?'

'Really.' I do my best to stand straight and sound calm. 'So, can we go?'

'Er, yes, of course. These guys can take you.'

'Thanks.' I begin to move out, awkwardly shouldering my rucksack. 'Oh.' I stop abruptly, and Kajal gives a little start. 'I forgot to mention: Rubio has Neha's book. In his PPK. So it's on its way to Mars right now, just like I promised. I thought you might want to tell her. I . . .' Kajal's stunned face makes me falter. 'I didn't want to let her down,' I finish quickly. Kajal clutches her hands to her chest, looking like she's about to cry. I turn quickly and gesture to the guys to lead the way.

'Bye, Kajal. And thanks.'

And I'm out the door, not giving her a second glance. My knuckles white around the handles of my crutches.

PART TWO

PART TWO

Rubio

I READ THAT GENE CERNAN ONCE SAID, 'FUNNY THING happened on the way to the moon: not much.' That was about a journey of only four days. He should have tried six months.

It's day eighteen on the way to Mars. We've done over four times the length of Gene's trip, and already we're resorting to kids' games to entertain ourselves. Dr Morin has decided that each Wednesday (or 'hump day', as she likes to call it), during R and R time, we should do something 'fun' as a team. So my assigned task? An *Argo* treasure hunt, with riddles leading the crew from one hiding place to the next. Paper, however, is a finite resource. I refuse to use the meagre supplies I brought with me, and instead am recycling the one thing we definitely won't need any more: our launch checklists. There's something both exhilarating and terrifying about defacing the papers we studied and relied on for so long.

I pretend I'm grumpier about this task than I actually am, especially as I've turned it into an opportunity to paint each clue. I've found a way of mixing the colours in a ziplock bag and it's pleasing to see the different pigments swirl and clash together in microgravity.

I push away from the wall I've been tethered to and using as my workstation and, as I float through the hab to hide my clues, a purple hue pulses over everything.

Without even looking up from her paperwork, Dr Morin calls across to me, 'Mic, Rubio!'

I grumble as I spin myself back around and grab the battery pack and wire that's Velcroed to the wall. I've gotten into a habit of taking my mic off whenever I can. I can't deal with the wire floating around and tickling me. It reminds me of the feeling you get when you walk through a spider's web. Most of the alerts and alarms we're trained to respond to are red or orange, and indicate an imminent threat of death. Purple, though, indicates that something is interfering with the broadcast: a camera is obscured, the feedback to Earth is broken or, far more often, someone (mainly me) has forgotten to wire themselves up for the entire planet to hear. Sure, there are mics everywhere on the *Argo*, just as there are cameras. But Abbey and his cronies 'want to hear every decibel of every belch', even though I remember Alyssa despairingly telling Abbey that we can't burp in microgravity. I smirk at the memory. She was never very patient with hyperbole or figures of speech. Then I feel a pang of guilt. We haven't heard anything about her since our launch day. I've asked a couple of times in my personal messages to Anders how she's doing, what happened to her, but he's evasive.

I try and shake Alyssa from my mind as I head to my first stop. The bio lab, which everyone calls the greenhouse. It's where Brun is cultivating our plants – or I should say, our future farm and pharmacy. We're all trained in basic biology – it's part of our contingency plans in case one of the mission specialists snuff it (the training for my speciality was a little less strenuous. People had to learn how to use the camera equipment and the basics of framing and lighting. I don't think I imagined the slight loss of respect from the likes of Brun and Lee after that) – but Brun is the expert and he spends most of his time in the greenhouse. The added carbon dioxide from human presence is good for them, and it's strangely comforting to see living things thriving and growing, day by day, in this man-made environment of metal and plastic.

'Hey,' he offers in greeting as I make my way through the airtight door into the lab. There are various artificial plant habitats lining the room, all cultivating the crops we're going to need when we get to Mars: dwarf wheat, radishes, lettuces, peppers, potatoes, and tomatoes. They glow the familiar white-yellow of Earth daylight, behind doors of glass, but the plants in the centre of the lab are out in the open and beginning to climb up to the magenta LED lamps above them. I don't exactly know why they glow pink – something about different wavelengths – but it lends the lab the vibe of a sleazy strip club.

'Mind if I hide a clue in here?' I ask.

'Be my guest.' He gestures to the lab.

'Close your eyes – I don't want you cheating.'

He smiles. 'Rubio, my friend, your secrets are safe with me.' He dutifully closes his eyes, but then he takes on a parental tone. 'Don't touch the tomatoes at the back. I just repotted them and they need to settle.'

Secrets. I instantly think of the one I'm still hiding in my sleeping bag, and my palms begin to clam up. Thank God Brun has his eyes closed, or he might see my flash of panic.

I push the thoughts away as I find a spot well away from the tomatoes, and tack one of my riddles underneath it.

'*Merci*,' I say, as casually as possible.

Brun opens his eyes again and goes back to work. '*De rien.*'

'Where's Ana?' I ask. I know she's supposed to be on duty in here with Brun today.

'Where do you think?' he says with more than a hint of disdain.

I check my watch. 10:17. Shit. She's tipped over into another hour now.

'I don't get why Morin doesn't do anything,' he says, irate.

'They're trying different lighting.'

'Pssh.' Brun finishes his data input and floats over to another hab, checking the readings on its panel. 'That won't work. I don't want to sound crazy, but maybe someone likes her being around late at night.' He glances up at the camera above him. His shoulders look tense, but he moves on to the next panel and pushes a few buttons. The show must go on.

I must admit, the same thought had occurred to me too . . . But we can't discuss it properly here. 'Don't miss dinner at eighteen hundred,' I say as I float over to the door.

'*D'accord*, although it will be lunch for some.' He raises an eyebrow.

When I make my way into our sleeping quarters and peer into one of the pods, it's confirmed. Suspended in micro-g, hovering under a halo of soft blue light, is Ana. The long golden locks, that I've seen Morin and Okeowo looking at dubiously, float around her in beautiful tendrils. Her pale arms lie slightly above her torso, which rises and falls softly. Angelic is the only word to describe her. Is she dreaming? Feeling safe in the oblivion that the darkness of sleep provides?

Either way, Brun's right: the blue light is doing nothing to rouse her.

Since the first couple of days, Ana has fallen into a twenty-five-hour circadian cycle. At first, she was simply a night owl – she'd stay up reading, or watching films, or would volunteer to clean. But as she stayed up later and later, she began rising later. We don't have a strict timetable on board, but one thing the medical team are serious about is sleeping; fatigue on a spaceship can be fatal. Last time I checked, she wasn't going to bed until around four in the morning. If she's sticking to our recommended eight hours of sleep, she won't be up for another hour or so.

I wonder what she does at 'night' when the rest of us are asleep. How lonely it must feel, being the only conscious human being within ten million kilometres. Do people on Earth watch her floating alone in the infinite darkness of space, while her crewmates slumber? Do they listen to her hum to herself as she eats her meals alone? Watching a person grow ever further apart from the only people they will ever be connected to – is that entertainment?

I realize I've been staring at her for a while. Now who's the strange voyeur? I push on, floating past our sleeping beauty and my own bunk. I try not to look at it as I pass. Denying the pull of what is still concealed there.

I propel myself towards my next hiding place: a storage area just beyond our personal pods, containing things we won't be needing until we land: thermals, camera equipment to set up on the surface, shoes.

I snap open the lid of one of the storage bins as I ponder how strange it will feel to encompass our feet in shoes again. Millions of years of evolution, and Homo sapiens never developed hardened feet. It's weird what evolution prioritizes—

My heart rate skyrockets. In about thirty seconds, someone in Baikonur will think I'm going into cardiac arrest.

In the bin, tucked among our shoes, is an electronic device with some sort of block attached to it. I stare at it, agape.

It feels like a snake might leap out at me if I reach in.

I look around me – not a soul in sight. I can feel a camera lens burning into my back, but it won't have seen what I've seen. Just the bulk of a body inexplicably freezing after I opened up the lid.

Do I touch it? My mind goes to the thought of fingerprints. Preserving evidence. I've been watching too many crime shows on our entertainment system. We haven't got the means to dust for prints up here. It wouldn't have occurred to anyone that we'd need to investigate a crime. Is this a crime? Why am I thinking of it like that? Then I chastise myself for being so naive. It's an unexplained piece of equipment, hidden somewhere that crew would have no reason to disturb for the next six months. Of course it's not above board.

I decide to pick it up. I shift my body and secure myself to the wall with a foothold, purposely obscuring the camera. I want to know what it is before the rest of the world sees it. Gingerly, as if the thing is a bomb (Christ, can you imagine?), I reach in and pull it to the top of the bin.

It's definitely a touchscreen. There are smudges of oily fingerprints over its dark, muted face. So it's being used. Or has been used. But by whom?

Something clicks in my mind, and I think I know what it is. In the event of a radiation threat, we're trained to seek sanctuary in a strengthened refuge within the ship where our water is stored around us. It's supposed to give us added protection, but in that scenario we have to take a mobile communication device with us – a last resort, in case a solar flare knocks out our main communications system. This basic bit of equipment would allow us to have typed conversations with Earth, in the hope that they would be able to help us get the comms systems up and running again.

I know that device, though. We check it every day as part of our safety protocols. It's mounted in the centre of the ship, for ease of access. It's a tablet, too, but it's a lot sleeker, more compact than this . . .

Holy shit. Is someone secretly contacting Earth without the rest of us knowing? Why would anyone need to do that? The implications make me feel sick. I let go of the thing like it's razor sharp. The motion sends it spinning at the mouth of the bin.

I cast around for a less terrifying explanation. It's a backup. Nothing sinister. But the Mars One crew are meticulous. Backup equipment would never be stored with a bunch of plimsoles. We've all read the manuals over and over. Always remember the boldface: the stuff they put in bold and underline; the stuff that will save our lives. A backup to the backup communication device would be in the boldface. But it isn't.

I have to tell Dr Morin. She's our commander. Anything like this has to go to her.

It's at this moment more than any other that I yearn for Alyssa. She would know what to do. And then I think about what she said to me, and what she screamed to us as we hurtled for space.

I shove the lid back on the bin, and place it back where it was secured. I need to show Morin exactly where I found it.

Taking deep breaths to calm my pounding heart, I spin and push back off towards the pod entrance, past Ana, still sleeping soundly. As I reach the doorway, I turn back one last time, almost to check it's still there. That I haven't made the damn thing up in my mind.

There's an eerie glow. A lightness forming at the top of the storage bin, creeping out where the lid is unsecured.

Now it feels as if my heart has stopped. Before I know it, I'm floating back towards the storage bins, my eyes transfixed on the glimmer.

My hands shake as I land up against the wall and reach out to peel back the lid once more.

More white light bursts out and I blink in astonishment. The device is staring up at me, floating among the innocent cargo.

It's a white screen, with just one small, black word centred in it – a word that makes my blood run cold.

THIRSTY?

I slam the lid shut and spin round. The camera is still boring into me. I wasn't as careful that time to obscure the view. Did it see?

Fuck.

Without thinking, I snatch the paper clue that is now spinning in an unseen eddy of the air system and thrust it beneath one of the bungees securing the storage bins, for all the world to see.

I need a moment. Some space to think.

Trying to move as calmly and slowly as possible, I make my way out of the sleeping pods and down towards one of our toilets. I squeeze into the tiny space and slide the door behind me.

As soon as I hear the door click, I claw at my back pocket and grab for the mic strapped there, pull out the wire from the battery pack.

A gargling noise comes out of my throat and I begin to gasp for air. That screen was so bright, it feels as if the word is imprinted on my retina. I squeeze my eyes shut to try and clear it. Over and over. But it's no use.

Heat rises up my throat. I grab the piss funnel and fumble to flick on the suction switch before I retch into the damn thing. I haven't eaten much today. Nothing comes out but water and bile and shame.

After my body finishes convulsing, I let everything go and just float, trying to breathe deeply.

The flask. They know.

Whoever that device connects to. Whether they are the people who conspired to smuggle it onboard or not. They clearly know my darkest secret.

Which is that most nights, when I am alone, my back to the cameras, I have been taking the tiniest sips of that damn flask. Drop by drop, night by night, I've been destroying the evidence of my addiction, while simultaneously fuelling it.

And now, after seventeen tiny sips, the flask is almost empty. Whoever placed it there – be it to mock me, shame me, or maybe even help me – none of that will matter when it's finished.

But they know.

I glance at my watch. 10:39. Even with our current thirty-second lag, that's more than enough time for someone on Earth to have seen what I was up to, and then send a message back to the communication device.

What happens if I reveal the device to Morin? Will whoever is messaging from Earth somehow reveal my secret? That's what it means, doesn't it? It is a threat. Blackmail.

I've been in this toilet for quite some time; I don't want anyone asking questions. I take another couple of deep breaths, undo the latch and float out.

I drift back down to the hab, where Morin is buried in paperwork. So blissfully unaware of everything. I hover for a moment. I can see what her face will be like when I tell her. The furrow of concern, her forehead wrinkling.

'Dr Morin,' I say. 'Commander.'

A purple hue floods over the two of us. She glances towards the alert light and then back to me. 'Again?'

At first, I'm not sure what she means, but then I realize. I've left my mic unplugged. My hands shoot to my backside and I feel around for the loose wire and battery pack.

'Sorry. I must have caught it when I was in the toilet.' I connect it back up.

'You can deal with Abbey next time,' Morin says, rolling her eyes. Then her head tilts as she looks me up and down.

'Are you OK?' she asks. There's that hint of concern on her brow I was anticipating. She's too perceptive.

My mouth feels very dry. I cough. 'Yes, sorry. I'm fine. I, err,' I stumble. 'I've hidden all the clues. And Ana is still comatose, by the way.'

Her face softens and relief spreads through me.

'Thanks, Rubio. And don't worry about Ana, I'm working on it.' She smiles warmly and turns back to her work.

I spin, faster than I intended. But I have a plan. I won't tell anyone about what I've found just yet. Instead, I'm going to keep an eye on the storage bin. I'll work out who is using that thing, and then talk to them. Find out what they're up to. You never know, it might be totally innocent. Or it may be that their secret is far greater than mine.

One thing I am certain of: I am going to be paying a lot more attention to Ana and her sleeping patterns. Her circadian cycle may not be so erratic after all.

Alyssa

THE TELEVISION WARNS ME IT'S GOING TO GO INTO STANDBY again due to inactivity.

Judgemental asshole.

I bat around for the remote, finally finding it between two pizza boxes, and slam a button so that my vigil can resume.

Day nineteen of the Mars One mission.

Day sixteen of my self-imposed internment in Jacob's apartment. And I haven't turned the TV off once. The *Argo* is ever present, as my body becomes part of the couch. I eat there, brush my teeth there, sleep there. The only thing I don't do is piss there, and even then I turn up the volume so I can hear what's going on. The only things that interrupt the livestream are the adverts and occasional studio bits, in which polished presenters explain space travel for dummies.

The crew are on Baikonur time, so I find myself slipping into that pattern, too. When the daily routine winds down and the majority of the crew head to their sleeping pods, I usually try to get a couple of hours' shut-eye, but then I wake up throughout the night so I can see what *she* is up to, in those dark hours while the rest of her crew sleep. The only conscious human being for millions of kilometres.

Most of the time, she's fulfilling her duties studiously. Checking her experiments, running through her maintenance tasks. It's clear Morin has resigned herself to this set-up and given her the tasks that can be completed solo. I watch her clean the toilet, stir the oxygen tanks. And sometimes, when she's worked through her list, she'll just float in the middle of the communal area, above the 'dining table' and Anders' moon rock, her hair spreading out around her head like Medusa.

The presenters and the press have picked up on it, too. Some have named her the 'Argo Angel'.

It doesn't seem angelic to me.

It's deeply worrying.

A human being, purposely isolating herself from the entire human race and embracing a feeling of . . . nothingness. That's what it looks like to me.

Perhaps we aren't so different after all.

I didn't know what to expect when I first arrived here. I directed my car to take me to the address that Jacob had suggested. It was a restaurant in a little town outside Indianapolis called Noblesville, which made me smile. It seemed apt for Jacob, even though I hardly know him at all.

The restaurant was open when I arrived, but quiet, with no diners to be seen. The decor had seen better days, but there was an undeniable warmth when I opened the door and the little bell pinged above it. A plump, middle-aged Native American woman appeared from the kitchen. She wore her dark hair in a long braid, and her deep-brown eyes smiled when she saw me, her hands wet and soapy.

'Hold on just a second!' she cried, dipping back into the kitchen before re-emerging suddenly with a towel in hand. 'How can I help you? You want some lunch?' She moved towards the menus on the counter.

'No,' I rushed. I glanced over my shoulder to check that the dark-tinted car was still waiting for me. 'My – er, colleague – told me to come here and that you would help me. Jacob Kindred?'

Her face broke into an even bigger grin. 'Ah yes, he said you might be coming. Lyss, right?'

'Alyssa,' I automatically corrected, bracing myself for her to start talking about Mars One. But she didn't.

'I'm Martha. So pleased to meet you.' She took my hand and shook it hard and fast. 'How are you?' she asked, her brow furrowed in concern as she looked at my leg. 'Do you need to sit down?'

'No, thank you. I'm just here to get the keys for his—'

'For his mawmaw's apartment, yes, of course. Hold on just a second!' She scurried over to the register and popped the cash drawer open. Right at the back, she dug out some keys, and scribbled down the address on a scrap of paper.

'Here you go,' she said. 'Are you sure you're not hungry? I can pack something up for you real quick? I have some chicken that—'

'I'm fine thank you.' I waved the slip of paper as I headed out the door. 'I think I just need to sleep right now. Maybe some other time.'

'I'll hold you to that!' She waved enthusiastically as I escaped out onto the street.

The apartment itself was colourful, busy and had a distinctly feminine touch to it. Books and pictures were neatly placed along every surface, and the worn woven rugs that covered nearly all the hardwood floors muted the sound of my crutches and bulbous cast as I made my way into the living room. In the corner was the kitchen, small but neat. A round antique-wood table sat by one of the windows, all but one of the three chairs around it stacked with what looked like photo albums. In the centre of the room was an over-large deep-green velvet couch that looked like it had been there for decades. It faced a small television, above which were several shelves crammed with yet more photos. One of a younger Jacob caught my eye, grinning from ear to ear in a cap and gown, with an older woman sat beside him – probably Mawmaw – and a frail-looking woman standing on the other side, clutching his arm and beaming.

I found the bedroom at the back of the apartment, an old-fashioned fire escape outside one of its windows, which I opened to get a breeze through. The bathroom had a retrofitted walk-in shower with a seat. Men's shower products stood out against the bright pink shower mat and floral tiles.

It was the second bedroom where Jacob had made his mark. The walls were alternate dark blue and white, and someone had lovingly stencilled the Colt's horseshoe on one of the white walls. The room was bare other than a shelf with sporting trophies, and an old exercise bike squatting in the corner. The closet was ajar, full of weights, ropes and other exercise paraphernalia. As I moved closer to the door, I noticed the marks scratched into it.

JACOB - AGED 9
JACOB - AGED 10 1/2
JACOB - AGED 13

All the way up to eighteen, Jacob's height was recorded in uneven increments, showing short, sharp growth spurts between each one. Until eventually, he was slightly taller than me.

Over the next few weeks, I gradually pieced together Jacob's life story. The picture on his bedside table was the most revealing: a teenage Jacob next to the frail woman I'd seen in all the albums and other photos – his mom. She was propped up in bed, looking horribly thin, a tube coming out of her nose and trailing off camera. And that telltale scarf wrapped round her head. Both were smiling, but there was an undeniable sadness to it. I could tell it was a last photo.

I felt a newfound admiration for Jacob. He'd opened up his home, knowing his whole life story would be laid bare. He was happy to be living in among his mother and grandmother's memories. There was no embarrassment in the way he seamlessly laid his own life on top of theirs, only shifting their belongings where necessary. Letting their presence linger on this planet just a little longer. In fact, the only thing he'd truly erased was his very own bedroom.

Over those initial weeks, I left the apartment only once, for an appointment for my leg. Gwynne, one of the only human beings on this planet to know where I am, arranged it. After I managed to use the stairlift that Jake must have had installed for himself, an anonymous car whisked me to a private clinic, where they told me to come back in three weeks to have the cast removed.

All I have to do is wait.

Watch and wait, and ignore the crushing sense of helplessness within me. Shut out the nightmares that have me clawing at my chest and gasping for air as I rush back to consciousness. Push away that haunting feeling of the vacuum of space opening up and swallowing the crew whole, as I scream at them, but they can't hear me, they're too far gone—

A loud bang jolts me from my sleep. For a moment, I can't remember where I am. Then more banging, on the door.

'Coming!' I croak. When was the last time I spoke to anyone?

I slide out from underneath my blanket and curse as I remember I'm naked. My hands find a dark, striped dressing gown on the back of the bathroom door. It smells musty, but seems clean.

I limp to the front door and fumble it open, to find Martha grinning at me. She looks me up and down and laughs. 'Is that Jake's?'

I hug my arms around me, self-conscious.

'Err, yeah. Sorry. I was sleeping,' I mumble.

'No problem. I see you're moving around without the crutches. That's great! Can I come in?' She holds up some paper bags.

'Sure . . .' I say, baffled, and hop out of the way. She heads straight to the kitchen like she's been here thousands of times before.

'My gosh, it's dark in here,' she calls out, as I shut the door and follow. She places the bags on the kitchen counter and hurries to open the drapes, which makes me wince.

The light reveals the state I've been living in. There are take-out containers on all the surfaces. Unwashed cutlery and plates. And an open photo album on the coffee table. My cheeks flush as I hobble over to close it. Martha's quick, bright eyes definitely clock it, but she doesn't say anything. She sweeps round the room, picking up the detritus.

'I hope you don't mind me dropping by, but it's been so long and you said you'd come have dinner!' She turns on the tap and squirts some detergent, her bubbly voice rising over the noise. 'Plus, Jake's asked me to bring you up a few things.'

'Jacob's been in touch?' I ask, surprised. I realize there's nothing I can do about the mess, she's seen it now, so I collapse on the couch and watch her whirl about the kitchen.

'Oh, he's always calling. But this time he gave me a special message to give to you. He's asking if you've been into the restaurant yet.'

'I'm sorry.' I search for an excuse. 'I've not been feeling great.'

'Oh, it don't matter,' she chirps. She's made quick work of most of the plates, and moves on to her bulging bags, from which appears a mountain of groceries and several plastic containers.

'We know you've been through a lot.' She gives the television, where the *Argo* crew are sleeping soundly, a stern look, before turning to the fridge and busying herself making room for her new supplies.

So she does know who I am, then.

'Let me pay for that.' I reach for my wallet on the coffee table.

'Not a problem. It's all taken care of. I insist. As does Jacob,' she says without looking back at me. 'There,' she declares. 'Better already. Now I gotta run, but here's what Jacob sent for you.' She scoops up the bags and pulls out an envelope, which she hands to me. 'I printed it off and didn't look at it,' she says with a sparkle in her eye. 'I don't want to pry.'

I feel his dressing gown close to my skin, my bare chest, suddenly aware of what this could look like. 'We're not—'

'Well, I'll leave you to it – and see you soon,' she says pointedly. 'I'll see myself out.' And with that, the whirlwind of Martha is gone. I'm alone, in a much cleaner room, with a well-stocked fridge and a message from the other side of the world.

Dear Lyss,

A belated welcome to Indiana. Hope you settled in all right. I figured you'd need some time to yourself at first, but I've sent Martha round because there's no more excuses for moping around in my apartment all day. You have to keep moving now, to get that leg back up to strength.

To help with this, Martha's brought you some of her cooking. It's the best. If you want more where that came from (which I know you will), you'll have to go down to her restaurant and she'll feed you up. Think of it as an incentive to go outside.

And if you're worried about being mobbed – don't be. You're out of the news cycle and things are cooling down. I'm going to be in touch a bit more from now on.

So, eat! And then go to Martha's for more.

Jake.

Not for the first time, I wonder why Jake is doing all this, why he's gone to so much effort. But then my stomach rumbles. I hobble over to the fridge and pull out a couple of Martha's containers. Without looking at what they are, I ram them in the microwave and hover impatiently until the ping.

I take them out and the smell makes my head spin. It's some sort of stew, with meat and vegetables. The other box contains something stodgy that I should probably have warmed in the oven – the microwave has obliterated it. Oh well. I throw it all in a bowl and park myself at the breakfast bar.

Holy shit. It's good. So good, I burn my tongue shovelling as much of the stuff in my mouth as I can. The meat is tender, with sweet peppers cutting through the salty yet caramelized stew. And the obliterated stodge, whatever the hell it is, is doughy and warming, and pillows up nicely in my stomach, like a hug. It reminds me of my mom's cooking.

*

I last a couple more days before all Martha's containers run out and I feel the call of her restaurant. But I hold out because the more I think about it, the more annoyed I become at Jacob. Who is this guy to come into my life and tell me what to do? Just because he's provided me with a sanctuary, does that mean I have to do what he says? I feel like his pet.

The anger and resentment bubbles up inside me until I can contain it no longer. So I decide I will head down to the restaurant, but only to settle my bill and tell Martha that I'll be leaving soon. As soon as this cast is off, I'm going to move on. I have the payoff money. I'll find my own place, in a city where I can slink into anonymity and the night sky is bleached out by lights.

When I get down to the restaurant, it's packed. I hadn't even realized it was lunchtime, let alone a Saturday. The sights and sounds of it instantly take the wind out of my sails. I've not been around this many people in a long time. I hover in the doorway, considering turning back, when a friendly voice calls out over the din.

'Alyssa!' Martha beams at me, weaving through the tables.

Before I know it, she's taken me by the hand and is dragging me towards the back of the restaurant, where a small table tucked in the corner bears a reserved sign.

'This is the staff table,' she says, giving it a quick wipe down. 'What you after?'

'Er . . .' I look out across the dozen or so rammed tables. Couples, families, friends, all of them chatting, laughing, eating. They're too wrapped up in the delicious food and company to even register my existence.

'Don't mind any of them,' Martha says, reading my mind. 'Ain't no one expecting to find you here.'

I pull my eyes away from the crowds and look up at Martha, who is smiling so kindly I almost forget that burning pit of anger in my stomach. I can't bring myself to say what I'd planned.

'Don't worry, I'll get you something.' And she's off, weaving expertly back towards the kitchen. I look down at the menu in front of me, the words swimming and making no sense to me.

What if someone does recognize me? What if they talk to me? Or if the press gets hold of where I am? I'm not ready to face other people yet.

A plate slides in front of me. More glorious stew, and the doughy rounds that I obliterated in the microwave, but these look fresh and golden.

'Thank you,' I say quietly, looking up at Martha, who places an iced tea by my plate.

'No problem. You let me know if you need anything, OK?' But my eyes are distracted by the television behind her. Mars One isn't on. It's the news. Something about growing tensions with Russia as the G7 gather for an emergency summit.

I feel a sudden pang of panic. Like the crew might disappear if I'm not watching.

'Martha!' I blurt. 'Could we . . .' I look around and lower my voice. 'Is there any chance you could change the channel, please?'

Martha watches me, wary.

'Sure . . .' she says, slowly. 'Let me just go find the remote.' She starts to move back off towards the kitchen, before stopping abruptly. 'Oh,' she exclaims, turning back to me. 'I forgot, he told me to give you this when you finally came.' And she drops another folded letter onto the table.

Something jolts through me and I instantly forget about the TV screen. My hand darts to snatch at the paper and I unfold it quickly.

> Told you you wouldn't be able to resist. Welcome back to the
> real world, Lyss. Hope you've at least had a shower. I'll call you.

My cheeks flush. Martha smiles and bustles away.

Not taking my eyes from the note, I stab at the food in front of me and take a bite. My God, it tastes even better fresh.

Before I know it, I'm devouring the whole thing, taking great gulps of iced tea in between mouthfuls. Reading Jake's words over and over.

Lyss. There he is with that damn nickname again, like he's known me forever. No one has ever called me Lyss. My mom calls me Lyssa, sometimes. Or, she used to.

'The real world', as Jake calls it, hums around me. As I lose myself in the food, the cacophony turns from repressive to soothing. When my plate is clear, I sit back and watch the other diners. Two female friends gossiping close together; a toddler dropping potato chips on the floor; an old couple eating happily together, the woman stealing a fry from her husband's plate. Little pockets of humanity going about their lives.

I'll call you. Something about that makes me smile.

For so long, I've wanted to be alone. To shut everything and everyone out. Scared of what others might say to me.

But with Jake, the thought of hearing his voice – even if he calls me by that damn nickname – is reassuring. It's something I might even look forward to . . .

Another full plate is placed down in front of me, and I look up.

'You look like you need it,' Martha says.

'Thanks.' I pick up my fork with great enthusiasm. 'What is this stuff?' I ask, pointing to the stodgy discs.

Martha beams. 'That's Jake's favourite, too.' She lights up whenever she talks about Jacob, almost like a mom would. But then she sees my eyes snag on the TV remote, and places it down in front of me.

'Here you go, hun,' she says, softly. 'You sure you wanna change the channel?'

I look up at the TV screen and then look back to Martha, her eyes full of worry, her apron stained by the food she makes so lovingly. The same food that's beginning to fill the great void within me, along with Jake and his maddening note.

Maybe I can stay here a little longer.

Just until my leg is sorted. Until I'm healed.

'Actually, no,' I reply, pushing the remote back towards her. 'I'm good. Thank you.'

Jia

LUNCHTIME IN THE NORTHERN PACIFIC SUBTROPICAL gyre – or, as I've learned, the Great Pacific Garbage Patch. For the last few days, the scientists onboard have been abuzz with excitement: they're finally able to conduct their experiments. But for me, this is just another long day of the ship moving slowly through the water, trawling for samples, while I wonder what the hell is happening to Kai and when we'll ever make it to shore.

Turning on my burner phone, I do my daily check to see if there's any signal on this damn thing to call Agnes and Erica, find out what they've done with Mom. But the phone remains blank. As usual.

I slam it down on the worktop as Mike curses behind me. I'm not the only one in a bad mood today. He hates making pizza, but it's a crew favourite so every now and then he has to condescend to prepare 'such a basic meal'.

Thirty-five days into our voyage, and neither of us is having fun.

I fled Hong Kong to rescue my brother, and instead, I'm stuck here.

'What do they even do all day?' I lament as I pick up a dirty ladle. The galley is a total mess and steaming hot.

Mike sighs, exasperated. 'I told you. They're putting a shit-tonne of nets in the water, trawling to see the concentration of microplastics in—'

'I know!' I cut him off. Throwing the ladle into the sink. 'But it's taking so fucking long!'

'Christ,' he mutters. 'What the fuck is wrong with you today, eh?'

'Sorry,' I mumble, shoving my hands into the dirty dishwater and scrubbing furiously at a pan, taking all my frustrations out on the allegedly non-stick surface.

'You're almost as annoying as those bastards out there,' Mike snaps.

'We can hear you!' calls out one of the researchers from the mess.

'That's the point!' yells Mike, right back at her. He doesn't really mean it, and everyone knows it. At first, I took it personally when he yelled at me; now I just ignore it.

He swears, pulls the first batch of pizzas out of the oven and slides them in front of me. I dry my hands off and slice them up.

'That's for the bridge. They want lunch up there.'

I scowl. I hate going up there. The captain either ignores that I exist or makes it clear that he wishes I didn't. But I know my place, so I grab a tray and arrange the pizzas, swiping the captain's favourite sriracha sauce from one of the shelves as I pass.

'Don't forget the—'

'I got it!' I cut him off and slip through into the crew mess.

On the far side, the researchers have set up station. Laptops and paperwork are strewn over one of the large dining tables, along with glass bottles of samples and a microscope. I stare at the little bottles as I move past. They contain ocean water, but floating at the waterline is a thick layer of multicoloured plastics: pinks, greens, blues, black, also some bleached white by the sun. When the light hits them through the portholes, they glint and sparkle, the colours swirling behind the glass, like tiny snow globes. If you didn't know they were suffocating the ocean, you'd almost think they were beautiful.

With sturdy legs, I navigate the rolling deck and relish the moment of fresh air. Even just a couple of weeks ago, the motion of the ship would have sent me vomiting over the side. Now I'm just bored of the rocking. I look to the horizon, yearning to see land. If I'd have known it would feel so excruciatingly slow . . .

Erica warned me, said this wasn't a good idea. I wonder what she's doing right now. Is she still stuck at Agnes's? Are her beautiful eyes staring out over the bay? Someone yells further down the deck, snapping me back to reality. Even though no one is here, I blush. I'm being ridiculous. I barely know Erica, and she sure as hell won't be thinking about me any more. I have to focus. Get through this journey, find Frybread. Find my brother. Then we can all go home.

As soon as I enter the bridge, I can tell something's up. The captain is standing by the window, a pair of binoculars glued to his eyes. Penny stands next to him, her arms crossed. She turns when I enter with the food and gives me a nod of thanks.

'How many can we see on AIS?' he barks at Penny, as I set the tray down and lay out the pizza.

'Just one,' Penny replies.

'Doesn't mean there's not more of them. I'd have my AIS off too if I were them.'

'Looks like drift nets.'

'What's your bet on length?'

'Gonna be over two and a half k, right?'

'Definitely,' he growls. 'Think we have enough time?'

'They'll have seen us already.' There's a warning in Penny's voice.

'But they're quite a distance. I think the *Scorpio* will manage a slash and grab.'

Lunch set up, I turn to see the captain grabbing his radio. 'Captain Sigurðsson to deck crew. Scramble the *Scorpio*. Kyle, report to the bridge. Potential drift net sighted. Prepare to intercept.'

'Are you sure you want to engage?' Penny asks, looking concerned.

The captain ignores her. 'Tell the scientists to pull up their experiments. We need manoeuvrability and speed.'

Penny looks like she's about to say something, but nods and backs away. She picks up her own radio as he heads out, but grabs me before using it.

'Jia, you need to go below and stay there.'

'What's going on?' I ask.

'We think we might have spotted some illegal drift nets.' My confusion clearly shows on my face. 'Illegal fishing nets. Very bad ones. Their owners aren't around right now, and we can only see one potential ship on the Automatic Identification System, but there may well be more in the area. These ships don't tend to work alone.'

'You're going to sabotage the nets?'

Penny grimaces. 'We're going to seize them, take them in as evidence. But things might get a bit heated. You should stay in your cabin until I send word, OK? I told Agnes I'd look after you.'

I must look unsure, because she carries on. 'It'll be fine. Captain's just craving some action.' I think she's reassuring herself as much as me, but then Kyle, the bosun, calls for her and it's clear our conversation is over.

As I head back down into the heart of the ship, the bells ring out a message to the crew that I don't understand, but they get immediately. Chairs scrape and footsteps pound. A call to action, then.

'For fuck's sake!' Mike cries from the galley. I bump into a load of scientists filing out of the mess to retrieve their nets, looking extremely miffed.

I don't hang around to take Mike's wrath, but instead head down to our cabin. Orion is having one of his crazy half hours, leaping all around the room and chasing something that only he can see. Every now and then he freezes and looks at me, then scrambles off to the other side of the room, before starting the cycle all over again.

At least someone is having fun.

I climb up to Mike's bunk to get away from him.

An engine thrums. It's not the constant din of the *Dolly*'s, so it must be the *Scorpio*. I duck down and peer through the salt-stained glass to see it swinging around this side of the ship.

In the very corner of what the window allows me to see is a small black boat racing to catch up with us. It's a RIB, but it's not the *Scorpio*. It's travelling fast, and soon it's in line with Mike's window.

Onboard are several men, their heads and mouths covered, gesturing wildly above me, at the deck or the bridge. Then there's a loud THUNK as something hits the metal of the *Dolly*.

I gasp. Are they throwing stuff at us?

There's another THUNK, somewhere further along the ship, also above me. And another.

Three of the men on the skiff are hurling things now. Shouts erupt from within the *Dolly*, out in the corridor and above. Another alarm sounds. The panic is infectious and Orion gives a loud meow. I look for him below me, but a loud smash of glass brings me back to the window. The men on the RIB cheer in triumph.

I'm thrown to the side, and by the sound of it, Orion is too, as the *Dolly* suddenly slows. The boat begins to disappear ahead – they're now going too fast – but first something glowing flies from it up above my window.

There's another almighty SMASH and the ship's alarm starts wailing, one long, continuous ring. *Shit*. Even I know what that means.

I jump down from my bed and scramble to get my boots back on. Orion is practically bouncing off the walls. The alarm must be too loud for him.

'Calm down!' I plead. Partly to him, but also to myself. Fire. A real fire. We've done drills, so I know to go to the muster station on the helideck.

I leap towards the cabin door and slide it open, check there's no smoke. The alarm is even louder out in the corridor.

But then an orange blur dashes past my feet through the gap.

'NO!' I scream, as Orion's tail bobs down the hall and he leaps up the stairs in sheer panic. 'Orion!' Heart-stopping images fly through my brain. Him leaping off the edge of the ship and into the water. Him getting squashed by a stray fender—

I blunder up the stairs, but when I get to the top, there's no sign of him anywhere.

'Orion!' I yell above the din of the alarm.

A helmeted crew member runs past, fitting a gas mask. 'Get to your station!' he yells, like I'm insane.

'My cat!' I cry back at him. He dashes through another door and leaves me to my madness.

Turning around, I realize the door leading out to the boat deck is wide open, daylight blaring through it. My stomach sinks. I push myself through the hole in the metal and out onto the deck, where all hell has broken loose.

A gaping space is left where the *Scorpio* RIB usually sits. There's water all over the deck. Someone is aiming a huge firehose at a spot past me, near the bow, where the last remnants of smoke and oil can be seen.

Suddenly, the wailing fire alarm stops, replaced by the buzzing of what sounds like dozens of high-speed engines all around us.

I scour the deck for signs of Orion. Could he be cowering under the shelter of the other skiff, covered in tarpaulin? I dash across the deck and grab the skiff as soon as I reach it. Daring to look around its bulk, I see another two strange RIBs running along the port side of *Dolly*. Further down the ship, *Dolly*'s crew are using the water cannon to fire at the two boats. The men launch another projectile, which smashes down a few feet from me. I dart back around the skiff for protection, crouching down with my head in my hands.

Then I think of something hard and heavy hitting Orion and my panic sets in all over again. I pull up an edge of the black covering over the skiff and duck down to see under its shadow.

'Orion?'

Something hard yanks my arm and pulls off the cover. I fall back. Kyle, wearing what looks like full combat gear and a black helmet, comes round the side of the RIB, crouching low. He blinks at me, surprised, as other deck crew prepare the crane arm behind him to launch the RIB.

'What the fuck are you doing?' he yells, over the din.

'My cat!' I yell.

Another THUNK echoes around us as yet another projectile hits the deck. There must be enemy boats on the starboard side, too.

'Take cover!' he screams, gesturing behind him across the deck towards the bridge. 'And get a helmet on!'

He pushes me out of the way as he goes back to his work, his duty to me fulfilled.

THUNK. A lead weight misses one of the deck crew by centimetres. He's right: I need to get out of here. Surely Orion won't have stayed out here. Unless the force of the fire hose swept him—

I push the thought from my head and scramble back onto my feet. Ducking low with my arms over my head, I run with all my strength to the door that I know lies beyond the remaining RIB.

'Helmet!' A female deck hand screams at me as I pass her. She swings a wooden shield in front of the person manning the port water cannon, a second before another projectile lands square on it. She absorbs this hit and braces herself for more.

I yank open the heavy metal door and clamber inside, pulling it shut behind me, my breathing fast and shallow.

A grunting sounds behind me and I turn to see a bloody hand grasping a plank of wood, coming up one of the tight stairwells. The figure gets to the top and drops the wood down, grasping at his other arm, which is also dripping with blood.

'Mike!' I cry, as he considers his lacerated arm.

'I thought Penny told you to stay below?'

'Orion got out,' I explain.

He rolls his eyes. 'That bloody cat.' He tries to pick up the wood again, but grimaces and lets it fall.

'What happened?'

'Galley window,' he says. 'I've patched it up but I heard the bridge has a window smashed too. Thought they'd need this.' Once again he bends down to pick up the wood.

'Let me help,' I cry, rushing forward.

Mike looks a bit surprised, but I don't have time to be offended. I haul up the other end of the plank and together we carry it up the next set of stairs.

Our boots crunch over shattered glass as we move into the bridge. Mike was right about the window up here, then. Captain Sigurðsson and Penny are talking while the second mate – I think his name is Chen – sits with his back to one of the walls, the medic, Giovanni, holding a cloth to his head as blood drips down his face.

Penny doesn't look happy to see us, until she sees the wood. She heaves it from us with ease and places it up against the broken window frame.

'Mike, go see Giovanni. Jia, get me those hammer and nails.'

I do as she says, gingerly moving around the captain, whose hands are on the ship's controls as he talks quickly into his radio.

'Here.' I brace the plank as she hammers nails into the bridge's window frame.

'That'll do.' Penny says, then she grabs me by the shoulders and forces me to crouch down. She pulls a helmet from a shelf and thrusts it on my head.

'Stay down.' Then she's back by the captain's side again.

I secure the helmet around my chin. To my right, Mike sits on the floor as Giovanni moves over to him and rifles through his medical kit.

'You OK?' Giovanni asks. I wait for Mike to answer, but the medic is looking at me as he moves back to his bag to get more gauze.

'Oh. Yeah.' My voice is shaky. 'Who are they?'

'Fucking Chinese bastards,' Mike says through his teeth, as Giovanni wraps a bandage round his arm. I try not to react to the racism.

'They came out of nowhere. Must be pissed that we started hauling in their drift net. Even threw some Molotovs at us,' Giovanni whispers.

I gasp.

'It's OK,' Mike interjects, 'only hit the boat deck. And the hoses stopped them from boarding us. Thanks, doc.' Mike inspects his newly bandaged arm.

'Is this . . . normal?' I squeak.

'Not really.' Mike winces. 'Illegal boats do get pissed at us getting in the way of their activities, but this level?' He shakes his head.

'Why don't we run?'

'Because the *Scorpio*'s in trouble.' Sigurðsson's voice booms over everything. My eyes widen.

'Captain, Captain, Kyle.' The radio squawks.

'Go ahead,' replies the captain instantly.

'Our cannon has hit one of the hostiles into the water on the starboard side. Hostile skiff has retreated. Request we pick him up?'

The captain says something low under his breath, before then clicking back on the radio.

'Copy that. Retrieve the hostile.'

'We'll require language assistance.'

Captain Sigurðsson and Penny look to the second mate, but he's clearly in no state to stand. Then the captain turns to me.

Shit.

'You.' His voice is like steel. 'You speak Mandarin?'

I hesitate – should I lie? – but then nod.

'Captain—' Penny begins, but he holds his hand up to her.

'We'll rescue the bastard but he may be danger to the crew. She can try and calm him down. Then we use him to negotiate.' He puts the radio to his mouth again. 'Sending assistance. Stand by.'

The captain pulls me to my feet. He grabs a life jacket and thrusts it into my arms.

'Time to earn your keep. Giovanni, take her down to Kyle.'

Giovanni hauls his kit bag over his shoulder, before gently taking my arm.

I suddenly remember why the hell I was up here in the first place. 'Orion! I don't know—'

'Now!' shouts Sigurðsson, and Giovanni steers me out.

We head down the stairs and out onto the boat deck, which is now clear of RIBs. Giovanni is already heading to the railings on the port side.

'Come on!' he calls.

I follow him and look down, seeing the second RIB, the *Seafang*, bobbing in the waves. The water cannon on the port side is fending off the hostile boats, which have now retreated further.

'Put your life jacket on!' Giovanni yells over the roar of the cannon and *Seafang*'s engine.

I obey without thinking, but then I start to realize what I'm doing. 'I can't go down there!' I shout.

Giovanni just grimaces. 'You have to! There's no one else!'

Knowing he's right doesn't make it any less terrifying.

'What's going on?' Kyle yells from below, yanking the rope ladder he and his crew descended.

'Jia's coming with you! Language assistance!'

'What about Chen?!'

'Injured!' Giovanni yells back, holding out a hand to me like an old-fashioned gentleman.

My legs feel like jelly, but I step up onto the railings. The wind whips around me. I tell myself not to look down.

And to think, half an hour ago I was bored.

'The ships are heading this way!' someone screams from below.

Giovanni holds me as I turn to face him and put my feet on the first rung of the ladder.

'Go!'

With a screech, I take my foot off the first rung and plunge it down into nothingness. It flails in the air, my knuckles white with terror as I try to find the next rung down.

There!

I put my weight on it and it swings. Far below me, the waves pound against the boat. My other foot rushes to join its partner, my whole body swaying.

'Again!' someone shouts. I thrust my foot out into oblivion once more. With a jolt, I make it down to the next rung.

'Again!'

We do this I don't know how many times, until I feel hands on the small of my back. I hurl myself off the ladder and slam into the people behind me, on the boat at last.

'Finally!' Kyle scowls down at me. 'Go, go, go!'

I fall to the floor as the bow rises to what seems an impossible angle. The wind whips around us as we speed away from the side of the *Dolly* and then take a sharp turn to wind back round the stern.

Although the ocean looked calm from the *Dolly*, every wave feels like a speedbump as *Seafang* slams across them. Spray flies everywhere and I can hardly see anything. We emerge on the starboard side of the *Dolly* and I can just about make out the arc of another jet of water snaking in pursuit of another RIB, far up by the bridge.

'Can anyone see him?' Kyle screams, looking out, away from the *Dolly*.

'There!' one of the four other crew yells. *Seafang* turns tightly to the right. As we swing round, the sea rises up to meet me and I cry out in horror at the Pacific froth yawning up. I swear I'm about to tumble in when we level off again and resume bouncing over the swell.

After a few seconds, the engine powers down and we slow. Now I see him. He's not wearing a life vest, and is yelling and spluttering in Mandarin.

'*Help!*' No need for me to translate that.

Seafang heads past him then swings round again. He's just a few metres away now – close enough for me to see the panic in his eyes.

Kyle throws out a flotation device tied to the boat. It lands perfectly beside the man, who launches himself at it, water flooding his mouth. Once his chest is on top of it, he gasps, blinking.

'Reel him in!' The man turns as the rope comes taut, a mini wake fanning out behind him towards the *Dolly*, which is still firing water at his comrades.

When the float hits the side of the *Seafang*, Kyle and one of the others lean over into the water and grab the man under his arms. They haul, with others in the boat bracing them to ensure they aren't also pulled over. Water floods in with the man, deathly cold, and I cry out as it splashes all over me. The man rolls to the floor, shivering and retching. He flops around, gasping for breath, then pushes himself into a corner, yelling wildly, looking terrified. Even I can't make out what he's saying.

'Jia!' Kyle gestures at me.

'*You're safe. We won't hurt you.*' The Mandarin feels strange. I haven't spoken it in so long, only with Mom . . .

The man looks at me for the first time and stops, stunned.

'*You're safe*,' I say again, no idea if it's really true.

'Tell him we're taking him back to the ship to see our doctor,' Kyle yells. The bow of the boat lurches up in the air once more.

I repeat what Kyle said. The man looks at me, wide-eyed, then at Kyle. He turns to Kyle and says in English: 'No. No.'

'Yes,' Kyle says to him, before pointing out to the water again.

We turn again, but away from the *Dolly*.

'You said we were going back to the ship!' I scream.

'We need to help the *Scorpio* first!' shouts Kyle. I follow where he's pointing. The *Scorpio* looks stationary, most of its crew leaning over the back of the boat, working on the engine. One figure is at the bow, leaning into the water.

We zip across the ocean again at full speed. The Chinese man doesn't say another word, just shivers, his eyes darting to each of us until someone pulls out a silver foil blanket and throws it at him. He looks down at it warily, but then his survival instincts kick in. He pulls it around himself, watching us all the while.

Once again, the engine pulls up and we coast close to the

Scorpio, which appears to be entangled in the drift net they had been trying to reel in.

'The engine's fucked!' one of the *Scorpio* team cries. 'We need a tow.'

'We've got you,' Kyle replies, throwing him a rope. 'Pull us in. Balkwill, watch those lines, make sure we can get out of here.' The driver nods and pulls the engine out of the water, our propeller now above the waves.

The *Scorpio* and *Seafang* crews work together to draw the boats side by side. Kyle jumps over from the *Seafang* to inspect what's going on.

'Who's that?' one of the *Scorpio* crew asks, pointing at the Chinese man.

Our driver grins. 'Our prize catch.'

'Jia,' Kyle shouts over, without looking at me. 'Tell him no funny business and he'll be safe.'

I look back at the man. He looks young, but thin, unwell. He has bags under his eyes and his cheeks seem hollow.

'We're . . .' I hesitate. '*We're fixing our boat, then we'll head back to the ship. Stay calm and we won't hurt you.*'

He blinks at me.

'*What is your name?*' I try. His eyes dart behind me and I turn to see what he's looking at. Three dots on the horizon, growing larger every second.

I turn back to him.

'*Your ship?*' I ask. He nods. '*We'll get you back to them. Just do as we say.*'

We're interrupted by cheers and the roar of an engine – the *Scorpio*'s back up and running. Kyle looks pleased as he wipes his oily hands on his life vest – but when he sees the Chinese ships looming, his smile drops.

'Let's get going,' he says. 'We need to get free of these lines.'

'No!' cries out a high voice from the front of the *Scorpio*, and the figure that was leaning over the front of the bow comes back up. It's Marnie, the science liaison officer.

'Look!' Marnie gestures out towards the water. 'It's a right whale dolphin!' she cries.

'Shit,' Kyle says as he turns to look at the Chinese ships and then back to where Marnie is pointing.

'We can't leave it!' Marnie exclaims, close to tears. Kyle looks at the horizon and the looming ships.

He turns back to the skiff teams. 'You have two minutes.'

The two crews launch into immediate action.

'Balkwill, bring us round.' Balkwill nods as the rest of the crew untie the bonds holding the two boats together. As soon as we're free and given a soft nudge, Balkwill lowers the skiff's engine back in the water and we skirt around the edge of the net to get closer to the dark bulk of the dolphin.

The *Scorpio* does the same, until the dolphin lies between the two boats. I lean over to look. The ocean foam is tinted red as the net's lines slice deep into the dolphin's flesh. It's entangled in multiple places, but it's worst at the tail. It can't be alive. It's so still. But then, as though in answer to my panic, there's a sudden breath out of its blowhole, and I see life in its eyes. It's alive, but barely.

Marnie is at the dolphin's side first. She expertly thrusts her hands into the water and saws. The dolphin jolts, and suddenly it can move its head more. Marnie pulls away one of the lines that was slicing into its neck, and more crimson seeps out of the wound.

'Jia, come here!' Kyle shouts from the other end of the boat. He and his team are focusing on the tail. I tear my eyes away from Marnie's tender work and stumble down to the end.

Kyle thrusts a Swiss Army knife into my hand.

I stare down at the blade, and then at the mass of netting bunched around the dolphin's tail. It's impossible, surely. And those ships are only getting bigger. What happens if they catch us? It's too late.

'Cut, Jia!' Marnie shouts from the dolphin's head.

Sensing we're trying to help it, the dolphin finds a last reserve of energy and starts to wiggle, but that just makes our job harder. The crews try to hold it in place.

No idea if I'm doing the right thing, I thrust my hand into the icy water and seize on some strands of net and start cutting. The ocean churns more and more with our slashing and the dolphin's thrusts. At first, I feel like I'm getting nowhere, but then netting strands start to fly away from my blade and I feel a dart of triumph.

'One minute, guys. Come on!' Kyle yells.

I hardly hear him. I'm drenched, frozen, my arms aching and my fingers numb, but I keep hacking as though it's my life, not the dolphin's, that depends on it. It's slackening; the dolphin has more and more room to move. My heart is racing, my breath jerking out of my throat with every fibre cut. Elsewhere, eight sets of hands are doing the same.

There's still a large ball of netting clumped together to the right of me. It looks as though it's now free of the main drift net, so I start hacking at it. There's only a few lines tying it to the dolphin's tail and if I can just—

'We've got to go!'

Balkwill lurches towards the engine, thrusting it back into the water again.

'Jia! Stop!' Kyle calls.

'No!' I shout. Just a few more lines. We can do this. I can do this.

'We're so close!' screams Marnie. We both keep sawing at the net. One more strand . . .

'Stop,' he yells back at her. 'They'll kill us!'

But then Marnie yelps – the dolphin's head is free.

'Come on!' she cries, urging me on.

With a final *snip*, the dolphin thrashes its tail up and back down, splashing us all with frigid water. I scream. Another jerk and the dolphin bolts away, quick as a flash. My heart soars and my scream turns into a laugh, and then a cry of triumph.

'Yes!' Marnie cries. But as the dolphin surges to freedom, her joy is strangled in her throat. 'Wait! There's still netting!'

I can see it too: another small ball wrapped around its tail, being dragged along by just a few lines wrapped around the end. But it's too late. It disappears along with the dolphin.

'Go, now,' Kyle screams at the drivers.

'Kyle!' Marnie wails across the boats.

'It's gone, Marnie! We have to move!' Kyle pushes the net out of the way of the skiff's rudder, and the engines roar into life.

Suddenly exhausted, I clamber back to my seat as Balkwill navigates us away from the net. I look at the knife in my shaking hand, which is red raw from the cold, and place it down next to me. Flexing my aching fingers, I wonder if anyone has found Orion. What if one of the missiles hit him? What if he was washed overboard in the panic? What if he—

'Woah!'

I'm jerked sharply backwards by my jacket. Kyle, Balkwill and the rest of the crew leap up, their eyes wide. And then, there is cold steel at my neck.

The Chinese man's breath is ragged, ruffling my hair as he glares from behind me, over the top of my head, at the rest of the crew. Balkwill cuts the engine, and after all the noise, the silence feels ominous.

My eyes dart out to the *Scorpio*, completely unaware, zooming back towards the *Dolly*.

'*Take me back to my ship and I'll let her go,*' he says in rushed Mandarin, pressing the knife closer to my neck.

The knife I just put down.

God, I'm an idiot.

Kyle shifts his weight a little towards us in the bow, but the man flinches and Kyle stops.

'He wants to go back to his ship,' I blurt out. Am I imagining the feeling of the knife breaking through the top layers of my skin? Like the netting searing the dolphin's flesh . . .

'He will.' Kyle's voice shakes with rage. 'When he lets you go.'

I take a short gasp of breath, close my eyes and translate.

'No!' he cries in English.

My fear spikes at the terror in his voice. His hold on me tightens. Behind Kyle, one of the other crew members brings a radio to his lips.

'*Dolly*, this is—'

'NO!' he yells again, and my neck stings as he jolts. Something warm trickles down my throat. Is this what happened to my brother just a few weeks ago? I thrust that from my mind, but the images of the dolphin's frothing blood and Kai's ransacked room won't be suppressed.

Kyle turns back and signals for the crewman to stop, before focusing back on me and my captor.

'OK!' Kyle says. 'No radios.'

'*Seafang*, why are you stationary? Over,' the radio barks out. Kyle waves his hand behind him, not taking his eye off me, and the radio's volume dies down to nothing.

It's a standoff. The man's hold on me loosens a little. Is he losing his nerve?

I lick my lips. Taste the bitter salt of the ocean. I'm thirsty, and so tired.

'*Please*,' I manage to breathe. '*This isn't going to help. You have to let me go.*' He shifts behind me. I push on.

'*I'm scared. You're scared. But I'll make sure they don't hurt you.*' Out the corner of my eye, I see the *Scorpio* speeding back towards us.

'Look,' I whisper to him. '*The other boat is coming back. It would look so much better if you let me go on your own.*'

The knife pressure lightens. My voice gets stronger.

'*Can I tell them you're letting me go?*' The RIB is almost here.

'Jia?' Kyle says. I widen my eyes and hold up my free hand to silence him.

'*Your crew didn't come for you,*' I whisper. '*We did. We want to do the right thing. Please, let me go. And then—*' I feel tears welling in my eyes as I think of Mom, and our apartment, and Orion, chirruping as I come through the door, the familiar clacking of my brother's computer. '*And then we can all go home.*'

Home. That seems to do it. The arm holding the knife drops to his side and he sags behind me. Instantly, Kyle lunges forward and grabs me, throwing me behind him, then leaps onto the man and snatches the knife. Balkwill pulls me to him and two others throw themselves over Kyle.

'Don't hurt him!' I shout.

I hear a struggle behind me, and the man cries out. Then, quiet. Balkwill raises his eyebrows in a silent question.

'I'm fine,' I reassure him, before turning round to see Kyle tying the man's hands behind his back.

'Ungrateful motherfucker,' Kyle growls as the man hisses in pain.

Another crew member throws a foil blanket at me and hands me a bottle of water. But, surprisingly, I'm not shaking. I feel strangely calm. Kyle bundles past the captive and pulls out his radio.

'*Dolly*. This is *Seafang*. We're heading back now. Get the doc ready. And tell those fucking ships we have their man.'

'He's fine. A little cold. Maybe some bruised ribs, probably from where the cannon blasted him.' Giovanni looks at Kyle. 'At least that's what I hope it's from?'

Kyle shakes his head. To be fair to him, they didn't handle him that roughly, and he did hold a knife to my neck.

'Jia, could you tell him he's going to be fine, please?' asks Giovanni.

I relay the doc's diagnosis. I can't bear to look him in the eye; he keeps staring at me, like it's my fault they haven't let him go.

'Did anyone find Orion?' I ask Giovanni, who looks at me sadly and shakes his head. I suddenly feel a huge pressure on my chest, and struggle to breathe.

The sound of feet on the stairs, and Penny bursts through the door to the med bay.

'You OK, hun?' Penny asks. I nod and she seems satisfied. 'Doc, we need Jia and Kyle up on the bridge. Are you good with our guest?'

The doc smiles, and for the first time I realize how tall and muscular he is. How do all these men do that on a diet of tofu? The Chinese guy seems to notice his strength too, and his thin, wiry body shrinks back on the bed.

Kyle and I follow Penny back up onto the bridge. The wood nailed to the windows still holds firm, and the odd shard of glass glints on the floor here and there, but the *Dolly* appears relatively unscathed from the attack. Beyond the salt-frosted windows, the three Chinese fishing boats sit silently, just under a mile away. Their multiple RIBs buzz around them, waiting. But for what?

'*Liming*. This is the *Dolly*. We believe you are fishing illegally and have reported you to Interpol. We also have one of your crewmen aboard,' Captain Sigurðsson states over the radio, out towards the fishing boats.

'No English,' comes back the reply.

The captain turns, looking frustrated.

'*Liming*. Mean anything to you?'

'Bright thunder,' I translate.

'It's not on any of our lists, but could be a new moniker. I speak. You translate.'

I nod, and Penny smiles at me warmly.

'Tell them my original message, then.'

I do as he says. There's a momentary pause, and then a gruff male voice speaks back to me on the radio.

I hesitate, eyeing the back of the captain's head.

'Well?' he turns and barks at me.

'He said . . .' Oh boy. 'He said, "Give us our man back, you . . ."' I wince. '"You piece of shit . . ."' Blood rushes to the captain's face. He looks like he's about to boil over. '"And . . ."'

'And what?' he demands.

'He asked who I was.' My eyes dart to Penny, who is frowning.

'Tell them they must pull their RIBs out of the water and allow us to pull in their illegal drift net as evidence. Only then will we place him in a life raft for them to collect.'

Wary, I relay his message, but something in Penny's frown and my gut tells me not to tell them my name.

The message we get back makes me wince again.

'He says, "Fuck you. We are both captains. I demand your respect. Deliver our man."'

Sigurðsson curses under his breath, then turns to Penny. 'Let's haul in that net.' Then to Kyle: 'Get ready on the hoses again.'

'Captain,' Penny steps forward. 'We're on a science mission, and these guys are acting much more aggressively than we've ever—'

'Do it,' he growls back at her. Penny stiffens, and for a moment looks like she's going to refuse, but his rank makes her shrink back and she moves to handle the ship's controls.

Over the crackly PA system, the captain explains the plan. As the *Dolly* begins to turn to where the RIBs wrestled with the entrapped dolphin earlier, the Chinese ships swing out of sight.

'Keep them behind us,' the captain barks at Penny. 'I want to be able to outrun them if necessary.'

I shuffle behind Penny as the Captain barks more orders into his radio.

'Penny,' I whisper.

'What, Jia?' Her tone is unusually harsh.

'I need to find Orion, so—'

'You stay here. In case I need you,' says the captain, coldly.

I scowl up at him, but he's not even looking at me.

It doesn't take long for the *Dolly*'s powerful engines to pull us alongside the illegal driftnet. The winch system begins to crank it in, complete with rotting sea life, while the crew diligently haul and fold it. Every now and then, crew members look back towards the stern of the ship, checking to see if the poachers are approaching. Only twenty minutes in and the answer is: yes, they are.

Kyle and his team turn the cannons back on as the rival RIBs once again approach. It looks like they're out of ammunition, so the cannons do their job in holding them off, forcing them to circle in a wide perimeter, unable to stop us hauling in the evidence of their illegal activities. The crew pays no attention to their gesticulations and insults, just keeps going. Metres and metres of netting pool on the deck. Every couple of minutes someone retches at what they're having to pull up, mangled and half-decomposed fish slopping at their feet. I imagine them hauling up Orion's little body, and the world spins.

Penny raps her knuckles on the ship's console. 'Captain,' she clips, gesturing to the three ships, which are in motion again.

'Yes, thank you, but right now that net is not long enough to get a conviction.' His eyes dart between the approaching ships and his crew on the deck. 'Just a little longer,' he mutters.

The radio comes alive again with Mandarin. The captain looks to me, eyebrows raised.

'"Stop. Thieves,"' I recite. '"Give us our man, you motherfuckers."'

He just nods.

'The *Liming* is taking a very wide berth, sir,' Penny says, her brow furrowed. 'I think they're turning.'

I look out to the horizon and she's right. The lead fishing boat is turning towards us, a huge wake billowing out behind it.

'They're less than a mile off our port side, Captain.'

He eyes his crew, and the mound of netting that is piling up on the deck.

'They're coming fast,' Penny barks, her hands hovering over the ship's controls.

'Wait for it,' Captain Sigurðsson whispers. He looks at the radar, back out to the water, then back to his crew. I can practically hear the calculations whirring in his brain.

I stare out at the approaching *Liming*. It looks so fragile compared to the bulk of the *Dolly*, but it looms larger and larger with every second.

'Now.' He grabs his radio. 'Cut the lines. Brace for impact.'

Straight away, the crew throw themselves to the side of the ship and begin hacking away at the net. Others secure what netting they have procured and head back into the centre of the deck.

'Lines severed,' barks the radio.

'Now, Penny.'

She slams the ship's throttle to max. The *Dolly* jolts forward, clamouring to pick up speed, the *Liming* boring through the waves towards us. The whole ship rattles. I grab the table for support and brace myself for what feels like the inevitable. The *Liming* is so close now. We can see the figures on the bridge – men hell-bent on ramming our ship.

And then we begin to pick up some momentum, and the *Liming* seems to slide across the windows, its bow sweeping just ten feet behind our stern.

It's behind us.

And then it's shrinking. As we surge away from it, the radio comes alive with Mandarin expletives.

Captain Sigurðsson breathes out a huge sigh and slumps over the ship's console. I slip down the wall to the floor, too exhausted to stand any longer. I feel the blood surging through my neck, the pressure of it pounding against my wound dressing.

Penny stands, stiff. She watches the *Liming* fade away from us, then turns back to her captain.

'Permission to leave the bridge?' Penny clips.

'Granted.'

Penny heads over to me. She scoops me up under the arms and throws her jumper around me, then leads me towards the door. My body feels like jelly and I lean into her strength. At the door, she pauses and turns back to him.

'Don't ever put our lives in danger like that again,' she says, her voice like steel.

We're down in the crew mess, drinking strong tea, when Mike comes in through the doorway, holding a bundle of a towel, his face puckered with concern.

'Jia?' His voice is unusually soft. I jump up, knocking Penny's cup as I go.

'Orion?' I cry.

Mike nods, and I throw myself around the table towards him. As I move closer, I see the tip of a tail, and black spots appear in my vision.

It twitches.

'He's OK,' Mike says as I rush to take the bundle off him. I peel back the towel and cry out at the sight of a shaking Orion, covered in black, his hair all matted.

'I found him down in the engine room, covered in oil. He was terrified. Scratched me to shit.' He holds out his arms, which are red raw.

'I'm sorry,' I mumble, as I look down at the congealed ball of fur and oil in my arms. Orion isn't making any noise in his throat, but he's shaking and his heartbeat is pounding through the towel.

'It's fine,' Mike says, steering me to the galley. 'We need to get the oil off him right now. If he licks himself . . .'

I let myself and Orion be guided to one of the sinks, where Mike runs the water. He finds some washing up detergent and rubs it on his palms.

'Hold him steady, OK?' He's talking to me like I'm a child, but this time there's kindness there instead of condescension. I nod and peel away the towel, before lowering Orion into the water. His heart races even more and he flinches, but allows himself to be partially submerged in the warm water.

As Mike carefully rubs the detergent into his fur, Orion's eyes remain locked on mine. Usually he blinks slowly, or turns away, but now he just stares right back at me, his green eyes expressing so much sadness. My eyes sting. Kai would kill me if he knew.

Mike carries on rubbing Orion with a tenderness I would never have thought possible, especially after all the moaning he's done about Orion sharing our cabin.

'I cleaned birds,' he explains, apparently sensing my surprise as he flushes the muck off Orion's back. 'After Deepwater Horizon. One of my first missions with Greenpeace. Before they chucked me out.' He winks at me. 'I was just a teenager then. Thought I knew everything.'

'What's changed?' It slips out of me before I can take it back, and I grimace, waiting for the explosion.

'Ha!' Mike barks a laugh that makes Orion twitch. 'You made a joke, Jia!' He seems genuinely pleased as he applies more detergent and gently massages my brother's cat. I make hushing noises as Orion shifts around, getting impatient. The black oil and grey suds congeal and slide down the plug hole.

After helping dry him off, Mike leaves me and Orion to it. The crew need feeding after their ordeal today. Adrenaline and relief have given way to exhaustion and hunger.

Orion is now curled up on my lap in my bunk, a light purr vibrating through his body. At first, I felt awkward with him on me. But now . . . I stroke his still-damp fur. He nuzzles into me and I smile.

There's a soft knock on the cabin door.

'Come in,' I call softly, not wanting to disturb Orion. The door slides open.

Penny peers in. 'How's he doing?'

'Still a little shaken I think, but fine.'

Penny nods, as if she can relate. 'You know,' she says, 'it's the ultimate sign of trust, an animal falling asleep on you.' She smiles and we both look at Orion, his little paw draped lightly over his eyes. Seemingly content. Oblivious to the fact that his owner has now been missing for nearly eight weeks.

Eight weeks.

And I've been stuck on here most of that, unable to do anything to find him.

The *Dolly* rocks.

'Could you come with me? We need your help with our guest again.'

As I scoop Orion up and lower him onto the bed, he barely stirs, and I feel a surprising pang of reluctance at leaving him. But it's been good to feel useful today. It feels good to have them need me again now.

'Sure.'

I follow her back through the ship to the med bay. The captain is there, eating from a bowl of pistachio nuts, his eyes never leaving his prisoner. Kyle stands in the corner of the room, arms crossed, watching everything. The Chinese fisherman has been given a bowl of soup, although by the looks of it, he hasn't touched it.

'Here she is,' Penny clips, the atmosphere still frosty between her and Sigurðsson.

'Jia,' the captain says. 'We need you to translate.'

I nod.

'He's claiming to not speak any English.' The captain sounds dubious, but it's probably not a lie; I can't imagine this guy ever got much of an education.

'You can start by asking him why the hell his friends tried to ram our boat.'

I ask him, but the fisherman just looks at me.

'Again,' Sigurðsson demands.

Still no response.

Quick as a flash, Kyle is there, spinning the guy round and yelling in his face. 'Why the fuck did you try and ram us?!'

The man winces, but still he says nothing.

'Kyle,' Sigurðsson admonishes, and he backs off like an obedient dog. 'Jia, ask him if his ship is known by another name.'

The questions go on: who is his captain, where are they registered, what are the names of the other ships? The man just looks back at me, blankly.

Kyle fizzes with rage. 'We all know this isn't normal,' he eventually snaps. 'That many ships and only one drift net? And the way they attacked us? Captain, there's something else going on here.'

Sigurðsson nods.

'I know, Kyle. Why do you think we're here?' It's clear his patience is wearing thin, too.

An awkward silence hangs over us. My desperation to leave makes me bolder than usual.

'*What is your name?*' I ask the man. He doesn't reply, but looks at me, curious that I'm not simply doing what's asked of me now.

'*I'm Jia,*' I push on. '*Just tell them what they want to know.*' He doesn't say anything, but he leans forward, just the tiniest amount. '*If you talk, they might tell the authorities you escaped and asked for help.*' I doubt this, but I've heard about young men from mainland China who are tricked into going to sea and then stuck there for years. He's probably a victim as much as anything. Then I remember what chimed with him earlier. '*We can help you go home. Just tell us what you know. Please. Home.*'

He leans further forward and finally opens his mouth.

'*My name is Wang Wei,*' he says, his voice croaky. Stunned, I relay the information to the others. Penny sighs, relieved at the small sign of progress.

'Thank you,' I say sincerely, to Wei. '*Now, could you tell me the name of your ship?*'

'*Liming.*'

'*Did it have another name before that?*'

The man shrugs and replies. I tell the team his answer: he doesn't know; he only just joined the ship.

'Convenient,' Kyle mutters. I ignore him.

'*Why did your captain try to ram us?*'

Wei gestures for me to come closer. I look to Penny, who places a warning hand on my arm. I lean in anyway.

He stinks of the ocean and sweat, and smiles as he gestures for me to get even closer. Pointing to my ear, as if to tell me a secret.

I turn my ear to him, suddenly very conscious of how exposed my neck is. Still sore from where he held the knife to it.

'*My captain,*' he growls in my ear, '*is after you, Li Jia.*'

I gasp and throw myself backwards. Penny lunges forward and pulls me back from Wei, as if he were a wild animal.

Kyle leaps up. 'What did he say?'

I can't bring myself to say it. The man looks at me one last time, almost as if he's wondering what all the fuss is about, then turns to the soup and starts spooning it into his mouth.

'What did he say?' the captain repeats.

Penny crouches down so her face is level with mine, trying to read me. But I'm too stunned to say anything.

'Jia, what did he say?' she pleads.

'He said—' I clear my throat, trying to force my voice to be more than a whisper. 'He said, his captain is after . . . after me.'

Penny closes her eyes, as if she was waiting for me to say that, and wished I hadn't.

'You?' Kyle barks.

'Calm the fuck down,' Penny snaps, standing up again.

'Who are you?' he says, glaring at me. All the anger he was directing towards Wei now comes piling down on me.

'Nobody,' I blurt.

'Well, clearly you are, if three Chinese ships want to ram us to get to you!'

'Kyle, go get something to eat. Or cool off out on deck.' Sigurðsson says, brushing his hands off and rising slowly. 'Penny, Jia, come up to the bridge.'

The bridge is quiet now. Out over the ocean, the sun is setting behind us and the sky is tinged an eerie pink-blue hue. The *Dolly* hums along, and deep within her bows I can hear the crew clearing up the debris of the day.

Sigurðsson checks his monitors before gesturing for me to take a seat.

'So, Jia, you want to tell me why three illegal Chinese fishing ships are chasing you across the Pacific and are willing to sink my ship and kill all my crew just to get you?'

It sounds even more crazy when someone else says it. I look down at my hands; there's still some oil under my nails from where we bathed Orion. Is the *Liming* after him, too?

'I don't know.'

Sigurðsson's face is a mask. 'Tell me everything you do know, otherwise I am calling the authorities and when we next land, you'll be arrested and deported right back to Hong Kong.'

Deported, extradited. Words that strike fear into any fugitive's heart.

So, once again, I tell my story.

Sigurðsson listens silently through it all, his hands folded. A couple of times he glances up towards Penny, who still stands beside me, shifting uncomfortably under his gaze. He rolls his eyes when I get to the bit about Agnes bringing me onto the *Dolly*.

'Penny, it seems like I'm not the only one who has taken a risk with our crew's lives.'

'Captain, I—'

He holds both hands up. 'I'm sure Agnes played fast and loose with the truth. But this one is on you, and now it's on me, too. We have to decide what is best for the ship and the crew.'

He mulls things over a little longer.

'There must be a bounty on your head, Jia.' He frowns at me. 'The only thing those trawlermen care about is cash. They'll strip this planet of every resource for it, so I think they'd also stretch to kidnapping. Now, *who* is fronting the reward for you, that's anyone's guess. If the police and NS are involved, it sounds like the Chinese government have skin in the game. But frankly, I don't give a shit. All that matters is you're clearly wanted by some powerful people.'

I gape at him as he stands and looks out across the horizon, his hands folded behind him.

'As long as you're on the *Dolly*, you're a liability.'

Penny takes a step towards him. 'Captain, what do you propose we do? We can't just dump her in the ocean.'

He shrugs. 'It's not like she'd die. They're probably still trailing us – they'd find her.'

Penny glares at him. 'If you give them what they want, they'll have yet more money to line their filthy pockets. They'll buy up more boats, and enslave more men, to strip this ocean of every last living morsel—'

'Or, more of them turn up and send us into an early grave just to get their hands on her. Penny, even as we speak, there's probably another dozen trawlers in the area that have now got wind that we've got a huge cash prize sitting on our ship, and only a few water cannons for protection. How many more rounds of ammunition do you think we can dodge?' He gestures at the broken window, his voice rising. 'We were lucky – this time it was rocks! Next time—'

'No one can match our speed. If we blitz towards the West Coast, we'll outrun any other hostile ships.'

'And, what, you leave me to explain to the universities we've finally partnered with that our first legal mission in years had to be abandoned because we had an illegal runaway onboard who was being pursued by Chinese militia?'

'Don't act like you suddenly care about this mission, Sigurðsson. You don't give a shit about the science—'

'I do when it's the only goddamn chance I have to sail, Penny!' Sigurðsson's usually steely composure snaps, his face flushed with passion. 'When it's the only chance we have to take any fucking action! Everything we do is tied up in legal red tape from here to the moon and back. We can't stop these bastards from raping our planet and leaving it to rot any more than she can outrun the bastards who killed her brother, and—'

'Sigurðsson!' Penny cries.

I shrink back into my chair. He said it, what I've been thinking for so long, but never wanted to voice. Of course, Kai must be dead. Whatever this is, those people are willing to kill for it. The room spins, and bile rises in my throat.

The captain throws his hands up. 'I'm just being realistic. As much as I hate to admit it, this is the only chance we have to do anything. Science missions. Research. Yes, I am willing to push things. Out here, we can get away with taking some risks. I'll make a calculated decision to pull in a drift net if I think it can nail some of these fuckers. But I cannot put this entire ship and our entire organization under threat for just one person. This is bigger than that. The world is bigger than that.'

The whole ship seems to have gone silent. Can the rest of the crew hear? Sigurðsson storms outside and leans on the railings, the ocean breeze tugging at his hair.

Penny sighs and turns to me. 'I'm so sorry, my darlin'.'

All I can do is nod. 'I'm sorry, too.'

She gestures for me to stand up, but before we can leave by the back stairs, Sigurðsson pulls open the door and shoves his head back into the bridge.

'Confine her to her cabin and call all crew to the mess. We're going to vote.'

Rubio

MOVEMENT. SOMEONE SHIFTING AROUND ME. PASSING BY.

My eyes shoot open and in an instant, I'm awake.

From my floating sleeping sack behind my pod's curtain, I see a shadow. First, my hands grasp for the flask, which is still hidden, still safe. Then I nudge myself close to the curtain so I can peep through the gap, breathing as quietly as possible. My eye finds the storage bins, right where I've been staring night after night, desperate to unmask the clandestine visitor. But once again, I'm disappointed. There's no one.

Except, to my left, Okeowo rifles through her sleeping pod in the darkness. She's sniffling. I glance at my watch. It's early, but not what we would call night any more.

'Ruth?' I croak.

She turns quickly. It's dim in here, but the *Argo* is never completely dark. The low glow of emergency lighting and equipment shows her raw eyes, her moist cheeks.

I scramble to get out of my sleeping sack.

'So sorry, Rubio. I didn't mean to—' She pats self-consciously at her cheeks, then blows her nose into a handkerchief.

'Don't apologize.' My voice shakes. This woman is like a rock; nothing breaks her. 'What's wrong?' I ask.

'Oh it's . . .' She sniffs, looking like she might cry again. 'Honestly,' she scolds herself. 'I don't know why it's got to me so much. I just . . . When you look forward to something – well, it's just taken me by surprise, that's all.'

Still none the wiser, I move over to her and rub her shoulder in what I hope is a reassuring manner.

'What's not there, Ruth?'

She turns to me, her face grim.

'The personal messages,' she says. 'They're gone.'

When Okeowo and I emerge into the hab, everyone is there, even Ana. It's clear she's been crying too. There's a steely silence in the room, and Morin is at one of the monitors, her back to me, scrolling through files on the screen.

When Ana sees me, her eyes widen and she floats over to me.

'Rubio!' she cries. 'I'm so . . . I don't know what happened!'

'The PMs?' I ask.

'Yes. They were there,' she replies, doe-eyed. 'I looked at them earlier, when you were all sleeping. I'd seen the notification that they had been uploaded to the system. We all had them. You too!'

Now that *is* a surprise. Out of everyone on the ship, I'm the only one without any family. Both parents gone, and not many friends to speak of. It must have been from Lars.

'I saw the messages were in. I made some dinner, ate it, then went up to the cupola to read, and fell asleep there. Then—'

'Then when Morin got up this morning to check her PMs, they were all gone,' Brun finishes, his face like thunder.

'Have they been accidentally moved somewhere? Hidden among the other uploads? What about the star references we use for telemetry?' I offer, but Lee shakes his head.

'I checked the system. They were received, no doubt. There was plenty of data, more than enough for video messages for all of us, but now there's no trace.' Morin is clearly still looking on the system, not wanting to believe that they are gone. But if Lee – our computer and engineering expert – can't find them, there's no hope.

'So what happened?' I ask the room.

'I don't know. I was just—' Ana pipes up again, but Brun cuts her off.

'They were deleted, weren't they?' he snaps, glaring at Ana.

'Brun, no! I saw them, but I didn't—'

'You heard him!' Brun barks, gesturing at Lee, who shrinks back from the group. 'He said they've been wiped. They don't just do that by themselves.'

'Brun!' Ana is crying again. Okeowo moves to comfort her, and gives a squeak of shock as Ana launches herself into her, sending her spinning. But Okeowo's caring nature kicks in, and she puts an arm around her, while Ana sobs into her armpit.

'I didn't! They were there,' she wails. 'I watched mine, I ate dinner—'

'You *watched* yours?' Brun erupts.

Ana freezes. We stare at her, and her face emerges from Okeowo's embrace.

'Yes,' she squeaks. Even Okeowo frowns at that.

'You see!' Brun throws his arms in the air, as if this proves his point even more.

'But Ana's message is gone, too, now?' I ask Lee, who seems to be the calmest in the room.

Brun nods. 'Well, she couldn't keep her own PM, could she? That would be far too obvious! But of course, she got to see it before it mysteriously disappeared. What did it say, huh? Another note from precious Daddy. Where is he today? On his superyacht with all the other oligarch scum?' Brun spits.

Ana's wails grow louder and she says something in Russian. Okeowo raises the hand that's not taken up by cradling her weeping crewmate.

'That is enough, Brun!' she says, loud and firm.

'Don't you defend her, Okeowo,' Brun growls. 'She's either stupid or she's lying, but either way, she's responsible. And don't try and be all calm and magnanimous about it. I saw your face when Lee told you. Thanks to her, your nieces' message is gone.'

'They'll send new ones,' Lee says meekly.

'It doesn't matter!' Brun cries. 'She did it. And now we all have to wait even longer before we hear from Earth. And who the hell knows what else she gets up to in the dead of night.'

This is madness. As Lee said, it's not the end of the world. We'll contact Control, explain the problem, and they'll re-upload the messages. We'll wait a day or two at the most. But Ana's broken sleep cycle has made an outcast of her. She's an unknown. Rogue. And I think of the tablet glowing in that bin, and the word: 'THIRSTY?' I've been trying to watch her movements. See if she has shown any interest in the storage bins, my sleeping pod. But so far, nothing, from anyone.

'But, why?' I cry, the question that's haunting me for many more reasons than the rest of them realize. 'Why would Ana do that? It must be a mistake, Brun.'

'A mistake, or something else.' Brun points towards one of the cameras that is soaking all this in. 'This is what they want. The drama! The conflict! And they're using her to get it!'

'Don't be ridiculous,' Okeowo hisses. 'You sound like—'

'Alyssa,' Lee quietly says. 'He sounds like Alyssa.' His wide, innocent eyes stare at Ana.

'Okeowo,' Morin says, and we all whip round to face her. Her expression is completely neutral. 'Take Ana back to the pods. Ana?'

Ana's pink face emerges from Okeowo's shoulder.

'Go and calm down for a moment. You must be exhausted. I'll come and talk to you later, OK?'

Ana zooms out of the hab, but Okeowo turns back briefly.

'Commander, are you . . .?' she half asks.

'I'm fine, thank you,' Morin says in a clipped manner. Okeowo hesitates a moment longer, but heads out.

'Brun.' Morin turns to him.

'Yes, Commander,' he says, an edge to his voice.

'The messages are gone, but I've already contacted Control. I'm sure they will be re-uploaded very soon.' Brun scoffs. Morin continues, her voice louder now. 'There are, I'm sure, a number of ways the messages could have been lost. A software error; yes, maybe even human error. But I see no evidence of foul play. We are a team, Brun. We are a crew. We are a family. And I will not have you brutally accusing other members as you have just done.'

'Commander, this—'

'That is the end of it,' Morin speaks over him, like a mother scolding a child. 'Once Ana has calmed down, I would like you to go and apologize. I am giving you the benefit of the doubt, Brun, and am assuming that you are only acting like this because you are missing your wife, your friends. We are all disappointed. But this is not a mission-critical issue, and we should treat it with the proportion it warrants.'

Brun glares at her, then seems to deflate. I realize I've been holding my breath, and finally let it out.

'Maybe you should take some of that . . . energy . . . and fulfil your exercise quota for the day, hmm?'

For the briefest of moments, it looks as though Brun might say something, maybe even do something. I swear I see his hand twitch. But then the fire in his eyes dies down and he kicks himself off in the direction of the treadmill and weights.

As soon as he is out of earshot, Morin lets out a huge sigh. She closes her eyes and takes some deep breaths. I watch her as she tries to centre herself. Whatever messages were deleted, she has lost the most out of this. Even if it is just another day of waiting, it's another day of her children's lives slipping past her. Okeowo told me a couple of days ago that Morin's son, Ben, had been charged with a DUI back home. But then again . . . this is what she signed up for.

'Commander.' Lee makes his way over to her and she opens her eyes. 'To wipe the messages from the system completely like this would take knowledge that Ana just doesn't—'

'I know,' Morin says, squeezing his arm. 'Thank you for your help. Let's . . . let's look into how we can ensure the system is always backed up as soon as it's uploaded, maybe? Could you liaise with the coders back in Baikonur?'

'Of course, Commander,' Lee says, heading off to the command module. Morin turns to me.

'Rubio,' she breathes, attempting a smile. 'How are you doing?'

'I'm fine,' I shrug. I'm not, but I'm terrified of telling her anything else. Because the truth is, things are even darker than she realizes.

The truth is: I found the tablet fifteen days ago. We are now thirty-four days into our mission and the flask ... The godforsaken flask that I think of constantly throughout my day. That I cling to every night ...

Well, the flask hasn't run out.

She studies me, her intelligent eyes boring into me. Can she see what a mess I'm in?

'A message for you, though,' she nudges. 'You think it's Anders?'

'Most likely,' I say.

She nods, grabbing herself a juice box from one of the refrigerated drawers.

'You know, most of my briefings at the moment are coming from Abbey. Anders seems to have gone very quiet,' she says, in a leading manner. Her eyes flick to one of the cameras as she sucks from the juice box. 'When you do get your message from Anders, I'd love to know how he is. It feels like it's been too long.' She peers at me, her eyes saying more than her words.

'Of course,' I reply, and make my excuses.

As I head off to my ablutions, I eye the cameras that pan to follow me. It's clear that Morin is concerned, as we all are, about who is really in charge down in Baikonur. The quieter Anders becomes, the louder Abbey and his TV minions get. Could it be that they're the ones who deleted the messages? Is Brun half right? Are they messing with us? Stoking the tensions that are naturally growing? But as Lee said, it would take some technical clout. And the TV production crew have nowhere near that level of access to our ship's software.

Do they?

One thing I do know, however: they can't hack their way into that flask.

But someone is topping it up.

It took me a few days to accept this. I kept convincing myself that my sips were so tiny, so minuscule, that the contents were lasting longer than I'd anticipated.

But it was another lie.

A lie confirmed a few nights ago when the taste distinctly changed.

Before, it was vodka.

Now, it's hooch.

And the gut-wrenching, stomach-churning thing is, now that I know it won't end – that it's being replenished – I'm drinking more of the damn stuff. My tiny sips have become a gulp each night, a swig. Still not enough to spike any readings, but enough to scare the shit out of me.

Whoever is blackmailing me, whoever is behind this . . .

I'm dependent on them.

And they know it.

Is this another trick, like the messages? Are they testing me? Hoping I'll break?

My last lapse was good for ratings.

As my shaking hands squeeze toothpaste onto my brush, Ana's sobs still echo down the ship from our sleeping pods.

We've heard they're calling her the Argo Angel. A magical, floating being, imbued with mystery and magic, operating when no one is awake.

That's not an angel.

Feels more like a demented tooth fairy, to me.

A flask fairy.

I choke on a laugh, like the madman I am.

I stare at myself in the mirror, more desperate than ever to see Lars's message. I just need some reassurance that all is well; that back there, everything is under control.

Because up here, it's anything but.

Twenty-four hours later, the lost messages finally arrive.

But there is nothing for me.

Alyssa

THE HEAT AND STEAM OF THE RESTAURANT BILLOW AROUND me as I wait for the phone to connect. Marvin, the chef, gives me a nod as he carries a big pot to the stove.

'Hey,' Jake's warm voice finally comes down the line.

I slump down into the chair by the emergency exit, almost giddy with relief. It's late in Kazakhstan, but this is the time we've pre-arranged, once Jake is off shift and alone in his apartment.

'What the hell is going on over there?' My voice comes out sharper than I intended.

'*Oh hey, Jake, how are you?*' he mocks in a high pitch. '*I'm good thanks, Lyss, a little tired, but cool other than that, how are you?*'

'Hilarious,' I retort. 'And it's Alyssa. Come on, what's everyone saying?'

'I won't talk about it until you tell me how *you* are.'

I breathe out.

We've started like this the last couple of times we've spoken on Martha's landline, with him insisting on me telling him how I am. It makes it feel like a therapy session. A therapy session where the therapist is calling on a burner phone and making it look like he's calling his aunt, for fear of losing his job . . .

'Fine,' I reply. The first time I said this to him, it was a lie. But now? Martha emerges from the walk-in refrigerator and hands me a slice of pie with a wink, before heading in to help Marvin. Beyond, the hustle and bustle of the restaurant floor bleeds through the open doorway. I look down at what I know will be a delicious treat.

'And the cast?'

'Comes off a week on Monday.'

'That's great! How you getting on with the weight training?'

'Good.' I smile, just a little. His enthusiasm is infectious, even when I'm trying my hardest to resist it. 'The thigh's pretty strong, and the other leg is pumped, so hopefully I'll have a bit of a running start.'

'Amazing what a couple of weeks can do, right?'

To be honest, it is. The exercises I've been doing have given me a lot more energy and sometimes the TV has actually gone off. I'm no longer sleeping on the couch and have even had some dreamless nights. Although what I saw yesterday brought my nightmares right back to the surface.

I put the pie down, pull the cord of the landline out a little further and step through the fire escape, inhaling the fresh air deeply. It's a shitty day. Damp and overcast.

'I'm sorry, Jacob, but I think something is wrong.'

'You're still watching, then,' he says quietly.

'Of course I am. Come on, you know it's fucked. The crew are fighting. There are so many mistakes. And what happened with the messages? That was deliberate. Haven't you heard anything on your end?'

'Lyss—'

'It has to be Ana. She must have found a way to delete the messages, to rile things up a bit, probably on Abbey's orders. Didn't you guys look into it?'

'Lyss, no one knows what happened to the messages. It was just a data glitch. There's been quite a few of them recently, the ship's software has been a little . . . temperamental. They've got us pulling double shifts trying to patch a few things.'

I push off the wall I've been leaning on, everything in me alert.

'What do you mean, "temperamental"?'

'We've just been finding quite a few bugs, that's all. The message issue was just one of them. It's fine, we're fixing it – just the consequence of lazy assholes not paying attention, or it might even be caused by radiation flipping some of the bits—'

'The software's compromised? Fuck, Jake.'

I start pacing outside the door, but the phone cord pulls taut and I stumble backwards. Then I remember something that sends a thrill right through me.

'You know she's a computer scientist?'

'Who?'

'Ana.'

Jake sighs.

'What if she's hacking at shit?'

'Lyss—'

I barely register him; my mind is going at the speed of light. 'That must have been how she deleted the messages. Maybe even how she wasn't seen. Are you guys monitoring what she does at night, what she has access to?'

'You're starting to sound a little . . .'

I freeze. 'A little what, Jake?'

He doesn't say the word. He knows how much it will hurt. Instead, he clears his throat.

'I know this is all really tough on you,' he starts, slowly. 'And you're still working through everything, but—'

'No!' My voice has risen, my face is hot. 'I know what you think. What everyone thinks: I'm crazy. Obsessed. But what if I'm right? Anders used to spout on about how the *Argo* software was some of the most advanced in the world. There's something going on here. You have to check what Ana has access to, what she's been doing . . . I can't be the only one who is seeing this?'

'I think you might be.'

'How can you not—'

Martha emerges from the restaurant with a glass of water. Her eyebrows raise at the sight of me pacing, yelling down the phone. She puts the glass down carefully and retreats. I take a deep breath.

'Please just humour me, Jake. Find out if she's accessed the code in some way.'

'And while I'm at it, see if she's been planted as a mole and there's a conspiracy to cover it up?'

My silence is enough of an answer.

He sighs deeply. 'Did you see the stuff I sent you?'

I blink, wrong-footed by the change in tone and subject.

I shake my head to clear it. In the last care package from Martha, there was a printout of several apartment listings in Houston. I haven't even looked at them.

'Look, if you want me out of here, all you had to do is say.'

'I don't want you out,' he says, sadly. 'You can stay as long as you like. But I think it's good for you to see what's out there for when you're ready. I guessed that you've spent a lot of time in Houston in the past, and . . . well, I figured maybe you might want to go back to NASA, eventually.'

I scoff. 'And you think I'm the crazy one?'

'Lyss, there's only so much I can do to help you. You also need to help yourself.'

'You think not believing me is helping me?'

'Alyssa, all I'm trying to do is look out for you.'

'What, because I'm some crazed woman who can't take the fact that my life was destroyed and now there seems to be all these things happening that suggest I'm not the only victim in all this, I suddenly need looking after?'

'Yes, Alyssa. You do.'

'Screw you.'

'That's no way to talk to someone you're asking to spy for you.'

'Fine, don't help me, Jacob. I'm fine. I don't need your help. God knows why you even offered me your apartment in the first place. Probably because you have nothing else going on in your sad little life. Just your code and your daily calls to Martha. So you saw me and thought you'd get in on a piece of history, instead of being sat behind a fucking screen all day, and now there might actually be something wrong and you have a chance to do something about it, you're calling me hysterical and being a fucking coward.'

A heavy silence follows. I readjust the weight on my cast, waiting for him to shout back. But nothing comes.

I look down. In my anger, I've knocked over the glass of water Martha left me. Its contents are pooling by my feet, the glass is cracked.

My rage subsides, leaving piercing remorse in its wake.

'Look, Jacob, I'm—'

'It's fine. Alyssa,' he says, his voice cold. 'I'll ask around and get word to you if there's anything suspicious. Just make sure you give Martha your keys before you go.'

And he's gone.

I smash the tranquil surface of the puddle with my right boot. I've really fucked it. But if he'd just trusted me, believed in me, then—

Someone clears their throat behind me. I turn to find Martha, standing in the hallway. She tilts her head.

'Alyssa?'

I wipe my nose and step back inside, placing the receiver back on its holder.

'Sorry,' I mumble. 'And thank you.'

She glances at the phone, then takes off her apron.

'I'm heading out, Marv,' she yells. 'Cover for me!' She grabs my discarded crutches and holds them out to me.

I look at her, puzzled.

'Come on,' she says, her voice both kind and sad. 'We're going for a walk.'

I let her lead me down the street, across a couple of blocks. We don't say anything, she just gently guides me until we get to a small park, with a playground and a rundown basketball court. She makes her way to a bench and sits, gesturing for me to join her.

The bench faces the little playground, but only one parent and a child have braved the weather today. The child slides down the slide, then rushes back round again to climb the ladder to it once more, before starting the whole thing again.

'Jacob used to love this park,' Martha breaks the silence. 'That would be him – even in the rain – going up and down. Getting his pants soaked, and not giving a damn. That was back before he found computers, of course. His mawmaw preferred it here. It was much cheaper.'

'What happened?' I surprise myself by asking.

'Breast cancer. His mom died when he was fourteen. His grandmother raised him after that. She was a good friend of mine.'

'And when did she—'

'She passed away two years after Jake's accident.'

A pigeon swoops down in front of us and picks at a packet of chips near the garbage can.

'I'm sorry.'

'For our loss? Or for tearing Jake a new one just now?'

I glance at her, but she stares straight ahead, though a little smile creeps across her lips. I look back to the playground and shift uncomfortably.

'Both.'

'I thought so.'

We sit in silence, until the mother's head snaps up and she calls to her child. She gathers her things, and the boy reluctantly follows her out of the park. The paper she was sitting on is left on the bench, the wind teasing the pages.

'After his mother died, Jake really went into himself. Only natural, of course. It's a small community – everyone knew what had happened. People used to cross the street when they saw him or his mawmaw. They used to choose a table further away in the restaurant, too. People are scared of loss.'

'Jacob said something similar to me once.'

She nods. 'He knows true loneliness, that boy. And yet, he has so much to give. I think that's why he's fallen for you.'

I laugh. 'What?'

'Oh, I know you barely know each other. But I know him, and he likes you. So what you said to him just now . . . that's big.'

The laughter is snatched right out of my throat. How much did she hear?

'Alyssa.' Her old, wrinkled face turns to me, and she looks deadly serious. 'I know you've been through a lot. And it's not fair.' She takes my hand and squeezes it tight. 'You are an incredible woman to make it to where you did, everyone in the world knows that. And I can see why Jake likes you. But please, don't lead him on. He's done everything in his power to help you get back on your feet, and I'm glad I could help him in that. But you're stuck on this Earth now, and you need to realize you have a responsibility to those around you. If you don't like Jake, please tell him. He deserves the truth: are you keeping in touch with him because he's your last connection to your old life? Or are you keeping in touch with him because you want him to be a part of your new one?'

I peer at her, mouth hanging slightly open. 'I . . .'

She smiles and shakes her head gently. 'You don't need to answer now. Or even to me. He'll call you back. I know he will. Take the time until then to think.'

She gives my hand one last squeeze, then she stands up and starts walking back the way we came.

'Martha!' I call out. She stops and turns, only kindness in her face.

'Yes, honey?'

'Thank you.'

She smiles, big and warm. 'You're welcome.'

She turns and makes her way across the park to the street. As she crosses, the sky opens up again and rain begins to patter the sidewalk, adding to the already full puddles.

I don't move, though. I let the rain fall on me, dousing my burning guilt.

Jia

IT'S LIKE WE'RE ON MARS. THE SKY IS A VIOLENT SHADE OF orange, hanging low and heavy over the land. Everything sounds muffled and the sun is nowhere to be seen as we make our way towards the marina. The forests of California are burning again.

Mike stands next to me on the deck, his face creased with concern.

'I've never seen it like this. Not here, anyway.'

Nausea roils in my stomach. After thirty-nine long days, I'm finally about to make landfall.

Mike claps a reassuring hand on my shoulder. 'It's fine. Unless you have asthma, it won't hurt you too bad.'

'It's not that I'm worried about,' I mutter.

'Captain trusts the Marina Del Rey. We'll get you on your way to fuck-knows-where.'

As if on cue, Penny appears. She's in full Sea Saviour branding and looks like she hasn't slept a wink in the last few days.

'You ready to go down?'

'Yeah.' I give the fiery hellscape of California one last look. It's hard to believe this country might be the answer to my brother's disappearance. I just hope I'm not too late.

'Jia,' Mike calls out.

I turn back and the big Aussie thrusts himself at me, wrapping his huge arms around me. Before I can figure out what to do, he lets go.

'Look after yourself, yeah? And that cat of yours.'

'He's my brother's,' I say automatically.

Mike laughs. 'Sure he is.' He hits my arm affectionately then turns back to the horizon.

There was quite a debate about whether to help me get to shore, and it was clear where the captain stood. But Penny said everyone agreed in the end that they didn't want the illegal trawlers to win. 'Plus, the stunt with the dolphin and Wei impressed them – they reckon we can make an eco-warrior out of you after all.'

Wei was going to be the key, apparently. The explanation for why the science mission had been abandoned and they had to call into shore early. As soon as I get off the *Dolly* and am on my way to the state border, they'll call up Interpol and report him: an accidental hostage from an unprovoked attack.

Penny hovers as I pick up my meagre belongings and scoop up Orion. Just as I drop him into his bag and turn to leave the tiny cabin, my pocket begins to vibrate.

The burner!

I almost drop Orion's bag in my rush to get the cell phone out of my pocket. I utter a whimper of joy at the sight of the signal bars on the screen, and the messages and missed calls from the only number programmed in: A.

'It's Agnes! She's called!'

Penny pulls the door closed again and squeezes into the cabin with me.

'What does she say?'

My fingers shake as I click onto the messages.

'There's no voicemail. Just some missed calls and messages . . .'

But each one makes my stomach sink.

CALL ME.
RESPOND ASAP.
PLEASE CALL.

Then there's another text, the most recent one to come into the phone, from an unknown number.

**Agnes has been arrested. Her family are fighting it.
Me and Mom are OK. Hiding and plan to leave v soon.
Your mom's home is being watched, but she is safe. The news says they think you fled the country. Don't call this number. Thinking of you. E x**

Erica.

I suddenly feel so small, like everything is bearing down on me, and there's not much more I can take before terror completely takes over. Only the kiss after *E* is holding me together.

Penny reads the text over my shoulder and looks at me, aghast, my fear reflected on her face. She folds me into her arms.

'We need a new plan,' she says, firm.

'I rang the marina,' Penny breathes as we enter the med bay. Captain Sigurðsson stands rigid, looking furious, as always.

'There are two men claiming to be police officers at the dock, although they have refused to show any credentials.'

'So someone *does* know she's here,' Sigurðsson grunts.

'Are you ready for this, Jia?' Giovanni, the doc, asks.

I nod, but can't bring myself to say anything. I place Orion down on the medical bed and stroke him. He sniffs the air, curious.

'I promise you, I've done the math. This should be just the right amount to sedate him. He may not be fully unconscious, but he'll be drowsy.'

He shuffles about some of his kit, before pulling on a pair of latex gloves and opening up a syringe.

'*Should?*' I squeak.

'The plan will only work if you and Orion can keep still and silent for as long as possible – we have no choice. Trust us.'

Giovanni plunges the needle into the top of a vial and withdraws what looks like a huge amount of clear liquid. My heart hammers.

He moves over to Orion, who turns on the bed and then crouches as though to jump off it. I readjust him.

'Shhh,' I soothe.

'Here we go,' whispers Giovanni. He grasps the scruff of Orion's neck and gently lowers the needle into his skin.

As soon as the liquid floods into him, Orion goes floppy and the doc uses his other hand to ease him down onto the bed, onto his side. Orion's eyes half close, and his mouth slackens. His belly rises and falls more slowly with every passing second.

'You gave him too much!' I cry out.

'No, look, he's fine.'

As I stroke his fur, I realize his breathing is no longer slowing, but is now coming in deep, steady breaths. My relief goes beyond my awareness of his importance to Kai, and I do something I've never done before: lean down and kiss his soft little head.

'How long do we have?' asks Penny.

Giovanni shrugs. 'At least a couple hours.'

'We're about to dock,' Sigurðsson growls.

'Let's go,' Penny mutters.

The stench of rotting fish makes me retch silently. I try to inhale the faint scent of peppermint from the handkerchief I've stuffed into my facemask, but it does nothing. Instead, I go back to breathing through my mouth, although the air is warm and damp.

Above me, beyond the heavy layer of confiscated illegal drift net, I hear muffled voices. They've moved the crate with the net concealing Orion and me onto the back of a pick-up truck. Meanwhile, Captain Sigurðsson is answering the questions from the men who met the *Dolly* as it docked; the guys claiming to be police officers.

'That must be the tip you were given. We picked him up after they tried to ram us. It's all on the ship's log. We have no objections to you taking him. Now, can I see some form of identification?'

I can't hear the rest of the exchange. Only Sigurðsson is loud enough. I have a tarpaulin over most of me, and my shoes and hair are soaked through with stuff I don't even want to think about. It was my idea to use the drift net as cover, but I never appreciated how torturous the wait would be. Orion is protected in his bag at least, but I wish I could feel his little chest expand and contract, to know that he's still with me.

Someone slams their hands against the side of the truck.

'Officers, would you excuse me?' It's Penny. 'The stench is bad and I'd like to get this net down to the bureau for processing so we get charges out for that fleet.'

More mumbling, but they must agree, as Penny opens up the door to the truck.

Just a little longer, Orion. Just a little longer, and then I can get out of here and make sure you're all right.

'Li Jia!'

Terror shoots through me.

'Li Jia!' My name again, yelled out loud for everyone to hear. And I recognize the voice: Wei.

'Li Jia. Hide! Net!'

Banging, on the truck.

'Get this down, please.'

'Sure, hold on. It's just the net, like we said. Evidence of the illegal fishing that—'

The vehicle shifts as someone climbs onboard.

'Jesus!' The officer – if he really is an officer – chokes at the smell, as they sift through the net.

'Like I said, officers, it's an illegal drift net, with several pounds of rotting fish. Also, this is not standard procedure. Please identify yourselves at once.'

The officer thumps round to the side of us. The net's weight shifts around me. How long until they find me? Just a matter of seconds. They'll grab me, restrain me. And then what – extradition? If the Chinese government are after me, I'll never see anyone again. Everyone knows that once they have you . . .

His hand nearly scrapes past Orion's bag and adrenaline thrills through me.

The old Jia would have let the inevitable happen. But I've just spent forty days on a barely legal eco-warrior ship and helped the crew navigate a hostage situation.

And I won't let them take us.

I take a huge breath and heave with all my might, my hand gripped around the handles of Orion's bag.

'What the fuck?' the man cries, as the mass of rotting net and decaying sea life heaves up in front of him, and I push with all my might to get out of the pile.

Fresh air and sunlight hit my face, but there's no time to revel in it. I clasp Orion's bag with both hands and heave again, setting him free, too.

For a moment, I lock eyes with the man standing a couple of feet away, fish slime streaking down my face. He looks horrified, as though he's seen some kind of beast.

'Hey!' Penny screams, snapping me out of it. I shoulder Orion's bag and launch myself over the side of the truck, just as the officer lunges for me. I cry out as I land hard, my ankle twisting. But now is not the time to feel the pain.

I throw open the passenger door of the truck and thrust Orion's bag in.

'Stop!' The pickup jolts as the officer jumps down as well.

I scramble in and slam the door behind me. Penny's already in the driver's seat, and locks both doors behind us.

'Go!' I yell, hauling Orion's pack onto my lap.

Penny floors it and our backs slam into our seats as we screech off. In the wing mirror, the two officers dart away from the captain and Wei, back to their own car. We have a small head start, but it won't last long.

Penny sends the truck flying towards the ramp for the freeway. Huge signs are flashing: Warning: Wildfire.

But we zoom past them. Smoke sits on the horizon to our left as we head east, away from the coast.

Suddenly it hits me what we've done, and I give a shout of deranged laughter. Penny looks at me like I have two heads.

'I can drive you to Albuquerque and you can bus it from there.'

She swerves around a slow-moving vehicle, and I twist in my seat. Through the rear window of the truck, the officers' silver car is gaining on us.

'Shit,' she breathes, glancing in the rear-view mirror.

Up ahead is an interchange. Penny's eyes dart between that, the car behind, and the smoke to our left.

'Fuck it.'

She flings the wheel to the right and the truck swerves across the lanes. For a moment I'm certain we're about to hit the barrier, and I scream and clutch Orion's pack to my chest. Then we're past it, spinning onto another freeway.

Behind, the silver car does the same. They just make it, too.

But now I realize we're heading north. Straight into the smoke.

'I know!' Penny yells, as if reading my mind. 'We have to lose them. The freeway will cause a firebreak. We'll sail right through.' The tremor in her voice tells me she's trying to convince herself, too.

Up ahead looms a wall of smoke, smothering the whole of the freeway.

'Penny?'

'It's just smoke.'

The world outside dims ever darker.

'Just a little further. They'll turn back.'

'Then what?' I cry, but Penny doesn't answer.

BANG. BANG. BANG.

Penny and I scream and instinctively shrug right down in our seats. Something has hit the truck, but we're still moving.

'Are they shooting?' she screams.

I lift my head just high enough to look at the wing mirror. The silver car is coming to a stop, and a figure sticks halfway out of the passenger window, gesturing. The figure takes aim again. *BANG.* A bullet ricochets off the side of the truck.

'Yes!' We brace ourselves as they fire again, but this time no sound – they must have missed. 'They're going for the tyres!'

As we near the wall of smoke, panic rises in me. It looks solid, impenetrable. Like we'll crash into it. Penny's knuckles are white on the steering wheel.

We both take a breath, as if we're about to dive into the ocean.
WHOOMPH.

We're inside the cloud. Everything goes dark. The lights on the dashboard glow and I hope to God that the road stays straight. All the sounds are muffled; the engine seems far away.

And then what sounds like thousands of grains of sand start hitting the car. Then flares and specks of light, embers flying past.

All at once, an ominous orange glow seeps around us, until the world is no longer dark, but blinding. As if we were driving into the centre of the sun. There are flames to the left of me. A ball of fire billowing.

A little more of the road is visible now, a lone strip of grey ignited by our headlights, while all around us everything glows.

'Shit,' Penny utters again and again as she fights to keep the car steady, only able to see about five feet ahead.

'What do we do?' I ask.

She never takes her eyes off the road, hardly blinks. 'If we turn back, they'll find us,' she says simply. 'If we push through, we can find a way up past San Antonio to join the I-40.'

I have no idea what she's talking about.

'Drive through the night,' she continues. 'We can be there by morning.'

The intensity of the embers hitting us suddenly increases and an almighty roar erupts.

'Woah!' cries Penny as she battles with the steering wheel. A huge gust of wind-driven fire sweeps over us. There are balls of flame on the road and it feels like we're driving over them, through them, swerving all over the place as the blazing gale bats the truck across the tarmac.

'FUCK!' screams Penny, pulling the wheel with all her might. I can hardly hear her over the din of the wind and the sparks crackling against the glass.

Outside, the windows whiten as the world gets hotter. The engine groans. Lights in the truck begin to flash, every dial flaring into red, and the moisture on my skin begins to crackle.

Penny floors it. A last-ditch attempt to pull us out of the inferno.

Everything is blinding. I close my eyes, the light still burning my retinas even as I pull my entire self into my chest, along with Orion. There's no way Penny can have her eyes open. She must be driving completely blind. It's just too bright. Too hot. This must be it.

I feel thuds from underneath us and we jerk upwards. Then the roar disappears. Are we dead? Is everything over?

But no, the engine is still growling, the truck is still pinging at us as Penny's breath comes in gasps.

'Jia,' she breathes, 'we're through.'

I open my eyes, feeling as though my whole face has been screwed up within itself. The whiteness is gone. It's orange, but a dull glow. And more smoke is muffling the light. It's black as night, but now we're driving through the devastation the fire has already wrought. Nothing here is left that can burn.

'So.' She turns to me, and I gape back at her, my face a mask of terror. 'Welcome to America.'

Alyssa

DESPITE EVERYTHING I SAID, AND HOW I SAID IT, THREE days later Jake rings me on the restaurant landline, as promised.

He opens with, 'Are you done being an asshole now?'

'I think so.'

'Good. It doesn't suit you.'

I think I can hear him smiling through the phone. Martha's words are rattling around my mind, and I probe my feelings towards him. I do feel strangely calm when I hear his voice; grounded, in a good way. Is that because of him? Or because he's my only connection now to Baikonur?

'I looked into it and there's no way Ana has been fucking with the software. She doesn't have the access. I also looked into her degree and there's nothing that suggests she has the required level of coding skill.'

'OK . . .' I say, scuffing my shoe on the floor.

'You don't sound convinced,' he says, his tone less chirpy.

'But what about the glitches? If there's something wrong with the ship, people should know. The crew should know.'

'Lyss, they're just bugs. Nothing sinister, and we're patching them. I've heard they may even be bringing other people in.'

I take a breath, trying to calm myself.

'Hey, I said I would look after your crew for you, and I am. I'm keeping an extra ear out for anything, OK?' He sighs. 'It's probably no good for you to hear this, but I've heard that Abbey is holding some emergency meetings. Ratings aren't what they expected since the launch and some advertisers are threatening to pull out . . .'

'So the revenue will dip?'

'I think it already has. I haven't seen Anders for over a week and more Valdivian execs are flying in. Abbey and his cronies are terrified about their shares – they'll all be ruined if this fails. They want to make a big thing about breaking the *Mayflower* distance on Saturday.'

He says it so casually, like it's no big deal.

Of course, he has no idea.

The *Mayflower* disaster was just a news story to him. A simple tragedy.

But I know the reality of it.

And soon my crew will be passing that point where disaster struck over four years ago. Without me. The furthest any human beings have ever been. Beyond the place where my dreams take me to, night after night.

Jake is right. Me obsessing over conspiracy theories is not going to help them. Their fates are tied to forces I can no longer control. They're gone.

'You know,' I start tentatively, keeping my voice low even though I know we won't be heard over Marvin's loud rendition of 'Defying Gravity' from the kitchen. 'I started looking at some listings yesterday.'

'Oh?' He sounds genuinely shocked.

'Just to see what's around.'

'That's great, Lyss. If you do end up back at NASA, then—'

'I wasn't looking in Houston.'

'Oh.' Again, he's surprised, and I smile. 'You thinking of heading back to Illinois?'

I laugh. 'Back to my parents? Hell no.'

'Where then?'

I glance up at my surroundings. I'm sat round the back of Martha's in the small corridor between the restaurant and the kitchen. Up on the wall in front of me is the staff noticeboard, which has news clippings stuck all over it. Marvin has taken great delight in keeping track of where the press are speculating I am. Every couple of weeks a new article pops up: '*Mars One Reject Spotted in South Africa*', '*Russia Offers Safe Haven to Beleaguered Astro-nought*', '*The Not So Wright Stuff: Why Ex-Nasa Astronaut Snapped and Where She Might Be Now*'. Martha offered to take them down, but I find it reassuring how wildly off the mark they are.

'I thought I might stick around here, for a bit.'

Silence.

My foot twitches as I wait for him to say something, anything.

He breathes out. 'Wow. OK. How come?' he finally says.

'Purdue has a decent geology department and they may have some openings in the fall semester, plus I've got hooked on Martha's cooking. I don't think my leg will recover without it.'

He laughs and I'm filled with a warmth that has nothing to do with the sunshine outside.

'She'll be real pleased to hear that, I'm sure.'

'And maybe when you're done . . .' I shift a little in my seat. '*Over there* . . . you could take me to a Colts game. I'm pretty good at coping with loss now.'

'I would really love that,' he says, softly.

Something within me stirs.

'Me too.'

There's a pause, loaded with . . . something.

'It's so good to have something to look forward to,' he says.

And for the first time, I think maybe he might just be right.

Rubio

'YOU HAVE TO BE UP FOR THIS ONE, I'M AFRAID,' I SAY AS I pass a coffee to Ana through the curtains to her sleeping pod.

'I know,' she replies, clutching the Thermos close to her.

She sips silently, avoiding my eyes.

This is the first time we've been alone together in weeks – and I plan to make the most of it.

'How are you?' I ask.

Ana pauses. Despite the sleep deprivation, she looks beautiful.

'You're the first person to ask me that in a long time,' she replies, soft and quiet.

'Who'd've thought it would be possible to feel lonely when sharing a tin can with five other people, huh?'

She finally looks at me with a hint of surprise. I study her eyes, her expression. Is this woman responsible for everything she's been accused of? Is she my tormentor?

I lower myself a little, so I'm closer to her.

'I'm sorry,' I say. 'That you're not able to spend more time with us.'

'I get everything done,' she rushes. 'I'm pulling my weight, achieving my daily—'

'I know you are. We can all see that. It's just—'

'You don't think I want to be on the same cycle as you all? I'm trying.'

'I know,' I reassure her. If I'm to get anything out of her, I need to gain her trust. 'Morin said she found you floating in the hab earlier this morning?'

She nods. Takes another sip of her coffee.

'I was trying to stay up all night. I thought if I stayed awake, I'd be able to fall back in line with you all. But I just can't seem to. When you're awake, I feel so tired. And when it's time to sleep, my mind . . .'

Once again, she looks away from me. I lick my lips, my own thoughts whirring.

'What do you think about?' I ask. 'When you're totally alone. What do you do?'

She shrugs. 'I think of home. Of what brought me here.'

'And what was that?' I nudge.

Her lips twitch into a bitter smile and for the first time, I sense something raw. Something that can't be performance. She's tired, she's sad. She's vulnerable.

Slowly, as if trying not to startle a wild animal, I reach down to the mic pack around my waist and unplug it.

Ana's eyes follow my every movement.

I give a tiny nod towards her pod. She shifts herself a little, and then I'm inside, the curtains drawn. We're practically nose to nose; I can feel her hot breath, the hint of the coffee on it. It's been long enough for my own not to give away my nightly indulgence. But then again, perhaps she already knows.

We have sixty-eight seconds before Earth sees this and the purple warning light goes on, and they switch their live cameras to inside Ana's sleeping pod.

'I came here to escape,' she says simply.

'Escape what?'

'My world, my life, decisions that had been made for me.'

Usually I would probe gently, delicately. But there's no time.

'What kinds of decisions?'

'Bad ones.'

I wait with bated breath, but she doesn't elaborate. How much time has passed? Fifteen seconds? Twenty?

I need to push her. I have to get more.

'I was trying to escape from something too, you know.' I try to stop my voice from shaking. 'But even up here, I can't get away from it.'

I search her face for a sense of recognition, a flash of guilt, a moment of hesitation. But her beautiful eyes show nothing but sadness.

'I know how that feels,' she says, then her eyes flick towards the camera mounted in the corner of her sleeping pod. 'We left our planet behind, but we carry so much more with us.'

Our time must almost be up, and I have nothing. I'm vibrating with panic. I have to go all in.

'Ana,' I say. 'What Brun has been saying, what Alyssa . . . you can tell me. If someone asked you to—'

Her face hardens. I look behind me and see the light blinking on the camera.

Out of time.

We stare at each other.

Her face flushes. From shame? Anger?

'Ana—'

'Thank you for the coffee,' she clips, pulling back the curtain and letting the light stream in from the rest of the ship. 'I'll be ready in a moment.' Then that signature smile – the one that doesn't reach her eyes.

Clearly there's no chance of getting any further today.

Back in the hab, we're all in our M1s – our more formal uniform of dark chinos and branded polo shirts. Pinned to those shirts is the symbol for the *Mayflower* mission. Today, we're holding their memorial.

'How we looking?' Okeowo asks Dr Morin as I head back into the hab for my own coffee Thermos. Lars's moon rock shines in the soft light.

'Baikonur's put up a countdown for us.' She gestures to a small screen on one of the walls. Our distance from Earth is rapidly clicking upwards, while a new timer clicks downwards. We're approaching the final distance *Mayflower* made it to before disaster struck.

'The live memorial broadcast will begin an hour out. They'll start with studio stuff and VTs, then they'll join us live ten minutes before we drop the wreath.'

'What about the lag?' Lee asks, spinning in the air as he puts on a pair of black socks.

'We're not to worry about it,' Morin replies, taking a biscuit Okeowo offers her. It's a Tunnock's Tea Cake – one of Okeowo's luxuries she's been rationing out. 'When we hit the distance, we go. Sixty-eight seconds later, they'll watch.'

Lee rights himself and returns to his breakfast, crunching loudly on some Cheerios.

'What about, her?' Brun asks, looking up from his tablet.

'She's here,' Ana says, from behind me, and I turn. Her cheekbones are still a little flushed, but her eyes are perfectly framed by subtle liner. The bags under them look less dark, too. She must have something in her PPK that hides them. No one can look that good on only two hours' sleep.

The atmosphere in the hab shifts. It's been a long time since we were all in one room together. Lee ceases his crunching.

'Good morning, Ana.' Morin, ever the diplomat, smiles over to her. She dips into her pocket and floats over to her.

'Here.' She holds out a *Mayflower* badge to Ana, who looks down at it sombrely.

'So nice of you to grace us with your presence this morning,' Brun drawls. 'I see it's only an audience of millions that you deem worthy enough to wake up for.'

'That's enough,' Morin shoots, scowling at him. He spins and pushes himself away from the hab.

'Where are you going?' Okeowo calls.

'I have some readings to take!' he shouts back, disappearing off towards the greenhouse.

'He'll be here when it matters,' Morin reassures us. 'Rubio, could you check we're all set up by the airlock? The wreath is already in place, but make sure there's nothing blocking the camera.'

'Of course.' Lee resumes his breakfast as Okeowo goes back to some paperwork and Ana heads to the kitchen.

Crunch crunch crunch.

'And take Lee with you,' Morin adds, with only the slightest hint of irritation.

As I float out, Okeowo approaches Morin and leans in close to her, gives her a reassuring squeeze on the arm. I'm glad someone is also thinking of her. The comms have not been kind these past few days, and I think all of us have noticed how red her eyes are every morning.

The service will be held just outside the airlock. We've spent the last couple of days moving equipment out of the kit room that leads to it, so we all have space to hover and listen as Morin gives her speech, before we release the wreath. Inside the airlock, a mechanism will allow us to override the external doors and flush anything within into the vacuum of space.

Lee floats over to inspect the camera rig as we enter the room, still crunching on his last few Cheerios. I peer out into the airlock. There in the centre of it sits the wreath, shining in the harsh artificial light. It's a gold-plated copper laurel wreath, with a central plaque, and a radio communication system mounted behind it powered by solar panels. It's essentially a tiny wreath-shaped satellite. A beacon that will float through the solar system until it's smashed apart by meteoroids or knocked off course by some unknowable force.

The thick glass of the airlock door, coupled with the shine of the plaque, make the inscription illegible from here, but I know it reads:

IN GRATEFUL AND LOVING MEMORY OF THE BRAVE CREW
OF THE UNITED STATES SPACECRAFT
MAYFLOWER.
21 DECEMBER 2026.
FOR THE BENEFIT OF ALL.

Behind the solar panels there are also engravings of codes, numbers and schematics, to help any extraterrestrial intelligence who may pick up the wreath in the future decipher its meaning and its origins. It's not just a memorial; it's a message in a bottle.

It feels strange to think that soon, the object in front of me will be left behind us in the vacuum of space as we continue on our trajectory. We've checked time and again that nothing other than the wreath is in there. I had thought of placing my flask inside, disguising it as a piece of space junk left by accident. Or even strapping it to the wreath somehow. I'd be rid of it, for ever. But I quickly talked myself out of such madness. It would definitely be noticed, either before flushing or afterwards. And I couldn't taint the memory of the poor souls who died with my shame. I still sigh, though, at the missed opportunity. One like this won't come around again.

'I do feel sorry for her.' Lee's voice makes me jump – I'd almost forgotten he was here. I busy myself, pretending to buff the glass with a cloth.

'Oh?'

'She's alone most of the time. And Brun is being harsh, I think.'

I turn to face him as he tightens a screw on the camera mount.

'You've changed your tune,' I say, unable to keep the astonishment from my voice. When we first met her, he was the coldest towards Ana, his loyalty to Alyssa palpable in every word he uttered.

He shrugs. 'We're a team now. It's no good being hostile to her. We must help her instead – give her a reason to want to get back in sync with us.'

He glances at me, almost to see how his words have landed. My thoughts go to the moment I just had in Ana's sleeping pod. I felt like I was almost there. Within touching distance of finding out what was going on with her. If I can't do it, maybe he can. I adopt an encouraging expression.

'That's very wise, Lee. We should do more to bridge the gap with Ana. Extend the olive branch, so to speak.'

Lee's voice takes on much more confidence. 'I completely agree.

I'll . . .' He pauses, just slightly. 'I'll speak to her, make her feel more included.' He straightens up and gives me a little smile as he stows away his screwdriver.

I smile back. 'I'll do the same.'

Lee gives a thumbs up before spinning around to survey the rest of the room.

'I think this is good to go, so I'll just check the comms . . .'

And he's gone.

Did he just ask me for permission to get closer to Ana? It felt like it.

The *Mayflower* memorial distance is close now. We're assembled in a line facing the camera, our feet hooked onto footholds off-camera so we appear to be standing. Morin stands in front of the airlock, her hands behind her back, eyes focused just left of camera, where Okeowo has fastened some prompts for her speech. I am to the right of Morin, between Lee and Ana. Okeowo and Brun flank Morin on the other side.

We haven't spoken much since entering the room. It's like that moment at a funeral when the general mourners are waiting for the procession of those who are truly grieving. The family, the friends. We are merely witnesses, well-meaning supporters to those who are back on Earth who yearn for a sense of closure they'll never get.

'Here we go,' Morin says, as a light above the camera blinks.

Okeowo rubs her sleeve over the screen of the tablet computer she's holding. When the time comes, Morin will use it to open the airlock, which we've already depressurized.

Blink. Blink. Blink.

A breath from Morin, and then she begins.

'Good evening to our fellow people. Thank you for joining us this evening. As we approach the final distance the crew of the *Mayflower* reached on their mission to Mars, we honour them. On December twenty-first, 2026, seven intrepid astronauts lost their lives: John Robinson, Sam Rutherford, Joseph Rawkins, Temi

Okorafor, David Lynch, James Halligan, and Abigail Fukuhara. Together, we mourn their loss and great sacrifice.

'To their families, we feel your loss. Your loved ones were heroes, and their courage and commitment to exploration and discovery are an inspiration to us all. They worked for the greater good of humanity, and the people of Earth will forever be grateful. They will always be remembered.

'Nearly eighty-nine years ago, a fighter pilot in the Royal Canadian Air Force died while serving. The poem he wrote, just months before his death, has long been treasured by both aviators and astronauts. But the words of John Gillespie Magee Junior have never been more relevant than now. "*Oh! I have slipped the surly bonds of Earth . . .*"'

As Morin reads the poem, I feel strangely breathless. Who's to say that in the next few months our ship won't rip itself apart like the *Mayflower* did. Will anyone come this far ever again, to lay a wreath for us?

'"*. . . The high untrespassed sanctity of space, Put out my hand, and touched the face of God.*"

'As we approach their final distance, we will lay a wreath in their memory, which will stay at this orbit for eternity so that fellow explorers in the coming centuries may find it, and know what they achieved. Before we lay this wreath, please join us in a minute of silent reflection.'

Morin shifts to the side, to allow the camera a view of the wreath in the airlock. As I bow my head, I can see we're exactly seventy-five seconds out from the *Mayflower*'s terminal distance. It's mind-bending that in this sixty-second silence, we will travel thousands of kilometres. By this point, nearly all the *Mayflower* crew were gone. It was just Rutherford, scrambling to get back inside. It was when his communication cut off that the mission was officially lost. What must it have been like? The image of Lee's *Toy Story* alien spinning out into the nothingness of space flashes before me; a figure in M1s rotating round and round and round—

'And now . . .' Morin's voice breaks through my dark thoughts.

I snap my eyes open and return to the world of the living, and the brightness of the *Argo* kit room. The countdown is almost over.

'I lay this wreath, on behalf of all the people of planet Earth, for the brave souls who lost their lives on the *Mayflower*. Per aspera ad astra. May they rest in peace.' Morin places her finger on the tablet computer, and we all turn to look through the airlock's window.

The outer doors begin to slide open, and the slight difference in pressure does the trick as our wreath is released and begins to move out into space. It looks as though we're leaving it behind, gradually moving away from it as it edges out into the inky blackness, growing smaller and smaller. Some selfish inner voice also reminds me that we're now the furthest any human being has been from planet Earth. We six are the greatest explorers of all time . . .

I hear a sharp gasp, and a second later realize it's come from me. Something has come away from the bottom of the wreath. Have the others noticed it? Lee has: he thrusts his neck forward and one of his feet comes unhooked as he moves to get a better view.

Shit.

I glance across the room at Morin, whose eyes are wide. Okeowo's hand is covering her mouth, and Brun is frowning furiously.

I follow Morin's glance back towards the camera. The light is off; the broadcast has obviously switched to another angle, or back to the studio.

She unhooks her feet and launches herself to the airlock window. 'Lee, get us a close-up from the hull cameras. Now.'

Lee shoots out of the room and up to the command centre. Okeowo drifts over to take his place at the window.

'It looks like the plaque. Or is it the casing?' She squints.

No doubt Baikonur will be seeing this now. It's been more than sixty-eight seconds. They probably know more than we do.

Morin and Okeowo are still watching the wreath and the unidentified object recede. Brun unpins his *Mayflower* badge and looks at it thoughtfully, while Ana just stares out into space, a shocked expression on her face.

'I have it!' Lee yells, and we all propel ourselves to the door.

I let Morin and Okeowo through first. Brun nods at me as he leaves, and I turn back to see Ana hovering, hesitant. What's wrong with her?

'Come on.' I try to say it gently. She gives me a tight smile and precedes me out of the doorway.

Lee is zooming in on the image when I make it to the flight deck.

'Fuck,' Okeowo says, which is very out of character. A couple of us glance towards the nearest camera.

'It's the landing plaque,' Brun announces, moving away from the monitors.

'How can that be?' Okeowo asks, appalled. With Brun out the way, I move and look over her shoulder. There it is, clear as day: the commemorative plaque we are supposed to lay when we land on the surface of Mars. It reads:

HERE HOMO SAPIENS FROM THE PLANET EARTH
FIRST SET FOOT UPON MARS,
JULY 2031 CE

Followed by all our signatures, along with Anders'. His one bit of vanity in the whole thing: his name in the place where Nixon's signature was on the Apollo 11 lunar plaque.

It should be in storage. Instead, it's turning around and around in space, next to the *Mayflower* memorial wreath.

'How the hell did it get there?' I ask.

Morin hovers next to Lee, who's strapped himself into a chair.

'Pull up the airlock log,' she commands, and Lee begins to type. 'And shut the damn thing,' she adds, turning away from the screen and looking back at all of us.

She's not wearing her usual composed expression. She's angry. Furious. She looks at each of us in turn, her eyes boring into Brun, who returns her gaze, looking resigned. Then Ana, who hovers nervously. She's pulled her hair out of her bun and is twisting it between her hands. Then Morin looks at me, and I cringe away from the heat of her gaze. I have no idea how that thing got out there, of course, but I hate when she looks at me like that. She's a shrink, and it feels like she's analysing me, drawing out everything from within me until I confess all my sins in a blubbering wreck. And I have sinned. But not this.

Lee taps some more, then stops, reading.

'The airlock was last accessed at three forty-seven a.m. today,' he says, glancing back at Morin.

'A couple of times . . .' Okeowo adds as she peers at the data on Lee's screen.

'But it doesn't say who by.'

Morin's gaze sweeps over the group. 'Who did it?' The coldness in Morin's voice makes my stomach drop.

Silence. My mouth feels dry, all the way down my throat. Like sandpaper. I can't think of anything but the flask still tucked in my sleep bag.

'Whoever did it, must have done it on purpose,' Brun says almost lazily. 'That's no accident.'

A sniff from Ana, who is still twisting her hair round and round.

Morin's eyes rest on her.

Ana's eyes go wide, her eyeliner and mascara making her look like a cartoon character. Her mouth turns into a tiny 'o'.

'It wasn't me!' she cries. 'I was up, but I was looking at the *Perseverance* surveys, trying to stay awake. I was there, in the hab. Why would I do that?' Her voice is getting higher and higher.

'Well, who the hell else was it?' Brun growls, his eyes burning.

Ana turns back to Morin. 'Look at the cameras!'

Morin takes a few breaths then turns back to Lee, who's looking over the back of his chair at the rest of us, seemingly terrified.

'Lee?'

He nods and turns back to the monitors, typing again.

'The airlock first, please,' Morin says.

The footage of the airlock and kit room appear side by side

on the central monitor. The timestamp says 03:46:00:00. The seconds roll on. There's the wreath, exactly where it should be. The footage moves into 03:47:00:00 and onwards. 03:47:15:12. I blink. 03:47:16:02. I blink again. And then blackness blinks onto the screen.

Everyone flinches.

Then the brightness of the airlock and the kit room pops back up on screen, with the time stamp reading 03:54:00:00, before the seconds tumble on again once more.

Lee rewinds the footage. Plays it back again. And again. Each time, those seven minutes are missing.

Brun throws his hands up in the air, growls something in French and leaves the room, presumably off to his greenhouse. We hear a bang as he punches something on his way. Ana winces.

Morin says nothing. She stares at the monitor for a while, then puts her head in her hands.

Okeowo takes over in a motherly tone. 'Lee, my dear. What can you tell us about the blackout?'

'It's just . . . blank. The feed skips.' He sounds even more perplexed than when I confessed I'd never seen *Star Wars*.

'What about the other feeds?' Okeowo says. 'Why don't you run through—?'

'Check the hab,' Morin interjects. She's turned back to look at Ana, whose eyes widen again.

'I was there! You'll see.'

'Shhh,' Morin hisses.

Ana looks like she's been slapped in the face. Even I'm stunned. Morin has never acted like this before. She turns to Lee's screen like a woman possessed. His hands shake as he pulls up the hab feed and clicks to 03:35:00:00.

An image of Ana appears. She's floating, her blonde hair spread out around her head, curling in tendrils as she stares intently at a tablet screen. She's spread like a starfish, hovering over the surface we use as our dining table.

The seconds click by, and still she floats. I glance over to the real

Ana, who watches herself with a small frown. Is she concerned about what she'll be seen to do next? Or is she just worried about what she looks like on camera?

I turn back to the screen. At 03:43:13:00, Ana suddenly jolts and grabs for the table beneath her, pulling herself down to it and attaching the tablet to a small square of Velcro. Her blonde mane rolls to one side as her head turns towards the right-hand doorway. Almost as if she is looking at something . . .

And then at 03:47:16:50, black.

Lee is already tapping at his keyboard when the image of Ana pops up again. This time, with the timecode at 03:54:00:00, she's on the other side of the dining table, reading something on her tablet. But her body language is less relaxed, her hair not languishing as much in the microgravity.

'Shit,' I hiss.

'See!' Ana cries out. 'I was there.'

'We can see that, my love,' Okeowo says carefully. 'But there is seven minutes missing, still.'

'Just under seven minutes,' Lee corrects, as he cycles through all the camera feeds. They all go black at the same time.

'And it does look like you moved, my dear,' Okeowo says, careful to keep her voice neutral.

'I didn't do it!' Ana cries, thrusting her hands on her chest. 'I swear, on my life!'

'Ana,' I say as softly as possible, but everything within me is frozen. 'Did you leave the hab at any point?'

'No!'

'Not to go to the loo?' Okeowo asks, as if teasing the truth out of a child.

'I . . .' Ana falters. She must have pissed at some point. But when? Does she know she's being rumbled. 'I mean, yes but . . . not then . . . I'm sure. I moved, yes, but I think that's when I heard a sound. I thought someone else was up. But I couldn't see anyone, so I went back to my work. It wasn't me! Why would I do this?'

'I don't know,' is my honest reply. She's crying now, tears

clinging to her eyes. Is it true? Did she hear *someone else* moving about? The real perpetrator?

A noise breaks the tension. An alert. Baikonur is calling. Morin throws herself at the wall and picks up a headset, her back to us. The sixty-eight-second lag means we can't call directly with Baikonur, so we communicate in brief voice notes, and wait for well over two minutes between each recording. She listens for a while. We all wait, hoping she'll play it out loud to all of us.

Instead, she turns to us and quietly says, 'Get out.'

Lee scrambles to unstrap himself from the chair and launches into the air. Okeowo and I push ourselves off towards the door. On her way out, Okeowo takes hold of Ana's arm and tugs her along.

'But, it wasn't—'

'Come on.'

Morin straps herself into a chair in front of the monitors, her back hunched over, the weight of the whole mission on her shoulders.

Lee slides the door closed behind us.

'I'm going to check the cameras,' he mumbles, then heads back to the airlock and kit room.

'Ana,' Okeowo says, brightly. It must be taking her a lot of effort to sound cheery. 'Why don't you head back to sleep for a bit? This is going to take a while, and you must be knackered.'

'I can stay . . .' Ana says, glancing back at the door and the terror that is Morin behind it.

'No, dear. Best to stay out of the way, don't you think?'

Ana seems to wither and collapse in on herself. She nods, and floats down the tunnel back to the sleeping quarters.

Okeowo's shoulders slump. We look at each other, the two oldest on the crew. The two most tired.

'Cup of tea?' she asks.

'Sure,' I breathe. My mouth still feels so dry. It's not tea I'm yearning for. But it will have to do.

We make our way towards the hab, our minds whirring.

'You know,' Okeowo says over her shoulder, 'whoever did it has bloody balls.'

'Oh?' I say, only half listening. Trying to bury the thoughts of the flask.

'That plaque was stored in the bins by our sleeping bay. Whoever it was would have floated right past us while we all slept.'

My stomach flips. I was trying not to think about it, but deep down, I knew. I knew our landing plaque was kept in one of the other long-term storage bins, right behind the very one I'd been obsessively watching for the last couple of days.

Thirsty?

God, yes.

A blue and white sphere hangs in the abyss in front of me. The haunting tinkling of the piano on the folk track I'm playing floats through the recycled air. It's beautiful, nostalgic – earthy. The lunar eclipse retreats through the window as the artificial lights glare above, and the life-support systems hum on.

I'm in the cupola, a cubby-hole jutting out into the vacuum of space to the rear of the ship made purely for viewing. As I float, I'm acutely aware that this is both the furthest away from home I have ever been, yet I will never again be closer to that pale blue dot than I am right now. My mind can't comprehend it.

I place another tea cake in my mouth, not taking my eyes off the view.

I become aware of Dr Morin lowering herself down next to me. We don't say anything for a while; she, too, seems to be absorbing the sights. Then I push the ziplock bag containing Okeowo's tea cakes towards her.

She eyes them, then me, eyebrows raised. She knows I didn't get them legitimately, but she takes one anyway. The current song fades into the next.

'Why folk music?' she asks. 'You're not even British.'

I smile and take another bite of my tea cake, careful not to let loose any crumbs.

'Does there always have to be a reason why someone likes a particular thing?' I ask.

'With you? Yes.' Morin laughs, tucking into her treat.

'It's green and grounded. Everything Mars won't be.' I lean over to steal back the packet of tea cakes. 'Spaceflight has always been accompanied by overblown, dramatic music, like Holst's crescendos, and huge horns. Or, did you see that one where that stranded astronaut was stuck listening to disco? I can't think of anything worse.' Another song begins, this time a chirpy fiddle. 'No. This is the music of Earth. And we are creatures of it, so it feels right that it should accompany us on our journey.'

Heather nods her understanding, and we munch companionably for a while.

'What did they say?' I find myself asking.

'Hmm?' she replies, distracted.

'Baikonur.' I reposition myself so I can see her better in the faint Earth-light.

'They're investigating.'

'And?'

She turns to me. 'And I'm not obliged to tell you everything that Baikonur communicates with me, Rubio.'

I hold my hands up in surrender, and she turns back to Earth. She doesn't leave, though. I push the ziplock back her way. It turns over and over and hits the inside of the cupola window before ricocheting off. Morin watches it tumble.

'Alyssa told us not to trust her,' I say.

'Alyssa was displacing her frustration and anger onto someone else.'

'Or, she was onto something.'

Morin bats the cakes back to me, untouched.

'They said the launch after us is delayed.'

My eyebrows shoot up my forehead. 'The supply capsule?'

'Yes.'

'Why?'

'Revenue hasn't been what they expected. They're merging two missions into one to save expenditure and reassessing the timelines for when we build the second research base. And the second crewed launch has been delayed. Indefinitely.'

Fuck. That was our next chance to see other human beings. Without that . . . well it will be just the six of us for a hell of a lot longer.

'Why the shortfall?'

'Ratings.' She grimaces. 'You're just not exciting enough, Rubio.'

I could have told her that years ago. We both look to the planet we're discussing. The one that, apparently, isn't looking back.

'Has Anders been in touch?'

'He responded after I requested it. Finally.'

'And . . .?'

'He says he's not worried. That this was to be expected, there was always going to be a period like this. *"The problem with epic journeys is that they're long, but the destination is worth it."* Or something like that.'

I nod. That sounds like my old friend.

'The memorial mishap caused a spike. Just like Alyssa's . . .' she searches for the right word. 'Episode.'

'Makes sense, I suppose,' I say gloomily.

'I'd just prefer it if we didn't need to rely on shit going wrong for us to get the supplies we need.'

An alert goes off deep within the ship and Brun shouts French expletives at Lee. Morin rolls her eyes.

'You know, seeing how grumpy he is, I'm starting to wonder why Brun ever agreed to come. He seems to find us all so frustrating.'

'I think all of us have probably questioned why we're here at one point or another,' I reply.

'People down there can't seem to stop speculating about my reasons,' she says, bitterly.

'What are they, really?' I ask, intrigued.

Morin floats closer to the windows, staring intently at the planet where her children remain. 'Neil Armstrong had two boys when he went to the moon.' She places a finger on the window and taps it lightly. 'For centuries, fathers left their families behind and set off for a new life across the Atlantic. Or across the world to Australia, never looking back.' Her voice is low, perhaps trying to defy the mics, or maybe she's just talking to herself. 'I don't remember people ever asking why they did it.'

I float closer to her and gaze out at the tiny blip of colour, at the very oceans she's speaking of.

'It was Max who wanted the kids,' she continues. 'He'd let me pursue my career for so long, heading off to the Antarctic once a year for long-term isolation experiments. I felt like it was his turn to fulfil *his* purpose. And I love our children. I was surprised by how much I loved them as soon as they arrived. Is that a strange thing for a mother to say?' She glances at me, but I keep my face neutral. Who am I to judge her? She shakes her head. 'Once I went back to work, though, I was so frustrated that I couldn't be part of the missions, that I was now analysing data collected by others. But when this came in . . . this once in an epoch opportunity to ensure humanity has a future . . .'

As a sad flute echoes around us, I wait, hoping she'll carry on. But the moment is gone.

'Heather, do you think that Ana . . .' I begin, hardly knowing how to phrase what I'm about to say. 'Do you think that Ana—'

'Don't even finish that sentence.' She looks mad all of a sudden. 'Baikonur are investigating. Until we know what happened, I will not have accusations flying around. This ship will only function if we all work with each other and trust each other.'

She pushes herself away from the window, and away from me, turning her back on our home planet. As she leaves, she calls back over her shoulder. 'And put those cakes back where they belong.'

Guilty, I snatch the bag out of the air and glance out at the darkness. A new melody begins, and a woman's voice surges. It's beautiful, but I don't speak Irish so don't know what it's about.

Yet another thing that is lost to me.

Alyssa

I EMERGE FROM THE DOCTOR'S OFFICE, FINALLY CAST-FREE. It feels bizarre, as if my foot has been born anew. It's like what I was anticipating after months in micro-g. Almost. But I'm still not entirely unencumbered; I have to wear a boot for a few weeks. But I can walk. I can move. I can rebuild the wasted sinews of my muscles.

I spend the next few days working out on Jacob's old exercise bike, determined to build up my strength. My leg still struggles to support my full weight, and every morning the moisturizer I put on the night before has congealed into gross lumps with the dead skin. But I'm making progress – in more ways than one.

The more exercise I do, the hungrier I get, and the more I crave Martha's cooking. So once again, I'm heading down to the restaurant on a Saturday night, even though I know it's going to be busy. I purposely go late, hoping I can miss the rush.

Martha seamlessly switches the television from Mars One over to a news channel as I enter the restaurant. She doesn't think it's healthy for me to watch. By the sounds of it, not many people are. Martha's seems to be one of the few public places that plays it – after all, her beloved Jacob is involved.

Feeling a couple of eyes on me, I take my usual seat in a booth at the back. By now my presence hasn't gone entirely unnoticed by the locals, but Martha's made it clear that no one is to bother me, and the threat of being banned from the restaurant is enough to keep tongues from wagging to the press.

On the TV, the news is reporting on protests in San Francisco, where the Golden Gate Bridge has been blocked for days by Terra Revolution. I watch the futility of it all, as army experts attempt to scale the bridge's supports to detach the hanging nests of protestors suspended in the Bay mist.

Martha weaves her way to me. She looks tired tonight. 'Usual, honey?'

'Please,' I say, and she smiles wearily before moving back over to the kitchen doors.

I settle in, watching the people around me. Chatting. Looking at their phones. Showing their companion a video. One person does seem to be watching the television, perched on the edge of her seat, gripped by the chaos.

She looks a state. Her hair is pinned up in a bun on her head and her clothes look well-worn. Her sneakers, perched on the metal bar of the table in front of her, are practically falling apart. By her feet lies a big rucksack, patched with duct tape.

I watch her a while, wonder what her story is. Perhaps she's one of Martha's strays – sometimes she offers a free meal to someone who looks in need of it.

As if to confirm it, a plate is placed down in front of her and she begins to stuff it into her mouth. Then she picks up a rasher of bacon and rips it into pieces.

She's attracting quite a few stares now from nearby diners, but she seems oblivious. Eyes glued to the television, she reaches down to the pack beneath her feet, fumbles to open the top and throws in a few bacon shreds.

I frown, intrigued.

A minute later, her hand moves down to the pack once again. This time, she bends right down as though about to stick her whole head in.

I do a double take. I swear I saw a little white paw batting at the bacon as it fell in.

The girl seals the bag back up and returns to her dinner as if nothing has happened. Then a man comes in and sits down at the vacant table next to her. Martha signals that she'll be with him soon. He nods at her before burying his face in the menu.

The girl turns and for the first time I can see her whole face. She's East Asian, and looks young, but tired. She looks at the man next to her with an unnerving intensity. There's tension in her shoulders as she leans over and speaks to him. He looks up, startled, taking in her threadbare clothes. She smiles nervously and says something earnest. I shift forward in my seat, trying to hear her, but she's speaking so quietly and the rest of the restaurant is so loud.

Whatever she says, he shakes his head and her face falls. She looks devastated. She says something else to him, her head bobbing, and he leans away from her. In apparent desperation, she reaches into her bag, fishes out a scrappy piece of paper and unfolds it, moving towards him again.

'I'm sorry.' He raises his voice above the din. 'I have no idea what you're talking—'

But my attention is snatched by the ball of ginger and white fur that is creeping out of the young woman's bag. A tail flicks underneath the tables, and then—

CLANG.

A cat is on the man's table, blinking up at him before tucking into the previous diner's leftovers Martha has yet to collect.

The man cries out, pushing himself back from the table. The cat seems unfussed, and continues chomping on some fish skin.

The girl looks mortified.

'No!'

Martha rushes over.

'You can't have that in here!'

'I'm sorry, let me get him,' the girl blurts. She clearly speaks good English, but it's not her native tongue. She lunges for the cat, but he springs over to the next table.

'You have to go.' Martha turns to the gentleman. 'I'm so sorry Mr Webb. Shoo!' Martha flicks her towel at the cat, which drops down off the table.

'Please let me stay,' the girl begs, her face creased with anguish. 'I need to find someone.'

But her cries startle the cat and it darts under another table. Diners jump up at the feeling of something rushing past their legs. The poor busboy making his way to the kitchen is knocked by a man thrusting his chair back and the whole bowl of soapy dishes he's carrying flies into the air. It splashes over several customers and the blur of fur leaps and bounces off a wall and onto a table, plates and cutlery flying everywhere.

'Orion!' cries the girl as she chases the ball of fur.

Martha stands in shock as her beautiful restaurant descends into chaos. I grab some bacon from the girl's plate, which has miraculously managed to stay on the table, and snatch a towel from the busboy.

As the cat circles back round towards me, I throw some bacon in its path. It doesn't stop, but there's a moment of hesitation and I pounce, wrapping the towel around it, and it freezes.

The girl turns to me, tears streaming down her cheeks.

'This yours?' I ask her.

She nods and takes the bundle from me, hugging it close, whispering to it.

In the renewed calm, Martha recovers her senses.

'I'm so sorry, everybody. Dinner is on the house. We'll have it back to normal for you in no time.'

She heads over to the girl and her bundle. 'Needless to say,' she says quietly. 'You should leave.'

The girl sniffs, resigned, and picks up her pack, all the while clinging to the bundle as though her life depends on it.

'Sorry,' she mumbles as she picks her way out towards the front door. She looks so small, so helpless.

'Great catch, Alyssa,' Martha says. 'Ready for your food?'

I can't take my eyes off the girl skirting around the people and avoiding their judging gaze.

'You know what, Martha, don't worry about the stew. I'll just take the frybread to go.'

The girl's head snaps up and she looks directly at me, her mouth open.

'Give me a moment, yeah?'

Martha nods then hurries off to help one of her customers who has soda all over her lap.

I move towards the door and nod at the girl, who can't seem to stop staring. Without a word, she follows me out into the night. I duck under the awning, away from the rain that's pounding onto the sidewalk. The girl drops the cat back into her bag and pulls her jacket tight around her.

'I don't know much about them, but I don't think cats are supposed to be carted around,' I say, regarding her curiously. She shoulders the backpack again and shrugs.

'He likes it now.' The 'now' sounds heavy, like she's come a long way. Before I can work out what the hell I'm doing out here with a stranger, she says, 'You ordered frybread.'

I fold my arms, my natural defences rising. 'What's it to you?'

'Is that your name?'

'What the hell?' I laugh. But from her expression I can tell she's deadly serious.

'No, my name is not . . . Frybread.'

She sags, her head falling into her hands.

I sigh and take out my wallet. 'It looks like you and your friend need a few good meals. I don't know the area, but how about—'

'I'm not a beggar,' she barks.

'Can I help you with anything else, then?'

She shakes her head, and I don't think I've ever seen someone look more defeated. Then she jumps up. 'Actually, do you know anything about this?' She rummages in her pocket and pulls out the same tatty piece of paper she showed the man inside.

I peer at what looks like a senseless stream of numbers, and shake my head.

'It's code,' she says, like it might help.

'I'm sorry,' I say again. 'I really wish I could help.'

She gives an almighty sob. 'I'm looking for my brother.' She blows her nose loudly. 'It's his cat. His code. He was looking for errors in it, but he's missing and I don't know where he is.'

I freeze as a thrill of adrenaline shoots through me.

'What did you say?'

'My brother,' she repeats, taken aback at my intensity. 'He's missing.'

'You said he was looking for errors in a code?'

She nods slowly, holding out the scrap of paper. 'This is something he found. It mentions this restaurant. I thought if I came here, I might find him.'

'And he's missing?'

Her heart looks as if it's breaking as she says, 'Yes.'

I step back and rub my face. This is madness. She's a random girl in a restaurant who happens to have a missing brother. And yet . . . he was working on a code, with errors. And it led her here . . .

Coincidence is just a matter of probability. But what are the odds?

Then my eye snags on a car on the other side of the road. It has no lights on, but two figures are sitting in the front, one lit up by the light of a screen. Is that a camera he's aiming towards me? It's hard to see through the rain.

'Shit.' The girl frowns in confusion, then follows my eyeline. She tenses.

'*Diu!*' she cries, clutching her bag closer.

I grab her arm at the same moment she grabs mine. We look at each other, her eyes wide.

'They've found me!' she breathes.

'What?' I ask, eyes darting back to the car. 'They're after me.'

'No!' she insists. 'They're after me.'

Clearly there are some crossed wires here, but I refuse to stand around and let those bastards spy on me. I yank at her arm. 'Come with me.'

I duck out into the rain and she trots along to keep up with me. Even with my limp, she takes two strides for every one of mine as we head off in the opposite direction to Jacob's flat. We'll go down an alley between two shops further down and then loop back round.

'Where are we going?' she sounds scared now.

'My place. Don't worry, I just want to talk to you.'

'Who are you?' she asks, her breath quick.

'Alyssa,' I tell her. 'Come on, this way.'

'I'm – I'm Jia.'

I don't respond, too busy checking both ways as we emerge out of the alley and I march us down a different street.

We make it back to Jacob's apartment without anyone following us – that I could tell, anyway. It's only when we're through the door and I've shut it tight behind us that I realize I've been holding my breath. I dart through to the living room and peep through the blinds before shutting the curtains. I keep the main lights off and click on one of the low lamps. My leg throbs from the burst of movement.

When I turn back around, the girl – Jia – is still standing by the door of the apartment, looking terrified, soaked to the skin, and clutching the bag.

'Do you want a glass of water?' I gesture at the kitchen.

She makes her way into the room to join me, casting her wary eyes around the place. I hand her a glass and make my face as reassuring as possible.

'No one followed us.' That's not something I can guarantee, of course, but it seems to do the trick. Her shoulders drop and she accepts the water, places it down on the table in front of her, then bends down to her bag. She looks back up at me, a silent request for permission.

'Sure.' I head to the fridge to grab a Coke.

I hear the scrambling of the cat, and turn back round to see its tail disappearing underneath the couch. The girl perches there, shivering. I swipe my old NASA sweatshirt from the back of a chair and toss it to her. She catches it and swaps it for her own sodden jacket.

'Do you want something to eat?' I ask. She nods again. She's very quiet all of a sudden.

I utter a curse as I remember I didn't pick up my order from Martha's. I peer into the fridge gloomily. There's some salami. A couple of bites of cheese. Some crackers. I make up a meagre plate – my mother would be so ashamed – and place it on the coffee table for Jia. I hold up an extra couple of slices of salami. 'For your friend?'

'Thank you,' she replies with a small smile, and I leave the meat by the corner of the couch then sit down on the armchair opposite her.

The silence drags on.

Jia looks to her left and sees some of the pictures on the side table, then looks around the rest of the room.

'This isn't your place?' she asks.

'It's a . . .' I hesitate. 'A friend's place. He's abroad.' She looks down at the plate on the table. 'In Kazakhstan.'

Am I hoping that she'll recognize it? That she'll suddenly put two and two together and know who I am? It's astounding she hasn't recognized me already, given the news coverage over the last month.

In the corner of my eye, a little paw darts out from under the couch and pats at the salami. After a couple of attempts, its claws sink in and the salami disappears. As though synchronized, Jia takes a chunk of cheese from the plate and nibbles on it. As soon as it goes in her mouth something is unleashed and she pulls the entire plate onto her lap and proceeds to devour everything on it, like she hasn't eaten properly in days.

I watch, fascinated, sipping my Coke.

She looks embarrassed after she's finished, and places the plate back on the table with precision.

'Thank you.'

A car roars past outside and she jumps about a foot in the air. She eyes the curtained windows nervously.

'Earlier, on the street –' She snaps back around to face me – 'you said "they've found me". What did you mean?' The cat emerges and rubs itself around her feet. She bends down, picks it up and places it on her lap. It stares at me as she strokes it, its eyes never leaving mine. It's a little unnerving.

'I thought it might be . . . them.' The way she says 'them' makes me put my drink down.

'You're not from the US, are you?' I lean forward. She shakes her head in reply. 'So is it ICE? Immigration?'

'No,' she says. The cat is purring now, but is still looking at me like it wants to kill me.

'The police, then?'

She stops stroking and tenses up.

'I . . .' I think she's considering lying, but then she slumps as though defeated. 'I don't know.'

I look at her expectantly, hoping she'll elaborate, but she just carries on stroking the damn cat.

'OK,' I sigh, leaning back. 'I'm sorry, Jia, but either you're having one hell of a fucking week or you're lying. Or maybe both.'

Jia barks a bitter laugh, which makes both me and the cat jump. I sit forward again, encouraged at this sign of life. Eventually, she looks back at me, and smiles, almost in apology.

'You have no idea,' she says.

'I'm pretty sure they weren't after you, by the way,' I try and reassure her again. 'They were likely after me.' She looks quizzical. 'Do you honestly not know who I am?' I ask.

She shakes her head again.

I click on the TV and there it is. The *Argo*. Rubio and Okeowo are eating in the communal hab. The sound is off, but it looks like they're making light conversation as the camera shots cycle around from different angles. Lee hovers in the background.

Jia watches, then looks at me, her face blank.

'Mars One,' I say simply. She looks back at the screen.

'Yes, I've heard of it,' she says slowly.

My turn to laugh. 'I would've thought so. That's my crew, on the *Argo*.'

She turns back to me, curious. 'Did you build the spaceship, then?'

Wow.

Where has she been the last few months? Evidently my incredulity is clear on my face, because her cheeks flame red.

She shrugs. 'I haven't been following the news recently.'

No shit.

Where do I even begin? But there's something inside of me that feels relieved. There are some people out there who don't know my tragic little story. For the first time, it feels like there might be a time, a world, in which I won't feel like a dead woman walking.

'It's a long story, but essentially, I was one of the astronauts who was meant to go to Mars. I was actually the commander of the mission. But I got injured and err . . . I left.'

Jia absorbs all this in silence. The cat closes his eyes, as if I'm boring him.

'Anyway, it's getting a lot of press attention and I've been avoiding people so I can get some privacy. I'm pretty sure the people in that car were looking for me. So please, don't worry. You're safe, for now.'

She runs a finger up the bridge of the cat's nose, and its purrs deepen.

'Why?' she asks, after what feels like an age.

'I'm sorry?'

'Why would you go to Mars . . . for ever?'

I open my mouth to answer, but I can't seem to find the words. I push up off the armchair and grab my empty Coke.

'Do you want another drink?'

'No, thank you.'

I open another drink and take a swig, considering Jia as she watches me.

'Enough about me. Your turn for explanations.'

Jia

'AND HE DISAPPEARED WHEN?' ALYSSA ASKS, STARING ME OUT.

'Just over two months ago.' Saying it aloud makes me breathless.

Alyssa moves around the back of the couch and begins pacing. 'Your brother's friend – Ella?'

'Erica,' I blurt, reddening at her name. I've tried calling the number so many times, but it doesn't even ring any more.

'She said your brother is hired to find errors in big projects.'

'Yes.'

'And there's code, presumably with errors, inside that cat.' She gestures towards Orion.

'We think so. I'm trying to find the person who wrote the code, and apparently there's some connection to that restaurant.'

She stops pacing and stares intently at Mars One on the screen.

'Is there anything in this code about Mars One?'

I blink at her, then turn to the TV.

'Or does it mention the *Argo*?' She comes close to me, crouching down to my level.

I shrink back from her burrowing stare. 'I have no idea. There was just one bit Agnes recognized – the signature, they called it. Frybread.'

'Frybread,' Alyssa repeats. I nod.

Orion rolls over, batting at me to keep stroking. I smile down at him, reassured by the warm weight of him on my lap. Kai wouldn't recognize either of us.

Alyssa moves over to the dining table and toys with some papers. I peer over the couch. They look like apartment listings.

She pushes them away.

'I need to call someone,' she says, almost to herself. She strides over to a drawer in the kitchen and pulls out an old cell phone.

Her fingers fly as she types something into the phone, then waits. I peer back at the screen, at the people travelling to a new world. What the hell could they have to do with my brother and his cat?

Both Alyssa and I jump out of our skin as the landline trills. It's mounted on the wall, like something out of the early noughties.

Alyssa dashes over to it.

'Hello?' she pauses. 'Martha? Yes, put him through. Thank you.'

She holds the handset flat and hits speaker.

'Lyss?'

'Jake!' Alyssa says breathily. She's slightly flushed, and there's a new warmth in her words. 'Thank you so much.'

'Why the urgency? I can't speak long.'

'I know, listen.' Her voice is fevered. 'The code, all the bugs you've been finding—'

The voice groans. 'Lyss, not again. This is not health—'

'There's a missing coder who found errors in some sort of confidential project.'

'What are you talking about?'

'I've got someone here with me now. Her brother is a bounty hunter, with code. Do you know what I mean?'

'Well, yeah, but—'

'He disappeared two months ago and this girl, Jia, has a section of the code he was trying to fix.'

'Lyss—' he says slowly, almost like a warning.

'Listen to me, Jake! He's a missing coder, who found something wrong in a code and who disappeared just before the mission kicked off, and now she's turned up here. This can't be a fucking coincidence.'

'He could have been working on anything, Lyss. Look, I can't be talking to you right now, I have to go—'

'You said they were considering bringing others in to deal with the code,' she blurts. 'What if they already did and they found something you missed? Come on, Jake. Please hear me out?'

A tinny sigh sounds through the phone.

'Fine, I'll bite. Does this girl know what the code says?'

Alyssa looks at me pointedly.

'Err . . . hello?' I say, my voice small.

'Hi. I'm Jake. I'm sorry about Lyss, she's . . .' Alyssa shoots a filthy look at the phone. 'Jia, is it?'

'Yes.'

'I'm sorry about your brother. This, er, code. Do you know what it refers to?'

'I'm sorry. I can't read it.'

He breathes deeply again. Alyssa looks almost heartbroken.

'Lyss, I'm sorry but this is crazy. If you want, I'm happy to look at the code and see if I can help this girl find her brother, but I really don't think this has anything to do with Mars One.'

Alyssa closes her eyes and bites her lip.

'Lyss,' he says, much softer now. 'You were doing so well. Please, don't let this ruin the progress you've made.'

'I know,' she says, her voice breaking a little. 'Believe it or not, I don't want to be right about this. But she said there's one thing her friends could make out. A signature from the original coder.' Her voice is pleading. 'It's what led her to Martha's. Tell him, Jia,' Alyssa begs.

'Frybread,' I offer. 'The signature is for someone called Frybread.'

The phone goes silent.

'Frybread?' Jake says, razor-sharp.

Alyssa and I stare at each other. Even I can tell something has shifted in Jake's voice.

'Yes,' I answer.

'Jia,' Jake says, shakily, 'can you send me the code?'

Alyssa looks at me.

'Sorry, I can't. It's on my brother's cat's microchip. I can't get at it. And what I do have . . . it's not a lot. It's just a small section with the signature—'

'Can you find a way to get all the code out?' he cuts in.

'No!' I cry. Alyssa jumps at my sudden shout. I shrink back. 'Sorry, but if we take the microchip out of Orion, the chip will wipe. And Orion has to be alive. He's the chip's power source.'

'Fuck,' he mumbles. 'Maybe if you scan it, you can send it to me, or even read it to me. If—'

'Jake,' Alyssa interrupts, her voice shaking. 'What's so important about the signature?'

A long, unbearable pause.

'It's me,' Jake says, almost sadly. 'I'm Frybread.'

Alyssa

'HOLY FUCKING SHIT!' I HEAR MYSELF SAY, THE IMPLICATIONS spinning out faster than I can keep track of them. If what Jia is saying is true, and people are chasing her halfway across the world for this, the bugs in the code aren't just glitches. There must be something wrong with the ship. Something huge. And the key to what that might be has just turned up on my fucking doorstep. All we need is the chip in the cat.

The cat.

Where's the damn cat?

I dart over to the couch. There he is. I manage to get my hands around him and he cries out as I pull him towards me. His claws find my flesh. FUCK. That hurts, but I hold on.

'Let him go!'

I turn to Jia, who looks shocked and furious, and I shove the cat into her arms. He melts into her chest, glaring at me.

'Hold him!' I command, and then go for his neck. 'Where is it?'

The cat flinches again, but I've got it. There. Beneath the fur. It's hard.

'You're hurting him!' Jia says.

I steer her and the cat back to the kitchen, still holding the lump on his neck. I head straight to one of the drawers and just as my spare hand seizes a knife, Jia realizes what I'm doing.

'No!' She yanks him away from me, squeezing him tight. 'Are you crazy?'

Actually, I'm not. I'm perfectly calm. This is the obvious next step.

'I told you,' Jia says. 'It'll wipe if you cut it out. It needs Orion to be alive. It relies on his heartbeat, or something. Besides.' She glares at me, voice raised. 'You can't cut him open! What the fuck is wrong with you?'

And so we stand there. Frozen. Her with the cat in her arms, and me with a knife in my hand. If the entire existence of my crew weren't at stake, it would be laughable.

I look down at the cat, its chest rising and falling so rapidly.

I slump. The knife goes back down on the counter.

'What do we do?' I ask.

'I don't know,' Jia mutters, burying her head in Orion's fur.

'Jia,' I say, a wheedling edge to my voice. 'If there is an error with the *Argo*'s code . . . I don't even know how to finish that sentence. It could be fatal to the mission – and to the crew.'

Jia relaxes her grip on the cat and it takes the chance to jump onto the kitchen counter, down the other side and back under the couch.

'Fine.' Jia steps forward. 'We send a picture of the code we *do* have to Jake, and in the meantime he can tell me where the fuck my brother is.'

Jake. He's still on the line.

'It's not as easy as that,' I say to Jia as I stride back over to the phone. 'Jake? Did you hear all that?'

'Yeah. Lyss, are you all right?' His voice is full of concern.

'Yes, sorry. What do you think we should do?'

He pauses and I imagine him running his hands through his hair, his eyes full of concern. I wish half the world weren't between us right now.

'I think this is serious,' he says. 'If people are willing to kidnap for this code? Something about it must be mission-critical.'

'I don't care about your mission!' Jia calls out, marching over and snatching the phone off me. I'm too shocked to object. 'You're Frybread. You wrote this damn thing. Where's my brother?'

'I'm sorry, Jia, I don't know! I didn't even know they had other people looking at this. Whoever took your brother, it's not us, I swear. Not that I know of, anyway.'

Jia seems to take a moment to absorb that, then hands the phone back to me and slumps against the wall.

'Then what the hell do I do now?' she whispers.

It's a good question.

'Lyss, send me what code you do have.'

I look to Jia and she wordlessly hands over her scrap of paper. It takes a few goes with the shitty camera on the burner phone I've been using to talk to Martha, but I finally manage a clear photo.

'OK, I have it,' I tell him.

He breathes out heavily. 'You're gonna have to send it to me on this number. I'll wipe it as soon as I get it.'

I open up the encrypted messaging service Jake directs me to and hit send.

The seconds tick by excruciatingly slowly.

'I got it,' Jake clips.

More painful seconds crawl by.

Another sigh. 'This is the tiniest sample. It barely contains anything, mostly just my signature. I need to see more to know what it does.'

'It's in the damn cat,' I snap, even though I know none of this is his fault. Well, except for the fact that it's clearly his code that's fucked.

'You know, I have a friend. At Purdue,' Jake says slowly. 'He teaches coding now. If you could get the cat to him, I'm sure he could—'

'No.' Jia is up off the wall again, standing as tall as she can manage. 'No one else.'

I move forward, trying to calm her, to let Jake talk, but she pushes my hand away. 'Jia—'

'I said no.' There's a fire within her that I've not seen yet, and it makes me pause. 'There's already a bounty on my head, on my friends' heads, for all this. Whoever is after this, they've chased me across the world. Every time I've stopped, they've found me. I can't trust anyone.'

The way she looks at me, I know she's also saying, *Not even you.*

'So, no more strangers,' she continues. Despite her strong words, she's shaking. 'There's only one option: we go to Jake. With Orion.'

Despite the seriousness of the moment, I burst out laughing.

'Jia, he's in Baikonur.'

She just crosses her arms.

Fuck. She may almost be as pig-headed as me.

'She might be right,' Jake's voice calls out. 'I have to see this code in its entirety. And we don't know how long the crew might have before the error causes serious issues.'

I look back to the TV. If a glitch can corrupt the communications systems, what else could also be fucked? Guidance? The code that manages the fuel tanks? The life support? I feel a stab of fear.

'But I can't leave Baikonur, and it would help if I had access to the *Argo*'s software. If you can get it here—'

'They won't let me within twenty miles of there,' I scoff.

'Jia,' I turn to find her watching me, wary, 'is there any chance we could borrow the cat. Send it to Kazakhstan so that—'

'No!' she yells, jolting forwards as if I've just suggested we cut her arm off. I instinctively pull back. Is she going to blow? But then she closes her eyes and takes a deep breath, before settling a steely gaze on me.

'I get it, OK?' Her voice wavers, like she's suppressing a storm of emotion underneath, but she remains in control. 'Your crew might be in danger. But my brother *is* in danger. He is missing, and the only clue I have is in his cat. In fact, this cat is the only damn thing I have left in this world. And you want to take him? No. He is my brother's. He is mine. Where he goes, I go. And you only get us to go anywhere if you promise to help me find my brother.' She chokes on that last word. It reverberates through my bones. Even Jake is silent.

BANG BANG BANG.

'OPEN UP!' someone yells. My head whips around to the door of the apartment, but it's not coming from there. It's coming from outside. I run to the window, part the blinds. There are people outside, as well as cars and vans. Lots of them. And figures are rushing into the first floor. 'Shit!' I run to the apartment door and open it a crack. More yelling. More bangs.

'*Down on the ground. Hands in the air!*' The terrified sounds of Jake's neighbours in reply.

Then the lights go out.

We have to get out of here. I slam the apartment door shut, bolt it and head to Jia.

She is still. So still.

'Jia!' I shake her. 'Now is not the time to freak out on me. Who did you say was after you?'

'I – I don't—'

BANG. Louder. Closer.

'People with guns?' I ask.

She nods.

'Fuck.'

I grab the phone again.

'Jake. We have to run. Someone is here!' I slam it down and run to the dresser in the hall, dragging it in front of the apartment door.

'Jia!' I call. Footsteps on the stairs outside. 'Grab the damn cat!'

She stares at me for a moment, and then she's calling the cat's name and grabbing her bag. I do the same, scrambling for my wallet.

BANG. The loudest yet. On Jake's door, this time.

'*Open up!*'

I can't let them take her. Not when she might be the only thing that can save the *Argo*.

I take deep, calming breaths as my mind whirrs. The fire escape is out – they'll definitely be covering it. The bathroom window? It's on the other side of the building and there are dumpsters below it. That could work. But where the fuck is Jia?

'Jia, come on!' I grab her and try to drag her through to the other side of the apartment but she won't budge. 'Orion!' she calls, swiping her arm under the sofa. 'We can't go without him!'

Explosions thunder in my ears, and wood flies from the apartment door. I smell burning. Smoke.

I drop down to the ground, covering my head.

'They're not fucking messing around. They'll shoot us!'

'Orion! Please!' Jia cries, on her belly now.

It's too late. I grab her by her legs and pull.

'Noooo!' she yells. 'Orion!'

I wrestle with her and pull her onto her feet. I drag her out of the room, the bag still in her hand.

'Orion!'

Something flies through the hole in the door.

CLANG CLANG. PSSSSSSSS.

I cry out in horror. They're gassing us. I throw my arm over my mouth as I drag Jia to the bathroom. We only have seconds.

'Orri— hgghhgh—' she calls, coughing and spluttering.

And then we're at the window, and I leave Jia retching as I use the bath caddy to smash the glass open. The fresh air that hits us is glorious.

But then the apartment door breaks and they're in. I grab Jia and thrust her over the bath.

'Go!' I scream.

Suddenly, all her resistance falls away and she clambers through. I glance behind us. In the bathroom mirror, black figures with guns are sweeping into the living room. More smoke grenades fly.

And then Jia is through and I'm launching myself out of the window, using my sleeves to cover my wrists as I scramble over the broken glass. The damn boot is a dead weight as I heave it over the ledge.

And then I'm falling.

My injured ankle screams as it hits the garbage bags, but we're out. I push Jia's ass with all my might as she hauls herself over the edge of the dumpster.

'Go,' I urge, my heart pumping hard enough to leap out of my chest.

'Orion!' Jia still yells, even as she makes it onto the sidewalk.

I look up at the sound of gunshots from above, and am astounded to see a shadow launching itself from the window. It tumbles, but rights itself in the air and sticks the landing.

Jia screeches and runs towards it as I tumble out of the dumpster, throw myself towards her, grab her jacket and drag her down the alley.

We duck at the sound of two more gunshots in quick succession. They hit brickwork – and then we're round the corner.

We run.

I want to run further, but it's clear Jia can't and my leg is throbbing. So we huddle in an emergency fire door a few blocks from Jake's apartment, just about managing to stay out of the relentless rain.

She checks the cat over with shaking hands.

I take a moment to process all that just happened. I can practically feel the synapses firing in my brain and everything slotting into place.

I look at Jia, huddling on the ground, cradling the soggy bundle of fur.

I could grab the cat now.

If those men are after her, and not me, I could grab the cat. Despite my pain, I'm much more mobile now – I could run with this boot on and she might not be able to catch me. Then I could find a way out of here, find a way to get to Jake. Deliver the code.

But then I think of the guns, the men, and I know I can't leave her. As much as it is the most logical thing to do, I just can't.

'What do we do?' she rasps.

'We need to get out of here,' I say, trying to quell my rising panic. When in doubt, talk through the problem. 'We need to find somewhere safe. Somewhere we can get access to transport, money.'

'Transport? Why?'

'We need to get to Kazakhstan now.'

'No! We need to get Orion checked over—'

'Right now, the only person who knows what is on that chip is in Kazakhstan, and that chip is the only clue to where your brother might be. You said it yourself: we have to go to Baikonur.'

She scowls, but she doesn't object.

'How are we going to get there?'

I give a heavy sigh – not because I don't have the answer, but because I just might. The problem is, it involves a visit to the last place I want to be.

'Just trust me,' I say as I pat down my pockets, relieved to feel my wallet still in place. There's a few dollars in there – not remotely enough, but better than nothing.

'Come on.' I pull Jia up off the ground, and hold open the bag she somehow managed to cling to in the chaos as she lowers in the bundle of fur.

'Where are we going?'

'To get a bus. Quite a few, in fact. Now, we have to move fast. You think you can do that?'

She nods, wiping rain from her face. Her expression is resigned now, rather than resentful, and I give her my best attempt at a reassuring smile. I pull her arm through mine and lead her and her damn cat into the night, hoping to God I've not lost my mind.

Rubio

A ROUTINE EVA. IF FLOATING OUT INTO THE DEPTHS OF space with only a thin cable keeping you from disappearing into the abyss can ever be called 'routine'.

Thankfully, I'm not one of the suckers scheduled to do it.

That pleasure belongs to Lee and Morin. Okeowo and Brun have been helping them suit up and will be on hand to get them in and out of the airlock. My job is simply to catch a few images of them traversing the outside of the *Argo* while it hurtles through space. Thank God this thing doesn't have any drag.

I sit down at the console showing the livestream from the suit cameras. Lee and Morin are strapped to the walls of the airlock opposite each other. They're flapping their arms about, looking a bit like young children misbehaving while their teachers tell them the rules of the school trip. In reality, they're doing light exercises as they breathe in pure oxygen to increase their metabolic rate. Soon, they'll be ready for depressurization.

Ana floats in beside me and I give her a surprised nod. I guess even she can't sleep through this moment. After all, this is the first EVA in the history of human spaceflight that is not under control from Earth. We're too far out now for Baikonur to direct it. We're up to two minutes forty-five seconds for two-way conversation – so we're pretty much on our own.

A lot can go wrong in nearly three minutes.

'Good morning,' Ana says quietly.

'Good afternoon,' I counter, watching Brun sliding back into the ship's hull and leaving Okeowo alone next to the now-sealed airlock doors, holding a radio mic that will allow her to communicate with the EVA duo.

It's almost time to purge and depressurize the airlock. We've checked it a dozen times, but never with living beings in it. This feels like one of the first real tests of our engineers' work. Although I suppose the fact that none of us have perished yet is already proof that they got some things right.

With a *CLUNK*, the airlock begins to depressurize.

'Chief Engineer Lee, Commander Morin, you have eight minutes before PSI is at the correct level. Best of luck out there.'

'Thank you, Dr Okeowo,' Morin fires back over the radio. We're on rank and title terms now. That's when you know it's serious.

'How is it looking?' Ana asks me. Her hair is plaited to the side this morning and she looks contained, efficient. Astronaut Barbie.

'I think Dong-hyun was a little nervous. I saw him stashing away a packet of Imodium.'

Concern flashes across Ana's face.

Over the comms, Okeowo conducts with her crisp British accent. 'Your suits are now switched to internal battery power. The EVA has commenced at zero-seven-zero-nine standard time.'

'Copy.'

'Here we go,' I say more to myself than to Ana. She nods and secures herself properly to one of the footholds in front of the console, eyes riveted to the screen.

'Switch water on. O. N.'

'Water on, EVA 1,' Morin calls back.

'And EVA 2,' says Lee, not a hint of nerves in his voice.

'Copy all. Temperature control valve set as desired.'

I turn my attention to the camera mounted on the outside of the *Argo*, showing the exterior of the airlock. In just a few moments, we'll see Morin and Lee emerge from it. The thought sends a shiver down my spine.

'Four hours, right?' Ana asks.

'Yeah, although Lee was hoping it might take a bit less.'

The final checks bounce back and forth over the radio.

'He needs to take his time. I told him this,' she almost hisses, scowling at the tiny Lee on the screen. I raise an eyebrow – who knew she cared?

'Pressure at the right level. Ready for you to detach.'

'Copy,' Morin's voice rings out loud and clear. 'Releasing our harnesses and heading to release the outer hatch thermal cover.'

My palms clam up. I think of my little secret in my sleeping bag. An occasion such as this deserves a toast. And the flask has been filled again.

I tried to access the camera feeds this morning, to see who had access to my sleep pod yesterday, but there was nothing. Not even a jump in the timeline.

Someone is getting better at covering their tracks.

'Lee, you'll be stowing the hook on the stiffener tether point, cinching the strap until snug.'

'Copy.'

On the screen, what looks like nothing more than a large hula hoop with some filter paper stretched across it, swings open.

'Thermal cover is open.'

It's comical how flimsy it looks, and I bark out a half laugh.

'Affirmed, Commander. You can egress the airlock with EVA crew lock bag number 1. We'll have you verify the forward hatch pickpin is engaged.'

'Copy.'

Morin's spacesuit emerges from the hatch, and suddenly I'm not laughing any more. I'm not thinking about my flask, either. Both Ana and I lean in, surrounded by silence as we watch our commander float into the inky blackness.

Not long after, Lee's suit follows. Both the human figures seem oddly large in comparison to where they have just appeared from. Like a strange robotic birth. It's all so . . . quiet and calm.

Which, I suppose, is exactly what you want a spacewalk to be.

As my crewmates prepare to traverse the ship, I pick up my camera equipment and move over to the cupola, leaving Ana floating in the command module. I enter the cupola and peer out of the window. There she is, Planet Earth, hanging peacefully in mid-air. Dwindling and diminishing with every day. I let the chatter of the EVA comms wash over me as I set up my lenses and wait for my subjects to arrive.

And then I see them. Slowly and methodically making their way over to the solar panel array they're checking on this side of the ship. I wait until the bulk of their bodies are in view and begin snapping, all too aware that this is the furthest picture ever taken of human beings in the history of our species. It's almost incomprehensible that the two figures in front of me are from the tiny world that sits behind them. That everyone they have ever known, ever loved; every ancestor they share DNA with; every organism we have ever known to exist, has come from that blue disc. And I am here to witness it.

I can't see Morin and Lee's faces and I'm relieved that they can't see me because, inexplicably, I'm crying. Tears well in my eyes and spill over as I click, again and again. I glance down at my camera's display screen to check that this is real.

I unhook my foothold and move over to the wall where a radio sits.

'Okeowo, I have eyes on EVA 1 and 2.'

'Copy that, Rubio.' I can hear her smiling through the airwaves. 'Morin and Lee, Mission Specialist Lindroos has eyes on you in the cupola. Wanna give him a little wave?'

I thrust myself back over to the windows in time to see Morin and Lee push back off the side of the *Argo* and lift their arms in my direction.

The universal signal of hello, from the farthest flung known life in the universe. *Click click click.*

And for the first time, I finally understand what Anders has gone on about all these years. All my stresses, my concerns, are melting away and I am utterly lost in this moment. This is what we're here for. This is exploration. It's our species' greatest endeavour, and we are making it possible.

But then the moment is over, and like the professionals they are, Morin and Lee are back in work-mode, moving hand over hand towards their next destination on the body of the *Argo*.

Lee heads right to look at some bolt heads that Baikonur were mildly concerned about, while Morin clambers over the cupola up to where the solar arrays are, out of my sight. I capture some images of Lee's cord streaming out into space, running below the Earth. I wish I could reach out and sculpt it so that it surrounds the Earth completely – his artificial lifeline encompassing humanity's ultimate one. But all I can do is observe and marvel.

'Uh-oh.'

I drop my camera. Lee is pushing himself away from something, fast, his hand reaching out for his tether. In the space he's just left, a jet of snowflakes streams out, fluttering in the sun- and earthshine, like a flock of silvery butterflies.

'I think we've got a leak here,' Lee's voice rings out on the radio. Flat and matter-of-fact.

I hover a moment, pulse pounding, then grab my camera as it spins in front of me and dash back to the wall.

'Lee? Are you OK?' Morin, her voice deep and serious.

'EVA 2, your heart rate and oxygen consumption have spiked. Just breathe. What's going on?' I'm so relieved Okeowo is on duty, not me.

'*Argo*, this is EVA 2. I've found a leak. Or I started one, I'm not sure.'

My mind instantly jumps to the *Mayflower*. It was during an EVA that they met their fate. Is it happening again? Is this it for us too?

I snap myself out of it with a growl in my throat and open up the mic.

'Okeowo, it's Lindroos. I have eyes on the leak too.' I detach the radio from the wall and fly back to the window. 'Starboard side. Err . . .' I close my eyes and try to dredge up memories of all the damn diagrams we were made to memorize. 'It's above the greenhouse. I think it's a coolant line!'

I open my eyes again and focus on the leak. The flakes are surging out into the darkness like sea foam being launched up and over rocks, a cloud of vapour blossoming above Lee and the *Argo*, swirling in one large flurry.

'It's beautiful,' I whisper, then wince, hoping they didn't hear that on the radio.

'Affirmative. I think it's ammonia,' Lee calls out. His breathing is rapid as he hauls himself back towards the *Argo* by his tether.

Shit. Ammonia. That's bad. But before I know it, I'm looking at the scene through my camera's eyepiece and my index finger is clicking.

No one knew what exactly happened on the *Mayflower*, but I'm sure as hell going to make sure the world knows what happened to us.

'I'm coming to you now,' Morin says. 'Is the ammonia on you?' There's tension in her voice – and I know why. First, this ship gets very hot, and ammonia is what cools us down and keeps our life systems online. Second, it is extremely corrosive and can be fatal. It should be fine on Lee's suit, for a while. But we can't bring it inside the ship – and we can't bring in Lee without his suit.

A moment's silence.

'Yes,' Lee replies. He's back on the body of the *Argo* now, a few feet from the leak. He braces himself as he moves towards it.

'Lee, wait for me,' Morin calls. I glance above me, hoping her figure will appear any minute.

'No.' Lee's voice is cold and steely. 'Need that ammonia. I have to seal it off now. And you have to stay away – we can't contaminate another suit.'

With that, Lee launches himself back into the stream of ammonia and reaches for the bailer bar – the locking device on the male QD, a part that protrudes from one of the plugs that connects the coolant lines – where the ammonia is leaking from.

I capture the whole thing. What else can I do?

Lee strains, trying to get purchase on the bar in microgravity. Morin bounces into view from above and traverses the *Argo* towards him.

'It. Won't. Budge.' The strain in his voice is clear. Morin hovers a few feet away, avoiding the deluge of ammonia.

'Use that footplate as leverage, to your left,' she calls. Lee repositions himself and begins to jolt and heave again. Meanwhile the cloud of ammonia mushrooms.

Seconds click on, minutes. Ever more of the stuff pours out and blasts Lee as he battles to close the valve.

'You're going to have to take a break soon,' Okeowo warns. 'Brun and Petrova are shutting down the coolant system from in here. We can limit the loss.'

'No. I. Have. It!'

'Lee, you're burning through your oxygen,' Morin cries. 'Stop. That's an order.'

'Gaaaaaahhh!'

Lee jolts down suddenly. The stream stops.

Lee slumps for a moment, then straightens back up and gingerly moves, away from where the leak was just moments ago.

'Leak is contained,' he breathes over the radio.

'Affirmative. Well done, EVA 2.'

Lee floats away from the *Argo*, his foot hooked onto a restraint bar. He's clearly exhausted. As he turns towards me, I gasp aloud. Because his ordeal is far from over.

All over the front of his suit, his helmet, his visor, is a thick layer of frost. It glints in the sunlight. I click.

'Okeowo. This is EVA 1, EVA 2's suit is covered with a layer of frozen ammonia an inch deep.'

'Copy that, EVA 1, I have eyes on it. Lee, how are you doing?'

'I'm OK, *Argo*. Levelling out my breathing,' he says, between deep, calming breaths.

'Good. EVA 1, stand by for instructions.'

That's my cue. I push off from the cupola and fly back through the *Argo*, to the command module, where I know Okeowo and the others will be assembled.

As I make my way into it, there's a stream of French expletives.

'What the fuck do you mean, we need to get him inside? He'll kill us all if he comes back in here like that. Who even are you? Why the fuck are you even here? You're destroying this mission. Get out!'

'Woah!' I cry, at the sight of Brun screaming at Ana, who looks surprisingly calm in the face of his tirade.

Okeowo zooms in front of Brun.

'Enough! Shut the fuck up, all of you. We need to think.'

As if sensing her crew's turmoil, Morin calls out on the radio.

'*Argo*, we need to terminate this EVA and work out how to get Lee back in safely.'

'Affirmative, Commander.'

'I'm going to brush him down.'

'Commander, you may also—'

'I'll be careful.'

Through Morin's feed, we see her awkwardly turning as she attempts to access one of her tools – a white brush. Then, she and Lee coordinate their movements so she can get closer to his contaminated front.

'OK,' I say. 'We bring Morin in first. Then we bring in Lee. We depressurize the airlock. Purge it. He comes on in.'

'There'll still be traces of the ammonia,' Brun mutters.

'Fine. We ditch the suit – just get Lee out of it.'

'You can't get him out of it without exposing him,' Ana squeaks.

'And we can't ditch one of our only pressure suits,' Brun growls.

I raise my hands in submission. 'All right, all right.'

'And why did we even have a leak in the first place, huh?' Brun barks. 'They said "you'll never have a male QD leak", and that is exactly what we have!'

'It doesn't matter how or why right now, Sébastien,' Okeowo says soothingly, but he rounds on Ana again.

'Where were you, when all this was kicking off? Sleeping Fucking Beauty?'

'Hey!' I yell. 'This isn't going to help Lee.'

'I was right here. Rubio, tell him!' Ana turns her pleading eyes on me.

'You were off taking fucking pictures, Rubio. What the hell do you know?'

'And where were you, then, Brun?' I snap. 'If you weren't here?'

Brun puffs up. 'How dare you! I spend every waking moment making this ship function. What the hell do you do? Paint and take fucking polaroids?'

There. He's said it. What I knew they'd all been thinking. But before I can react, Okeowo's calm, measured voice cuts through it all.

'EVA 1 and EVA 2. I've had a thought. If you get enough of the ammonia off with the brush, then get out of *Argo*'s shadow and into the sunlight—'

'We can boil it. Yes, Okeowo!' Lee's voice rings out, triumphant.

'I'm going to help get him up to the solar array, *Argo*,' Morin says. 'He'll get more exposure to the sun up there.'

'Copy that.'

Brun crosses his arms grumpily and I eye him as Okeowo turns her attention back to us. 'We're going to evaporate the remainder of the ammonia. If he stays out there long enough, and gets enough of the sun's rays, we might pull this off.'

Brun huffs. 'Might.'

'How long does he have?' Ana asks in a quiet voice. 'How much oxygen?'

Okeowo looks at her readings. 'At current consumption, he has just over three hours left in the tank.'

'Is that enough to boil it all off?' Ana whispers.

'Don't be ludicrous,' Brun snaps. 'He won't be sunbathing that whole time. He needs at least forty-five minutes to get back down from the solar array, through the hatch, into the airlock, and through the venting processes.'

Ana's eyes widen.

'So,' I jump in, keen to reassure her, 'that gives him two hours, twenty minutes up there to burn it off. That's enough, right?'

Okeowo's lips press into a thin line. 'It's going to have to be.'

'Bullshit!' Brun cries. 'God knows how much damn ammonia is on that suit. It could need hours to evaporate. And if there is anything still on him once we open up that hatch—'

'We just have to limit the contamination as much as we can,' Okeowo says steadily.

'We'll need oxygen masks, then. And to run an extra filter cycle in the life-support systems,' Ana says quietly.

Okeowo looks pleasantly surprised. 'Do you want to get the masks and other equipment ready?' she asks. Ana nods and zooms off down the *Argo* towards the airlock.

Brun shoots a dirty look at Okeowo. 'You're really going to trust her after—'

'Enough with your paranoia, Brun. If we don't get that stuff off Lee, she dies just as much as the rest of us. So yes, I trust her. Now, do something useful. Prep the filters.'

For a moment, it looks as though he's going to explode, but then he utters another French expletive and heads off towards the life-support control panel in the storm shelter.

Okeowo deflates a little, now the rest of the crew are gone.

'Ruth, are you all right?' I ask quietly.

She looks up at me, looking older yet again. 'We will have to time this perfectly. He's burned through a lot of his oxygen – he won't be able to sunbathe for long.'

'What can I do?' I ask.

She gestures to a panel that's flashing red.

'You can answer Baikonur – they're desperate to know what's going on and act like they're saving the fucking day.'

'Commander, you need to come in now,' I hear Okeowo say as I move towards the airlock. My briefing with Baikonur has been painfully slow – over two damn hours – and yet they still couldn't come up with a better plan than ours.

Ana, Okeowo and Brun are outside the airlock in full protective clothing, eyes glued to the screens showing Morin and Lee clinging to the solar array above us.

Okeowo doesn't look at me as I approach. 'And?'

'They gave some suggestions on how to make the airlock pressurize faster if we need it. Might come in handy if he's out of air,' I say, handing my tablet to Brun.

'Merveilleux,' Brun mutters acidly, before begrudgingly looking at the instructions.

'And Abbey's arranged for the live feed to go directly to several news channels, so we've been asked not to swear.'

'Well, thank fuck he's told us,' Okeowo says, straight-faced.

'Morin's oxygen levels are good, right?' I ask.

'They're enough. She didn't burn through hers like Lee.'

'What time are we on?' Ana asks.

'Only fourteen minutes left until he's critical,' Brun states bluntly.

'Fuck!' I blurt. 'They're leaving it too long.'

Okeowo clicks back on the comms. 'Commander, Lee's oxygen is dangerously low. You have to start moving now.'

Finally, Morin replies. 'Copy that, *Argo*.'

'I can make it back inside in under ten minutes,' Lee barks. 'I can't risk having any of this shit on me when I come in.'

'In fourteen minutes, Lee,' Okeowo clips into the comms, 'you'll be hypoxic. You'll be risking your life and Morin's, as she'll be forced to drag your unconscious arse back through the hatch with not a second to spare.'

'That's enough, Lee,' Morin cuts through. 'Move. Now.'

'Heather!' Lee cries.

'That is an order!' We glance at each other, taken aback. None of us has heard that tone from Morin before. She's angry. She's scared. We see her yank at Lee's tether.

'Imbecile,' Brun mutters.

Lee cries out in frustration, and we finally see him moving. He rolls onto his front, and gradually, ever so carefully, begins to crawl back towards Morin, in the direction of the hatch.

'Thank God,' breathes Okeowo. I touch her shoulder lightly, but she's back to business already. 'Brun, get that coding bypass ready. We will need to vent and repressurize the airlock to purge any remaining ammonia as quickly as possible. He won't have anything left in the tank once he's inside.'

'I still don't think—'

'Fucking hell, man!' I cry, snatching the tablet back from him and heading to the nearest control panel, fighting the panic rising in me. My mouth is so dry. I'm so hot, so thirsty. Jesus Christ, I need a drink. My hands tremble as I tap in the codes.

Hold it together, Rubio.

Ana thrusts an oxygen mask into Brun's hands. He snarls at her in French, but Okeowo jumps in.

'Don't you dare, Brun,' she barks. 'Get that mask on.'

An alarm begins to sound on Okeowo's tablet, pulsating red.

'Time?' Ana gasps.

'He has nothing left in his tank,' Okeowo confirms, her voice shaking. 'All he has is in his suit. From here on in, he's suffocating.'

I finish up the coding bypass in minutes, despite my shaking hands. The rest of the team are still watching Lee's painfully slow progress. His breathing sounds strained now.

'He's heading through the hatch now, *Argo*,' Morin calls over the comms, a moment before we see it for ourselves.

'Copy that,' Okeowo replies, calm. 'Lee? We need you to attach your suit back to the wall. We're enacting a shortened venting process. It'll be a bit rough.'

'Copy. Thaaat. Argooo,' Lee replies, his speech slurred. Every cell in his body is screaming for oxygen now as his suit fills with carbon dioxide. How much longer does he have left? Usually the venting and repressurizing would take anything up to ten minutes.

I know he hasn't got that.

Excruciatingly slowly, he manoeuvres himself back to the wall mounts. But he struggles to get his arms into the loops.

'You OK in there, Lee?' Morin calls out over the comms. She's retreated back a safe distance. With more in her oxygen tank, she can afford to stay out until Lee is safely inside.

'Yeaaahhhh,' he replies. But we all watch helplessly as he flails with the straps and buckles.

'Okeowo?' I prompt, no idea what I expect her to be able to do about it.

'Lee, just focus,' she says, her nose almost touching the glass into the airlock. 'Move your right arm down. That's it. Almost there.'

'He's going to black out,' Ana cries.

'*Argo*, status update?' Morin calls.

Okeowo winces as Lee thrusts his arm towards the loops again, but fails. 'He's struggling to secure himself in the airlock, Commander.'

'I can dooo iiiit!' Lee calls out, but his head is lolling to one side.

Then Morin moves, fast. She untethers, re-tethers, and swings herself around the side of the hatch.

'*Argo*, I'm entering the hatch. I'll secure him. Prepare for venting.'

'Commander, we don't have time for you to secure yourself—'

'I'll get in, strap him, get out. You vent,' Morin growls, hurling herself into the airlock, towards Lee. 'OK, buddy. Here we go.'

Like a mother dressing her toddler, Morin thrusts Lee's floating arms into the straps and cinches him in, talking to him the whole time.

'Just breathe. You're OK,' she drones softly. 'Okeowo?'

'Airlock systems primed,' I call.

Morin pats the last buckle on Lee's suit with finality and pushes back off towards the hatch.

'He's in!' she cries.

'Lee,' Okeowo says. 'Prepare for venting and pressurization.'

But there's no response. Through the glass, his head lolls to one side, eyes closed.

'Lee!' Ana whimpers.

'Shut up!' Brun bites at her. 'Get your damn mask on.' We can't get the airlock open unless we're all protected. Ana is the only one not wearing her mask yet, but she ignores him.

'Lee!' She's crying now.

Morin is clear of the hatch, shutting it behind her before tethering herself to a hold on the outside of the ship.

'Clear!' She calls.

I push the button and instantly the pressure starts to build in the airlock. I see the contents moving around as the room floods with gas again. Then, almost as quickly as it started, everything is sucked towards the vents in the room.

'Pressure dropping back to zero again,' Brun reads, over my shoulder.

'Ruth?' Ana sniffs.

'He still has a pulse,' Okeowo says, her eyes not leaving the tablet showing Lee's vitals. 'But it's slowing.'

We hear another loud clunk, and the system reverses itself again.

'Repressurizing,' I call out, needlessly.

Brun grabs Ana and roughly pulls her oxygen mask over her mouth and nose. She cries out in pain, but finally, she's protected.

'I watch the numbers tick upwards on the control panel. Then it clicks.

'Done!'

Okeowo launches herself for the airlock door mechanism, yanks it open, and flies through. Within seconds she's by Lee, her tablet floating off into the air as she scrambles for his helmet.

'He's flatlining,' she calls out.

Ana flies into the airlock with another oxygen mask. 'Here!' She thrusts it at Okeowo as Lee's helmet floats ethereally upwards.

Okeowo snatches the mask and rams it onto Lee's face.

'Brun!' Morin calls out, from outside the ship. 'Filter the life support.'

Brun does what he's told, as I watch Okeowo with Lee.

We're too late.

He's not moving.

It's over.

But then, there's a rasping gasp.

'Lee!' Ana cries.

His eyes flutter open.

'Holy shit,' I cough.

'Commander, Chief Engineer Lee is conscious and breathing,' Okeowo states calmly over the comms.

'Copy that,' Morin replies, relief suffusing her voice. 'Well done, team. And the ammonia?'

I turn to Brun, who's squinting at some readings.

'No traces yet, Commander,' he says. 'But let's keep these masks on for the next twenty, while the systems cycle.'

A raspy cough snaps my attention back to the airlock.

'That . . .' gasps Lee, colour coming back to his face. 'Was fucking close.'

An hour and a half later, Okeowo has Lee in the hab and is checking him over. All seems well.

Having zoomed in straight from the airlock, Morin is now up in the command module with Ana, assessing how much ammonia has been lost. Baikonur are doing the same from their end, but they don't seem overly concerned.

Even Brun seems relieved. He's busy making dinner for everyone: we've experienced something extremely stressful, so we need to get everyone's blood sugar levels back up. As he pops a bag in the microwave, he notices me hovering, watching Okeowo check Lee's vitals.

'I . . . I'm sorry about earlier,' he says, quick and low.

I don't really want to look at him right now, so I turn my focus to tidying away some packaging that he's left spinning in the micro-g. 'Don't worry about it.'

'No.' Brun grabs my hand as I move away from the waste bins. He looks me in the eye, and I can see he's tired, anxious. Today has taken more out of him than I realized. He's even shaking a little. But that might also be me. 'It was uncalled for. I apologize. We are all of us up here, all of us, invaluable.'

I pull my hand away and give him a smile, which feels more like a grimace. His words make me feel a bit sick.

'Thank you, but honestly, I'm fine,' I reassure him. But I feel the sudden urge to get out of there, to be alone.

I pull myself away, past Lee and Okeowo, and out of the hab, my clammy hands slipping on the metal bars. As soon as I'm away from the others, my body begins to let itself go. I'm shaking so much I can hardly hold on to things as I pull myself through to the sleeping pods. The panning cameras whir as they follow me.

Must get out of shot.

Must be alone.

I don't even try to mask my face, which must look a picture of anguish, as I enter the sleeping quarters and dive into my pod. Drawing the curtains, I turn my back to the camera, blocking its view just enough for me to reach into my sleeping bag and grasp the flask.

My hands seem to be spasming as I unlock the cap and bring it to my mouth, sucking with all my might. The burn hits my tongue and the back of my throat. I swallow, gulping it down, savouring every moment, every last moment, before it's gone. I suck once more. But my flask is finally empty.

Breathing hard, I thrust the bitter disappointment into my sleeping bag, then float in silence.

Behind me, the lens pulls focus.

Look at me. I'm pathetic. A weak, pointless man craving alcohol to assuage the burning humiliation of being utterly useless. Lee could have died today. We all could have. If the ammonia leak had continued . . . that could have been the end of us.

Brun's words just now made me feel sick because he is wrong. I'm not invaluable. I don't know the boiling point of ammonia. I'm not a doctor or an engineer. I'm just an observer. And when faced with a true emergency, I don't offer anything, other than another pair of hands. And weak, shaking ones at that.

I close my eyes and lick my lips, searching for any remnants of the alcohol upon them.

I think of the tablet and the taunting message. At least one person knows my true worth. Knows who I really am.

But I can stop it.

This could be the last time.

I reach down into my sleeping bag and unscrew the flask. If I destroy the lid, then it's useless. No more refills. No more temptation.

It will finally be done.

With a yank, I pull hard on the little arm that attaches the lid to the main body of the flask.

And it's free.

Such a small thing, so easy to conceal. I'll hide it with our trash. We expel a limited amount of waste each week, out into the vacuum of space. An entire hip flask would be spotted. But a small cap like this? It could fit in an empty food pouch.

I pocket it, feeling better already.

I take another deep breath and push back my pod's curtain, moving directly towards the storage bin, searching for the tablet I've been too scared to touch again. I'm going to smash it, destroy it, and then I'm going to take it to the crew. At least then I am doing something. At least then—

But it's not there. My hands scramble around, but I can't find it.

My mind begins to race. Am I going mad? Was it in another—

'Rubio?'

I freeze.

'What are you doing?' Okeowo moves towards me, rests a reassuring hand on my back.

'I . . . I've lost something . . .' I fumble.

She nudges the lid of the storage bin back into place.

'Well, whatever it is, I'm sure we'll find it later.'

She pulls my face round to meet hers and her eyes flit back and forth between mine, staring straight into me, concerned. I hold my breath, petrified that she'll smell the fumes on it.

'Come on, dear,' she says, smiling kindly. 'Lee is fine. The coolant levels are OK. We've got away with it. You need to eat something.'

'But I—'

'Come on,' she says, firmly, and I notice a flash of annoyance before the empathetic face of a doctor reappears just an instant later. 'This has been a difficult day for everyone. We all need to eat, together.'

'Ruth,' I manage to croak out. 'There's something I need to—'

'Shhh,' Okeowo soothes. 'Rubio, listen. Between Lee, Morin, Brun, Ana, I have so many people to look after. Please. I need you.'

My breath hitches. I believe her. And I so want to be needed. I could tell her about the tablet and the flask. But both are gone now. What good would it do to tell her now?

You have to tell them, a small voice inside of me urges. *It's wrong.*

But the rest of me – the broken, tired, drained rest of me – lets Okeowo lead me away. She's right. There's already so much for her to carry. For all of them to carry. How can I burden them with more now?

PART THREE

Alyssa

THE HOUSE IS UNUSUALLY DARK AND QUIET. NO WARM GLOW in the kitchen, no sign of my dad's car on the drive. Everything is still. It feels strange to be back here, not just because I haven't been here in so long, but also because we're hiding in a goddamn bush, watching the house like robbers.

It's taken several Greyhounds to get here. Luckily no one recognized me – we kept our heads down, sat at the back when we could. The cat has been quiet, although he won't let Jia really touch him, other than to get him in and out of the bag. She's worried, but that seems to be a perpetual state with her.

'Shall we go in?' she whispers, crouched next to me, watching the house with wide eyes. She's built my parents' house up in her head as some sanctuary. I haven't got it within me to break her dreams; she'll find out the reality soon enough.

'I don't think they're home. Better to wait.'

As soon as I say that, headlights flood the road and swing themselves onto my parents' drive. My heart starts hammering even before my father emerges from his car. He looks much older in the dim light from the street, bent low. I wait for the other door of the car to open up, but nothing. My mother must already be in bed.

He pulls a bag of groceries out from the passenger seat and makes his slow way to the front door. He fumbles and drops the key. It looks like it causes him agony to bend down and get it, like it's in some deep ravine that he might never reach, but he does and is finally able to let himself in.

I watch the pattern of the lights switch on as he makes his way through the house, into the kitchen and breakfast room. I can almost hear the clock ticking in the hall. The jangle of his keys setting down on the table. The clunk of the fridge opening, my mom calling down in greeting. My feet feel like lead. Is there really no other way?

But the truth of the matter is, no. There's no other place for me on this planet right now. After everything I've been through, I've been sucked back here.

I nudge Jia. 'Come on.' If I don't go now, I never will.

We look around as we make our way across the street. It's deathly quiet.

My hand hesitates just a little before I knock softly.

My father gives a hacking great cough and a chair scrapes back, then he pads towards the door. I gesture for Jia to step back a little. She fingers the straps of her bag nervously. We squint into the blinding light as the door cracks open.

'Alyssa?' There's bafflement in my father's voice and I steady myself. I will not let him see me be scared.

'Dad.'

The door is fully open now, and he stands in front of me, an almost amusing look of shock on his face. He's definitely aged. It's his hands that seem the most alien to me; so deft and strong before, now they look withered.

'Who . . .?' he asks, peering at Jia.

'A friend,' I say, and instinctively look behind us. 'Can we come in?'

Still looking stunned, he nods and moves to the side to allow us to pass. The smell of the place hits me like a brick wall. Leather and cedar and spices. It's rich and heavy. My head spins.

The door shuts behind us and I turn to find myself standing next to my father, as he looks at the two of us with a blank face.

The silence stretches out for a long time. The floor creaks as

Jia shifts her weight uncomfortably. Has the clock always been that loud?

Then, he seems to come back to himself.

'What are you—'

'Can we close the blinds first?' I interrupt.

He shrugs. 'Sure.'

I rush to the window, extinguish the porch light and draw the drapes. Then I move into the kitchen and breakfast room and do the same, before turning around and taking the place in. It's neat, orderly. A cup and plate out on the breakfast table, waiting for something to be served. Everything in its proper place, as if I never left.

Jia and my father follow me in. Exhausted, she collapses on a cushioned seat by the table. She takes off her bag and opens it up, cooing softly to the cat. My father stays in the doorway, and I feel the weight of his gaze. Looking at me in a way I can't quite understand.

'Do you want a drink?' he says, with such uncharacteristic warmth I can only gaze at him, mystified. He shuffles to the refrigerator. 'I think I have some Snapple or something.' The refrigerator doors clunk open. It's looking pretty bare.

'Or a beer?' he asks, turning to me.

'No. Thank you,' I reply slowly.

He nods, shuts the refrigerator door and stands there, once again at a loss. 'Does anyone know you're here?'

'No. And it needs to stay that way.'

'Of course,' he replies.

Silence yet again. My eyes drift to the hall and the stairs. Everything is so quiet. My father notices the direction of my gaze and takes a step forward. The kitchen counter stands between the two of us, but it might as well be the Grand Canyon.

'Where's Mom?' I ask to break the awkwardness, taking a seat opposite Jia, who's still trying to coax the cat out.

No reply comes and I turn back to my father, who is statue-still. Not even blinking. His hands placed heavily on the counter.

'Dad?'

He swallows loudly. 'Mom . . . Mom died, Alyssa.'

I know it's not possible, but I feel Earth's rotation judder a little. I feel the magnetosphere slow, too. All the atoms within me shift and sway as they adjust to this new reality.

'What?' I hear my voice say. But my father knows I heard. I shake my head as I stare at a tiny scratch in the wooden surface of the table. 'No,' I say. 'No.' I look back at my father, whose petrified face watches me.

I push up, and Jia gapes at me as I stride across the kitchen, through the doorway and into the hall. I speed up the stairs, flick the light on as I move through the hall, past my old room, down to the end of the corridor and push open my parents' bedroom door, to reveal two neatly made single beds. Both empty. My mother's bedside table, also empty. No creams, no crossword puzzles. No coffee mug. No glasses.

No.

I dart to her closet and pull open the heavy wooden door to reveal a chasm. A few hangers. An empty shoe box on the floor.

No.

I flit to her dresser, pull open every drawer. No sweaters, no vests. No bras, panties or socks.

When I see that her slippers aren't tucked under the bed, my chest tightens, my breath coming in wheezes. I gulp as I collapse into the chair by the window. I look out across the room, where my mother's presence, so eternal, so irrefutable, is no more.

I breathe, in and out, hoping there's something in the air that I can inhale, subsume. Some essence of her that still lingers that might fill the void that is now expanding within my chest.

No one has followed me up here. He's left me to confirm everything on my own.

The corners of the beds are sharp, crisp. Military corners. Beds made by my father's aged hands. Not her calloused, warm ones.

It had been tough, living with my father. But she had always softened things. She had always thawed out the frost.

The moment of realization traps me, almost suffocates me – and then, after seconds or minutes or hours, my breathing eases. I inhale shakily through my nostrils again, levelling myself out. I stand and shuffle back down the hall, the stairs, and into the kitchen, where my father hasn't moved. Jia's no longer in there, though.

'When?' My voice comes out cold and steely.

My father makes his slow way to the table and sits down. He seems to have shaken off his astonishment and grief, and is back to his usual, practical self.

'Six weeks ago. Aneurysm. Nothing to be done. We contacted the program, but by then . . .' He raises an eyebrow.

By then, I'd lost my mind, gone off-grid. Refused to answer when they told me my parents had called.

I feel a flash of guilt. The message about the medal, when she had said she was sorry – it must have been just days before . . .

'Where is she?'

'With your grandmother.'

'And her things?'

'Goodwill.'

Of course. For him there'd be no sense in keeping her things around. No point in being emotional about it.

'Where's Jia?'

He raises his eyebrows. 'Is that her name? She's in the living room. Said she'd give us some space.'

I pad across the hall and jut my head into the room. Through the darkness, I see her, collapsed on the sofa fast asleep, curled up in my NASA sweatshirt. A small dark shadow, suggesting a cat, snuggles behind her in the crook of her back.

I move back into the kitchen and busy myself making a pot of coffee, which I gesture at, and my father nods.

'Please.'

He watches me move about the kitchen. The empty refrigerator now makes a lot more sense. I take out the milk and place it down in front of him.

I sit opposite and stare at him as he pours and stirs in the milk.

'Was she . . .' I croak. 'Was there any pain?'

Dad places his spoon neatly beside his cup.

'No,' he replies, voice soft. 'It was quick. She wouldn't have known.'

The clock ticks on for many minutes as we drink.

'Why are you here, Alyssa?'

It takes me a while to remember what it was that brought us here in the first place, when all I want to do is run right out of that door again. A set of headlights flashes past the drapes, reminding me what is out there.

'We . . .' I shift uncomfortably, feeling like I'm twelve again. 'We need your help.'

'And why is that?'

'Because we need cash and a car.'

'Why?'

'Because we need to get out of the country.'

'Why?'

'Because Jia, and a lot of other people, are in trouble.'

'And why is that your problem?'

I slam my coffee down.

'Enough questions. I didn't ask any questions of you, did I? I haven't asked why you've ignored my existence for the past four years, or why you never apologized to me for what happened that night. I never asked why you lied. And why you let Mom live a life so fucking miserable and false for so long. Have I? So spare me all the damn questions and just tell me: are you going to help us, or not?'

A ringing silence falls, broken only by my loud, panting breaths. I've never yelled at my father like that, so I have no idea what to expect. He leaves me waiting a few seconds, then calmly places his coffee down on the table, spreading his palms out across its surface. He stares at them, contemplating, before finally lifting his head and locking eyes with me. And then I see something in them that surprises me more than anything else that's happened over the last few days. Could it be . . . remorse?

'Alyssa,' he says, his voice cracking. 'I'm sorry.' The weight of that word is so heavy, I can almost hear the *clunk* of it landing there on the table between us. 'I'm sorry for . . . well, everything really. But most of all, I'm sorry I never explained anything to you. I . . . I was a coward.'

'Explained what?' My voice comes out small.

'What you saw that night . . . your mother knew. We never really spoke about it, of course, but that was more my fault than anything. But believe me, your mother knew everything about me, and while I cannot say whether or not her life with me was miserable, I can at least say that it wasn't false. Not in the way that you think, at least.'

'Mom knew about you and Mike?'

He winces at the name. 'She knew enough, yes.'

'Then why pretend? Why make me feel like . . . like, you never wanted to see me again?'

His spread-out hands contract into fists. 'You've always seen the world in black and white. It's not as simple as that, damn it. I wasn't born into a world where a woman could go into space, or someone like me could be a pilot in the damn US Air Force. I wasn't even in a world where people wanted me to exist, let alone thrive. I made choices. I made sacrifices. And so did your mother. Was it easy? Was it right? No, but this world was neither of those things. It still isn't. And your mother and I carved out a life for ourselves that worked. That got us through. I had my work, my service, my pride. She had her family, her duty, you.' He shakes his head.

'Should I have done things differently? Probably. Do I wish I'd forced myself to have conversations with your mother, with you? Definitely. Do I wish that I'd let your mother have one more moment with you before she . . . before she passed? More than anything.'

I let him sit a moment. Absorbing everything pouring out of him.

'I thought . . .' I trail away. I don't know what I thought.

'I know this is hard for you to understand, but you need to accept that all of us are flawed. My weakness? My pride, my stubbornness. My refusal to be honest with the people I love, with myself.'

He sniffs loudly. Swigs at his coffee, then stares down at it.

'Your mother loved more than I even knew was possible. She was so brave, so strong. And so loyal. Too loyal. While I remained silent, so would she, even if it broke her own heart. And you leaving? Well, for our own reasons, that was just too much. For both of us.'

He looks back up at me, then. My father. The man who has shaped my entire life, for better or worse, and who – I'm only just realizing now – I never really knew.

'Well . . .' I croak. 'I didn't go, did I?'

He smiles, sadly. 'No.' A pause. 'And I'm sorry about that too.'

I believe him. And I realize in that moment just how damn similar we really are. How flawed I am, too. How I could have done so many things differently. How stubborn, full of pride, and loyal I've been, to a fault.

'Dad,' I say quietly.

'Mmm?'

'Grandpa's medal is on the *Argo*. On its way to Mars.'

He looks down into his coffee again, playing with the handle. I think back to how proud I was when he gave it to me. A piece of our family.

The clock in the hall ticks on.

The house feels so empty.

'You know,' he says finally. 'I can't give you a load of cash or a car.'

I sigh, stretch and head to the sink to get a glass of water.

'OK, thanks, Dad. I get it.'

'No,' he says, getting up and rounding the counter to stand with me. 'I mean, I can't *just* give you a load of cash and a car. You might get across the border, but what good will that do you? You're still six thousand miles from where you need to be.'

'What are you talking about?'

He barks out a laugh. 'Alyssa. I may not have been the best father, but I know you. I saw your outburst. Hell – the whole world saw it. You still think there's something wrong with your ship, don't you? Or your crew. Or maybe both? And cat lady through there –' he gestures to the living room – 'has something to do with it, doesn't she?'

'Yes,' I say weakly. Perhaps we do know one another after all.

'So you need to get back to Kazakhstan?'

'Yes.'

'And I assume, from the fact that you rock up here in the dead of night, draw all the damn drapes, and tell me you need to get out of the country, that something very dangerous will happen if you're caught?'

I shift my gaze from his. 'Yes, Dad.'

He grabs me by the shoulders and leans in, looking deep into my eyes. 'Alyssa, are you sure about this? Are you absolutely certain there's no other way to solve this? No one *else* who can solve this?'

Who is this new person standing in front of me? He's simultaneously a stranger to me, but also someone I feel like I've always known.

'Yes, Dad. Trust me, I've thought about this. I've thought about going public, about speaking to the press. But after what I did, what they've said about me, Valdivian could easily dismiss or discredit me. Besides, I don't trust them to save the crew. So I have to get Jia to Mission Control. Although I have no idea how. I—' I take a breath, steadying myself. 'I've made some mistakes, but this is something only I can fix. It'll save everyone. Myself included.'

'I just don't want you to put all this on yourself. Like last time.'

'This is not like last time.'

'Because you know that wasn't your fault, don't you?'

I take a half step back, wrong-footed. I didn't know he knew . . . had no idea he'd heard. But of course, NASA, the military – they're all in each other's pockets.

'I know,' is all I can say.

He holds me there, a moment longer, then gives one big, definite nod. He releases me and marches out through the doorway, into the hall, and down towards his study, moving with his old strength.

'Dad?'

I follow, limping, baffled. In the study, by the light of his desk lamp, he rifles through his desk drawers, searching for something.

'You're gonna need a plane.'

I gape at him. 'What?'

'A plane, damn it.' He looks up at me. 'You think you're gonna swim across the damn Atlantic?'

'No, but I—'

'Ah!' he cries, pulling out an old map. He checks his watch and hesitates a moment. 'Screw it,' he growls, and picks up the old house phone resting under the desk lamp. He dials and puts the receiver to his ear.

'Dad, it's too early, whoever you call will be—'

He holds up a hand to silence me. Then the ringing stops, and I hear a deep rumble on the other end of the line.

'Mike? It's me.' A rumble again. 'Yeah, I know. Listen, I want to call in that favour. You still have that old Cessna?' Another rumble. 'Well, we need a ride.' Rumble rumble. 'No, I'm not kidding. It's for Alyssa. She's a commander and she needs a plane.'

Rubio

IT'S A SOMBRE MOOD AS I FLOAT INTO THE HAB AND FIND the entire crew waiting to begin.

After concealing the hip flask cap in the trash compartment, I did not sleep well last night and the rest of the crew have allowed me to catch up this afternoon. I woke just now to find a bag of popcorn floating in my pod, along with one of my water pouches freshly refilled. I know it will have been Okeowo, and I give her a small smile, which she returns.

The rest of the crew are all hooked in around the central area we use as a table, apart from Ana, who's looped her delicate arms through some handles on the far side of the wall, to be as far away from Brun as possible.

'This looks serious,' I say, as I settle next to Brun, whose whole body seems to be fizzing with what I can only assume is anger.

'It is, Rubio,' replies Morin. She's tight-lipped. My stomach flips over. Has someone found the cap? I try to still my shaking hands.

'Brun has made a request,' she clips, and all eyes turn to him. I notice how heavy his eyes look. Someone else has clearly not been sleeping well either.

'I think we should turn back. In a few weeks, we should initiate the termination procedures and, when the time comes, fly-by Mars and head back to Earth.' He stares down at the table as he says it.

The seconds tick by as shock reverberates around the room.

Not land? Return to Earth, after all this? Never set foot on Mars?

Finally, Brun looks back up at us all, making eye contact with each of us in turn.

'This mission is broken. We are not safe. Someone among us is putting us all in danger, and I do not want to spend the rest of my life trying to build a new world with someone I do not trust.' His eyes bore into Ana, who doesn't blink. She even raises her chin in defiance. I admire her for that.

'Those are some very big words you've just used, Brun. You cannot take those back,' Okeowo says.

'I know,' Brun replies. '*C'est ça.*'

'No,' Lee says firmly. 'We can't abandon this. We always knew there would be problems, mistakes—'

'Not like this,' Brun fires back.

'What are you really saying, Brun?' Okeowo asks softly.

'Come on, you know. The memorial, the ammonia, our messages – hell, even Alyssa's original accident.' Okeowo winces. 'They're fucking with us.' He throws his hands to one of the ever-present cameras. 'She's fucking with us.' His finger thrusts out to Ana.

'Brun, we all know Alyssa's accident was my fault, and mine alone,' Okeowo rasps.

'It wasn't, Ruth.' I place a reassuring hand on her shoulder.

'You're wrong, Brun,' Lee says, sounding heartbroken, exchanging a look with Ana that I can't quite read. 'You're going crazy.'

'CRAZY?!' Brun launches himself at Lee. 'You're the crazy ones, to be ignoring the fact that we have a traitor among us!'

'ENOUGH!'

Morin shoots between Brun and Lee, pushing them apart. The two men float away from one another, glaring. The air stills. Some items Brun disrupted spin innocently in front of us. A pen, some chilli sauce.

'We will have a vote.' Morin declares.

'Do we—' Ana starts. Brun's head snaps towards her, and she

falters, then steels herself again. 'Do we even have a say on this? Surely it is for Baikonur, Anders, Abbey to decide whether we—'

'Of course we have a fucking say,' Brun spits. 'They're twenty-five million kilometres away, they won't even know what we've done for minutes. We could be dead and they wouldn't fucking—'

'Brun!' Morin raises her voice again and gives him a deathly stare. 'Enough. Please.'

Brun looks as if he's about to object and say more, but then decides against it and hunkers back down in a sulk. Okeowo turns to Ana.

'Of course, we need to coordinate with Baikonur – they'll know what's safest. But Anders always said we had autonomy—'

'Ha!' Brun barks.

'They are our support, not our masters,' Morin says as Brun mutters something in French under his breath. 'We shall vote about whether we request this from Baikonur. I trusted you all with my life the moment that we lifted off. I trust you all to make the right decision now and we, as each other's crew members, should respect whatever that decision may be.'

Lee tentatively hooks himself back to the table and Brun slowly moves away, seemingly resigned to see how this plays out.

'I'll go round each of you in turn, and you can say what you think. We will go with the majority.' She turns to Okeowo next to her. 'Doc?'

Okeowo takes a moment. I feel a sudden glow of warmth towards her, always so considered, always so careful.

'Brun, I understand your concerns – this has not been a smooth ride. But I cannot believe that—'

WEEE-OOOOWW. WEEE-OOOOWW.

The colours in the room have plunged to red.

'Shit.' Morin pushes herself away from the table and checks the nearest screen on the wall. 'It's the radiation assessor. We have a solar energetic particle event.'

'Fuck!' I yell, as we all catapult ourselves into action.

Okeowo dives for her med bag. Brun zooms off towards the

greenhouse. Lee heads to prep the shelter, and Ana and I join Morin in prepping the modules and life-support systems.

'Yep, electron spike. It's a solar flare. Radiation will be with us in a matter of minutes,' Morin clips.

'Closing module doors,' Ana says calmly, tapping away on the screen. She clicks onto the ship's comms. 'Module doors closing in thirty seconds.'

'LS re-routed,' I confirm to Morin.

'Baikonur informed. Re-routing the main comms. Let's go.' Morin finishes on her screen with a flourish and pushes off just as we see Brun up ahead dart down towards the shelter with key plant samples under his arm, Okeowo on his tail.

Morin counts us in as we all float down into the belly of the ship, towards the service module and main storage bunkers and in through a circular hole, surrounded by huge tankers. The red makes it feel like we're heading underground. Lee pulls us through from the inside. Morin comes in last behind me and pulls the shelter door shut.

We're all in a bizarre tangle. There's no up or down in here, and it's a very tight squeeze. Faces are by feet, shoulders by crotches.

'Bags!' she calls, and in the reddened darkness we scrabble about to pass up the water bags that attach to the door for added shielding. Morin breathes heavily as she secures them in place.

'Punch it, Lee.'

Lee taps a few buttons on his tablet and the sirens stop. It feels like all sound has been eliminated from the world in an instant.

'We've got space down here, team,' Okeowo calls, and we begin to manoeuvre again, further down into the tunnel. The lighting has turned back to a normal, off-white/blue. Now it feels less like we're underground and more like we're all squeezed into a tiny cupboard. Which I suppose we are.

At one end, Okeowo, Brun and Ana are parked almost in a triangle with each other. Brun does not look pleased at his close proximity to Ana, but with space so limited, there'll be no place changes until we can get out of here – and that could be anything up to twenty-four hours. He busies himself finding a home for his plant samples among the emergency supplies.

'Good job, everyone,' Morin congratulates us, checking her tablet. 'No news from Baikonur yet about expected size, so let's just sit tight and see what happens.'

Easier said than done. First, it's hard to ignore the fact that right now, without us even feeling a thing, ionizing radiation could be searing through our ship and our flesh, destroying critical mechanisms, both electronic and biological. And second – well, let's just say our morale is not what it used to be.

'Brun, perhaps you could just . . .' Okeowo indicates he could shift slightly, to give Ana some more room, as she seems particularly cramped up against the wall.

'Fine,' he grumbles, but complies.

'Thank you,' Ana says politely. Her hair, thankfully, is in one long braid today. She tucks it into her shirt, clearly aware of how much it will irk Brun if it keeps floating around him.

The lone camera in the corner follows her movement automatically.

'They even put one in here,' Lee says, watching it warily. He's upside down to my orientation, as is Morin. They look like bats, hanging.

'Of course,' Okeowo says. 'Don't want to miss our hotboxing.'

'What would happen if we just, like, covered it?' Ana whispers. There's a stunned moment of silence.

'Well, there's no purple light to piss us off . . .' Brun concedes.

'They're not just Valdivian's cameras,' Morin says. 'They're also the only way Mission Control can see what's happening. Without them, they just have instruments and data readings.'

Of course, we all know this, but it's Valdivian and Abbey's presence that looms largest.

Okeowo suddenly lurches and leans over me, reaching for something above my head.

'Sorry, Rubio,' she says, opening up a drawer. Dehydrated food packets float upwards.

I try to avert my gaze as she leans further into the drawers and her chest approaches my face. Lee catches my eyes and suppresses a laugh, despite the palpable tension. It's the first time I've seen him smile in ages.

'Aha!' Okeowo cries, batting a box back out towards us all then clearing up the other floating packets.

Morin catches it.

'Brownies?'

'Yes.' Okeowo smiles broadly as she nestles herself between Ana and Lee again, taking the box off Morin. 'Ana, dear, these were supposed to be a treat for your birthday, but maybe you won't mind if we indulge a little early?'

Ana looks surprised, perhaps even a little touched, and she smiles.

'Not at all.'

Morin hands them out and we rip into them. The brownie is sweet, very sticky, and has that unmistakable taste of long-life, but it's still better than some of the other dessert options we've been served up recently.

'What day?' I ask Ana. We're going to be in here a while, so we might as well try at small talk.

'Friday,' Ana replies, picking a small amount of brownie off with her fingertips.

'We should do something to celebrate,' Lee offers, having already devoured his brownie. Brun's lips curl.

'Yes, we should,' I jump in, not allowing Brun the space to make a snide comment. I feel a bit of a thrill at forcing him to listen. 'What do you normally like to do, on your birthday, Ana?'

Ana smiles sadly. 'Oh, I haven't really celebrated it recently, with the training and my studying . . .'

'Well, what was the best birthday you've ever had?' Lee asks. I'm not sure if it's the sugary treat, my awkward moment with Okeowo's bosom, or simply this conversation, but he suddenly seems more animated.

Ana takes a thoughtful bite of her brownie, while Okeowo

gestures to me for something. I realize she's after my water pouch, which I'd attached to my belt without thinking earlier. I pass it over.

'My sixteenth. It was my best and my worst.'

'How come?'

'Best, because my mother took me to the science exhibition I had been begging to go to for weeks. We ate English scones in the museum cafe for lunch. Even my mother had one. She coated it with clotted cream, and laughed. She was having a good day. A stable day.'

Ana's words are loaded. I remember her mentioning, many weeks ago, that her mother was unwell.

'But when we got home, my father had arrived from Russia. He was furious. Had a whole dinner planned with his English friends at a private club in Mayfair. A young woman like me shouldn't be spending her sixteenth in a dingy museum, he said. He hit my mother that night. Said she wasn't worth the money he sent to her. And then put me in a designer dress and I spent the entire evening stuck between an elderly politician and his son. All of them remarking on how I looked so much older than sixteen.'

She lowers her half-eaten brownie, staring down at it.

'We ate caviar and Kobe beef. But nothing tasted as good as that scone did,' she says wistfully, her face serene, lost in her memories.

Okeowo coughs a little and I notice her eyes go wide as she pulls my water pouch away from her lips with a jerk. Her eyes dart at me, her face suddenly taut. She looks back at the pouch and holds it away from her as if it were poison.

The top of my stomach goes cold.

'That was back when he lived in Chelsea,' Ana continues. 'With his wife. He would only come over for big occasions. It was a relief when he could no longer visit.'

But I can hardly hear her through the sound of my pulse raging in my ears as Okeowo gingerly bats the pouch back to me and I grasp it in my hand.

'Because your father was exiled for his connections to Putin,' Brun interjects.

'Brun, assez,' Morin hisses.

We all feel the shift once again, the heavy weight of our earlier conversation bearing down upon us. And yet something else is now terrifying me. I place the straw mechanism of the pouch to my lips and squeeze . . .

'It's true,' he says. 'Her daddy is a fucking oil criminal.'

I cough.

That is not water. Not even remotely.

Even through my dulled sense of taste, I can feel it burning through my sinuses, I can tell what this is. That undeniable fire of ethanol.

I look back to Okeowo, her eyes boring into me.

'He was *wrongly* accused. My father fled to the UK—'

'Sure, he suddenly grew a conscience, but when Ukraine kicked off, his assets were frozen and he disappeared with his millions to the UAE where he continued to feed our species' filthy addiction to oil. And guess what else he invested in?'

Ana says nothing.

'He invested in media companies, my friends,' Brun says, triumphant. 'And guess which one young Ana's father happens to have many, many shares in?'

'Why don't you just leave her alone?' Lee snaps suddenly, his voice so earnest that even Okeowo and I are distracted. Any hint of a smile is now gone from his face. 'You have no right to bully and insult her all the time!'

Brun laughs bitterly. 'Please don't tell me you've fallen for it? The pretty looks. The beautiful performances?'

'Brun!' Morin and Okeowo both shout his name, but he ignores them.

'Don't you see? He bought her way on here. She's the perfect Trojan horse. A mole for Abbey and his cronies. Hell, maybe even a Russian spy! We all know Russia, China, America hated Anders and this mission, scared they'll be beaten to the post. Her father is an oil baron – what other valuable resources could be discovered and exploited on Mars?'

'Enough!' Ana cries, right in Brun's face, and for once he shuts up. 'I know you think I'm some sort of spy or saboteur, but I'm not.' Her cheeks are flushed, her eyes furious. 'I don't know what else I can do to convince you otherwise, so I give up. You will either come to the realization by yourself, or you will have to live with your suspicion and bitterness. Commander?'

Morin looks like a deer in headlights. 'Yes?' she manages.

'I think we should resume the vote. I would like to know whether the rest of the crew agree with Professor Brun.'

'None of us agree with—' Lee starts, but Ana cuts him off.

'Thank you, Lee, but we will do this and that will be the end of it.' Another charged look between them. Then Okeowo catches my eye again. God, I wish we weren't in here. If I could just say something to her, try to explain . . .

'Fine.' Morin says. 'As long as you promise to accept the result, Brun?'

Brun stares at Ana, eyes narrow. But then he waves as if to say go on.

'So, Okeowo? Terminate, or continue?'

Okeowo keeps eye contact with me for a moment longer. It's impossible to tell what she's thinking. I urge her not to say anything, beg her in my mind.

She turns to Morin.

'I vote we continue,' she says simply, before looking back at me. I breathe out with relief. For now.

'Thank you. Lee?'

'Continue, of course,' Lee says instantly.

'Lindroos?'

All eyes are on me.

'Err . . .' I croak. The poisoned pouch is still in my grasp. This is insane. Here I am, being tortured by one of my five fellow crewmates. Taunting me. Spiking me. Trying to frame me as an alcoholic . . . Which of course I am. 'Continue,' I blurt.

There. I've resigned myself to this fate, this one chance of redemption. If we make it to Mars, if we start a new world, it will all be worth it.

'Petrova?'

'Continue, of course. And I will prove to you all that I am worthy of your trust.'

All eyes turn to Brun, whose face is twisted with resentment.

'Fine,' he barks. 'We continue.'

Lee's body slumps a little in relief. Okeowo looks down, refusing to meet my gaze again.

'Then it's decided,' Morin says. 'And Brun, as commander, I want to remind you of what we've spoken about before. I will not have you antagonizing or insulting the rest of the crew. When we get out of here, you're on bathroom duty for the next two weeks.'

Brun just stares sullenly at his feet.

'And I want you to say sorry.'

'Commander, it's fine.' Ana's voice has returned to its soft, lyrical lilt.

'No,' Morin says firmly. 'Brun?'

Brun turns to Ana and smiles, but his eyes don't follow suit.

'Specialist Petrova, I am sorry,' he says, robotically, before looking at us. 'And to you all, I am truly sorry. But if things continue as they are, I really believe we will never set foot on that planet.'

None of us speaks after that. What is there to say?

And still, Okeowo won't look at me.

After a couple of hours, both Okeowo and Lee have nodded off. Ana looks as though she is reading a book on her tablet, although she seems not to have turned the page for a long time.

Brun, too, seems to be asleep. At least, his eyes are closed and he has turned away from the rest of the group.

Morin occasionally talks to me. We quietly discuss the upcoming schedule, she asks me when I'm next due to be interviewed. How my art is going – whether I've caught many images from the cupola recently. I answer mechanically.

I also take a couple more sips from my pouch. Feeling that undeniable rush through my brain. That sense of something solid hitting my stomach.

Then we hear four sharp beeps.

We all blink, dazed, as the lights brighten in the room, and Morin confirms what we already know.

'We're in the clear.'

'Thank God,' Okeowo breathes, and we unfasten the water bags and pass them back down to be stored. Morin unlocks the hatch and pulls herself out first, heading off to check the dosimeter in the command module.

The fresh air hits my face, making me realize just how hot and thick the shelter's atmosphere had become, even with all the filters and life support. Of course, we will never feel true fresh air ever again. But I guess it's all relative now.

We pull ourselves out of the shelter as quickly as possible and go our separate ways. Lee follows Morin up to the command module, Ana heads straight to the sleeping pods, Brun takes his samples back to the greenhouse. I hover, waiting for Okeowo, who still looks groggy from sleep.

'Ruth?' I ask, as she floats out into the corridor.

'Rubio.'

My water pouch bumps on my hip, where it's clipped once again to my belt. I wait for her questions, her disappointment, her chastisement, but nothing comes.

'The pouch, it's not—'

She raises her hand, then smiles at me, tired. 'Why don't you head off to the cupola?' she suggests gently. 'Take some pictures?'

She looks sad, but resigned. Is that how *I* look right now?

'Ruth, I can explain—'

She shakes her head and stops me. 'I know we could all do with some perspective right now,' she sighs.

And then she pushes off to the hab, leaving me adrift in space.

Alyssa

'HERE'S OUR RIDE,' DAD SAYS AS HE SWITCHES ON THE lights in the old barn we've driven out to. The place is pristine. Car parts, aircraft schematics and drawings adorn the walls and, right there in the centre, a gleaming Cessna aircraft, just big enough for four people.

'Since when—' I start.

'It's Mike's. He bought it for me, years ago, so I could take him flying some time. Even hooked up an extra-large fuel tank so we could make a trip out of it . . .'

From the way he tails off, I can tell the trip never happened. I wonder if that night put a stop to their dreams. Another loss that stems back to me.

Dad busies himself with the aircraft, and I place down the bags of supplies and start sorting them. Then I remember Jia, and turn to see her standing nervously by the barn door.

'Can that fly all the way across—'

'The Atlantic?' Dad calls from the back of the plane. 'No, not direct. But I have a few old contacts we can hit up on the way. People whose runways we can use, help us avoid *official* channels.'

Dad seems to be moving a bit lighter on his feet. There's an energy, a buzz about him that I can't remember seeing for a very long time. He emerges from the shadow of the plane, wiping his oily hands on a rag.

'Mind you, we may need to help persuade them to keep quiet,' he says to me, raising an eyebrow.

'I don't have much cash on me,' I reply. I used the entire contents of my wallet to get us here, and something tells me I shouldn't be using my cards any time soon.

He frowns. 'Me neither.'

'I have cash,' Jia pipes up, finally coming further into the room.

'My father appraises her. 'Enough to buy our way halfway across the world?'

'Would eighty thousand dollars do it?' she asks, shakily. My mouth drops. She's got $80,000 in her cat bag? She's never mentioned that before.

Jia looks sheepish in the face of our clear astonishment.

Dad laughs. It's a strange sound. A bark of surprise, triumph, maybe also a bit of relief.

'Well, that'll do it. Leaves plenty for fuel, too. Let's get going, then. Get your cat onboard, Jia. I'll find something that will work as a litter tray.'

The gesture seems to please Jia, and she smiles shyly as she walks past us towards the plane.

I look at Dad as he watches her go and I'm hit again by how fucking weird this all is. The man who shunned me for years, whose disappointment perpetually haunted me, is about to risk everything to take me and a crazy cat woman across the world.

'You don't have to do this,' I say. He turns sharply and looks at me, surprised. But I need to make sure. 'You don't have to make up for Mom . . .'

He moves over to me, and his old hands take mine in an act of intimacy I don't ever remember experiencing from him before.

'Yes, Alyssa, I do,' he says, so quietly I have to lean in to hear. 'I've spent a lot of time on my own these past six weeks. That's a lot of time to think. And I thought I'd lost everything: your mother, you. Well, this is my chance to try and make it up to you. I spent my life in service – but I realized recently that I never really served you. Let me do this for your crew.' He smiles, reaching up to my cheek, which is now moist with tears. 'Let me do this for you.'

I nod. It's all I manage.

Then he's pushing off towards the plane.

'Now, are you flying first shift, or am I?'

I cough. 'What?'

'Well, it'll be quicker if we both fly. One of us sleeps, one of us pilots. Save us a tonne of time, which I know you don't have.'

I gawp at him. In all these years, I've never flown with my dad. Sure, in a past life, I trained on T-38 jets. But he never showed the slightest interest in flying with me.

'What?' He smirks. 'You can fly a spaceship, but you can't fly this?'

'No. I can fly,' I blurt.

'You take second shift, then. I'll show you the ropes.'

Jia

THE WHIRR OF THE ENGINES IS THE FIRST THING I HEAR AS I'M dragged back to consciousness. The cockpit is a soft orange glow as we float towards the rising sun. Alyssa and Bill sit in silence, looking ahead into the sunrise. I blink at the brightness as I push myself up.

Orion.

I look around, but there's no sign of him. He's stopped sleeping up against me now. Since we escaped Alyssa's apartment, he's hardly let me touch him at all. I fumble around for my water bottle and top up the plastic box I've been using as his water bowl. It seems to be going down pretty quickly, so at least he's drinking.

As I search the cabin for him, my eyes catch a flash of white outside the window. I lean over and put my nose to the warm glass.

It's breathtaking. Below us, and as far as the eye can see, are rising and falling peaks of mountains, looking almost like clouds lying on the dark surface of the ocean. The early morning light glints off the sheer white faces of the hills and gullies of snow. And there must be glaciers, too. Veins of wrinkled ice meandering through the white rock.

I put my headphones on.

'Where are we?' I ask, looking back out the window.

'We're flying over Greenland,' Bill calls over the microphone from the pilot seat.

'It's beautiful!' I call back, mesmerized.

'It's changed,' he growls.

Alyssa is leaning out over her window too. Ahead, a dark ribbon approaches, weaving its way through the landscape like ink seeping across a page. A channel of water, frigid and deep, seeping into the ice shelf. Then I see a stark line, where darkest blue meets white. It's so strange to see such a straight line in this untamed landscape.

'There below us,' Bill says. 'That's the terminus of a glacier. All these wider ice sheets are draining into it.'

'There's a lot of them,' Alyssa replies, looking further ahead, where more dark ribbons creep.

'Last time I flew this route, the whole thing was sheer white. Far as you could see.'

'It's all melting?' I ask.

'Looks like it.'

'The Anthropocene in action,' Alyssa says, almost bitterly. Before I can ask what she means, Orion emerges and sniffs around the water bowl tentatively.

I lean over and pick him up, facing him towards the window, both of us bathed in sunrise and snow-glow.

'Look, O,' I whisper to him, stroking his back. He purrs, but when I pass over a certain spot, he flinches and I have to grab him to keep him on me. Frowning, I run my hand back over his spine again and there, about two thirds of the way down, towards his tail, he jumps again. I thought I'd caught all his scrapes from the other day. His paws and legs are healing nicely. What is this?

Clenching him firmly but not too tightly between my legs, I begin to feel around his back. His fur is dense, and he gives an almost silent meow as I begin to part it. And then an awful smell hits me. Bitter. Decay.

A bit of red and yellow.

And then I find it: a small circular hole of pus and dried blood, bright against his pale grey skin.

'Fuck,' I hiss.

'What is it?' Alyssa calls.

'Orion is hurt! He has a cut or a puncture or something on his back.' I tentatively put my finger to the wound. It's hot. Moist. Orion squeals and launches himself off my legs, dashing under a seat and arching his head round to lick at the area. I look at my finger, a tiny amount of pus on its tip. I put it to my nose, then recoil.

'It's infected,' I call to Alyssa, as I try to stop Orion licking himself. I don't know much, but I know he shouldn't swallow that stuff. He retreats further under the chair where I can't see him. 'Bill, do you have a medical kit?'

'Under the back right seat. Why?'

'Her cat's injured,' Alyssa explains as I scramble over our bags. 'You need help, Jia?'

I find the kit, and take it back to my seat, keeping one eye on where Orion is as I sort the contents, looking for some sort of antiseptic.

'I need to clean it. He must have been hit by something and we didn't realize. His fur is so thick.'

A bottle of surgical spirit and some gauze emerge. That will work . . . now just to get him.

In the cockpit, Alyssa is rummaging herself.

'What are you doing?' grumbles Bill.

'Do you need this?' she asks, holding up a laminated document.

'No, it's an old flight plan.'

'Great,' Alyssa says. Holding a couple of the laminated sheets, she takes off her headphones and clambers over the seats to join me in the back.

'Cable ties,' she says, her mouth moving exaggeratedly, in case I can't hear. 'In that crate.' She points to it, and I set the gauze and antiseptic down and unbox the crate. I turn back to her with a handful of the ties, finding her puncturing the edges of the laminated sheets with a pair of scissors.

'What are you doing?' I ask, raising my voice over the hum of the engines and propellers.

Alyssa threads the cable ties through the holes, joining the two sheets together. Then she curves it round.

'A cone,' she yells, leaning over for her headphones, placing them back on. 'For his head.' Her voice comes back over the system again. 'If he has a wound, we don't want him licking it, do we?'

I smile at her and she smiles back.

'He'll be fine. Here, I'll help you get him.'

Together, we manage to coax Orion out from under the chair enough for her to hold him, while I search again for the puncture wound. Alyssa grimaces too when I reveal it. How could we have missed that smell? I pour a little antiseptic onto the gauze and begin to lightly dab at the wound. Orion's claws scratch at the floor as he writhes in pain.

'Shhh, I'm sorry!' I hush. As I clean it, a deep red hole emerges, where something has really dug down into his flesh. There's a glint in the sunlight.

'There's glass!' I call.

'Get it out, then,' Alyssa urges. I take up the med kit again, and snatch up the tweezers.

'Hold him,' I breathe. Trying not to think about it too much, I pull his skin taut and insert the tweezers, picking at the glint of glass with shaking hands. It doesn't come out. Orion howls.

'I've got him,' Alyssa says.

I pluck at the glass again, and again, until I feel purchase, then jerk my hand up.

'Got it!' I say, holding it up to the light. It's a thin shard, almost the length of my fingernail.

'Help me get the cone on, now,' Alyssa says. I take over holding him as she slips a cable tie over Orion's hissing head and loops the cone onto it, before tightening it as much as she can without hurting him. She then leans past me, grabs the gauze and antiseptic, and deftly dabs at the wound once more.

'Let him go.' I do as she says and Orion dashes forward to get under the chair again, but the cone stops him dead. He tries to reverse out of the cone, but of course he can't, and he spins helplessly, thrashing his head about.

I instinctively move to help him, but Alyssa holds me back.

'Let him get used to it,' she says.

After a minute, he clumsily jumps up and over some bags, and settles himself in a corner, his heavy head resting on the lid of a crate, staring sadly at me.

Ashamed, I look down at the floor at the little shard of glass. Alyssa sees it too and picks it up with the bloody gauze, spiriting it away into a plastic bag.

'He's had that in there for days. How did I not realize?'

'It's fine,' Alyssa says, as she tidies the med kit away again. 'We got it out. He'll be fine.'

'But the smell . . .'

'Just a little pus. We cleaned it, he'll be fine. It wasn't that deep.' She squeezes my shoulder and then climbs back into her seat. 'We'll keep an eye on it, OK?' she calls back to me as she fastens herself in. I look back over at Orion, who looks miserable as sin and is now trying and failing to lick himself.

Kai is going to kill me. How could I let him get hurt like that? And what if it's really infected? Can cats have antibiotics? And where would we get them, anyway?

Alyssa senses my anxiety and tries to distract me.

'We don't have long until the next stopover, right?' she asks her dad.

'Nope. Scotland next. Then it's just a hop and a skip to the continent.'

As the engines rumble on, I breathe deeply, trying not to panic. Maybe when we next land for fuel we can find someone to check him over. Alyssa must be medically trained – she would tell me if there's something properly wrong.

I look back out over the snowscape below. It feels colder, harsher now. And I'm suddenly aware of the water, the power, the life of the place, draining away.

Rubio

THE DAY OF ANA'S BIRTHDAY, WE ALL — WITH THE EXCEPtion of Brun, of course — make a special meal and gather together in the hab to watch *Swan Lake*. The rest of the crew sigh and gasp in all the right places. Lee has never seen ballet before and is entranced, much to Ana's pleasure. But it's like I am seeing everything through a pane of glass. A distance has grown between me and them, particularly Okeowo, who barely says a word to me now. I keep thinking of the pouch in my sleeping bag, and how there will be one small moment of solace at the end of the day. And even if I try to get rid of it, another one will appear in its place.

When the ballet comes to its tragic end, I say I'm heading to bed. There, alone in my pod, I drain the last of it as if I were a man emerging from the desert.

As I let the sensation wash over me, I consider calling it a night.

But I find myself pulled in the direction of the cupola. The utter blackness of space feels like it's calling to me. Another way to submerge myself in the illusion of oblivion, if only for a moment longer.

I don't know how long I'm in there for. It is well after I hear Okeowo, Brun, and Morin making their way to their pods before I begin to consider joining them. But then I hear a scuffle, quiet voices. Ana and Lee.

I slink back into the dark recess, where I'm sure they can't see me. If they know I'm up and about, they'll ask why. And I just cannot face talking to anyone right now.

The two of them are whispering, low and soft. I can't make out what they're saying over the background din of the *Argo*. Hopefully I can find a moment to float past them; perhaps they'll only stay in the cupola for a few minutes before going to bed.

'Wait,' Lee urges, as they move up towards the panoramic windows. I flatten myself against the wall as he dashes past me and reaches up for something above. The camera. He turns it, then he moves to the other side and turns that one too.

Who'd have thought it? Lee having the guts to do what we've all been fantasizing about for months.

Ana's wide eyes sparkle in the starlight. 'Dong-hyun?' she gasps.

'Shh,' he soothes as he floats back to her. He fumbles at his waistband, taking off his mic pack and unthreading it from beneath his polo shirt, sending it spinning off behind him.

He holds out a hand to her, waiting. She looks at him for a moment, and then follows suit, rummaging at her waistband, slipping the mic out of her top and handing it to him. Without taking his eyes off her, he sends it spinning off towards his. The two gently clash in the air, and their wires snag and entangle with each other. No purple light glows. It will be well over a minute before Abbey and his cronies even know of their mutinous act.

They're much closer now. Lee's hand is cupped around Ana's head, his fingers entwined in her beautiful floating mane of gold. Their noses are practically touching. She places her hand on his waist, anchoring the two of them further as they float against a background of darkness and light. And then there's no light between them any more. They're kissing, now just a merged shadow, their shared outline picked out by starlight and earthshine.

I glance towards the exit – the tunnel leading back to where I should be, where they should be. But it's far too close to them. They'd see me, feel my disturbance as I dart past. Do I make myself known, tell them I fell asleep watching the stars, perhaps? What if they stop to speak to me, smell the guilt on my breath? My weakness oozing out of every pore . . .

I swallow hard, still able to taste the tang of the alcohol on my tongue. I can't be seen like this.

A small thud breaks my spiralling thoughts. The two of them have backed up against the central window in the cupola, Ana's back pressed against the quadruple-paned glass. Her hands grasp for handles above her head and below her feet, and Lee pulls himself against her, their shadow morphing as they explore each other's bodies. Light thumps sound against the window as they clumsily fight the lack of gravity. Buttons and zips unfasten. Their breathing heavy. Whispers of encouragement, of urging, of wanting.

As Lee's shadow moves into hers, Ana lets out a small gasp. Two lonely souls, entwined together, they move as one in the darkness, their breaths broken only by fast, low whispers.

They're further from me now, and their breathing is louder, ragged. Lee moans and I take my cue, launching myself sideways and out of the recess, towards the exit of the cupola.

I hear no cries, no gasps of astonishment. My hand stretches out ahead of me as far as possible, fingers straining to make it to the handhold on the side of the door seal. Finally, they reach metal and gingerly I pull myself through the doorway.

I'm practically through the hatch now, but I can't help but briefly turn back. From here, I can see the whole of the cupola. My crewmates have not noticed me. Their entire universe is wrapped up in each other as the expanse of the cosmos stretches out behind them. All that ever was, and ever will be, fades into nothingness in comparison to that moment. I cannot help but think of the Vitruvian Man. No. Vitruvian *people*. Limbs and essence outstretched. Ideally proportioned and totally complete, connected to everything and nothing all at once.

The purple light clicks on, but they don't stop.

I make my lonely way back down the ship towards the sleeping quarters, only the faintest of sighs echoing and dissipating into the hum of the life-support systems. As I approach the pods, heavy, dreamless breathing greets me. They're all oblivious. I slide past and hunker down into my sleeping bag, drawing the curtains to cocoon myself in darkness. My own breathing rattles through my head as I slide into my sleeping bag and turn from the relentless gaze of the camera.

There's a warmth and a pressure below and within me. I can't help but feel the rush of blood, the increase in circulation as I float in my bed, thinking of the two of them. How fucked up I am. How twisted and broken. And because of this, because of my despicable lack of control over anything, I reach down and silently, shamefully, give in and indulge in my perversion. Alone, consumed with envy at the two people who have managed to find one moment of happiness, of connection, in this cold, dark vacuum of space.

Jia

ANOTHER STOP.

This time there are raised voices outside as we wait for the plane to be refuelled. I'm in my usual spot, on the floor with Orion. Bill has told us to remain out of sight whenever we're on the ground. It's safer that way.

I scratch Orion's ear, trying to block out the raised voices for him. 'We're so close.' I whisper to him, but he just lies there, listless. 'Please don't be sick.'

There's a bang on the side of the plane.

I jump, wincing.

'We gotta go,' Bill hisses from outside, and Alyssa clambers up from her spot, cursing the boot that weighs down her leg. She stays low and crawls to the front, flicking switches and turning knobs, until the plane wakes up.

'We're not even half full!' she hisses to her dad, as he runs around the plane, climbs into the co-pilot's seat and slams the door.

'We have to go now.' He's tense as he scrambles with his harness, and I feel a dart of alarm.

The engines start whirring again, and we're moving. I put my head through the chairs at the front. 'What's happening?'

'I may have misjudged this one,' Bill mutters, looking out of the window and back to where we just left. 'Apparently not even money can get you a free pass in Azerbaijan any more. Come on!' Bill hits the dash of the plane.

A loud screeching sounds outside. Sirens.

'Fuck!' Alyssa cries, not taking her eyes off the runway as we taxi towards it. 'They called the police?'

'DO NOT TAKE OFF. REPEAT. DO NOT TAKE OFF!' A loud voice booms in a stilted accent.

My head spins. Oh God. We're going to be stopped. They're going to arrest us. They'll extradite me to China. And Kai? There'll be no one left to find him. And Mom . . .

I back away, into the corner. The plane vibrates, loud. The wind rushing.

'Come on,' Bill growls.

Alyssa keeps flicking things. 'Jia, strap in!' she yells. I do as I'm told. She looks calm, but scared.

BANG.

Something pings.

'Shit!' Alyssa yells.

I scream.

'They're shooting!' Bill barks.

'Hold on,' Alyssa calls.

The plane is so loud. We are moving so fast.

BANG BANG BANG.

More sirens. More screaming, although I think that's from me.

PING PING.

'Come on!'

The plane lurches up and then down. It lurches again – up, up and down. Then just up.

BANG BANG BANG.

The bags slide towards the back of the cabin. One flies at me and I bat it away. Boxes shift. And suddenly, Orion is jumping onto my lap. The most movement from him I've seen in days. I cling to him as the horizon tilts to an impossibly steep slope. We rattle, then slant to one side. I see green and grey out of the window nearest me. Blue in the one now above.

Then we turn the other way, everything flying and sliding. Orion's claws dig into me. It hurts, but I don't let go.

'Where now?' I cry.

'Straight out over the Caspian Sea, out of their airspace. Keep low to avoid the radar, right, Dad?' Alyssa shouts.

Bill nods.

'And then what?' I ask.

'Then we might just make it into Kazakhstan. Set us down somewhere. Get you a car,' he calls back.

'What do you mean, "might"?'

The old man is silent.

Alyssa gives him a worried glance. 'Dad?'

'I don't know about fuel,' Bill says, loud and fast.

We are not lurching so much any more but the vibrations are still too much for Orion. He tries to bury himself deep into my lap, but the cone doesn't let him. I scoop him up in my arms, holding him tight, whispering all the comfort I can.

The plane rumbles on, and I don't ask anything else.

Alyssa

IN THE CO-PILOT SEAT, DAD IS SCRAMBLING WITH HIS MAPS again, and I feel a twinge of unease.

'You OK there?' I call out on the headset.

'Everything's fine.'

'You sure?'

'I'm just . . . a little, lost.' He looks at the instruments, frowns, then looks back to the map.

'May I?' Before he can answer, I lean over and take the map. Instantly I see the issue. 'Dad, this map is over twenty years old.'

'I know. I haven't flown over Europe, let alone Asia, for years, but—'

'You're looking for the Aral Sea, right?'

'Yes, but do you see a damn sea?'

I look out of the window. Below us, our dark shadow flickers over an empty, barren landscape. Nothing but dust and dirt for miles and miles.

'Unfortunately, I do, Dad. This is it.'

My father rubs his eyes, exhausted. We all are. His eyes flicker again to the dial that I, too, can't stop looking at. Our fuel is terrifyingly low. We'll have to set down somewhere soon. If we're lucky, close enough to somewhere we can barter ourselves a ride.

'This ain't a sea.'

'It used to be.'

As if to prove my point, something up ahead begins to take shape.

I point and as it gets closer, it reveals more of itself. A huge hulk of rusting metal, hunkered down among the sand and salt, groaning under its own weight and the corrosive winds that drag past it.

'Well, I'll be damned. Is that a boat?'

More begin to appear on the horizon. We stare at them, wide-eyed, as they plunge past us, our shadow skimming over their rusting carcasses. Dozens of beached and abandoned ships and boats, scattered across the landscape.

'What the hell happened here?'

'We did.'

I've read about the Aral Sea. Some of the Martian images *Pathfinder* sent back in the nineties have been compared to it. I've studied those images of a long-dry, ancient body of water on Mars, its lack of a distinct shoreline. A rapid regression, so fast it didn't even leave a mark. That's what happened here, too. The world's fourth-largest lake, obliterated. Its tributaries diverted; an entire ecosystem left to die.

The sight of the dried-up seabed laid bare, salt glistening in the relentless sunlight, is astounding. Is this what I would have found on the Circum-Chryse region, all those millions of miles away? Something so alien, and yet it was right here in front of my eyes – and so close to the place I had once worked, trained, dreamed of Mars. My mom always wondered why the hell I was so fascinated with Mars. *Isn't this planet interesting enough for you?* she'd say, exasperated. The sudden memory of her, her voice, punches me in the gut.

'What's that up ahead?' Jia cuts through on the headphones system, making me start. She's been much quieter since we found Orion's puncture wound.

The horizon looks fuzzy, dark, a haze all along it, like someone has smudged it out.

'Shit,' Dad growls.

'A dust storm. Fuck,' I mutter, then turn to the back of the plane. 'Jia, wet a shirt and put it over your mouth. Do the same for me and Dad.' I turn back to him. 'What do we do?'

'Buckle up,' he says, pulling hard on his harness. 'You got this.'

I can count weeks, maybe even months of flight time. My father's got years. While his faith in me is touching, I can't help but wish he were in the pilot's seat right now.

Already the crosswinds are picking up. The dust storm looms.

I take my hands off the yoke and unclip my harness. 'Dad!' I call through the headset.

He looks at me, startled. 'What are you—?'

'Swap with me.'

His eyes meet mine, shocked. But I smile at him.

'It's OK,' I say. 'I can't take control of this one. I trust you.'

He looks once more at the storm ahead, and then he's moving fast, unclipping and taking the yoke. I fumble around him, slumping back into the co-pilot seat.

He begins to flick switches and turn dials, and I know I've made the right choice.

'Here.' We take the damp shirts Jia thrusts at us, tying them around our mouths and noses.

'Thanks.' I glance back at her. 'Strap in, and get Orion in the bag – he'll be safer in there.'

I tighten my harness and turn my attention back to the horizon. We can feel it now – the plane is rattling more than usual. My dad's hands and arms work hard to steady her. The ominous cloud ahead grows larger, sucking all the light out of the air.

'What about fuel?'

'Not good,' he says through gritted teeth.

A scream erupts from behind.

'Jia, calm down, we'll be—'

'No!' She grabs my shoulder and I turn to see her terrified face. 'Look!'

She holds a floppy ball of fur: Orion.

'He's not moving,' she cries. 'He's barely opening his eyes.'

Shit. His little body is rising up and down with quick breaths, and there's drool around his mouth. He's alive, but barely. The whole plane begins to shake.

'Jia, get in your seat!' Dad yells, but even through the headsets it's hard to hear one another now. The wind howls.

'Alyssa!' Jia pleads. 'What do we do?'

I have no idea.

'Put him in the bag, OK? Maybe cool him down with some water. We'll get him some help, but you have to sit down.'

'Now!' Dad yells.

Wide-eyed, Jia does what we say and straps herself in, then lifts Orion's body into the carrier.

I turn back to the front just as the cloud envelops us.

PHWUM.

The whole plane is cast in an eerie, dark-mustard light as the sound of millions of particles of sand, salt and dust hitting it fills our ears. We can't see even a foot in front.

My dad keeps as steady a hand as he can on the yoke, his eyes darting between instruments. He's flying blind now, the altimeter his only indication of where he is.

The air starts to get thicker in the cockpit as the dust infiltrates. My hands feel chalky, my eyes begin to sting and water. Dad coughs beneath the wet shirt.

'We need to get higher, fly out of it!' I scream over the din.

'We can't risk being seen on radar! We're right by the Uzbekistan border. We can't be seen!'

BANG.

The plane jolts on the right. 'What the fuck was that?'

'Larger debris!' he grimaces.

BANG.

Jia screams. Alarms bleep on the dash as the plane's engines stutter. I look out to the wing and the propeller. I can barely see it, but intermittent dark flashes reassure me that it's still spinning.

'An engine is overheating!' Dad calls out.

Then the whole plane shudders violently and slants left. My father expertly brings it back, but with a series of pops, and the alarms screeching even louder, it becomes clear: we've lost an engine.

'This thing can fly with one engine, right?' I yell.

'I got it!' he snaps, really fighting with the pull of the plane now, the asymmetry of her thrust an almost impossible burden.

The air in the cockpit clouds with ever more dust. My throat is so dry and I start coughing, heaving. I push the shirt closer over my nose and mouth.

'Should we bring her down?' I splutter into the microphone.

'We bring her down, we're down for good – especially with one engine!' he shouts. 'We've got to get as far as we can!'

I squint through the haze at the fuel dial. We're running on fumes.

BANG. Something else hits us. BANG. And another. A splitting CHINK and the window by me fractures into a starburst. There's a hiss of air on my arm, which burns from the corrosive dust.

We surge upwards, downwards, the wind tossing us about. At some point, I close my eyes and track on my closed eyelids the grooves and rivulets of the burned-out seabed that must still be racing beneath us.

'OK!' Dad shouts. My eyes fly open, stinging from the haze. 'I'm bringing her down!'

There's that unmistakable lurch as he relinquishes the plane to the Earth's gravitational pull. As we descend into the dust cloud, it gets thicker, darker, so that it feels more like we're a submarine than an aircraft. The place fills with white noise as we smash our way through the innumerable particles. The plane's remaining engine groans.

Then I see something. A glimpse of something solid. Whole. The ground? No, a reflection.

'Water!' I yell.

'I know!' Dad bellows, and the plane pitches harshly to the right. The dust takes over and we're flying blind again. Dad tears off the wet shirt in frustration. He's breathing hard, panting, his expert eyes searching for somewhere safe to land.

'There!' I scream, as something solid but dull hoves into view. Solid ground, it has to be. The altimeter is dangerously low. It's now or never.

Dad drops the landing gear. There's screaming, from the engine or maybe Jia, as we bounce up and down, buffeting in the wind, clambering to reach the safety of terra firma.

At the last minute, Dad tries to pull up but we're coming in too hard, too fast, and there's nothing he can do.

'HOLD ON!' he yells, before—

CRACK.

Metal screeches and snaps. Bangs everywhere. We bounce up, our bodies snapped back down again by our harnesses, and the plane spins. We've lost our wheels. We're on our belly. But it's land we're on, not water. Land.

Groaning, the craft judders to an ungainly stop.

We're down.

'FUCK!' my father bellows, smashing his hands on the yoke.

I breathe out. The dust cloud still swirls around us, but we are stationary within it, and I feel weak with relief.

'What now?' Jia's small voice calls out from behind us, still clutching Orion's bag tightly.

Dad unbuckles himself and grabs a water bottle, taking a swig before throwing some over his face in a futile attempt to clear the dust.

'Now,' he croaks. 'We wait.'

Jia

BILL MANAGES TO DRIFT OFF SURPRISINGLY QUICKLY. SOON, his snores are competing with the sandstorm outside. I huddle down in my seat, suddenly feeling really cold. It's still dusty in here, so I'm scared to take Orion out of his bag. Instead, I reach in and feel his paws, his little chest. His heart is still beating, but I swear it's fainter than it was. His paws are so small. I lift them up, and there's no resistance. He's like a big fluffy doll. Kai would be out of his mind with worry right now.

I'm out of my mind with worry right now.

I wish Erica were here. She would have found the wound, cleaned it, and sealed it days ago. Soothing both me and Orion at the same time. I shove the thoughts of her dark, smiling eyes from my mind. How can someone I only spent eight days with occupy so much of my brain? I should be thinking about Kai. It's been over eleven weeks now, and what the hell have I achieved?

I hunker down, enveloped in frustration.

'How's he doing?'

I cough, and pull a blanket tight around me. How long have I been asleep?

'Here,' Alyssa continues, and hands me the meagre remains of the last bottle of water. I swig it down gratefully. It's not enough.

'I don't know,' I finally rasp. 'I think he's unconscious, or maybe in a coma or something.'

'Try not to worry. As soon as we've got the code to Jake, we'll find someone to help him,' she says.

'And find my brother?' I say pointedly.

Alyssa blinks. 'Yes, of course,' she replies. 'If there's a clue in the code, Jake will find it.'

The sandstorm flings something large at us and it rattles overhead. I wince, but Alyssa hardly notices. Lost in her thoughts, she glances over at her sleeping father. Perhaps she's thinking about her home, her mom. I'll never forget witnessing the moment she was told about her death. It made me think of my own mother. All alone. No one will have visited her in two months now.

'Who is Jake?' I ask, to distract myself.

She tenses up. 'I told you,' she clips back. 'He's a coder who works on Mars One.'

'I know,' I stop her. 'But who is he to you?' She looks at me, confused. 'You put a lot of faith in him, I can tell. And you're so desperate to see him. Why?'

'Because he's helped me so much already,' Alyssa almost whispers, and the strange shift in her voice makes me look up in surprise. She's turned away and is looking out at the infinite haze of the storm, and suddenly she doesn't look as strong, as commanding. She looks like exactly what she is: a woman stranded in the middle of nowhere with only hope pushing her forward.

'I'm sorry about your mom,' I try. 'You . . . you hadn't seen her for a while?'

'No,' Alyssa replies, still staring out.

I think of the fear and confusion when Mom last looked right into my face.

'My brother and I, we've lost our mom too, well – most of her. She has dementia. My brother hasn't seen her properly for nearly two years. He can't face it. You know, the more I think about it, I think he can't stand the idea of a problem he can't solve. It's like her mind is being slowly encrypted. All the data, all the little bits that used to make her who she was, they're all getting lost, hidden, corrupted. And it's the one code he can't crack. The only one that really matters. So, he's cut his losses, abandoned it as a lost cause. Abandoned her.'

Alyssa gives no reply, but I feel a sense of clarity. Like I'm finally starting to understand everything a little more than I did before.

I think of the *Dolly* – the crew, and the ship, and those endless days out on the ocean, completely isolated, imagining what it would be like if that had been the rest of my life. My whole world narrowed down to just those two dozen people, those steel walls. And yet we could still see and feel a whole world outside. There's no comparison, really.

'Why did you want to go to Mars and never come back?' I ask her, stroking Orion's soft and motionless paw.

CLUNK.

Something else hits the side of the plane and Bill stirs, before shifting onto his side. Alyssa remains silent.

I check in on Orion again. He's still asleep. Short, shallow breaths. Clinging on.

'I thought there was nothing left for me here,' Alyssa finally replies, looking at her father. 'I guess I was wrong.'

I sit back and watch out of my window as the sand whooshes past, creating strange shadows and shapes that shift and disappear as soon as you look for them. I think of Mom, and of Agnes and Penny, and Erica, and Kai, and everything before all this madness. How I'd curated my little life, built the existence I thought I should have, did the things I thought I should do, without ever realizing how little I knew, or even felt. Or how much I could lose.

'I'm wrong all the time,' I offer Alyssa, rolling up tighter in the blanket and hoping, more than anything, that soon this storm will pass.

Alyssa

IT TAKES SEVERAL MORE HOURS FOR THE DUST STORM TO dissipate. As we wait, my dad sleeps, as does Jia for a bit, but I can't drift off. I'm too thirsty, and I keep thinking about my mom, about Jake, and poring over Dad's old maps, trying to estimate how far we've come, where we might have landed. As the storm eases, I hope for something to emerge out of the windows that will help place us, but our landing site is just as desolate and featureless as the Aral Sea.

By the time the wind has abated, I think I can just about make out something in the distance, to the east. I wake up a groggy and stiff Dad, and Jia, who instantly checks on Orion, but by the look of her face, there's no change in his condition.

I point out the window.

'I think civilization is that way. We'll have to head off on foot and hope we find a way to work out where we are, or someone who is willing to help us. I have a few dollars left, but how much it'll take to pay our way to safety depends on how far from Baikonur we are.' I shift uncomfortably. I don't want to ask if Jia has any cash left – she's already given too much.

It doesn't take long to pack up everything. We're low on food, and out of water. It's going to be a tough walk in this desert landscape.

Clambering out of the plane, I gasp at the sight of the damage she sustained. Several bullet holes from Azerbaijan, multiple dents, the burned-out engine, and her crumpled belly from our crash landing. I imagine her lying here for all eternity, turning to rust like those long-abandoned ships. Another vessel, dead, lifeless. I think of the *Argo* and my stomach turns.

'Come on!' I say to myself as much as the others. 'Let's go.'

Jia doesn't need much convincing, but Dad hangs back. He runs his hand over the body of the plane, looking her over wistfully, muttering.

'Bill?' Jia says quietly.

'She was past her prime anyway,' Dad sighs, before giving her a final pat and shouldering his bag.

We start out slower than I would like. My boot is a real pain in the ass and Dad isn't much of a walker. Jia marches a little further ahead of us, Orion's bag in its rightful place on her shoulders. I get in step with her.

'You OK?'

'I'm just worried about Orion.' She sniffs, and squints up ahead.

I don't really know what to say to that, so I say nothing.

'If he . . .' She breaks off, looking down at her feet then returning her gaze to the distance. 'If he doesn't make it . . . my brother . . . and your ship, your crew – will they be OK?'

I sigh. 'Honestly? I think they'll be in real danger if we can't get Orion to Jake in time. Your brother sounds really smart but . . . the whole kill switch thing in Orion is a real fucker.'

She nods, looking miserable.

'But it's not going to come to that, OK? He probably just needs some rest, some antibiotics. Maybe even to not be carted halfway across the world for a bit. We'll get him to Jake. Get the code, work out what the fuck is going on with the *Argo* – what your brother knew, and we'll find out who took him and where he is.' Privately, though, I doubt that whoever faked his 'murder' really faked it . . .

A rumbling in the distance saves me from this train of thought. A little dust trail is being kicked up ahead of us. It looks like something from a vehicle. We all freeze. It's definitely an engine. Someone's driving towards us.

Before I know it, Jia is waving at them, jumping up and down.

'Hey!'

'Jia!' I grab her. 'We don't even know who the fuck it is.'

She pulls away from my grasp. 'What difference would it make? We need help! HEY!'

The sound of the engine changes and the silhouette of a jeep speeds along the horizon.

Jia runs further towards them, shouting at the top of her lungs. Next moment, Dad joins in and both of them are bouncing up and down like loons.

But the Jeep keeps on rolling, and soon the sound of the engine fades away.

Jia screams and kicks at the dust beneath her feet.

Dad turns to me. 'How much longer?'

I know without asking that he means until nightfall. Until the heat of the day dies off, and we have to contend with the chill.

I grimace in response.

'Come on, Jia,' he says, turning. 'We need to keep moving.'

Hours later, my head is pounding.

We've taken a break, sharing out a couple of oranges. The segment's sweet juices do nothing to quell my thirst. If anything, it makes it worse.

Dad has fashioned a headscarf from a spare shirt, while Jia's arms and chest are an angry shade of crimson. None of our phones have signal, and Jake has no idea where we are. We could not be in a worse situation if we tried.

I heft my bad leg up and shake it. The support boot is full of sand and itches like hell.

Fuck it.

I unbuckle it and pull it off, and my foot suddenly feels light as air. Dad eyes what I'm doing, but says nothing as I stuff the support boot into my bag.

I'm just debating whether to keep my sneaker on my good foot, or go with just socks on both, when a light sound reaches us on the wind.

All of us stop. None of us breathe.

There it is again, louder this time. The unmistakable roar of something mechanical. I shield my eyes and squint out towards the horizon, as Jia leaps to her feet.

'There!' she cries.

A pickup truck.

'Over here!' Jia screams, her voice hoarse and dry. 'Help!'

We all join in this time. I push myself up onto my freed foot. It's tender, but it feels so much better than dragging the dead weight around.

The sound of the engine shifts with a change of direction. It's getting closer.

'Thank God,' Dad croaks.

I keep waving, praying it's not police or armed forces. I'd take being stuck in a desert without water over them any day. But the closer it gets, the more I can tell it's a beat-up piece of crap so it must be someone local – wherever local is.

The truck pulls up several metres ahead of us. With a creak and a clunk, the door opens and closes, and a figure emerges from the other side. It's an old woman, small, bent over. She puts her hand up to shield her eyes and appraises us.

Silence.

I take a step forward, and brush off my Russian.

'*Hello?*' She doesn't move. '*We're looking for help. Please.*' I raise my arms to make clear I'm not a threat, and the other two follow suit. Still, she doesn't say anything. I shuffle a little closer. Maybe she doesn't speak Russian.

'*Hello?*' I try in tentative Kazakh.

She finally nods. I experience a fleeting moment of relief, then apprehension. I only know a few words. As I scramble for them, I inch closer to her. She's very old. Her facial features have folded in on themselves under decades of wrinkles. Her grey hair is hidden under a woollen scarf pulled over her head. She looks at me blankly.

I point back towards where the plane is.

'*Our plane*,' I say, reverting back to Russian. '*Crash. We need help. A telephone.*'

Her eyebrows raise at the final word. She looks past me, at Dad and Jia, and I see us as she must: bedraggled and exhausted. Desperate.

She looks back at me again, assessing, before nodding and gesturing for us to follow her. She coughs heavily as she clambers into the driving seat. She's barely tall enough to see over the wheel.

I dart towards the doors before she changes her mind, ignoring the pain shooting up my leg. Dad and Jia pile in behind me. As soon as the doors are shut, the old engine roars to life and she spins us around, more dust flying, heading east.

On the radio, Madonna is playing: 'Like A Prayer'. It's bizarre. The woman stares straight ahead, giving only the occasional hacking cough, as we bounce along the terrain before reaching something that looks a bit like a road. She turns onto it and soon we begin to see tufts of plants, some scrawny trees and one lone string of electricity pylons. Civilization. If I already weren't sitting, I'd collapse with relief.

Eventually, she turns onto a long, dusty drive that leads to a low-lying white building with a tin roof. A camel turns with a bored expression as we pull up near some old rusting barrels. The place is completely isolated, the windows dark.

She gets out and heads into the house, coughing as she goes. I look at Dad in the back seat and he shrugs, looking just as wary as I feel. She's left the door to the house open, so I can only assume she wants us to follow.

When my eyes adjust from the blinding desert light to the gloom of the room, it's clear that this is the woman's home. Small, but neat and tidy, there's a couple of armchairs, a basic kitchen with Soviet-era appliances, and a small table. A couple of doors lead off the main room. The woman is in the corner of the kitchen, pulling a dusty old cell phone off a shelf and unplugging it.

She turns back to us and holds it out.

I rush over to her. '*Thank you*,' I say in Kazakh. She nods, then turns and opens up her old refrigerator, pulling out a chipped jug. She takes down some tumblers from a cupboard and pours four glasses of water.

I turn back to Dad and Jia, who don't seem to know what to do with themselves.

'Why don't you guys sit and I'll . . .' I shake the phone and they nod. The woman shuffles over and hands them a glass each, before settling herself in a chair. Dad and Jia practically throw the water down their throats.

I lick my dry cracked lips and dial on the tiny keypad, the woman watching my every move.

It rings.

Come on, Jake. Come on. Pick up.

But I curse as it goes to voicemail.

I turn away from the others and lower my voice, still not sure just how much this old woman understands.

'Jake, it's me. I need to talk to you. Now. Call me back on this number as soon as you can.'

I hang up and turn back, finally helping myself to water. Jia has taken the floppy Orion out of his bag and placed him on her lap. She's trying to coax his head up, but he can't seem to lift it. The woman watches intently, no hint of surprise that Jia has just produced a cat from her bag.

'And?' Dad says.

'No answer.'

He throws up his hands. 'Great!'

'We need to know where we are,' I mutter, almost to myself as much as to anyone else.

'Why don't you ask our friend here?' Dad grunts. 'Although she doesn't seem much of a conversationalist.' The old woman coughs violently again as she stands up and shuffles past me to approach Jia. I stand too, though I'm not sure why. Jia shrinks back, her hands and arms shielding Orion.

The woman raises her hands over Orion and holds them there, looking into Jia's eyes, before slowly inclining her head, as if asking permission. Jia lowers her arm slightly, and the old lady reaches out and strokes Orion. Her touch is so gentle, and Jia relaxes a little.

'*I'm sorry,*' I say, trying Russian again. '*Where are we?*'

She just stares at me, although this time she looks slightly amused.

I gesture hopelessly around us and try in Russian again. '*Where is this?*' I point to the ground. Still nothing. Dad gives a dismal sigh.

I cast around for something else to try, my frustrated desperation mounting.

'*Your name?*' I try. I point to myself. '*My name is Alyssa. Alyssa.*' Then I point to her. '*And you?*' She smiles at me but she doesn't move, doesn't speak. This is infuriating. I wrack my brains for the word for name in Kazakh.

'Ati?' I try. She smiles again, then moves to a bookshelf, where she points at a small figurine of a fox.

'A fox?' I ask. She smiles and points.

Fox. I think I know the Russian for that.

'Lisa?' I ask, and she beams. '*Your name is* Lisa?'

She nods, satisfied.

So she does understand some Russian, then.

'Lisa,' I try tentatively. '*Do you have a map?*' She looks at me patiently, but no response. 'Dad – do you have a map?'

He pulls one out of his bag and I snatch it from him and spread it out on the dining table. I gesture for Lisa to come and join me, and her old eyes squint as she bends over it. After a moment, she taps at a small year printed in the corner.

I laugh. 'Even Lisa is pointing out how old your map is, Dad.'

Lisa chuckles as Dad grumbles, but it turns into a violent coughing fit. After a moment, she composes herself and turns back to the map. She points at a spot, just on the east of the Aral Sea.

My heart starts racing as I place my finger next to hers.

'*Here?*' I ask, urgently. '*We're here?*' I point at the floor. She smiles and nods.

'Dad!' I cry, darting across the room with the map. 'We're here.' My finger jabs at the spot Lisa indicated, and my father's eyes wander further east—

'Baikonur.' He breathes. It's just a few centimetres away.

'It's only three, maybe four hours' drive. We did it, we're nearly there!'

The woman's phone trills, making us all jump.

Jia

HE'S BARELY AWAKE.

His poor little chest rises and falls so heavily, and I've never felt so helpless. The wound doesn't look anywhere near as angry and infected as it did, but it still feels hot to the touch. Is it an infection? Not knowing what's wrong is killing me.

Alyssa and Bill sit huddled together, working out with Jake where we're meeting, where we'll hide when we get to Baikonur.

It's almost painful to look at them. The intimacy that's grown between them in these last couple of days, the warmth that has returned, just reminds me of what I've lost with Mom – and what can never come back.

Outside, the light dims. The sunset is mesmerizing, bathing the dusty landscape in a pink-orange glow.

'Can you not speak?' I ask Lisa, as she plays a card game on the table in front of us.

Lisa glances up at me, her face blank.

I stroke Orion on my lap as I watch her move the cards about at lightning speed.

'Why are you helping us, Lisa?' I ask. 'Why haven't you called the police?'

She stiffens.

'Police?' I ask again, softly.

She grimaces, suddenly angry. If she were an animal, she'd be growling. She coughs again, her whole body shaking. I offer her some water, and she accepts with a grateful smile.

At my concerned look, she points at her chest then at the medicine, and shakes her head again.

So she's ill.

'I'm sorry,' is all I can offer. She pulls the old map towards her, gesturing to the Aral Sea, as it once was. Then she taps Russia, before returning to the sea and making a sweeping motion.

'The Russians destroyed the sea?' I ask, before remembering she doesn't understand and can't answer.

She runs her hand along the table and turns her fingers over, revealing the dust. She rubs it, then holds her palm to her chest. It's only then that I realize this place is covered in a thin film of dust. It's in the very air we're breathing.

I squeeze her hand, trying to convey my sorrow that she's here, all alone, suffering.

'Is that why you can't . . .' I point to my throat and open and close my mouth silently. She nods slowly, sadly. Then, for the first time, she opens her mouth and I have to fight to suppress my gasp of horror. Where her tongue should be lies only the stubby remains of the muscle.

Cancer. It must be.

Finally, her silent tale clicks into place. This whole house is full of toxic dust she's been breathing in for decades. The memory of those rusty old ships stranded in the middle of the desert flashes suddenly. They were corroded, almost as if the metal had been eaten away. Something that destroys metal like that, imagine what it does to flesh. To organs . . .

'Fuck,' I whisper. That seems to translate. She gives an ironic laugh and turns back to her cards. Playing a game that has no purpose, that she will never truly win.

I trace the lines on the map, just a few decades old, but evidence of what once was. Looking down at Orion, lying so helpless on my lap, I think of the arid, barren sea, the seeping darkness along the glaciers, the dolphin's flesh being torn apart by netting, and of the signs I saw in Agnes's headquarters: ONE FUTURE. ONE PLANET. ECOCIDE.

'We're really fucking this up, aren't we?'

Lisa gives a long, rattling sigh and turns back to her cards, wiping out her own hand.

We head out just before midnight. Bill slips Lisa the last of his own cash supplies.

'For your troubles,' he says, low and soft.

Lisa seems to understand and she cups his hand in hers.

She turns to me and touches Orion's bag then places her hand over her heart. My vision mists.

'Thank you,' I whisper. 'I hope—'

Headlights break the darkness on the horizon.

Alyssa marches out to meet them, limping on her bad leg, and soon she is silhouetted in the bright white light. The car skids to a halt on the dusty road and the sound of a car door opening is like a gunshot in the silent landscape.

'Lyss?'

She drops her bag and runs towards the voice. I can't see it in the glare of the beams, but I imagine her embracing the speaker. Bill and I trudge up to the lights, him scooping up her discarded bag en route.

'I thought as much,' he mutters to himself.

'I'm sorry?' I ask, puzzled. He just shakes his head and smiles.

By the time we're past the hood of what turns out to be a pick-up truck, Alyssa is muttering to a handsome man in the front seat, who must be Jake. He looks simultaneously thrilled and devastated to see her.

'... fuck were you thinking?' he's hissing. Bill clears his throat pointedly, and Jake breaks off. Alyssa steps back, looking rattled.

Bill smirks. 'Can we catch a ride?'

Alyssa and Jake speak low and fast to each other in the front seats as we're shaken around on the barely paved roads. Alyssa peppers him with questions about the *Argo*, Baikonur, a man named Abbey, so many things I don't understand, and to be honest I don't really care about. Every pothole, every jolt, every leap of the truck makes me wince, and I think of Orion in his bag on my lap, barely breathing.

Bill squeezes my arm, and I start, head whipping around to look at him. He smiles down at Orion's bag sadly, and I can tell he thinks this is the end. I pull my arm away, breathing heavily to quell the tears. He's wrong. He has to be.

'Jia?' I stop stroking Orion's paw through the mouth of the bag and look up, my eyes meeting Jacob's eyes in the rearview mirror. 'I need to look at the chip in Orion as soon as we get back.'

'He's not well,' I croak.

'Alyssa said. I'm sorry, but it's urgent. Then I promise I will find someone who can help him, all right?'

'Sure,' I reply, suddenly exhausted beyond measure.

Within a few minutes, Jacob pulls over. 'I'm sorry, folks,' he says. 'It's time.' As planned, the three of us clamber out and haul ourselves into the cargo bed, lying low, our faces pressed to the warm, dusty metal. A spare wheelchair lies covered loosely by tarpaulin, and we do our best to hide in its shadow as Jacob pulls away – thankfully more slowly than before.

It's strange to enter a town glimpsing only the tops of apartment blocks and buildings, flickering streetlights flashing overhead, hoping to God that someone doesn't see us from a window. But it's late, and we manage to reach Jacob's apartment block undetected. He pulls in round the back, where his truck is concealed from the rest of the street.

After getting himself out of the car and into his chair, Jacob does a slow circle, checking for lights, listening out for any sounds. Eventually, he gives the back of the truck a light tap, then wheels himself up a ramp and opens the back door.

Alyssa drops down onto the pavement, then offers her hand to her dad, who clambers out. Then it's my turn.

We dash inside, and Jacob lets us in to his ground-floor apartment. It's neat and tidy, if a little sparse, with the exception of the dining table, which is strewn with wires and chip boards, scraps of metal and a soldering iron.

He moves over to it as Alyssa shuts the door behind us with a soft click. Picking up what looks like a hand-held metal detector, he turns to me. 'Once I knew you were coming, I got myself a microchip reader and got to work modifying it.' He takes a deep breath. 'We need to take a look at Orion now.'

I place Orion's bag down on the sofa as though it were made of glass, and slip my hands inside. Alyssa and Bill move over to the table behind me.

'What have you done to it?' Alyssa asks.

'A microchip wouldn't normally need a battery – it works on radio frequency ID,' he explains, but I barely listen. I place a trembling hand on Orion, and relief washes over me at the warmth emanating from his body, at the sensation of his little heart, beating fast. I scoop him out and hold him against my shoulder like a baby, and force myself to tune back in.

'. . . sounds like Orion's has its own power source linked to his bioelectricity. That suggests it holds a lot more data than a normal chip, which means I needed to retrofit this . . .' He waves the reader as I approach the table with Orion. 'To be able to process more data and display it on this . . .' He points to the tablet.

Alyssa leans in, riveted. 'Will it work?'

'I hope so.' Jacob clears a space for Orion and I lie him down, whispering comfort to him all the while.

For a moment, we stare down at him, this tiny creature breathing hard and low, drooling. I cross my trembling arms in an effort to hold myself together.

'It's not going to hurt him, I promise.' Jacob looks at me with such kind eyes that I know it's true, so I shift slightly to the left, allowing him the space to work.

Jacob strokes part of Orion's neck fur, then hovers the reader between his shoulder blades.

We take a collective breath, and Alyssa leans in, her eyes burning into the screen.

Nothing.

'It's fine,' Jake breathes. 'There's a number of frequencies this thing could be operating on.' He moves the reader away and adjusts something, before returning again.

Another wave.

Nothing.

'Jake . . .' Alyssa's voice is low, heavy with anguish.

What if we've come all this way with nothing? What if the information was wiped somehow, or it was never there to begin with? We've risked our lives, I've risked Orion, all for nothing. And Kai . . .

I jerk my head, trying to shake that thought from my mind. I can't believe it's over. I won't.

Jake adjusts the reader again. 'Third time's a charm,' he says, trying to sound breezy, but there's a line of tension in his jaw. His hands shake as he hovers the device over Orion's neck once again.

BEE-DUP.

Jacob's tablet is suddenly ablaze with light, and code begins to appear in chunks.

'Yes!' cries Alyssa, clinging to Jacob and watching wide-eyed as the data streams onto the screen. Jacob laughs, looking giddy with relief. Alyssa lets go of Jacob and turns to me.

'Thank you, Jia,' she breathes, and her words carry the weight of a thousand emotions.

I force a smile, but my eyes turn back to Orion, whose breathing is still erratic. And I know. I think I've known for a while, if I'm honest with myself. I just didn't want to believe it. Alyssa's eyes follow mine, and then she moves back to the table, and strokes along the length of Orion's body, smoothing out his ruffled fur so delicately, so kindly.

'And thank you, Orion,' she says, her voice soft.

'Mr Wright?' Jacob mutters. 'Would you mind holding the reader so I can . . .?' He gestures to the tablet.

'Sure,' Bill takes the reader, keeping it in place above Orion as Jacob begins to screenshot and make notes on the data streaming in.

'Ahh,' Jacob utters.

'What's up?' Alyssa rushes.

'The data has stopped after those initial five lines, and now it's asking me to input something. I tried finishing off the last line of code – I know how I usually sign off on something like that, to start the next line – but it's asking for more to allow us to access the rest of the code.'

Alyssa wheels around to face me. 'Did your brother give you a password? Some numbers? Anything that could unlock the rest of the code?'

'What?' My mind is a blur. I look back down at Orion. His breathing is faltering.

'Jia!' Alyssa barks. 'Look at me, please.'

I force my eyes back up to hers. She doesn't look angry, just determined.

'We have to get access to the rest of this code,' she says, 'otherwise, this was all for nothing. Your brother meant for you to have the answers. He must have given you a word, a sequence. Something.'

I think back over Kai's last message to me.

'There's nothing,' I cry. 'He never told me any numbers.'

'Think, Jia. It's always in the detail, just breathe and think.'

'But Orion . . .' My hand is still on his soft fur. 'I don't know . . . I don't know!' I wail. I can't feel his heartbeat any more, but he's still breathing. 'There's nothing! Nothing I can do.'

'There is always something you can do. Think.'

She's so wrong, though. Look at Kai – I couldn't do anything to protect him, to save him. And Mom – nothing can be done for her. I know that, even Kai knows that.

My hand freezes in its frenzied stroking.

Kai.

He did do something. Agnes showed me. Even when I thought

he'd given up on Mom, abandoned all hope, that's what all this was for. To get money. To help in any way he could. To do something.

'Rosenberg,' I whisper.

Alyssa leans in. 'What?'

'Rosenberg. The name of the alien in *Men in Black*.'

'She's lost it,' Bill stage-whispers, but I ignore him.

'Rosenberg is the name of Orion's owner.'

Jacob looks at me blankly, but Alyssa squeezes my shoulders and turns to him.

'Try Rosenberg!'

'Oh!' he gasps, finally cottoning on. 'With an e? Or a u?'

'Try both!' Alyssa says, exasperated. He hits enter, and suddenly the screen is full. Lines and lines of code, streaming onto black.

'That's it!' Jacob cries. 'Bill, hold it still!'

I scratch behind Orion's ears as Alyssa continues to softly stroke his back, staring at the screen all the while. We stay there for quite some time. Just the sounds of Jacob scribbling accompanies the rhythmic movements of my and Alyssa's hands. Little tufts of Orion's hair occasionally fan out, onto the white tabletop. I almost think I hear a small purr in his throat . . .

Yes. I'm right. A purr.

Quiet. Low. But it's there. A purr of happiness vibrating through him. His whole body letting me know, he's calm. He's happy. He's happy I'm with him.

'I'm here, Orion,' I whisper into his ear. 'I'm not going anywhere.'

But suddenly, his little body starts to convulse – and I feel my heart begin to break.

'Bill, do not move that reader,' Jacob says urgently. 'We need everything we can get.'

'Orion?' I hear myself say, my eyes welling with prickling tears.

He twitches again. Alyssa tries to cradle him, hold him still. His chest rises, sharp and shallow, as his lungs struggle for breath.

And then everything in him flops. All tension is gone, his chest is still. The little light that remained in his eyes goes out.

The tablet goes blank.

And finally. After holding it in for so long. After trying to stay strong for Kai, for Agnes, for Erica, for my mom, for Orion.

I sob.

Alyssa

WE PUT ORION IN JACOB'S FREEZER. JIA IS INSISTENT IN her grief that we somehow get the body back to her brother. Wherever the fuck he is. By the time I manage to convince her to go take a shower and try to rest, the sun is rising over Baikonur.

Jacob is still poring over the data when I come back into the room. His eyes are bloodshot as he pounds another coffee. Dad is snoring in the next room, where he crashed out on Jacob's bed, without invitation.

I shrug on one of Jacob's sweaters. It smells of him. 'Jake,' I say quietly.

'Mmm?' He doesn't look away from his screen.

'We need to decide what to do next.'

He pushes himself away from the table and rubs his eyes. He squints against the sunlight streaming in through the window and checks his watch. 'Ah, shit. Well, I should call in sick, then I can stay on this. Later, when everyone else has turned in for the night, I can rock up, explain I'm feeling better, that I want to catch up on work. I'll start looking at the ship's code, see if I can find anything similar. You guys can stay here until—'

'No, I'm coming with you,' I cut in. 'You'll need me to—'

'Yes, I *will* need you,' Jake exclaims. 'I know the code, but I don't know the ship or the crew like you do. When I work this thing out, you might be the only person they'll listen to. So we can't risk you coming onto campus and getting caught until we know what's up with the *Argo*.'

His stare dares me to argue with him. As much as I want to, I can't.

'Fine.' I say through gritted teeth. God, I hate admitting he's right.

'Great,' he says, visibly relaxing. 'Stay here, keep an eye on Jia and your dad.'

'No. I'm going out,' I say, pulling the hood up over my head and gingerly putting my foot back in the support boot. Fuck, it hurts.

'Are you insane?'

'Probably,' I wince. 'But I have to speak to Anders.'

Jake looks as if his eyes are about to pop out of his head. 'I told you, he's locked up in his ivory tower. Abbey would never—'

'This is Anders' mission. He has to know. And more importantly, he might be able to help get Abbey and the team to back off and get a message to the *Argo*.' I check my watch. *Shit*. 'I know how to get to him, but I have to go now.' Before he can stop me, I'm opening the door, checking the corridor and then softly pulling it shut behind me.

It takes a couple of streets for me to orientate myself. When I know where I am, I pull the hood of Jake's sweater close around my face, grimacing at my limp. In the past week I've definitely done some damage to my healing leg. I shouldn't be moving so fast on it but I know exactly where I need to be and when, and it's going to be tight.

As I round one corner and enter another typical barren Baikonur square, I see a car parked outside an apartment block and a slight figure on the phone pacing towards it. I've made it – just.

I speed up and leap off the kerb into the road just as the car begins to pull away.

The driver honks her horn and squints out, but before she can see my face, I turn and duck down low next to the car, where the window is already open.

'Gwynne. Open up.'

'Jesus fucking Christ!' Gwynne screams. 'Alyssa?'

'Yeah. Quick, open up.'

She snaps out of her bewilderment and feels for the button to unlock the car. I throw myself in, and tell her to drive.

As I knew she would, she obliges.

Crouching in one of the exhaust channels beneath Gagarin's Start, I breathe a sigh of relief at the sound of his car. It means he's accepted the meet I asked Gwynne to arrange. The engine quiets and a door slams, and I let my hands slide down the rough walls beside me. The concrete is still scorched down here from those first launches. Gagarin's fire and fury leaving a mark for centuries to come, until the desert dust erodes it all away.

He takes his time, meandering over to where Gwynne dropped me earlier. To anyone in the outbuildings nearby, he'll look like he's just admiring the historic structure, alone.

I look up as he approaches the edge of the channel and am stunned by how stooped he looks. How slumped his shoulders are, how pale his skin is. He squints in the bright Baikonur sun.

'I'm pleased to hear you're alive,' he begins in his distinctive accent. 'But I am saddened to see you back here.'

'You know I'd never have been able to stay away, Anders. This is my home.'

'Why are you here, Wright?' he growls. 'I'm watched like a hawk these days.'

'There's an error in the code of the ship,' I blurt, peering up at his face to discern his reaction, but he lifts his head up to the sky and I can't see it any more. Is that a look of despair? Anger? Resignation?

I wait for him to say something, but he doesn't reply.

'We're trying to work out where the fault lies, how to fix it, but we need to warn the crew. Their lives could be in danger.'

Still, nothing.

'Lars. Please?' I cry out. 'I truly believe this is mission-critical.

People have been willing to kill to stop us from uncovering this error. I need you to get a message to the crew, and you need to get Abbey to pull transmission. Cut the TV bullshit. Everyone should focus on fixing this, before it's too late.'

Finally, he looks down at me. Deep sadness and regret flit across his face, and I realize in that moment that he is a broken man.

'I can't help you,' he says simply.

'Why the fuck not?' I explode, moving closer to the wall he's standing on. His stooped shadow towers over me, like another remnant of Gagarin's Start.

'Two weeks ago, I signed over ninety per cent of my shares in Mars One to Abbey,' he says, so low I have to strain to hear. 'They have the majority now. Valdivian have more shares, more chairs on the board. I'm just a figurehead. I'm frozen out. I'm not allowed any contact with the crew. This is their mission now.'

'Why?' I cry.

'It was the only way. I'm out of cash. Out of favours. The legal cases in the States and the UK have bled me dry. Revenue and sponsorships are not what we expected. My credit lines are maxed out with all our contractors, the Kazakh government are turning on us. We needed the injection of cash that Abbey and Valdivian were offering. If we didn't get that, the mission would be over. No more launches. No more supplies. The crew would have to be abandoned on Mars, for ever. He has me right by the balls, Alyssa. And if I break any of our terms, if I speak to anyone, if I step out of line, he could ruin me. I did a lot to get this mission off the ground, and not all of it was legal.'

I stand frozen in the channel, horrified.

'There is a price, it turns out, for ideas,' Anders continues. 'For the future of humanity, the future of our crew. And I am paying it.'

I shake my head. 'You can't just give up!' I yell, not giving a shit if anyone hears me. 'Don't you remember what you said to me? It's bigger than me, than us, than Abbey. What about the crew? Your best friend, Rubio? Your damn moon rock? You can't abandon them. You started this. You put them up there!'

'A fool's dream,' he whispers.

'What?'

'Once Mars One was established,' he starts, his voice stronger now, 'I decided the time was right to finally protect my most prized possession. After all, only about eight hundred pounds of rock was brought back from the moon. What I'd spent years turning over in my hands was rarer than any diamond.'

The rumbling of an engine sounds in the distance.

'Lars . . .' I say warningly. But he carries on.

'But then, the preservation lab told me my rock was not a moon rock. It was just a regular, insignificant igneous rock from terra firma.' Lars flinches, as though he's bearing the brunt of that revelation all over again. 'Just another lie my bastard of a father told me as a child. But one that had grown so big, one that had underpinned so much . . . Well. I just couldn't bring myself to tell anyone. The company offered to dispose of it for me, but I asked for it back, unpreserved, and it returned to my desk, to my hands once more. I thought, why not make it what I'd always thought it was: extraordinary, extraterrestrial. So I continued with the mission, only this time, it was to make a lie into a truth. To make a belief into a reality.' He looks down at me once more.

'So you see, Alyssa, this whole thing started with a foolish belief, a lie, and now – now we're all facing the consequences of that.' He gives me a small, apologetic smile, before looking back out at the horizon, as a car door slams. 'I am truly sorry.'

'Anders,' Gwynne's voice rings out. 'We need to go, people are asking where you are.'

'Lars, please—' I beg, but he cuts across me.

'Abbey won't let anything, or anyone, stop his show,' he says. 'If he finds out you're here, he'll have you, and anyone else you're with, arrested. My private jet is leaving Yubileyniy Airport tonight – I'm getting Gwynne out of here. We'll make sure the crew are expecting you as well. They will have the paperwork required to land in the US and they'll ask no questions.'

'Lars, I can't—'

'Alyssa!' he barks, his eyes full of anger – whether it's at me, or himself, I can't tell. 'Please, just get out of here – while you still can.'

He turns away from the edge of the channel and walks back to his car, leaving me alone. Reeling.

Moments later, I emerge from the ground and slip into Gwynne's back seat. We don't talk the entire way back to Baikonur.

When I turn up back at Jacob's, both he and Dad are thrilled. But not for long.

'What the hell do you mean you're not going to take the plane?' Jacob cries.

'Dad will, Jia can if she wants, but I'm staying here. We need to find a way to contact the crew. Anders is not an option any more.'

He crumples his head into his arms on the table. 'Bill?' he says, muffled.

'I agree, Alyssa. This is madness,' my father leans in. 'You did what you came here to do, and now you have a chance to get out. Take it!'

'No, Dad. You of all people should understand that I can't abandon the crew.'

'And how, without the help of Anders, do you expect us to reach them?' Jacob says into his sleeves.

'I have a plan,' I tell him. 'I just need you to get me a book.'

'He's a smart guy,' Dad says quietly as Jake heads out to his truck. We're out the back of Jake's apartment, peering at the setting sun. Anders' jet will be leaving soon.

'I know,' I say.

'He might even be as smart as you.' There's a spark in his eyes, like the one he would get when regaling us with old military stories when I was a kid. 'Your mother would have liked him.'

'Dad, it's not—' My voice cracks.

He takes both my hands in his. 'Is it selfish of me,' he starts, his voice unusually shaky, 'to say that I'm so happy you never got on that damn ship?'

'No.'

He looks up at me and smiles, his eyes wet. 'Good.' He looks back at Jake, who has averted his gaze to give us some privacy. 'I'm just glad you've found something that might make you happy about it, too.'

I look at my dad, then back to Jake.

I feel my cheeks flush, and shake my head. 'That's not what this—'

'Sure,' he laughs.

I look at the ground, face burning.

'And what about her?' He nods indoors, to where we left Jia, sitting on Jake's couch, staring into space.

I shake my head. 'She said she won't leave here until she knows more about her brother.'

'She offered me the rest of her cash,' he says, letting go of my hands and shouldering his bag. 'For a new plane.'

My eyebrows shoot up.

'Looked like a fair bit too.' He laughs. 'But I told her to keep it. Use it to find her brother. I don't need to fly no more. And besides, family is more important.'

My breath catches in my throat.

Jake starts the engine. It's time.

I throw my arms around my father, and he squeezes me right back – our first embrace in what must be over twenty years. I don't think he's hugged me like this since I was a little girl, even before our estrangement.

'Save that ship, Alyssa,' he says, and then he's gone, back home where he belongs.

I hope I get to see him there again soon.

Rubio

'OKEOWO WANTS US TO RETURN. I KNOW IT.'

My hand shakes as I adjust the tiny dials on the starfinder. 'She's never said as much to me,' I reply.

Brun snorts.

'Of course she hasn't. She's too much of a coward. But I know she wants to abort. Her and Morin. Both of them.'

My hand slips again. *Fuck.* I hold the fingers in my right hand, willing them to still. Although it's only been a matter of hours, it feels like for ever since my last guilty sip of my water pouch. Am I really that reliant on it?

'Morin offered us the chance to vote,' I remind him. 'And we did.'

I resume my position and put my eye back to the eyepiece. Black infinity floods my vision until my pupil dilates and things come into focus. *There.* The star I'm looking for. A solid light, glaring back at me. I sigh with relief and return to my chart, recording the position. It's already taken me a half hour to complete the rest of the star references, something that should only take fifteen minutes. Has Brun noticed how much longer I'm taking to do routine tasks? The back of my neck feels clammy.

'Morin probably wants to go back for her children. You know, her husband is divorcing her. I've seen it in the news. Clearly she underestimated her own—'

'That's enough!' I cut across him. Everything within me feels taut, pulsating with pressure, craving for something to soften the sensation of just being. I cannot tolerate Brun's casual cruelty any more. 'Just stop it,' I glare at him, and his look of amusement at my reaction only enrages me more. 'Not all of us are as lucky as you, to have no true ties.'

Brun raises his eyebrows. 'Says the unmarried, childless, middle-aged man.'

I tell myself he's not worth it and move back to my chart. There's only one reference left to find, but I frown. It's not like the others. An asteroid, which can't be right. The whole point of taking the references is to ensure our trajectory is on track, but asteroids aren't fixed points so can't be used to determine that. Perhaps it's an error? I put my eye back to the starfinder's eyepiece and attempt to refocus.

'Honestly, Rubio. It's painful watching you.' Brun shoots over and grabs the chart from my hand. 'What are you looking for, anyway?'

Sighing, I push back from the starfinder and point to the chart. 'It says Asteroid B-612, but obviously it must be a mistake. The B should be at the end, so—'

Brun cuts me off with a chuckle, and I glare at him.

'*L'essentiel est invisible pour les yeux*.' He raises his hands in proclamation and pushes himself back to float in the middle of the room.

'Thanks for nothing,' I growl as I take back my position and my chart.

'You won't find it,' he calls gleefully.

'And why is that?' I snap.

'Because it doesn't exist.'

I turn to look at him, floating there with his arms crossed, extremely pleased with himself. They warned us that we would start to become irritated with each other at this stage. But nothing about the flash of loathing I feel towards him in this moment feels normal.

'Asteroid B-612,' he continues, 'is fictional. Someone back there must have thought it would be a nice little joke. I wonder who? They clearly like French literature.' He smiles, smug.

That's the last thing I need: more people going out of their way to expose me for the fool that I am. I cross Asteroid B-612 off the chart so hard the paper tears, and thrust it back into the wallet on the wall that stores our references.

Brun's voice follows me as I push off and away, down to the hab. 'You should read it some time – it'll be on the digital library. It's a children's book – *The Little Prince*.'

I slow to a halt. Why does that ring such a loud bell?

Then I remember.

Alyssa.

The Little Prince.

Alyssa.

Could it be?

I change direction, propelling myself away from the hab, moving as quickly as possible.

When I get to our sleeping quarters, I peer around to make sure I'm alone. My PPK lies abandoned in a storage well. I fumble around in it until my hands find the book that Alyssa asked me to carry.

And there it is: *The Little Prince*. I open the pages and flick through, until I find what I'm looking for. A picture with a caption beneath: *The Little Prince on Asteroid B-612*.

The bastard was right. Surely this can't be a coincidence?

The loose pages of the book quake in my hands. I have the shakes again, but this time I don't think it has anything to do with my shameful secret.

I study the picture closely. The Little Prince on his planet looks so lonely, almost bewildered. I turn the page, not wanting to look at him any more. My eyes skim along the words.

Once upon a time there was a little prince who lived on a planet hardly any bigger than he was, and who needed a friend . . .

As I read, I feel all the more certain this is no coincidence. Whoever sent up that data would have known the star references are on my rota this week. But no one else knew what Alyssa had asked me to bring onboard.

Could it be a message, from her? But how did she manage it? And why is she trying to get my attention?

Voices sound further down the tunnel and I snap the book shut. Either I'm going mad, or Alyssa is sending me a secret message. No one can know until I'm certain either way. I thrust the book back into my PPK and return it to the storage space. As I turn to leave, my eye snags on the camera, staring at me blankly. Is the camera angled in such a way as to show the world what I was looking at? I don't think so – but I'll be more careful next time, just in case.

I attempt to place a placid, neutral look on my face as my heart races and my mind swims with confusion, excitement and dread at the prospect of yet another secret.

It's been three days since I first realized the meaning of Asteroid B-612. Every day, I've rushed back to the star reference chart that has been sent overnight, and every day I've been disappointed to see nothing out of the ordinary. I'm starting to think it was an accident. An odd kink in the universe that made nothing look like something. Or perhaps just a joke, like Brun said. God knows we could do with a laugh. Since all the mishaps, the mood of the crew is approaching boiling point, with arguments breaking out over unwashed dishes, petty theft of food items. Last night, Brun refused to eat with the rest of us again. Ana's sleep cycle is still fucked, and Lee is also beginning to fall behind as he spends more time with her. When we eat, he sits quietly with us, joining in the small talk. But he eats most of his meals with her.

I haven't told anyone about what I saw, but I think everyone is aware they're fucking each other now. Sometimes I can sense Morin gearing up to talk to him, but she never quite manages to take the plunge.

They warned us. This dull, drudge-like phase of the journey was to be anticipated, but I don't think any of us realized it would be this hard. As we click through the millions of kilometres, with nothing to break up the day but maintenance tasks, sometimes I feel as though I've lost all sense of myself. Perhaps that's why B-612 hit me so much; it felt like finally something was happening to wake me out of my stupor.

All this bounces back and forth in my mind as I take the latest star reference chart and attach it to the clipboard in the cupola. I make my usual glance down the list—

It's returned.

B-612.

Adrenaline floods my veins. Thank God we've stopped wearing our heart monitors every day.

This is no mistake. And who would play the same joke twice? But if Alyssa was trying to grab my attention the other day, why not follow up straight away? Maybe because Brun and I drew attention to it. Control would have questioned the mistake, perhaps even checked the reference chart before it was sent out for the next few days. She needed to let the heat die down before trying it again.

Well, Alyssa, you have my attention now.

I make my way through the references, logging each one patiently, skipping lightly over B-612. But after that reference, I find myself once again struggling to recognize any of the stars. At first, I assume my foggy mind is failing me yet again, but soon I begin to suspect that there's more to it. The final reference on the chart is correct – I recognize it instantly. I find it, log it, and then – with a fleeting glimpse at the camera – turn to look out at the stars through the windows, my back to the camera. I fold up the paper, taking care not to move my arms too much, and slip it into my pocket. Then I take the clipboard back to the wall and slot it in, just as I usually would, my brain whirring. I need to get somewhere with no cameras.

Trying not to look rushed, I head down the tunnel towards the toilet cubicle. Pulling the screen behind me, I switch on the unit as if I were taking a shit and secure myself to the wall, before taking out the paper. It rips slightly as I pull it open, and I force myself to slow down. The list runs as follows:

P- – 3WS89.
P-37W9.
P-81WS5556
P-16W213.
P-51W87
P-21WS4849
P-14WS127-9

They're not fake asteroid names, and anyone with a modicum of knowledge would know they weren't star references. I've started reading *The Little Prince* in my pod at night, and none of these numbers have been mentioned. And why do they all vary slightly in their composition, with dashes and full stops in different places? Could they just be typos? But something in my gut is telling me no. There is no such thing as coincidence.

Could it be code? Something I have to type in somewhere to learn more? The only personal computer interface I have is my tablet. I resolve to try later during my downtime. Or there is, of course, the other tablet . . . But I haven't seen that in a very long time.

My mind continues to race faster than it has in my life as I try and fail to solve the puzzle.

What feels like eons later, I'm back in my pod, another day of dull checks and experiments over with. But it's not just another day, is it? My whole brain is consumed with the fake references. I'm utterly convinced Alyssa is trying to talk to me through them, if only I can work out how.

I've left the team in the hab, telling them I want to relax with a book and some music. None of them seem to care – we barely ever interact in the evenings any more. So I'm alone in the sleeping quarters, my pod closed around me. As alone as I can be in this place, anyway – just a camera on night mode for comfort. Luckily, it's pointing at my face.

I put on some music and attempt to look relaxed. Bored, even. Then I open up the command keyboard on my tablet and type in the first fake reference. I hit enter.

Nothing.

I try the second – also nothing. The third, and so on. I try all seven at once. Still nothing.

I search the references on our internal entertainment library. No results whatsoever.

I thrust my tablet into my sleeping bag in frustration and open the book back up, continuing where I left off last night. As a work, it's a curious thing; its meaning runs through my fingers, like the sand of the desert in which the aviator and the prince find themselves.

But everything comes back to this book. I come to the page where the little prince meets a drunkard. Is this it? Is she trying to tell me something about myself? A glum, red-faced man staring off into space confronts me on the page. Pages and words. Page and word. P and W.

I jolt as if I've received an electric shock.

I pull the references back out, and see the second is P-37. I'm currently on page 35, and I practically rip the page over. W9. I count: 1, 2, 3, 4, 5, 6, 7, 8 . . .

Mistakes.

My pod spins around me. My God. This is it. I've cracked the code. A harsh exclamation from Brun, down in the hab, snaps me out of my trance, and I'm suddenly aware of the camera again. I try to reset my face, thinking hard. I'm going to have to be careful about this. I let the book hover in front of me as I pull out one of my sketchpads and a pencil. I'll make out that I'm inspired by my reading to do some light sketching. Instead, I scratch out the word 'mistakes'.

I turn back to the book. Back to the first reference. P- – 3WS89. Page three? Word, no, maybe WORDS 8 and 9?

Range . . . which.

Range . . . which mistakes.

My heart sinks. I'd understand if the meaning was a little cryptic, but that just makes no sense. Frustration and disappointment bubble up within me. I'm a fool, a child trying to create meaning in the chaos. I'm about to give up for good when my eye catches on the double dash. I frown. That's not in any of the other references. Alyssa was always so careful, everything done with precision, with purpose.

P-– 3.

Minus 3? I grab at the dog-eared book floating above my head now. There are pages without numbers. I count back, 1, 2, 3.

It's the dedication. 'To Leon Werth.' And words 8 and 9? 'Forgive me.'

Forgive me. Mistakes.

My pulse spikes. There's no question in my mind now. My God, I could cry. From relief, happiness, astonishment, guilt, fear? All of them. My friend, my comrade, who I will never see again, her future stolen from her, her mind seemingly lost, reaching out to me now as if she knows that I, too, am descending into madness.

I sniff, suck back the tears, refusing to give the world the satisfaction of seeing me weeping in my bed. My body crackles with anticipation as I turn my attention to the other clues. There's a full stop after mistakes, another after the fourth. It must be new phrases, new sections of the message. I take my time, casually sketching between turning the pages.

That last word was the 213th on the page. I'm finding it hard to count. I'm having to scribble on the pages themselves, count and recount. But finally, I manage it and the second reference's meaning kicks me in the stomach:

And now urgency.

I plough on until I have the whole message:

Forgive me. Mistakes. And now urgency. Ship in danger from bad seeds.

I read it again and again, a sickness growing within me. A

fiery rage burns in my stomach. How dare she dangle the hope of connection in front of me, and offer of support, only to strike even more fear and suspicion within me? I throw the book as far and as hard as I can. It ricochets off the far curtain of my pod, and back again, its bouncing as chaotic as my mind, rocking the camera on its mount.

I feel as though I'm split in two. Part of me knows why it's only seven references: too many fake star references on the chart and we wouldn't be able to check our trajectory, and it would potentially draw suspicion. But the other part of me is furious.

She's taunting me with a book that makes no sense; with the story of a drunkard, shamefully drinking to escape his shame of drinking. I tear the page of the sketchbook off and rip it into as many pieces as I can, leaving them to float around me like snow. The slowing book drifts among them, its haunting Little Prince gazing out at me. I zip my sleeping bag right up, over my head, and feel for the flask. It's still there, empty and useless. But my water pouch is full.

I don't reach for it, though.

I won't.

Let the drunkard be without his solace tonight, able to forget neither his shame nor the bad seeds lying in wait, germinating, as he hurtles further into nothingness.

Jia

SEVEN DAYS.

Seven days since we arrived here.
Since we found Frybread.
Since we got a hold of the code.
Since Orion.

'Here.' Alyssa places a plate of toast in front of me and drops down onto the sofa with her own.

I stare down at it. The butter congealing and soaking into the bread makes my stomach lurch. I shift my gaze to focus on Jake's TV screen instead, where the Mars One channel is on, just as it has been ever since we arrived. Alyssa has decided it should be constantly monitored. For what, I'm not sure. Clues, I guess. Clues to whatever it is the code affects, and whoever might be behind it.

Once we had the code, I thought that would be it. That it would miraculously reveal what all this has been about – and where my brother is. But despite spending every night in the coding room searching through millions of lines of code, Jake hasn't been able to work out what bit of the system the code fits into. And if he has nothing – so do I.

The sound of Alyssa's munching sets my teeth on edge. I pull out my burner phone and hit the last called number – Erica's. Before I can even put it to my ear, a tone blares out. It's out of service. I cancel the call and throw the phone across the room.

Alyssa eyes me. 'Still nothing?' she asks, putting her empty plate down.

I don't reply. 'I thought I heard you speaking to someone, last night?'

'I tried Penny,' I murmur begrudgingly. 'On her friend's number. Said she left to catch another Sea Saviour mission. I hung up before she could ask who I was.'

Alyssa nods slowly. 'Jia, I appreciate you helping monitor stuff,' she starts tentatively, gesturing towards the screen, where the *Argo* crew are beginning their morning. 'But I really think we should get you out of here. It's not safe.'

I stifle a howl of rage. It's been the same thing, every day, since the plane left: *you're not safe, you should leave*. They just don't get it. I'm not safe anywhere. Not until I find Kai, and prove he's alive and that he's been kidnapped, and that I – and those who dared to help me – have been pursued and vilified so falsely, all for the sake of some code.

Code that may or may not be capable of killing six people millions of kilometres away, and jeopardizing humanity's first step towards what many think is our only hope.

'I'm not leaving,' I say through gritted teeth.

Alyssa knows better than to push. She gathers my untouched plate with hers and goes to stand, but her breath catches and the plates clatter to the floor.

Despite my frustrations, I dart towards her, the look of pain on her face breaking through my rage. I glance down at her injured leg, still swollen within its support boot.

'You OK?' I ask.

'Just twisted it again,' she winces, trying to shrug it off. 'It'll be fine in a moment.' But sweat glistens on her forehead.

'What can I do?'

She lugs the boot up onto the coffee table in front of us. 'There's an ice pack in the freezer.'

My stomach drops. I glance at the corner of the kitchenette, which I've been avoiding for a week.

Because of what is in there.

Who is in there.

I feel sick all over again.

Alyssa must see me judder. 'Actually, don't worry,' she rushes. Before I can say anything, she's up and hobbling to the kitchenette. 'I can get it.'

I suddenly feel a chill. The absence of warm weight in my lap, where I've got used to another being resting, purring, soothing me, suddenly feels like lead.

I scrunch up my face and grab a throw cushion, hugging it close to my chest – a pale imitation of Orion's presence. I ignore the sound of the freezer opening and closing, ensuring everything within remains frozen, still, cold . . .

I grab the TV remote and turn up the volume, just as keys rattle in the front door and Jacob enters.

'Lyss?' he calls.

Alyssa is there like a shot, looking expectant, ice pack in hand.

For once, Jake's smiling. 'I've found something.'

I snap to attention. 'What?' we ask simultaneously.

Jake's face drops, as though he suddenly remembers I'm here. 'Sorry, Jia, nothing on your brother.'

I slump back, letting the burst of adrenaline, of hope, disintegrate within me.

He moves over to the table, where Alyssa makes space for him and settles with the ice pack. He locks his wheels and pulls out a tablet. 'But I've worked out what the code Kai isolated is doing. It's counting how many times something opens and closes.'

Alyssa lets out a breath. 'How many times *what* opens and closes?'

Jake grimaces. 'That, I don't know yet.'

Alyssa gives him a fierce look and opens her mouth, but he jumps in before she can say anything. 'Listen, it took years to write this code – you can't just search through all 800 million lines of it. The system opens and closes shit all the time. Data, files. It's like looking for a needle in a haystack. I just don't know yet.'

'But you wrote it!'

'I wrote part of it. Coders use and recycle each other's basic work all the time. I have no idea who did exactly what on this thing. We all crossover. And then there's this one particular file structure.' He gestures to what I assume is a part of the code. Alyssa leans in. 'Inside the PE file – the portable executable file, which is what contains the information the operating system needs to perform certain tasks – someone's renamed one of the headings. It's set to *Ultra Hard*. That doesn't make any sense – it's not coding we use. I think someone else wrote this, or at least altered it.'

'Who?'

'I don't know. But I think it's deliberate.'

They're both silent for a while.

'That might explain why Kai extracted that bit of the code,' Alyssa muses, her voice low. 'It's not just an error he's found, but proof of hacking?'

'Yeah. Whatever it's counting, the system was never meant to keep track of it. It's counting and storing pointless data. Filing it away somewhere, probably where there's no allocated space for it. Which could cause real issues . . .'

Alyssa puts her head in her hands. 'It's such a shitshow up there, Jake. You can tell, watching them all. Arguing over every little thing, and if there's another mistake like the ammonia leak . . .'

Jake puts a comforting hand on Alyssa's shoulder.

Even as I avert my gaze from this intimate moment, a pang of jealousy rips through me. They may not have the answers, but at least they have each other.

I turn my attention back to Mars One.

The presenters are wittering on about what is on the astronauts' programs today. I let the banality of it wash over me.

'. . . despite their busy schedules, the crew also find time for R and R. In fact, our artist in residence, Rubio Lindroos, treated us to a glimpse of his talent this morning. Take a look at this.'

The screen zooms in on a sketch that Rubio has tagged to the wall of the hab. I lean forward. It's of flowers – trees? I scramble for the remote and hit 'pause'.

'Er, guys?' I say, not taking my eyes from the screen.

'Hmm?' Alyssa answers.

'I think Rubio is responding to your message.'

Alyssa leaps up and Jake throws his chair around the table, both surging towards the TV screen.

Rubio's drawn a seed beneath some soil, and then another germinating, and then another transforming into a full-bloom rose. It looks a lot like the style of the book that Alyssa made Jake borrow from her friend – the picture book she's been spending so much time poring over.

'There, what's that?' I ask, thrusting my finger towards the screen.

'What's what?' Alyssa asks, squinting, but Jake sees it first.

'There.' He moves right up to the TV and points. Within the seemingly insignificant swirls of the soil, there's a tiny but deliberate '?' right by the first seed.

'He gets it!' Alyssa cries, her face flushed with excitement.

'What does it mean?' I ask.

'He's asking what I meant by *bad seeds*.' She darts back to the dining table and rifles through her work. 'Jake, we need to get another message to him. If this thing's deliberate, he needs to talk to Ana. If she's involved in this, she must know something.'

'I can hack the star reference upload again tonight,' he says, sinking back into his chair, his many sleepless nights finally taking their toll.

'Good spot, Jia,' Alyssa calls, and I turn to find her looking right at me. 'I'm glad you're here. We're going to work this out, together. I promise.'

Hope stirs within me for the first time since I lost Orion.

Rubio

WHEN THE NEXT STAR REFERENCES COME IN, I RUSH TO the command module, like a kid on Christmas morning. When I see the list, I struggle to stop myself punching the air in triumph.

P-14WS128-9:
P-51W182.
P-22WS26-7
P-20W175.
P-3WS127133.
P-64WS157-169.
P-30WS25-9
P-22W140
P-40WS230-2.
P-35W86
P-61W51.

So desperate am I to decipher the latest message that today, I'm the one making excuses to the rest of the crew and taking my meal to my pod.

This message is longer, more complex. I can almost feel her straining to convey meaning within the limited words at our disposal. A sense of desperation, or perhaps that's just me. Eventually, a string of sentences comes together:

Bad seeds: Riddles. Row of numbers. Something broken. What are they looking for? Not even the engineer on the locomotive knows. Command you to ask beauty what orders are. Help discover.

It's even more cryptic this time, and I try my hardest to suppress my irritation and just work through it. That's the central tenet of astronaut training: stay calm and work through the problem, step by logical step.

Bad seeds: Riddles.

The colon suggests an attempt at definition. No idea what it means, though. *Row of numbers.* I'm translating this from a row of numbers – is it self-referential? None the wiser, I go back to *Riddles*. What's another word for 'riddle'? A puzzle. This whole damn thing is a puzzle. An enigma. Enigma. Code. And code is a line of numbers, too.

My mind suddenly jumps back to our mortality march. A room full of monitors and programmers, all staring at lines – or rows – of numbers, with Anders wittering on about code. Software. Suddenly the next two words are much more terrifying:

Something broken.

The code. The software. Is that broken? That's the bad seed? The seed isn't a person, it's a broken line of code hidden in our systems, that could grow into something more sinister? That would make more sense of Alyssa claiming she'd made a mistake. Her mistake was focusing on Ana as the problem, but instead it was the code?

What are they looking for? Not even the engineer on the locomotive knows.

This line is the most chilling. She knows there's a bad seed, a bad code, but they don't know what the damn thing is. The engineer. Is that symbolic of the coders? One coder? Maybe even Anders? Either way, the message is clear: if the engineer of the damn locomotive has no idea what they're searching for, the locomotive is fucked.

And it's clear what she wants me to do.

Command you to ask beauty what orders are.

I huff. It's so like Alyssa to still be commanding us, even from over thirty million kilometres away. It doesn't take a genius to work out who she's referring to. Our Argo Angel.

And then there's the last line:

Help discover.

I can't stay mad at her. Whether she's right, or she's wrong, she's mad or she's sane, Alyssa is back there, doing everything she can to help. She is determined to save us. I guess the question is: is there even something to save us from?

Several hours after I've translated Alyssa's latest message, everyone has gone to bed, with the exception of Ana and Lee, who are eating together in the hab.

As I pull myself through the ship towards them, my fingers jitter against the handholds – and it's not just from the nerves of what I'm about to attempt. By now, I'd usually have had my fix. But I still haven't touched the water pouch.

Hold it together, Rubio.

The two of them are giggling like children. They're the only ones that laugh at the moment. When I enter, they look up and the laughter dies.

'Rubio,' Lee says, looking nervous. 'I thought you were in bed.'

I grimace. 'Can't sleep.' That part's true. I head over to the refrigerated drawers and pull out a drinks pouch. I hope they don't see how much the straw shakes as I perforate it.

'Sorry to hear that,' Ana says, moving to clear up their food packets, leaving me and Lee hovering around the central table.

'Actually, don't mean to talk shop, Lee,' I begin tentatively. 'But I could use your help. I was on the Magnetic Spectrometer experiment today, but I'm not sure I got the readings right. Would you mind taking a look? Hate to ask.'

'Sure,' Lee says, as I knew he would. Always the team player. 'I'll look first thing tomorrow.'

I pull a face. 'Ah, don't worry. I promised Baikonur they'd have it by then. I'm sure I'm just stressing over nothing.' I slurp my juice.

'No, it's OK,' Lee says, his face full of genuine concern. My gut wrenches. 'I'll take a look now.'

'You sure?' I ask, painting a look of guilt and relief on my face.

'Of course. Ana,' he calls over to her. 'You good?'

'Uh-huh,' she smiles at him as he leaves.

I reckon I have five minutes, ten at most.

'You didn't have to do that, you know,' Ana says.

I pause. 'Do what?'

'You may be the person with the least letters after your name on this ship, but you're meticulous with your work.' She finishes packing away the disposables and utensils. 'If you wanted to talk to me on my own, you could have just asked.' She floats back into the centre of the hab, her beautiful blue eyes pinned on me.

I gape at her.

'Well?' she says, crossing her arms. 'Are you going to deny it?'

I clear my throat. 'No.'

She smiles and waits.

Fuck, she's stunning. And clever. A dangerous combination.

'Seeing as we're cutting through the bullshit here,' I begin, my voice low, in case Lee comes back sooner than expected. 'I want to ask you what you know about the ship.'

She raises a perfectly manicured eyebrow. 'Rubio, what are you talking about?'

I sigh and pull out my personal tablet. Ana says nothing, just watches as I pull up a music player and select a song I know that Abbey and the production company will never get permission to broadcast. The distinctive, mournful harmonica of Neil Young's 'Heart of Gold' rings out. Now we can speak more freely.

'What if I were to say that I knew there was something wrong with the ship?'

Ana frowns. 'Then I would say you should tell someone,' she says slowly. 'Commander Morin, Baikonur.'

I grimace. She's really good. I need to try another tack.

'But what if coming forward with this would expose someone? A plant. Someone who has been complicit in all this crazy shit that's been happening? What do you think that person would do? Would they confess, and tell the crew everything they know – exactly what they've been up to and who they've been working for – or would they deny everything, hide the evidence, perhaps even if it damned us in the process?'

Ana considers me. I can only imagine what's going on in that gorgeous head of hers.

Neil Young's voice quivers around us, singing about getting old.

'Rubio,' she says, ever so softly. I lean in. 'Is this . . . some sort of confession?'

'Really?' I exclaim. '*You're* questioning *me*?'

'Well, why shouldn't I? We can all see you're not yourself. You're not sleeping, hardly eating. Shaking like a leaf.' She nods to my hands, which I clasp together. 'And now you're asking me about sabotage and talking about being *placed* here.'

'I think you know precisely what I mean, Ana, when I talk about someone being *placed* here.'

'Well, what about you?' She raises her chin towards me, defiant. 'Not a scientific qualification to your name, a questionable history of substance abuse, best friend of the founder. If anyone has been planted on this ship, Rubio, you would be my prime suspect.'

That hits me right in the gut. Of course she can see it. Just like Brun, just like all of them. How much I question my position. How much I don't deserve to be here. But I'm going to prove my worth. Alyssa has trusted me, and I will find the truth.

'Just tell me, Ana,' I snap, too loud. 'What is Abbey getting you to do? What's happening to this fucking ship?'

For the first time, real anger twists Ana's immaculate face. 'I am fed up,' she says, moving close to me, her hot breath on my cheeks, 'with being bullied and threatened. You, Brun, Abbey, my father. You all think that I'm some pawn, a mole, a fucking secret weapon, but I would never put your lives at risk. I have trusted *you* with *my* life. The least you can do is return the favour. And if you can't, maybe *you're* the one who shouldn't be on this ship.'

'You're all good, Rubio,' Lee's voice calls out. 'Readings look perfect to— What's going on?'

My head snaps to the door leading towards the lab, where Lee now floats, a crease of concern on his forehead.

'Ask him,' Ana spits, pulling herself away from me. 'Anything else you want to get off your chest, Rubio?'

I watch her, floating, her face stone cold. Even if she does know something, she's never going to talk to me now. I've fucked it.

Lee moves into the room, and I notice he positions himself slightly closer to Ana, as though ready to jump in front of her. Once more, there's a stabbing pain of loneliness within me. Of isolation.

'No. I think . . . I'll turn in for the night,' I say, pushing off towards the sleeping quarters. 'Thank you, Lee. For checking those figures.'

Lee looks worried still, but he smiles at me all the same. 'Sleep well,' he calls after me.

I won't. I'll just float there in the darkness, while everything screams at me to touch that water pouch. But I will not give in. I'll have to deal with the bitter taste of failure instead – and hope for more from Alyssa tomorrow.

Alyssa

'I DON'T KNOW WHAT I'M LOOKING AT.'

'I'm not expecting you to,' Jake says, exasperated. 'But look how many times it occurs.' He pulls up multiple screenshots, with a particular line of code highlighted over and over. 'I've found it in well over forty places now,' he says, his brow furrowed.

We're both in his bedroom. He's been unusually quiet all day, barely catching up on sleep from the night before, emerging only to eat before heading back to his work.

It's intimate, being in here with him. Of course, when we first arrived, he offered up his bedroom like a true gentleman, but Jia and I insisted we share the pull-out couch. Back then, I'd hoped that it would only be for a couple of days, not ten. We're taking too long.

'So what is it?' I ask, trying to bite down on my frustration.

'They're patches. Fixes on bugs.'

'You said yourself weeks ago that you and the team were fixing stuff. That the code has been temperamental.'

'Yeah, but this isn't being fixed by the team,' he says.

'How do you know?'

'I've been checking in with them, cross-referencing their patches. None of them recognize it. And it's got its own style. It's really fucking untidy. Like someone is playing whack-a-mole. Patching holes that we aren't even aware of yet, fast and messy, then moving onto the next one.'

'Papering over the cracks?'

'Exactly.'

'Do you think it's the person who deliberately altered the code?'

Jake shakes his head.

'If someone *did* deliberately fuck up the code, I don't understand why they'd be doing slapdash fixes like this. No, I think this is someone else,' he says.

'Who?'

He glances at the closed door before pulling up another screen where yet more code is highlighted.

//TODO: remove this 'duration' (O.Cat=dick)

'O-Cat!' I cry.

'Shhh!' Jake hisses, darting a panicked glance at the door.

I match him by instinct. 'Is this Jia's brother?'

'Possibly.'

'When was this changed?'

'I was working on this system a week ago. It controls the cameras in the hab. It wasn't there then.'

'What does it mean?' I breathe.

'He's left himself a note, to remind himself about something that shouldn't be forgotten next time he enters that section of the code. And by the looks of it, he's chastising himself, too.'

'We have to tell Jia,' I say, moving to the door.

'No!' he yelps. I stop.

'Why not?'

He looks so damn tired. Working his day job and then sneaking back in at night is taking its toll. 'Because I'm worried about what this might mean.'

I peer at him. 'What are you saying?'

'Kai went missing, right? And then Abbey said he may be getting outside help in . . .' Jake looks at me, urging me to come to the same conclusion as him.

My mouth drops.

'You think they have Kai,' I breathe. 'You think whoever took him, might have him here, in Baikonur. Attempting to fix shit.'

Jake's lips thin and he turns back to his work. 'I can't prove it.'

'Which is why you don't want to tell Jia.' It's a statement, not a question, but Jake nods all the same.

'It's a wild theory among so many other wild theories. She's lost almost everything – we can't give her false hope. Not until we know more.'

'Where?' I blurt.

'Huh?' Jake says, still scrolling through the code.

'Where do you think they would keep him?'

Jake shrugs. 'Somewhere no one's been able to find him. Somewhere he hasn't been able to escape from.'

My heart leaps.

'Like somewhere you would keep people in quarantine?' I ask.

Jake looks at me again and then groans.

'Lyss—'

'The crew accommodation block would work. Built for isolation. Cut off from the rest of campus. And hell, there's no one moving in there soon, not with the rest of the crewed missions cancelled or on hold . . .'

'Uh-uh.' He waves his hands emphatically. 'We are not going to break into the damn accommodation block on such flimsy grounds. The code and the crew are our priority. You said yourself, we're taking too long.'

'But what if Kai can help us?' I move in front of Jake and push his screen down, forcing him to meet my eyes. 'He'll know what the error does – maybe he's even fixing it as we speak, or trying to. And he may know who put it there in the first place! God knows we have no other leads down here, and up there . . .' Rubio clearly isn't making any headway. We've had Mars One on constantly, and there's been no sign of further attempts to communicate with us.

Jake takes a few breaths, as if processing. Then he sighs. 'Fine,' he growls. 'I'll see if I can hack into the cameras in the accommodation block tonight.'

'Thank you!'

Without thinking, I grab him and kiss his cheek.

He blinks, as if stunned. My own cheeks blush at this out-of-character display.

I clear my throat. 'I, err, won't tell Jia. Not just yet,' I say, hoarse.

Jake gathers up his tablet and jacket. It's time for him to head back to campus, to spend another night trawling through the *Argo*'s code.

'Good idea,' he says, not meeting my eyes. But there's a hint of a smile on his face.

Jia

THE DOOR TO THE APARTMENT CLOSES QUIETLY.

'Jia,' Alyssa calls out as she leaves Jake's room and softly pads into the living area. 'You awake?' She peers over the couch at me.

I nod, my eyes barely showing out of the blanket.

'I'm going to take a shower. You OK with pasta tonight?'

I nod again.

For a moment, she hovers. It looks like she wants to say something, but then she gives me a tight smile and heads off to the bathroom.

I wait, coiled, for the bathroom door to shut and the sound of water hitting the shower basin.

Then I'm up, my eyes full of stars from the sudden movement after days of moping on the couch. But I'm at the front door in an instant and grabbing what I need, finding my shoes.

I heard it.

After Alyssa's cry of 'O-Cat' in Jake's bedroom, I made sure I heard every word. After all these days, weeks, months, finally, there's news.

Finally, there's proof he's alive.

And if there's even the slightest chance he's here, in the same damn town... Well, I can't pass that up.

I already lost Orion. I am not losing Kai.

But I only have a matter of seconds.

Jake's engine roars into life as I open the apartment's back door. Thanking the dense darkness that cloaks the landscape, I dart across the parking space and clamber into the back of his pickup truck. It's only as we begin to pull away that I realize I didn't shut the damn door behind me. The rectangle of light disappears as Jake turns onto the main road that will lead us to campus.

Alyssa will find it, when she's out of the shower. But by then, it will be too late. She won't be able to stop me.

Nobody will.

Just under fifteen minutes later, at the campus gates, the security men wave Jake's truck straight through and we're soon parking up. I hear him set out his chair and swing himself out of the driver's seat. I stay low, listening.

'Shit,' he mumbles. He rifles around in his car door, pats himself down. 'Shit,' he repeats.

He's looking for his ID lanyard.

I know, because I have it.

I took it from his jacket pocket by the door while he was in his room with Alyssa. At the last second, I grabbed one of the many tablet computers he has lying around the place as well, figuring I might need a prop to make me look legitimate if I have to go out in the open. The thought makes me nauseous.

I wince as he curses again. If he decides to go back for it, I'm done for. But after an agonizing minute, he slams the truck door shut, clearly deciding to try his luck without it.

Although it takes everything within me to hold on for even a second, I give it a couple of minutes, my heart pounding through my ears. Finally, I wriggle and roll my way out of the back of the pickup. My knees hit the concrete hard and my breath hisses out between my teeth.

I keep low, my eyes darting around. I spot some dumpsters and rush towards them, out of sight of the parking lot. My own speed surprises me. I'm a lot lighter on my feet than I used to be.

In the relative safety of the shadows, I try to take stock of where

I am. A campus of looming buildings surrounds me. Closest to Jake's truck is the biggest of them all, where I assume his coding room is. From what Alyssa said, that's also where Mission Control is.

Next to me is a building that stinks like chlorine. A pool?

Not the one.

Other buildings are ahead, but they all have lights on. People are working, people are in them. But Alyssa said the accommodation block would be empty.

I look behind me, trying to quell the growing panic. In the distance, towards the edge of the campus, stands a cold-war era concrete structure that is isolated from the other buildings. And most interestingly, it's dark, just one light emanating from the entrance.

It's my best bet.

I stand and begin to make my way along the edge of the pool building, keeping to the shadows and watching out for cameras, until a large stretch of tarmac reaches out in front of me, all the way to the concrete building fifty or so metres ahead. I squint in the darkness. Does that sign read 'Accommodation'?

Footsteps sound to my right and I pull back, heart thumping, as two figures stride past, talking to one another. They're heading home for the night, back towards the parking lot. Dressed casually, they seem relaxed, their security lanyards glinting in the floodlights.

I look down at my own outfit: leggings, a skirt, a hoody. I look like any one of them.

Before I can talk myself out of it, I'm slipping Jake's lanyard over my head. I make sure to keep the photo ID side against my chest, and hug the tablet over it. I smooth down my hair, brush off my knees, and stride into the open like I'm exactly where I'm meant to be.

Keep calm, I tell myself. *You're doing fine.*

After a few seconds, I can finally read the sign properly – and it does say 'Accommodation'. I swallow a yelp of triumph and trepidation. The entrance light glows, like a light at the end of a very long tunnel, drawing me closer.

And then I'm in front of the glass doors, which are shut tight. There's a security office to the left of the entrance inside, the bluescreen glow of a TV emanating from it.

I clear my throat and press the buzzer with a shaking finger.

A hacking cough erupts from the speaker, and a voice rasps out. 'Yes?'

'Hi.' My voice is smaller than I would like, and I push myself up a little taller. 'I'm here from coding. Is . . . is there a—'

'Speak up. This fucking thing!' the heavily accented voice barks out from the speaker.

The door buzzes.

I jump and dart in, the door slamming shut behind me. A wizened man hobbles out of the security office and eyes me up and down.

'Who the hell are you?'

'My name is . . . Erica . . . from coding . . .' I'm doing everything I can to stop my voice from shaking, but it's no use.

The security man eyes me suspiciously. His name tag reads 'Erasyl'.

'What do you want?'

'I err . . .' I wave Jake's tablet uselessly.

All the adrenaline drains from me. When I heard Kai's name back at Jake's apartment, I completely lost my mind. I was so hell-bent on getting here, on finding him. And now what? This is the craziest thing I've ever done.

Erasyl looks at me like he knows how stupid I am.

Fuck it. I have to say something. I have to try. 'Is there a coder here?'

Erasyl says nothing, just bores into me with his bloodshot eyes.

'I've been sent to speak with him. About the *Argo*'s code.' I gesture again with the tablet computer. This time, something changes on Erasyl's face. Is he . . . shocked?

Terrified, I clam up. And Erasyl doesn't say anything either.

The silence screams.

'Interesting jumper you have there,' he finally says.

I look down.

Crap. It's Alyssa's sweatshirt, with the logo with some weird cockroach and the words 'CLASS OF '24'. I had been covering it with the tablet, but now . . .

'It's – err,' I fumble. 'A friend's. A friend gave it to me.' Not a lie, exactly.

'A *friend*?'

'Please,' I gush, rushing forward. 'I have to talk to the coder, if he's here. There's something wrong with the ship. The crew are in danger.'

CLANG.

The door behind me slams shut and my head whips around to find a burly security guard blocking it, holding a takeaway container. Unlike Erasyl, he has a gun on his belt. The sight makes me wither inside.

'Another fucking meal he won't touch,' the man growls in an English accent, before noticing me and stopping. 'Who are you?'

I go to speak, but my mouth is so dry . . .

'Erica, from coding,' Erasyl's heavily accented voice calls from behind me. I spin to see him approaching. 'She's here to work with the boy.'

The burly man's head snaps at me and his eyes narrow.

'Shut your fucking mouth, *Borat*,' he spits. 'No one knows about the boy.'

My knees buckle. There is a boy here. It's got to be Kai.

Erasyl is beside me now. He doesn't blink at what I assume is an insult. Instead, he rolls his eyes at the guard like he's an idiot.

'Well, *we* do, and she does too. She's here to translate. He's been demanding to talk to someone these past couple of days, right? Well, Abbey sent her.'

The burly man eyes me up and down.

'Show me your ID,' he demands.

I finger Jake's ID lanyard, but Erasyl shuffles back to his security office. 'You want me to call Abbey? He's in a bad mood, but—'

'No!' The burly man starts, and even he looks a bit scared. 'I'll take her.'

And with that, he's barging past me and heading to the stairs, barking, 'Come!'

I blink disbelievingly at Erasyl, who's back beside me again.

'Your friend,' he whispers, so quick, so quiet. 'Is her name Alyssa?'

My eyes feel like they're about to pop out of their sockets. All I can do is nod.

'She was right about these *mudaks*. Go!'

The man leads me up several flights of stairs, past dark corridors. There are cameras everywhere, but none have the blinking light that would indicate filming.

With a grunt, he shoulders open a fire door and leads me down a hall, where fluorescent lights blink on automatically. We walk past door after door of what look like low-rent hotel rooms until we get to the only one with a faint light glowing beneath the door frame.

An extra external lock has been added, the workmanship shoddy.

I hold my breath.

The man thrusts the takeaway container into my arms, and I juggle it with my tablet. He takes out a set of keys from his pocket and unlocks the original lock, and the hurried-looking addition.

'Away from the door!' he shouts before kicking it open, his hand going straight to his gun.

I'm frozen as the door opens into a cramped room with breeze-block walls, a tiny single bed, a desk, a laptop.

And there.

My brother.

Kai.

He looks up resentfully, and it's a split second before he notices me. When he does, he surges to his feet. He's even thinner than I remember, and much more gaunt.

'Jia?' His voice seems so childlike.

The man tenses next to me. 'Thought you said your name was Erica?'

But I don't answer. I can't stop staring at my brother. Breathing. Standing. Here.

'Answer me!' The security man goes to grab me. He's huge. Once he has me, it's over. He'll see Jake's ID, know I'm a fraud. He'll lock me up, too.

I do the only thing I can think of: drop the tablet, pull the lid off the takeaway pot and throw it in his face.

'Gah!'

It's not scalding, but it buys me the few seconds I need. I dart to my right and lunge for the fire extinguisher mounted on the wall. With all my might I yank and swing round, just as the man charges at me, his face covered in vegetable soup.

THUD.

I smash the extinguisher into his side. He grunts, winded, crashing to his knees with a sound like a felled tree.

My breathing comes out in gasps and I'm suddenly exhausted, but his hand goes for his gun and I heave again, swinging the extinguisher around like a possessed shot-putter.

THWACK.

Right around the head.

His hand relaxes instantly and he slumps to the floor. I'm left panting, standing over him.

'Holy shit! Is he dead?' Kai stands in the doorway looking down at his jailer.

As if in answer, the man groans, tries to lift himself but collapses once more.

I kick him in his wounded side, relishing his pain.

Kai stares at me, utterly bewildered. 'Who the fuck are you and what have you done with my sister?'

In answer, I leap over the man's legs and barrel into my brother.

My arms make it too easily all the way around him. He smells wrong, like sweat and fear. But he's real. He's solid.

He's alive.

My brother is alive.

I pull back to see his face, just to make sure it's definitely him.

'Jia,' he blinks. 'What the fuck?!'

It takes me a moment to realize he's crying.

'You. Fucking. Asshole,' I choke, wiping the tears from his cheeks. 'You have no idea what you've put me through.'

'Well, it's been pretty shit here,' he says, gesturing back to his room. He thinks I'm different, but so is he. The usual laughter in his eyes is gone. Instead, he looks exhausted, broken. Like he did in the first few days after we moved Mom.

'Jia, I don't know how much you know,' he blurts. 'But I've been working on this code, for this ship. And it's totally fucked. And I've tried so hard to fix it, to counter what they're doing, but I can't. And I've tried to tell them, but they won't listen and if I don't fix it—'

'Shhh,' I hug him again, alarmed. I've never seen him so frantic. So lost. I pull back and hold his head firm. 'We have to get out of here, OK? We can worry about all the rest later.'

He shuts his lips tight, his eyes flying back and forth between my own.

'You're right,' he croaks. 'OK.'

The security man stirs again. We don't have much time. I grab Kai by the wrist and snatch the gun from the man's holster. I've never held a gun before. It's surprisingly heavy.

'Can you run?' I ask Kai, looking his scrawny body up and down.

'Can you?' he asks, stunned.

A joke, at my expense. Relief flushes over me. He is still my brother.

'Let's go!' I try to inject my voice with a confidence I'm not remotely feeling, and pull him back along the deserted corridor.

We burst out into the stairwell and I hurtle down the first

flight, but a door sounds below and I freeze. Footsteps. Someone is climbing, fast. I turn to Kai, whose eyes are as wide as mine. I turn and drag him upwards, moving as silently as possible.

'Up? Really?' he hisses, but I ignore him. We just need to find a place to hide. Work out a plan. If we can somehow get back to Jacob's truck—

We run out of stairs. There's a sign: ROOF ACCESS ONLY.

I push through the fire door and we burst out into the darkness.

It takes a moment for my eyes to adjust, but after a few seconds I see the whole campus stretched out before us and what looks like a launchpad out in the distance, covered with a blanket of the brightest stars. I'm momentarily struck by the beauty of the scene, but I shake myself out of it. We don't have time for that now.

'What the fuck do we do?' Kai whispers.

'I don't know!' I snap, pulling the fire door to behind us.

I round an air conditioning unit and freeze, terrified.

There, sat on the edge of the roof looking out towards the empty launchpad, is a man. He turns towards us. I can't see his face.

'Shit!' I scramble for the gun and raise it. The barrel shakes uncontrollably. 'Don't move,' I call out, but my voice comes out in a mouse-like squeak.

The man slowly pushes himself up. Kai moves slightly behind me, his breathing ragged.

The figure starts to walk towards us. He's tall, but old. In his sixties perhaps? A very worn, sad face.

'Stop! Or I'll shoot,' I blurt.

'That threat would probably work better on someone else,' the man says. Even through his heavy accent, I can hear the sorrow deep within him.

He's so close now that the gun is practically touching his chest. But he doesn't look scared. Instead, he peers down at me. His eyes take in my face, Kai, and finally my sweatshirt. He sighs and shakes his head.

'Let me guess,' he says. 'You know Alyssa Wright?'

All I can do is blink. Who the hell is this guy?

He smiles, but it doesn't reach his eyes. 'That woman is stubborn as hell.'

Alyssa

AS I STEP OUT OF THE BATHROOM, I KNOW INSTANTLY THAT something is wrong. The door is open, letting in a cold breeze. The living room is deserted.

'Jia?' I call out, moving to Jake's bedroom, but that, too, is empty.

'Jia?!' There's an edge of panic to my voice now. There's no sign of a struggle. The couch blankets are thrown back like she's just got up. But her shoes are gone.

Fuck.

I scramble to put on my support boot and find my other shoe. On the coffee table, I spot the burner phone Jake bought for use in an emergency. Well, this is an emergency if I ever knew one.

I hit the speed dial. Jake answers in one ring.

'Hello?'

'Jia's gone. She's not here.'

'What?!'

'I think she might have heard us talking about her brother. Did you look at the accommodation block?'

I rush to the back door and grab a bunch of keys off the hook, moving out into the night and pulling the door shut behind me.

'I just got here. I'll see if I can use the CCTV system to . . . Oh shit.'

'What?'

'I've got footage from the parking lot. I can see a shadow or something, moving out from the back of my truck. She must have stowed away back there. Shit!'

'They didn't check you?'

'They know me. Think they're embarrassed about harassing a guy with a wheelchair.'

I fumble with the bunch of keys and hit a button, and an alarm beeps. Jake stops.

'Lyss, you are not—'

'Yes, I am,' I bark as I hoist myself into the rusty jeep that Jake bought just a couple days ago in case Jia and I needed to get out of Baikonur fast, throwing some jump cables off the driver's seat. 'I can find her, stop her, before she blows this whole thing.'

The engine sputters into life and I roar out of the parking lot, the support boot making me heavy-footed on the gas.

'The CCTV cameras in the accommodation block are offline. Fuck. I'll go over there,' Jake says. 'Maybe I can find her.'

'No. We can't afford for you to get caught.' I glance at the clock on the dashboard. 'I'll be at the launchpad gates in ten minutes. Can you get the hack up by then?'

'I'll only be able to give you a few minutes!'

'That'll be enough. Wait by the fire escape in the coding room. I'll knock five times.'

'Fuck, Lyss!'

'Jake!'

'Fine,' he shouts. 'Just . . . be careful!'

We haven't just been sending messages to Rubio and trawling through the code these last ten days. We've been making contingency plans – one of which was how we might get me onto campus, in case I need to contact the ship without Jake. He's been hacking into the security cameras to set up a loop. The main entrance to campus is usually busy and there would be too many witnesses, but the engineering access gates, down towards the launchpads, are only used for wide loads. With no imminent launches planned, the area is lightly staffed.

I approach the gates slowly and pause, ducking down. I can't appear on the security cameras until Jake has activated his loop. If all goes to plan, no one in the central security office will even know someone is at the gate.

That just leaves the two guys emerging from the gatehouse . . .

Another minute clicks over on the clock. It's now or never.

I drive on, keeping my headlights on full beam, and stop in front of the barrier. One guard hangs back to man it, the other approaches, holding his hand up against the blinding headlights.

I step out of the truck.

'Can you turn those off?' the guard approaching me calls.

'I'm sorry!' I cry, my voice high, soft. 'It's a new truck, I don't know how! I need your help.' I move towards the back of the jeep. 'Do you guys know how to change a tyre?'

As the guard moves past the blinding beams, I turn so he can't see my face and lead him round to the back of the truck.

'Sure, but we're going to need to see some ID, ma'am.'

'Of course, it's in my purse, hold on.' I move to the passenger seat.

'Which one?' the guard calls.

'Back right!'

He bends down and shines his torch on the tyre, which is, of course, perfectly sound. But by then it's too late. I've got the jump lead around his neck and I pull it tight.

'Don't make a sound,' I hiss.

He freezes and obeys immediately, lifting his arms in surrender. I kick the back of his knees and he falls to the ground. I stuff a sock, which I took off my good foot a few minutes ago for this very purpose, in his mouth. The jeep's engine ticks over as we wait. The guy struggles a little, but I pull the lead tighter and he chokes.

Sooner than I expected, his colleague calls out. 'Kris?'

'Round here!' I call, so sweetly. 'He's just helping me with my tyre.'

His footsteps approach and his colleague bucks against me, trying to call out. Just before the second guard rounds the back of the jeep, I pull Kris's head back and smack it against the jeep's chassis. He's goes down like a bag of bricks.

'What the fu—'

I thrust my right foot out behind me, boot and all, and it makes contact with the guy's groin. He flies back and lands in the dust with an *oof*.

Kris groans. I turn back to him, grab the handcuffs and baton from his belt and whack him over the head, knocking him out cold.

Behind me, his colleague scrambles for his radio. I launch the baton at his arm with all my strength, hitting him right in the hand, sending the device flying. He rolls onto his belly, trying to reach it, but in three strides I'm there. I shove the knee of my good leg into the small of his back and pull his elbows together.

'That's enough,' I snap.

Finally, he lies still.

I take a few steadying breaths. My leg is killing me and I'm out of shape, but I'm a military brat. You grow up on air bases and you learn a thing or two about fighting and self-defence.

But there's no time for pain. The clock is ticking.

I click the handcuffs onto his wrists.

'I'm going to pull you up, onto your knees,' I say. 'Then we're going to walk *nicely* to the barrier. Can you do that?'

He nods. I breathe deep and then step back onto my feet. My bad leg screams and I wince.

The guy must sense me falter because suddenly he's spinning, trying to knee me in the gut. My right arm shoots out instinctively to block it, but his shoulder catches me in the face and my teeth bite down into my lip. I taste blood, but ignore it. I swing with everything I have and my left fist smashes into his face with an almighty hook.

He stumbles back and onto his ass, his head hitting the tarmac.

'Goddamn it!' I yell, shaking my hand, pain shooting up my arm.

I look back up and see he's lying still.

'Shit,' I hiss.

I hobble over and put a finger to his neck. There's a pulse – thank fuck – thumping like the ticking of the clock.

Growling at the effort, I grab the guy under the shoulders and haul him back towards the gatehouse. His key card is attached to his belt, so it's easy for me to bring the barrier up. Once more, I grab him by the arms and drag his sorry ass into the gatehouse, before returning for his colleague. Everything has to look normal for when Jake's CCTV loop stops.

By the end, I'm dripping in sweat and sick from the pain in my leg. But I can't stop now. I limp back to the jeep, haul myself in and drive through the barrier, then close it once more. Then I'm back in the jeep and hurtling into the night, towards the main campus, cursing Jia all the way.

Jia

ALL THREE OF US KNOW THAT I WON'T EVER BE ABLE TO shoot. But something about the way he just spoke about Alyssa makes me think that maybe he can be trusted.

So I lower the gun.

He just stands there.

'Who are you?' I ask him.

'Lars Anders,' he says. I know that name. He's Alyssa's old boss. The one she tried to get help from, but he said no. My blood runs cold as I realize that maybe we can't trust him after all.

'And you?' he asks.

I hesitate, but there's no point in lying. 'Li Jia, and this is my brother,' I gesture behind me. 'Kai. But I'm guessing you know that seeing as he's been locked up in your building!'

'Sadly, this is not my building any more.' Anders considers Kai. 'I'm very sorry, for whatever you've been through.' It sounds like he means it.

He reaches for his jacket pocket.

'Please,' I blurt. 'Don't tell anyone we're here!'

But instead of a phone, he pulls out a bottle of whiskey. He unscrews the cap, takes a gulp, then looks at us again, before turning and walking away.

Kai looks at me, his eyes bulging. I shrug in reply, then follow Anders.

'Stop! We need somewhere to lie low for a bit.' He says nothing. 'Where are you going?'

Anders stops at the edge of the roof and gestures to it. 'Here,' he says simply, taking another swig from the bottle.

I follow to where he's pointing, and see the outline of a rickety fire escape leading off the edge of the building. A route to freedom.

'Straight to the ground. No cameras,' he grunts. 'Just do me a favour? Get Alyssa out of here.' He turns his back on us and stares out once more at the empty launchpad.

Kai is over to the fire escape like a shot. He has his feet on the first rung of the ladder and calls out to me in a loud whisper. 'Come on!'

But my feet are stuck, my eyes glued on Anders, hunched, staring out into oblivion.

'She said you'd given up.' My voice is steady, calm. 'That there was nothing you could do. But that's not true.'

He doesn't look at me. But he doesn't move his bottle either.

'Come with us,' I say.

Kai is off the ladder now and grabbing my sleeve. 'Jia, this is crazy. Leave him!'

I shrug Kai off and edge towards Anders. He is listening. I know he is. And if we get off this roof, if we get back to Alyssa and Jake, I know he could help them – help us – warn the crew.

'Before my brother was taken, I'd kind of given up.' I pull level with Anders, but I don't look at him. I too stare out at the vast expanse of desert in front of us. The launchpad looks incredibly lonely, its bare metal structure glinting in the moonlight. 'I was stuck doing the same stupid shit every day. Serving coffee and studying late. Visiting my mom every couple of days, wasting away in a care home, not even remembering me. I didn't watch the news. I didn't care about wildfires, or protests, or space exploration. I just kept my head down, because what was the point in caring about that stuff? Nothing could be done. The world is fucked. I couldn't change that. Maybe some other people could. But not me.'

I can sense Kai behind me, and I realize I'm talking to him, too.

'But then Kai went missing, leaving me with his damn cat. And I realized that it was on me to find him. I had to do something. So I did. And even though I was accused of his murder, chased halfway round the world by NS agents and men with guns –' I ignore Kai's sharp intake of breath – 'nearly drowned in an ocean, burned in a wildfire and even though I lost . . .' My voice breaks, but I have to continue. I have to make them see. 'I lost something . . . some-*one* I loved along the way, I never gave up. I found him. I found my brother.'

I turn to Anders, willing him to look at me.

'And even though he is an arrogant jerk and a pain in the ass, he is also a coding genius. So with him, Jake and Alyssa working together to save the crew . . . It's not over. If anyone can do something to save the *Argo*, it's them.'

Finally, Anders' gaze breaks away from the horizon and meets mine. In his eyes there's a plea, for help, for forgiveness. For it all to be over.

'If you give up now, would you truly be able to say that you did everything within your power to save them?'

He looks away.

'I came here to save my brother,' I say. 'But I think we can save so much more. We have to try, right? Because otherwise, what is the fucking point of anything?'

Anders huffs a bitter laugh, staring down at his shoes.

'Come with us,' I say softly, smiling. 'And you can help save the crew.'

Within minutes, the three of us are almost at the bottom of the fire escape, the wind snapping at our clothes.

Kai is down first, and watches me, astonished, as I jump off the second from last rung.

'Seriously,' he laughs. 'What the hell happened to you?'

'I became a fugitive, thanks to you.'

But our smiles disappear as we really look at each other, for the first time, and I know he's thinking about everything I just said up on the roof. He grabs my hand.

'Jia, I'm so sorry. When I left that message, I just wanted you to get the code to Agnes, I thought she could handle it, she could sound the alarm, I never imagined—'

'You never imagined they'd frame me for your murder, hunt me down and threaten everyone we know?'

'I never imagined you'd be the one who would try to save me.'

'Well, I did,' I say, squeezing his hand back.

'And . . . Orion?' he asks. My stomach drops and my eyes fill.

'I'm . . .' Oh God, I can't say it. But I have to. 'I'm so sorry, Kai. He didn't . . . he didn't make it.'

Kai closes his eyes.

'I tried my best to save him,' I rush, 'but there was nothing we could do.' Tears fall down my cheeks.

My brother raises his hands to his face, covering his eyes. It feels like the longest time that he just stands there. Then he lurches forward and hugs me.

'It's my fault,' he whispers into my ear. 'It's all my fault.'

The sadness, the grief, but also the guilt in his voice breaks my heart all over again.

'I just wanted to hide the code somewhere no one would ever look. Somewhere safe. I didn't mean for him, for you, to be—'

He chokes up, and I squeeze him back. 'It's OK,' I hush. 'I know.'

A gruff cough sounds above us and we jump. We're blocking Anders' way off the ladder. Kai and I spring apart as he staggers onto solid ground.

'What now?' Anders asks, a little sheepish.

I take a deep, steadying breath. 'Can you get us to the coding room?'

Alyssa

I'M SO RELIEVED TO SEE JAKE'S FACE AS HE PULLS BACK THE fire door that I almost kiss him again. Almost.

'What the fuck happened to you?' he asks as I limp past him, dabbing at my split lip, and slump down into the nearest chair.

'Doesn't matter. Where's Jia?'

'I can't find her on any of the security cameras,' he says, moving back over to his desk. 'They may already have her.'

'We don't—' I groan as another shooting pain leaps up my leg. 'We don't know that. I'm going to find her.' I push up, wincing, but Jake pulls me back down with a thud.

'Don't be a fucking ass. Look at you!' His face is full of concern. 'At least wait a moment, have some water.'

He thrusts a bottle at me and moves away to a kitchen area in the corner of the room. I look at his console, where lines of data flicker in the dim light. It's silent in the coding room, just the low buzz of the machines and my pained breathing. I glance at the Colts horseshoe on Jake's desk that I righted, what feels like a lifetime ago.

'Any luck?' I gesture to the code on the screen.

'No,' he grunts, heading back with a first aid kit on his lap. He manoeuvres himself under the desk and turns back to me, banging his leg on a slightly open drawer. 'Arrrghhh!' he screams in frustration and slams his hand on the drawer front, pushing it back so hard it bounces back out again. 'Fucking thing!'

'Shhh!' I hiss furiously. Sure, it's the middle of the damn night, but he knows as well as I do that the security guards sometimes get off their asses and patrol the corridors.

'I'm not sure I'm going to get this.' Jacob's voice is serious as he opens the kit and finds some gauze and antiseptic. 'Find what system the error is in, I mean. We're working on a literal ticking bomb here. Fuck knows how much time we have. Hell, with the lag, we might even be too late now. We wouldn't know it. And now we've got Jia running loose somewhere . . .' He shakes his head in despondence, then raises the gauze up to my face. 'May I?'

I lean forward in acceptance as he tenderly dabs at my stinging lip. There's so much weariness and kindness in his face that I have to look away.

My eyes go to the feed up in the corner of the room. The *Argo* ploughs on, unaware that at any moment, something disastrous might befall it. But of course, we're watching what was happening nearly two minutes ago. The *Argo* is so far away now, that's how long it takes for any images or messages to reach us.

Jacob glances up to where I'm looking.

'You still wish it was you up there?' he asks, going for another clean bit of gauze.

'No,' I say simply.

'Really?' he says, disbelieving. Still gently cleaning my lip.

'Really,' I reply. 'If I were up there, I wouldn't be here. This is where I'm needed.'

He takes that in for a moment then leans back, handing me the gauze, and packs away the medical kit.

'I was having a really shit day when you came around on that tour with everyone,' he says quietly. 'I was actually thinking of leaving after the launch. Believe it or not, even with my charisma,' he throws a sideways grin at me, and my stomach twists, 'I haven't made many friends here. I think despite this . . .' he gestures to his chair, 'for a lot of the other coders, I just reminded them of the jocks who used to exclude them, bully them. So it was time for them to be on top, for me to be the outcast. I was pretty lonely.'

He snaps the kit shut, then pauses, like he's steeling himself.

'But then when you came and helped me, and when you smiled at me... all that disappeared for a moment. I knew who you were, of course, but until that moment, I thought you were superhuman. This intelligent, beautiful, commanding woman who was going to change the world, who I had the privilege of being vaguely connected to. And then that person had focused on me, just for a moment. I was buzzing after that. The other coders could all go to hell. For those few seconds, you made me feel like the most important person in that room. But after the accident, when I saw you in the cafeteria... I realized I was wrong. You weren't superhuman. You were painfully *human*. You were lonely, too. And you needed someone to be there, to make you realize you don't have to be alone.'

I look down to find that my hand has stretched out to touch his arm. He looks down at it, too.

'I think,' he says, dragging his eyes up to mine, 'that's what we have in common. The desire to matter to someone.'

His words hang in the air between us. I feel as though I should tell him that of course he's needed, of course he matters. Not just to Mars One, or Martha, or to his mawmaw and mom – but to me.

'Jake,' I say, my voice weirdly cracking. 'I should...' I lick my broken lip, nervous. Terrified. 'I should find Jia,' I blurt.

Jake closes his eyes in resignation and turns away from me. As he does so, his knee hits the drawer again, and his hand shoots out to bat it back in.

'Stupid fucking thing,' he hisses under his breath. 'It's never been the same since—'

He stops, his hand hovering in mid-air, like someone has hit pause. His face is frozen in an expression of complete astonishment.

The desk drawer rolls back out again.

Carefully, as if the thing were a trap, Jacob lowers his hand and pushes the drawer back in. As soon as he releases, it rolls back open again.

I stare at him, nonplussed. 'Jake?'

'I've got it,' he whispers.

My stomach flips. 'What?'

He leans right up to the screen, hands flying over the keyboard so fast I can hardly see them. The clack of the keys echoes in the silent room.

'I told you, the code from Orion's chip shows us that the *Argo* is counting something it shouldn't be,' he says. 'Something that would be a really large number if it kept going and going. Initially, I was thinking it was opening and closing files, memory, data, but . . .' He turns to me, breathing like he's just finished a marathon. 'What if it's not referencing software. What if it's opening something physical?'

I'm still not following him. He looks at me in frustration then shakes his arms at the set of drawers, one still ajar.

'Doors!' he cries. 'Look!' He turns back to the screen, cycling through the lines of numbers. 'Yes! It's here again and again. This same command. Open. Close. Open. Close. It's counting how many times a door opens and closes.'

'Which door?'

'All of them.'

'OK,' I say slowly, daring to feel a slight glimmer of hope. 'That doesn't sound so bad, right?'

'Not in itself, no. But I told you before, the problem comes when the system can no longer hold the count. When it can no longer handle that amount of unneeded, unaccounted-for data. It's like . . . I don't know . . . a river you never accounted for is feeding into a dam. And that dam can only hold so much water . . . right?'

Something about his tone makes my blood run cold.

'What happens if there's too much data?' I ask, heart hammering. 'What happens if the count hits the maximum number?'

Jacob shifts uncomfortably. 'I can't be sure. I don't know where it's being stored, what the limit is.'

'Worst case.'

He takes a deep breath. 'Well, the system will try and preserve itself. It will shut down, which could cause a domino effect. Other systems might also shut down. Things might fail . . .'

'What things?'

He raises his arms and looks to the TV screen of the *Argo*. 'The entire door system could fail. They could all get stuck shut . . . or they could all—'

'Open,' I finish for him, my voice hollow.

If the count hits a certain number – a number we don't know – every damn door could open. Pressurized doors for sealing off breached units, the door to the storm shelter – so many doors are mission-critical.

And then there's the two most critical of all.

The hatch.

The airlock.

'Fuck!' I cry.

'Exactly. And I can't just expand how much data the system can hold. I need to stop it counting.'

'But now we know what's broken, right?' I say, trying to compose myself. 'We can tell Rubio. They can . . .' Stop using the damn doors? That's ludicrous. They need the greenhouse to live, the pressurized doors within the hab have to function if there's an emergency. Hell, the hatch and airlock have to open to allow them to do essential works and walks – to let them fucking leave.

'We've never simulated all the door systems failing at once. Or the hatch and airlock being breached at the same time . . .'

That impossible, terrible idea hangs between us for what feels like eternity. The TV cycles through some more shots. Lee's green, three-eyed Martian sways under what must be the gentle breeze of the life systems.

'We have to tell Rubio. They can do something up there. Buy us more time.'

Jacob is rubbing his face in his hands.

'Yes,' he says, a little uncertain. Then: 'Yes!' His eyes snap back to mine. 'We can get them to individually take each door offline. Isolate it from the system. We have that failsafe in case of power outage. But I can't do it from here. They need to do that onboard.'

'We have to get a message to them. Tell them how to do it. Now.'

'How? None of us are getting anywhere near Control. Since Abbey took over, not even Anders can get in there. And you came bulldozing in here to find Jia, remember? What if she's in trou—'

'Jake!' I cry. 'My crew are in danger. The ship is compromised! We will find Jia, but we have to find a way to tell the crew, now!'

'Tell them what?' a voice asks calmly from behind us. Jake's eyes go wide and he takes a sharp breath.

I wheel around, stunned.

'Hello, Alyssa,' Anders smiles. 'I see you couldn't stay away.'

Before I can respond, he steps further into the room, leading another figure behind him. This guy is skinnier, shabbier, Asian. His eyes are wide as he stares at us. Who the hell—?

'Alyssa?' Jia follows on his heels.

Despite the fact that my crew are hurtling towards Mars in a ship that could expose them to the vacuum of space at any moment, a wave of relief washes over me at the sight of her.

'I found him!' she cries, ecstatic. 'I found my brother!'

Jia

'HE'S BEEN HERE, IN BAIKONUR, THIS WHOLE TIME.' THE words tumble out of me. I can hardly believe them myself.

Anders shuts the door to the coding room, Jake and Alyssa blinking at us in astonishment.

'Kai, tell them!' I urge him.

Kai looks to me again for assurance, before turning to Alyssa and Jake. 'Abbey and his guys have had me locked up. No phone, no Wi-Fi, just a shitty laptop and the code. Told me I had to come up with a fix before they'd let me go.'

Alyssa is on her feet now. She's limping more than the last time I saw her, but it doesn't stop her striding over to us, her eyes locked on to Kai.

'The error in the code – the doors – do you know how to fix it?' she asks, desperation pouring out of her.

'No,' Kai says. Startled by Alyssa's intensity, he takes a step back. 'I've been trying, but nothing works.'

'Fuck!' Alyssa throws her arms up in the air and turns away.

'Who is this?' Kai asks me, trying to be subtle, but Alyssa hears him.

'I'm the former commander of this mission. And this,' she says, gesturing to Jacob, 'is the guy who wrote the code in the first place.'

Kai's intelligent eyes flick between the two of them, then he settles on Jacob.

'Frybread?'

Jacob nods tightly.

'Man,' Kai breathes out. 'Someone has really been fucking with your code.'

'Abbey,' Alyssa growls.

'I know you want to blame him for everything, but I wouldn't be so sure,' Anders says quietly from behind me. Alyssa's focus zeros in on him for the first time since we entered.

'You,' she breathes, and she rushes up to him, pushing him roughly. 'What the hell does that mean?'

I move between them. Alyssa's eyes never leave his face, even as I slowly back her off. He smooths down his jacket. 'Alyssa, he could have given me and Kai away, but he didn't. He wants to help. He brought us here to find you and Jake.'

'This is *your* crew,' Alyssa snarls at Anders. 'You were supposed to protect them.'

'I tried,' Anders croaks. 'If you could just let me explain—'

'Did you know there was a flaw in the ship?' Alyssa snarls. 'That they could die at any moment?'

'Of course not.'

Alyssa looks like she's about to blow when Jake starts to move his chair over to us.

'Lyss,' he says, his voice soft. 'I think maybe we all need to take a step back, take a breath, and hear what Kai and Anders have to say.'

'But we have to warn the crew,' Alyssa says, her voice like thunder.

Jake reaches her side and touches her arm lightly. 'And we will. But if we know everything, it might help us fix it.'

Alyssa gives Anders one last lethal look, before turning away.

'Fine. Him first,' she points at Kai, who looks terrified. 'And make it quick.'

Alyssa

'YOU PROBABLY KNOW BY NOW I GOT A PORTION OF THIS code, the Mars One code, and I was paid to look for errors.' Jia's brother rushes. 'Well, I found a big one. It's counting something it shouldn't, and the memory space attributed to it is not big enough—'

'We know,' Jacob jumps in. 'It's counting each time the door system is activated, for no reason, and once we reach the maximum number, it will fail.'

Kai nods. 'Precisely what I found, although I didn't know which system. So I dialled it in and demanded payment. Even offered to fix it for them for a bit extra.'

'Who?' I ask. But Kai just shrugs.

'An anonymous employer – it's not how I usually run my jobs. Typically, a big company will get in touch, ask me to quietly look at a code before release, so someone like me doesn't hack and exploit them later. But this time, these guys insisted on doing everything off-book. No names. No context. They said it was safer that way. I'll admit, it spooked me a little, so I took some precautions in case they turned on me. But I never imagined they knew who I was. Or what they would do.'

'They kidnapped you,' Jia says quietly.

'They must have sedated me or something, because before I knew it I was waking up in a strange room in the middle of a fucking desert with a weird-ass British dude staring at me.'

'Abbey?' Jake asks.

'Yeah. I guess I better be grateful that it was him. Sounds like some other bastards were hot on my heels, if what Jia's been through is anything to go by. If it weren't for that piece of shit, I might never have seen the light of day again.' Kai shudders at the thought. 'So this guy – Abbey – asks me if I'd be able to fix the error I found in the code. I told him, sure, no problem. All I'd need is access to the whole thing, but I wasn't speaking to anyone until they proved that Jia, Orion and my mom were safe.'

Jia makes a small choking noise.

'Well,' Kai continues. 'The fucker comes back a day later with a livestream of Mom doing some calligraphy and shoves a laptop at me. It's not online, but it has the entire *Argo* code on it. Says he wants me to fix the error and check the rest of it. Only when I've patched the error will he let me talk to Jia and in the meantime . . . well, I hated the thought of him watching Mom.'

'When was this?' I snap.

Kai shrugs. 'Like weeks, months ago.'

Anger and hatred rises up my throat. 'He's known all along the crew have been sitting on a goddamn ticking bomb.'

'Until then, I didn't realize what the hell I was working on. Wasn't until I started going through the entire system that I put two and two together and realized this shit was responsible for people's lives. Even without the threat to Jia and Mom, I had to do something. But once I had access to the whole system, I realized there wasn't just an error in the part I'd been sent. There were issues throughout the whole damn thing. And they looked intentional.'

Jake curses under his breath.

'What did you do?' Jia says, aghast.

'I told Abbey. I said, *This whole thing is fucked*. He asked me if any of the other errors were mission-critical, like the one I found. I said I didn't think so, they were small. And he told me to leave them.'

'What?' I burst.

'He said to leave them. *Little glitches might come in handy. Drama is good for us. Just make sure they live.*'

'Little glitches?' I cry.

Anders looks mortified.

'Were you trying to patch the glitches?' Jake asks. 'I found your work in the system—'

'Well, I wasn't going to listen to *him*, was I? So every time I found a bug, I tried to fix it, yeah. It was infuriating. And more and more kept occurring, some even stopping me from working on the original error – like leading me down pointless rabbit holes.'

'Enough.' I try to temper my rage. 'Let's focus on what we can do. We know what's wrong now. We can fix this. We just need to tell them to take the door systems offline. We have time.'

'That might not be quite true,' Kai interjects.

Everyone's eyes shoot to him. He looks apologetic, disappointed with himself, even.

'I told you, I tried to fix it,' he explains. 'But every time, it kept changing. Mutating. Someone else was hacking as I was patching.'

'Who?'

Kai turns to Jake, pointing at his console. 'The section of the code on Orion's chip is the incriminating bit. It was supposed to be my insurance if they tried to fuck me. That code doesn't just have your signature in it, Fry. There's just one other instance I can remember where someone has set a PE's file structure to *Ultra Hard* – I recognize that from when I've been working on . . . other projects . . . mostly pissing off the Hong Kong administration.' Jia groans, but Kai ploughs on. 'Anyway, *Ultra Hard* – that's a dude who works for one of China's espionage units. He works out of Shanghai. He's the one who has your spaceship by the balls. I've been trying to tell Abbey, but he wouldn't fucking listen.'

'What do you mean?' Jake asks.

'When I first found the flaw in the code, I thought it was like a passive, slow-burn fuse. But now, like literally in the last few days, I've realized Ultra Hard can speed it up, bump up the numbers.

Someone from outside the system can bypass the counting. They've created an instant trigger.'

'What are you saying?' My voice quakes.

'I'm saying that whoever Ultra Hard altered this code for, if they wanted to, could strike a command here on Earth, and all the door mechanisms on that ship will fail as soon as the message hits.'

We all fall into silence.

I feel sick. Terror. Anger. Bile. All rising up within me.

'Why would someone do this?' Jia asks, almost to herself, sinking down into a chair.

Anders' head drops. 'Space means power. Russia, America, China – none of them want a private mission to take control of our next planet. They've all tried to influence or stop this mission in one way or another. They refused us, sanctioned us, sued us.' He smiles grimly. 'This is just the next step.'

Jia looks at me and it's clear she thinks he may be right. We all do. It makes sense: why National Security got involved with Jia straight away; how they knew so much about Kai; why she was chased for so long, so far; hell, how someone even managed to hack into the *Argo* code in the first place. TV producers and lone cybercriminals don't have the resources, the power, to do that. Nations do. And it looks like one in particular.

Jacob breaks the silence. 'We can still stop it,' he says, turning to Kai. 'If the crew take the doors offline, nothing can be operated remotely. It won't matter if the system crashes, triggered or not.'

Kai nods. 'Makes sense.'

'The quickest way to contact the *Argo* is via the comms in Mission Control.'

'But how do we get in there?' Jia asks.

'He can get us in,' I say, jerking my head to Anders.

He throws his arms up in exasperation. 'I told you, I'm frozen out. They're under orders not to let me in.'

'You're telling me that the founder of Mars One can't barge his way into his own damn control room?'

'But Abbey—'

'Fuck Abbey! Didn't you hear Kai? The crew could be exposed to space at the press of a button.'

Our eyes lock and he knows the moment has come for him to decide what history will know him as: the starry-eyed billionaire who sold his company and his team down the river? Or the visionary who fought to keep his crew and his hopes for a new world alive.

'I can get us in there,' he clips, and my heart leaps. 'But whether Abbey's team will let us get anywhere near the consoles . . . let alone send a message . . .'

'Will this help?' Jia chimes in, holding up a gun.

'Yes.' I choke back my surprise. 'I think it will.'

Rubio

IT'S BEEN TWO DAYS SINCE HER LAST MESSAGE.

I've considered telling the crew, breaking my silence. But as soon as I do that, the people on the ground will know, and they'll find Alyssa. I can't put her in danger, not when she's risked so much to contact me. But I can't sit here and do nothing, knowing that one or more of our many critical systems may fail.

But after spending almost an hour on the flight deck, I've found nothing. None of the read-outs, the data, the comms have anomalies, nothing that I could even vaguely interpret as code. I find myself floating through the bowels of the ship alone in the darkness.

The entrance to the greenhouse looms ahead of me. I hit the panel to open the door and pull myself through. In here, there's a whole set-up for Brun to do his experiments and log his data on the plant cultures. Most of the time he's independent, but I know he does communicate with some biologists on the ground. A message from Alyssa here is unlikely, but I'm desperate.

The place is simultaneously eerie and nostalgic, containing the only natural hues and textures for millions of kilometres. The tang of fertilizer and chemicals hits me as I enter. A computer system sits silent and blank in the corner. I'm just about to log on when I notice a bright, unnatural glow on a low shelf, behind dozens of dark plastic crates. It flashes, pulsates.

My heart leaps.

I've seen that glow before.

I reach into its hiding place and pull out the mystery tablet. It has a notification on it, a message icon, but when I try to open it, it asks me for a code. But I'm distracted by something else, hidden in the same spot, strapped under the glow of a grow lamp: a container of cloudy liquid. Pushing the illicit tablet aside so it spins beside me, I reach for it. As I disturb it, a mass of fragments swirl around, creating whorls in the cloudy substance.

I push the warm bottle down on an empty worktop with a sickening thud, and hold it in place. My heart slams into my chest. I pull hard on the lid, revealing an acrid, acidic smell, which I recognize instantly. Fermentation. Ethanol.

Alcohol.

I snap it shut before a globule can escape.

'For an alcoholic, you drank very slowly,' a smooth voice purrs behind me. I don't need to turn around. Who else could it be? I'm in his realm. A place the rest of us have left him practically alone in for too long. I let the container go and it floats off the worktop.

'Why would you do this?' I ask, reaching for the tablet. There are just a few planters between us now, and his artificially suntanned hands play with the fronds of one of them. 'And who are you speaking to?' I manage to bring my eyes to meet his. He looks calm, unbothered that I have uncovered his deepest secrets.

'I think the real question is, why would a scientific mission tasked with colonizing Mars entrust one of its precious places to an alcoholic, with no valuable accreditation to his name?' Brun smiles, cruelly.

Of course, I don't have an answer to this. No amount of postulating about the worth of art and documentation and culture has ever quieted the doubting voice in my own mind.

'Don't you wish you could just wash it all away, Rubio?' he asks, his voice like silk. 'That doubt? That guilt? I have been helping you, really. You would never have been able to cope without me. Without that.' He gestures at the container.

I say nothing.

'I can only apologize for the decline in quality. I must be honest with you, I thought the amount I smuggled on board would be more than enough to expose your weakness. But I underestimated just how sly an addict such as yourself could be. So I had to improvise. As you can see, I had everything I needed in here for fermentation. Or, more believably, *you* had everything you needed for fermentation.'

'What?' I break my silence, confused, looking at a man whom I signed up to spend the rest of my life with, but apparently do not know at all.

'No one is going to believe I've been secretly brewing alcohol for your consumption. Why would I do that?'

'Precisely what I would like to know,' snaps another voice.

For an instant, the smugness drains from his face, replaced with shock. We both turn sharply to see Commander Morin hovering in the threshold of the greenhouse. She looks dishevelled, as if she's just emerged from her sleep pod. Her usually soft features are harsh and angry in the eerie artificial light.

'Commander.' Brun slips the charm back on like a glove. 'I just caught Rubio—'

'Save it,' she snaps. 'Rubio, what do you have there?'

I hold the tablet up pathetically. She propels herself into the room and snatches it from me. She anchors herself to the wall as she looks it over, before narrowing her eyes at Brun.

'Would you care to explain this?'

'Commander, this is ridiculous. As I was trying to tell you, I caught Rubio sneaking into the greenhouse just now and discovered this.' He gestures at the fermentation container, still spinning innocuously. 'I've yet to find the still, but I'm sure we will uncover it.' His smarmy act makes me want to vomit.

'Spare me,' Morin says with admirable contempt. 'What. Is. This?' She punctuates her question with the tablet.

His face falters again. 'I . . .' He gapes, looking like a fish starving in oxygen. 'I have no idea, Commander.'

'Rubio?'

I can't understand why she's looking at me, questioning me. Then I realize, she might not have heard enough to know who to believe.

'Commander, it's some sort of communication device. With who, I have no idea, but it's not one of ours. It's Brun's—'

Commander Morin holds up her hand, and I fall silent. She lowers her voice, softens her facial expressions. 'I'm offering you the choice to come clean now. Please don't make me take further action.'

'Commander, I swear to you,' I jump in, panic tingeing my voice. 'I have no idea what that device is, but I genuinely believe it's Brun's. He's been blackmailing me with alcohol – but I swear, I don't know why or what the hell is going on.'

Next to me, I can sense Brun calculating, his scientific mind running all possible outcomes, before coming to a decision.

'I have no idea what that tablet is,' he says.

Morin suddenly looks as old as I've ever seen her, her brow furrowed with stress and regret.

'Fine,' she says almost to herself, before looking at the both of us. 'I'm going to escort you both to the hab, and we will wake the rest of the crew.'

'OK,' I reply, resigned, but Brun barks out a laugh, still playing dumb.

'Escort?' He grins mawkishly. 'Morin, you cannot be serious?'

'*Commander* Morin,' she snaps. 'And you know perfectly well what I'm doing, Brun. I'm enacting my emergency powers as commander of this mission, and I order you to accompany me to the hab, where the crew will demand you both tell us the truth about this damn thing.' She waves the tablet at him. 'And why you've been brewing alcohol to blackmail and poison your crewmate.'

'Ceci est absurde.' He laughs incredulously, backing away. But he looks panicked. Cornered.

Morin surges at him, grabbing his arm.

'Rubio!' she barks at me, and I realize I'm frozen. 'Wake the others, then go to the hab. Now.'

As I push off towards the door, I look at the container, bouncing lightly off a crate at the end of the room. 'What about the—'

'I'll deal with that,' she replies sharply. She begins to tug the protesting Brun with her before turning back to me again. 'Go.'

After I've roused them all, I fly back down the corridor towards the hab, where Okeowo has tethered herself to our dining table, brow furrowed and lips tightly clamped, waiting for more information. She's the only one in here. Damn it. I curse under my breath and push past Lee and Ana as they enter the room, zooming out towards the greenhouse.

I hear them before I see them.

'I refuse. This is ridiculous.'

'You have no choice, we're—'

'It's over, Brun.' My voice booms through the tunnel, audible to all. 'You can't lie to us any more.'

He darts a look of venom at me, but underneath it is pure fear. I realize with a stab of adrenaline this is when he will be most dangerous.

I launch myself at him, wrapping my arms around his body. I'm bigger than him, weightier. And I have the element of surprise.

He writhes against me, sending us flying off the wall and spinning. I jerk my head back and launch my forehead into his with all my might. Blinding white pain sears through my brain, but I hear a grunt from Brun and, through blurred eyes, see that it's had the desired effect. His nose is streaming with blood, the surface tension making it cling to his skin and eyes. He can't see a thing, and stops resisting.

'FUCK!' Morin cries out. 'Get off him this second, Rubio!' Hands grab my shoulders and pull me back, sending me flying past Lee, who has clearly heard the scuffle and come to help. He looks at me astounded, disappointed. But he'll know soon enough.

Okeowo zooms past me too, grabs Brun's spinning body and pulls him back to stability. She examines his nose.

'Broken,' she barks. 'Maybe concussed.'

'Lee, get Brun to the hab,' Morin orders.

I manage to secure myself to the wall, my head in my hands, trying to still the throbbing in my skull. Now I know why I've never headbutted anyone before.

Jia

THANKFULLY, ALYSSA TAKES THE GUN.

We move quickly. Anders knows the positions of all the cameras, so we can easily slip out of the fire exit and into the staff parking lot, where he tells all of us to stay hidden among the shadows.

When we make it to the central building, we pause. Watching, waiting. There are a few staff milling about, smoking. We wait for them to finish up.

Jacob nervously checks his watch, giving Alyssa a look that I can't read as he moves closer to us.

'Jia, Kai,' he says in hushed tones. 'I'm sorry for what you've both been through. And for Orion.'

Alyssa, her eyes on the building, the gun steady in her hands, nods. 'Me too.' She steals a glance at me. 'If you want out now, just say the word. In a few hours, you could turn yourselves in. Kai's already been held against his will for months. And Jia, you can say I coerced you into coming here. This isn't your fight. You can go home, back to the way things were.'

There's a warmth in her eyes that I don't think I've seen before. An affection, a gratitude. I can tell she means every word.

'Jia?' Kai says, turning to me, uncertainty suffusing his face.

I think about everything it's taken to bring me to this point. About how Kai never told me anything about his life, his work, about his donation to Mom's home. How he'd felt like, maybe, I wouldn't approve of it, would even fear it. And yet, how he trusted me with the thing he loved most in the world. I think of all I've done to find him, to save him.

'No,' I say, my voice almost unfamiliar to me in its strength and certainty. I like it. 'We're in. I want to help.'

Kai smiles. 'Me too.'

Alyssa nods curtly and turns back to watching the building. 'All right then,' is all she says, but Jacob grabs my arm and squeezes it, flashing me a smile in the darkness.

Up ahead, the smokers have disappeared, leaving a lone security guard manning the reception desk.

Anders takes out his whiskey bottle from his pocket and swigs, before dabbing some of the liquid on his clothes.

'What the hell are you doing?' Alyssa hisses.

He turns to her, scooping a rock up from the ground. He hefts it in his hand. 'I need you to hit me, right here.' He taps his temple. 'Enough to make it bleed.'

Alyssa balks. 'What?'

'Trust me.' Anders smiles grimly. 'I've learned a thing or two from a good friend about being a drunk. Hit me.'

Alyssa takes the rock in her hands and weighs it. For a moment, she looks like she's going to say something, but then her arm whips round. Anders' head snaps to the side with the blow and he crumples, but he doesn't make a sound. I clap my hands over my mouth to arrest my scream of horror.

He breathes out, then rights himself. A tentative hand reaches up to his head, from which dark blood is already seeping. He smears it a bit.

'Wait here,' Anders whispers, then moves out into the open, whiskey bottle in hand, doing an excellent job of seeming unsteady on his feet – although after the blow Alyssa just gave him, I wouldn't be surprised if he wasn't faking it.

He reaches the sealed glass doors and bangs on them. The security guard looks up, alarmed.

'Open up!' Anders growls into the intercom.

'Sir, I can't allow that.' The guard's voice is tinny in the speaker.

'This is *my* fucking building. *My* fucking mission. Let me in!'

'Mr Anders, sir, we've been told not to allow you access without—'

Anders slams a bloodied hand into the window. The guard leaps to his feet, mutters a curse under his breath and buzzes the door open. Anders falls through. The guard rushes to help Anders off the floor, and has him in a chair within seconds.

The doors swing shut. We can't hear anything any more, but can see Anders doing a great job of feigning discombobulation. He thrashes around, tries to take another swig of his drink, but the guard prises the bottle out of his hands. He looks at the cut on Anders' forehead and dithers a moment, before rushing deeper into the building.

As soon as he's gone, Anders is up on his feet, moving swiftly behind the desk.

The glass doors buzz.

Alyssa, Kai and I leap to our feet. Alyssa looks to Jacob, asking him a silent question.

'Just this once,' he says, and she hurries behind him and pushes at the back of his chair. Together, we hurtle towards the doors.

As we dart through, Anders throws the whiskey bottle outside, where it smashes on the concrete. He makes a bloody handprint on the inside of the doors, as if he's pushed them open and disappeared into the night.

Meanwhile, Jake grabs his pass from me and tries it on a set of double doors to our right, but the light flashes red. 'We can't get in!' he cries.

'Out the way.' Anders pushes through, producing the guard's pass with a flourish.

Alyssa raises an eyebrow.

'A billionaire can't know how to pickpocket?'

'Makes sense,' Kai shrugs, as he moves through the door. 'All you fuckers do is steal.'

And with that, we're out of the lobby, following Alyssa and Jacob down the corridor.

Alyssa

ANDERS SWIPES THE KEY CARD ON THE DOOR TO MISSION Control and moves out of the way so I can burst in first with the gun.

'Everyone on their feet!' I yell, as screams erupt around me. There's maybe a dozen people in here. The night shift.

'What the hell?' someone shouts.

'On your feet!' I point to a man sat frozen in front of his console. He jumps up and raises his hands.

Not so long ago, these were my colleagues. God knows what they think of me now.

'Anders?' Sophie from the medical team cries.

'Everyone to the back of the room.' I try to sound like I haven't lost my mind.

No one moves.

'Listen to her,' Anders calls out behind me. 'There is something wrong with the ship. We need to contact the *Argo* right now.' Everyone looks at us, agape. 'Please, do as Commander Wright says. We need you all to step away from your stations and move calmly to the back of the room.'

Most people begin to move out from behind their consoles and head to the back. But two stay put, a man and a woman. They're over in the corner, by the TV camera feeds. Abbey's people.

'You shouldn't be in here,' Abbey's man calls out, his voice shaking. He looks like a weasel. 'I'm calling security!'

He lunges for a phone, but I'm quicker. I swing the barrel of the gun round, flicking off the safety as I let my eyes bore into him. His hands fly up and he shrinks back. Anders herds the crowd as I edge weasel man and his colleague towards the back of the room.

'Now everyone must empty their pockets,' Anders says, grabbing an empty wastepaper basket and thrusting it into Jia's arms. 'No phones, no communication of any kind.' No one moves at first. 'Now! Please!' Anders commands and finally, nervous hands fumble and drop phones into the bin as Jia moves along the line, my gun still aimed towards them all.

'Jacob?' Sophie says in a small voice. 'What's going—'

'Commander Wright is here for the good of the crew,' Anders calls, marching over to the door and locking it as Jia deposits the basket of phones well out of reach. Anders and Kai drag a nearby table across the door, barricading us all in.

'You can't be fucking serious?' bellows Abbey's man.

I move towards him once more, gun aloft, and he cringes back into line.

'Alyssa!' Jacob calls.

I thrust the gun into Anders' hands and fly towards the comms desk. It's so strange to be back here. Nothing has changed. Instantly my eyes find the huge screen. There they are, my crew. Though none of them is asleep. A few of them are gathered in the hab while Morin and Rubio have seemingly cornered Brun in one of the corridors. They all have grim expressions on their faces. What the hell is going on? Without a headset on, I can't hear what they're saying.

'Alyssa!' Jacob hisses, and gestures at the CAPCOM position. 'Come on!'

I throw myself into the chair and scramble for the headset. In my ear, I can now hear some of what the *Argo* crew are saying, but it all washes over me as I fly through the onscreen options, turning on the emergency system for contacting every area of the ship.

'. . . *over, Brun, you can't lie to us any more.*'

There. I'm in. I hit the comms channel.

'*Argo*, this is Control. Control to *Argo*.' Of course, none of them hear. We're watching things from nearly two minutes ago. It's going to take just as long for them to hear this message. We won't see its impact on them for almost four minutes.

'This is an emergency announcement. There is an error in the code of the ship. I repeat, we have discovered an error in the code of the ship. All ingress and egress points – all the doors, both internal and external – are compromised.'

Even through the headset I can hear some of the Control staff react behind me.

'Immediate action is required to override the automatic software. Stand by for emergency protocols and details of the fault.'

Next to me, Jacob's hands whir over a keyboard as he uploads everything he knows to the ship's comms. Just then, voices and banging sound out behind us. I whip round. There are people at the door, trying to force their way in, and the crowd Anders is holding in place is looking even more panicked.

'Help!' Abbey's man cries out. 'Wright is in here. She has a gun!' Anders grabs him by the scruff of the neck, and the woman next to him screams.

'Shut. Up,' Anders growls in his face.

'Open this door, immediately!' a voice shouts from outside. British, and full of indignation. Abbey.

I turn back to the *Argo* feed and watch them, still oblivious. I punch the comms button again. 'Rubio, this is the error. Abbey, Valdivian – they knew the code was compromised. But it's not an error – the ship has been deliberately hacked, and the fault can be triggered remotely. I repeat. The doors can be compromised at any moment.'

A smash of glass and then several gunshots and screams from behind. I duck, but stay where I am, my eyes glued to the screen as Jacob continues to type next to me. How much longer do we have?

'You must get the doors offline before someone sends a signal—'

A crashing sound erupts behind.

Jacob rocks in his chair, urging the computer to process his instructions faster. With an air of finality, he hits three buttons.

'We're there,' he gasps, and the message is transmitted out across the cosmos.

Then there are strong hands around my arms, pulling me away. I let them take me without resistance this time, safe in the knowledge that we've done all we can. I keep my eyes locked on the screen, willing them to hear me. But someone grasps my chin and roughly yanks my face around. Abbey. His breath is rancid, his usually smarmy face creased with anger.

'What the fuck are you doing?' he snarls.

'Saving the ship,' I spit back, defiant. 'Saving my crew.'

Rubio

ANA GASPS AS I FLOAT BACK INTO THE HAB, WIPING BRUN'S blood from my face.

'What is happening?' she cries, her features fixed in angelic astonishment. The others file in behind me, with Okeowo leading a stunned Brun, whom she begins to clean up with her medical kit, strapping a plaster across the bridge of his nose.

'That is what we all want to know,' says Lee as he settles next to Ana around the table.

Morin comes in with the fermentation container and the tablet, deftly attaching pads of Velcro to each one and placing them on the table in front of us all, so they sit next to Lars's moon rock, like items on an altar.

Lee reaches for the tablet.

'This isn't one of ours,' he says, examining it.

Ana points at the container. 'Is that—?'

'A makeshift fermentation jar, yes. It appears Brun has been making his own brew, which Rubio has been drinking.'

All eyes in the hab turn to me, and I burn with humiliation. With guilt.

'Rubio?' Lee looks stunned. 'Is this true?'

I can't even make myself say yes. I just close my eyes, and it's enough of an admission for them all. When I open them, Okeowo is shaking her head.

'Why would Brun give you alcohol?' Ana asks, confused.

'He didn't *give* it to me. He planted it on me. I tried to drink it in tiny sips to get rid of it once and for all, but he kept filling it up. Then blackmailed me about it,' I spit, feeling as angry at myself as I do at Brun. 'I didn't know it was him until now.'

'How did he blackmail you?'

'With that,' I gesture to the tablet. 'It's his. He's been hiding it, communicating with people back on Earth without our knowledge.'

Okeowo looks at me with concern, before continuing to tend to Brun's face. He groans, no longer looking so dazed.

'Can you get into it, Lee? Corroborate what Rubio is saying?' Morin asks.

'I'll need some time,' he replies.

Morin looks at her watch. 'We don't have much of that – easier to ask him straight.'

'Why are we worried about time, Commander?' Ana's light, high voice sounds so childlike.

'Because by now, images of Rubio headbutting Brun are being received on Earth and I'd like a head start on figuring this out before Baikonur sticks their nose in.' Morin launches herself to the other side of the room. Her fingers fly on a computer nearby and a hidden panel clicks open. An emergency medical kit floats out, as well as something I never expected to see up here: a pair of handcuffs. Lee and Ana look startled, too. Morin closes the compartment and turns to me.

'I am giving you the benefit of the doubt right now, Rubio, because you're cooperating. But you can understand why I'm still not sure if I can trust you fully yet?'

I nod, staring at the cuffs in her hand. Seemingly satisfied, she floats back over to Brun, grabbing his arm to steady herself. 'Doctor, you can leave him now, I'm sure he's fine.'

Okeowo stops dead at the sight of Morin latching one of the cuffs around Brun's ankle.

'Qu'est-ce que c'est que cette merde?' he cries, jerking his leg, but Morin has already hooked her own foot under the table and she yanks hard. Brun cries out in alarm, and then pain, as she secures the other cuff to one of the footholds under the table. Brun tries to push away, but just ends up spinning pathetically as the rest of us watch.

'You've gone mad, the lot of you!' he cries out, thrashing around. After a few seconds, though, he seems to realize it's not doing any good and pulls himself down to the table, where he squats, staring intently at the tablet. Is he hoping it'll light up with a message for him?

'It was you,' Ana says quietly, her eyes burning into Brun's head. 'You've been playing all these tricks.' Her voice is getting louder now. 'The deleted messages, the memorial plaque. The ammonia leak!' Her face is full of fury, like I've never seen it before. Then she turns to the rest of us. 'And you all thought it was me!'

Lee places a hand on her arm. 'Ana,' he says quietly.

'No, Lee. I demand an apology!'

'He won't—' I start.

'Not from him!' she snaps, looking at me. And I feel yet another wash of shame. She's right, of course.

'Let's all take a moment,' Morin darts in. 'We need to know everything, all the facts. It's clear Brun has not been truthful to us. We need to assess the extent of his deceit, what else has been jeopardized, and how we can move forward from this.'

She turns to our captive. 'Who have you been talking to?'

He sits there, sullen, still staring at the screen.

'Brun, as your commander, I demand you tell me who you have been communicating with and why.'

He laughs. 'Commander? Such bullshit.'

Morin stays calm. 'Who have you been communicating with, and why?'

Brun lashes out, smashing his hand into the tablet, sending it flying. Okeowo ducks as it hurtles past her head and ricochets off a wall.

'Why?! Because this –' He waves his hands in the air – 'is utter bullshit. The worst crime in the history of our planet!'

He looks around at each of us, and we all gape back at him, amazed at the stream of hatred and contempt spewing from our crew member's mouth.

'Don't you fucking get it? I never wanted this mission to work. Don't you see? We're destroying our planet – and now we're on our way to ruin another. Spreading our stupidity, our greed, our arrogance, our flawed and dangerous biological material all over the fucking solar system and beyond! We shouldn't be up here, we should be down there, spending every waking moment, every single cent, on saving the one place we know is capable of sustaining us. This whole mission is an abomination.'

'You're with Terra Revolution,' I state simply. 'That's their rhetoric. That's who you've been communicating with, isn't it?'

He stares at me with cold eyes. An admission through silence.

Lee pushes himself away from the table and turns his back to us, his hands on his head. 'Fuck!'

Morin clears her throat.

'Brun,' she says, measured. 'You claim to be about maintaining life, but some of your actions could have killed us. The ammonia leak alone—'

He gives a humourless laugh. 'He survived, didn't he? I never meant to kill anyone. Scare? Yes. Create suspicion and malcontent among us all? Yes. Undermine the mission? Yes. Make people consider abandoning everything and turn back? Yes. Or at least, it should have done, if you hadn't all been so fucked up that—'

'Brun!' Ana breaks in, her face flushed. 'There are six people on this ship. Whatever your beliefs, by manipulating, lying, deceiving, sabotaging – you put every single one of us in danger. You had no idea what the consequences of—'

'Oh, shut the fuck up, you dumb bitch.'

Lee is a blur as he catapults himself into Brun, and there's a loud snap as the sudden force twists Brun's cuffed ankle into an unimaginable angle. His growl of hatred transforms into an animalistic howl of pain.

Morin piles in, getting her arm around Lee's neck and trying to wrestle him off Brun, who he's now punching with all his might.

'LEE! NO!' Ana bellows, an ear-splitting cry that makes him stop instantly. Morin slackens with relief and lets go, the three of them floating above the table, Brun weeping, attempting to claw back down to his foot. His face is smeared red once again where Lee has dislodged his nose. He turns his blood-soaked face to Okeowo.

'Please!' he wails. 'Ruth, help me.'

But there's something on Okeowo's usually calm, kind face that turns my stomach. It's contempt. She watches him, without moving a muscle. Her healing hands lie still.

'Lee, Ana, Okeowo, Rubio,' Morin says. 'Head to the cupola. We need to discuss this.'

She pushes off and out of the room. The others follow suit shortly after, but I linger for a moment, staring down at the man we all trusted with our lives. He looks up at me, through blood, tears and snot, and I search for any remorse, anything at all. But there's only hatred and obsession.

I turn my back on him and follow the rest of my crew out of the hab.

Sébastien

THE PAIN. LIKE NOTHING I'VE EVER FELT BEFORE.
It shoots.
Up my legs. My spine.
I writhe, I strain, I claw.

By the time they've all disappeared out of the hab, I've managed to pull myself down towards it, alleviating the pressure on my mangled foot. Every new twist is sheer agony.

I take a moment to scream. Left alone by the crew I have come to hate, and who now hate me in return. Everything on this Godforsaken ship sickens me to the bones. Every single nut and bolt, every piece of wire, the billions of dollars holding this whole damn thing together. I loathe it. And now, it is my prison.

What started as a flight of fancy, became a chance to make something right. To show the world that people will no longer stand by and allow billions' worth of resources, thousands of lives, and incalculable amounts of time, be squandered in humanity's ultimate vanity project, while the planet that gave birth to us chokes to death under the weight of our own arrogance and greed. I was done with funding and supporting tiny projects that barely scratched the surface.

I'd contacted Terra Revolution plenty of times before, and written to them about Mars One, asking what their plans were to stop it. After years studying astrobiology, I had come to realize how our very own biosphere was being neglected in pursuit of another. I struggled with my own part in it, but after realizing the error of my ways, I had to do something. Had to take action. They responded in the usual manner: they were forming a series of protests, disruptive action to their supply chains, partners, and headquarters; they also had lawyers working to lobby against it, to sue for human rights violations. But as every legal bullet was dodged and the aberration gained momentum, I did what no one would expect me to do.

I applied.

I thought their selection process would be a mockery. That it would expose the whole sham for what it was. I kept meticulous diaries of what I submitted and when, where they sent me for tests. I thought when the time was right, I could issue an exposé, bring the whole thing crashing down. But the further in the process I got, the more I realized this wasn't a joke. If no one did something drastic, they might just get this thing off the ground.

Terra Revolution started to take notice. What started as polite responses, became an ongoing exchange. When I went away for a week-long medical and psych assessment, I gave them the information they needed to cost it up, to run stories in the press about how much money was being wasted by these crazy billionaires on testing potential astronauts who had no previous experience, and on the type of people they were recruiting. I even fed them some of the application schedule, so they could protest the venues. But if anything, the publicity boosted the profile of Mars One, ensuring it remained in the headlines. Would the final TV deal have been so large if the concept weren't so controversial?

When I made the final round of the selection process, something shifted. I realized I could take this thing down from the inside.

I planned to wait until they went to strap us into the rocket. With billions of eyes watching, I would stand up and tell them that I had been a plant. That the real problems we were facing were here at home, and Mars One was committing crimes against humanity and the planet of the highest kind. And the final joke? The system was so flawed they'd allowed through the recruitment process one of their most extreme objectors. Who else would they be willing to send into space at the cost of billions? It would undermine the whole mission. They'd have to cancel the launch.

But then someone new from Terra Revolution contacted me, representing the more extreme end of the organization – they called themself Ultra. They'd heard about my plan and while they'd been impressed by my efforts so far, they warned me the people I'd been speaking to previously had no imagination, and our current plans would only have limited impact. Couldn't I see? This thing was already too far gone. By the time I revealed myself live on television, everyone and everything would be too invested. They would just replace me. I would make a splash, cause some headlines, but ultimately, it would all be for nothing.

Unless I was discerning about when and how I revealed myself. If ever. Ultra pointed me towards the likes of Kim Philby, Agent Garbo. These plants remained on the inside, infiltrating right into the heart of enemy territory. The key was the ship, the crew. Once they were launched, that was it. Up there, I would have the power to tear the whole system apart and force them to abandon the mission. To bring it back down to Earth.

And if the initial mission failed, Mars One would fail. There was no coming back from it financially. They'd never be able to fund another launch, and neither would any other private company. As for the national agencies, with the failure of Mars One coupled with the catastrophic disaster of the *Mayflower* so fresh in voters' memories, there would be no way that any elected official could justify spending taxpayers' money on something as risky and flawed as long-term space exploration. Not for a long while, anyway. It would allow us to refocus the narrative: place our future back on planet Earth; realize where our true investment as a species should lie. Imagine what could be done, if the money squirrelled away for private space exploration and national space agencies suddenly became available for green technology – reforestation, ocean clean-up, the destruction of oil-based infrastructure. And it could all start with me.

All I had to do was sacrifice a few more months than planned, and play the dutiful botanist who signed himself up to a one-way mission to Mars. Meanwhile, Ultra would feed me information from the ground, and suggest how and when to strike to maximize my impact. In return, they would ensure that, when I got home safely, I would be protected.

Things started well. Ultra was well connected. It was they who suggested we smuggle alcohol onboard after I told them about Rubio's vice. If he was unwell, Ultra said, it would be yet another reason for them to abort the mission. Ultra's contacts took care of slipping it into Rubio's launch suit, as well as smuggling the tablet in ahead of launch.

But how, I asked, would I be able to move around the ship without being spotted? The thing was rigged for a live TV show. Ultra seemed to find my concerns amusing when we spoke online. They assured me that, just as with our communications here on Earth, they had ways of infiltrating and covering their tracks – as well as other key people on the inside.

It was a terrifying leap of faith to so completely trust this person I'd never met. But on the first night, as I settled into my greenhouse, I found my stash. The alcohol disguised as components for my fertilizer, and a tablet with a simple message: '*Welcome onboard*'. After a couple of nights, before checking on the flask in Rubio's sleeping bag, I punched a couple of codes into my tablet. When I glanced up at the camera just above our pods, to my relief, the light was not on.

We thought Rubio would binge the first opportunity he got. But instead, the bastard consumed it slowly. I kept topping it up, but when that first batch ran out, I had to improvise. I was certain that, as the stresses and strains of the journey escalated, his willpower would buckle. When he found my communication device, I thought it was over, that I'd be exposed. But Ultra assured me that shame was a powerful tool, and they were right. Rubio kept his mouth shut, and seemed to have no idea that I was his tormentor.

I couldn't use my camera hack too often, though. It would arouse suspicion on the ground. It helped if something more interesting was going on elsewhere. If Ana was acting weird in the hab, why would anyone notice a momentary drop out of the camera in the sleep pods?

So I triggered a code that deleted personal messages. I also sewed tension within the crew by losing things, stealing rationed personal items, even planting dirty utensils on other people's cleaning rotation. Everything petty and infuriating to prevent us all settling into a comfortable harmony. Ana was an outsider, a natural scapegoat. Alyssa had already sewn the seed of suspicion for me, and her idiotic mistake with the powder and warped sleep pattern played right into my hands.

But as we got further away from Earth, and the comms became more fragmented, things became harder. As we neared the point of no return, the messages from Ultra became more demanding. They wanted me to take more risks, to shut down the camera feeds for longer, to push things harder onto Ana. The clock was ticking – I had to do more to convince the crew that the mission was no longer tenable, that we had to turn back, that it was too dangerous to continue.

That's when Ultra suggested the ammonia leak. They had someone on the inside who could rig a QD to blow on command . . .

Up until this point, everything I had done – blackmailing Rubio, framing Ana for mistakes, even the Mayflower Memorial fuck-up – had not been mission-critical. But deliberately contaminating a crewmate? Terra Revolution had promised to keep me safe. I was well aware, floating in this tin can, that any kind of ammonia leak could be deadly. Until we got back to Earth, I needed the ship and its crew.

Ultra and I had had a conversation about what might happen if our actions failed to convince the crew to turn around. And we agreed, if it looked like the mission was about to proceed past the go/no-go point, I would out myself: threaten to take the entire ship down if we didn't return to Earth. But that, of course, was a last resort. If I did that, I'd be imprisoned for life as soon as we hit the ground. And I had so much more to give. So much more to do for our planet.

It was then that Ultra asked me something that surprised me: *And if they refused, would you end it all?*

This was a test, I was sure of it. A hypothetical question to make sure I was dedicated to the cause.

I told them I wouldn't let it get to that point. My intention was never for this to be a suicide mission. If anything, I would be saving these people from years of eking out a miserable living on the barren red planet, wasting away underground, waiting for the radiation exposure to finally take its toll and kill them in cancerous agony.

No, I told my handler. My job is to save these people, just as I will be saving humanity.

They seemed satisfied.

But, months into the mission, the *Argo* was getting closer to the point of no return, yet no one seemed to realize what was at stake.

So I agreed to the leak.

For the first time, I was putting someone in actual danger. But it was for a purpose. I was endangering them, to save them. To save us all.

And all this brought me to this moment. Cuffed to the ship with a broken ankle.

My foot throbs and my nervous system protests at any small movement, but I force myself to breathe, to think. My tablet floats around the room, forgotten by the others in their shock and confusion. It's on the other side of the hab, but with my cuffed and broken foot, it might as well be a thousand miles away.

But I have to find a way to get to it. The feed to Earth is, of course, delayed, so by now the ground will know something's up, but the TV crew likely pulled the plug on the live broadcast when they realized the extent of the crisis. I have to let Terra Revolution know that I've blown my cover. The final night before the launch, Ultra gave me a code to input if I'm discovered; a signal to them that will trigger a release of the truth of everything that we have done and why. Enough to convince the world that the mission is a failure, before Abbey, Anders and all those other bastards try to twist the narrative.

I must send them the message.

With three large breaths, I steady myself, and I think of everything that led me to this point. Every sacrifice, every moment of pain, of despair. Of hope. I grab hold of my foot and the cuff and, placing my free foot up against the table, I twist and heave.

White light sears across my vision.

Pain like I've never imagined.

Metal scrapes against bone as I twist my mangled ankle further still.

Unbearable pressure.

Then something pops.

And I'm free.

Floating.

Floating on a sea of suffering.

My dislocated broken ankle dangles beneath me.

I have to get that tablet. Only then can I succumb to the darkness creeping into the corner of my vision.

I swim, scramble with my arms, trying anything to propel me closer to the device. It's feeble, useless, until my good foot finds purchase on the table leg and I kick, arms outstretched. My fingers touch the cold metal and it's in my hands. I pull it to my chest, hugging it close, like a life raft.

I careen into the wall with a jolt of searing agony. But I barely notice. I have my tablet. I can end this.

I unlock it with my fingerprints.

And I send my SOS across the stars.

Jia

THE BRITISH MAN — ABBEY, PRESUMABLY — HAS PLENTY OF security with him. Two men bash the gun out of Anders' hands and smash into him, his already injured head making a sickening crack on the floor. Three others grab Alyssa and Jacob, dragging him out of his chair.

Kai and I are next to be slammed down to the ground, so hard that all the air escapes my lungs. Cold metal bites into my wrists as someone cuffs me. Five of the security men haul us into line, as the other two guard the doors. We're forced to kneel in front of the Control staff, facing the big screen, with the exception of Jacob, whose legs are sprawled awkwardly as he's held up by one of the men. My eyes find Kai, who seems relatively unscathed, but next to him Anders' chin is against his chest and there's even more blood seeping from his head.

Abbey leans into Alyssa. Her eyes burn with hatred.

'Tell me,' he says, low and menacing. 'What you said to them.'

'The truth,' Alyssa says simply.

'She said . . .' a nervous voice speaks out. We all turn. It's one of the Control staff. 'She said there's an error in the ship's code and all the doors were compromised. She said you knew.'

Abbey blinks, then looks at the rest of the Control staff, as if just realizing that they were there. Then his face rearranges itself into disbelief. He scoffs.

'My God.' He moves away from us, towards the staff. 'Alyssa

Wright is hysterical. You saw how she was on launch day. We had to remove her from her post. This is all part of her delusional fantasy. And she's somehow tricked these others into believing her lies. But please, believe me when I say there is nothing wrong with the—'

'Sir!' the small man who challenged Alyssa earlier cries, pointing at the huge feed of the *Argo*, where one of the crew has just attacked another.

Abbey's head snaps to the screen.

'Fuck!' he cries, and his mask drops once again. He turns to the small man. 'Get me a fucking headset. Now!' The man scrambles to obey, thrusting them into his boss's hands.

'Abbey,' Alyssa says, her voice calm. 'It's over. You need to call in all the engineers. They have to fix the ship, and you need to turn off the livestream. It's not just a mistake. You've let someone compromise this entire mission. Someone has purposely hacked into the system – this thing could blow at any minute. Particularly if they're watching and see that everything's going to shit!'

The two men holding Alyssa try to move her towards the door, but Abbey stops them.

'No,' he says. 'Put the five of them back there.' He gestures to some desks and chairs right at the back of the room. 'I don't want them out of my sight.' My captors lift me right off the floor and carry me back to where some of the staff are still cowering. Abbey seems to see them again, too.

He smiles, like a crocodile. All teeth. 'Guys, come on. It's fucking mayhem up there. Back to your places, yeah? Help me work out what's going on, and get me back in touch with the *Argo*. I need to explain to them what's happened.'

The security men resort to cable-tying all our cuffs to the desks, but they don't bother with Jacob, assuming he can't move. I watch, fascinated, as the Control staff hesitate. Only two people emerge from the group: the small man dashing to a bank of monitors showing different feeds from the ship, and a woman back to a laptop next to him – clearly Abbey's team. Everyone else remains where they stand.

Abbey shifts on his feet. 'Get. Back. To work.'

'With all due respect,' a blonde man with a German accent says. 'You are not our flight controller.' The longer he talks, the louder his voice gets. 'I think I speak for all of us when I say that we do not feel safe, and—'

Abbey curses under his breath and turns to the small man.

'Find out what we've missed. I want someone monitoring the ratings immediately. And get Bob down here. If they want a flight controller, they can fucking have him.' He shoves his headphones back on. 'I can hardly fucking hear them, damn it!' Abbey yells to the woman at the laptop. 'What's going on?'

'None of them have their mics on, sir. It's the middle of the ni—'

'Well put the fucking light on!'

'We have, they're not—'

Abbey screams and turns back to the Control staff. He strides up to a woman and grabs her.

'Abbey!' Alyssa yells.

Some of the Control staff try to intervene, but two security men step up, their hands on their holsters, and they stop.

'You.' Abbey drags her to the comms station. 'Bring the house mics up! And put them on speaker.'

The woman, shaking like a leaf, begins to tap away. Within seconds, a buzzing, throbbing sound blares through speakers in the walls and we can suddenly hear everything on the *Argo*.

'*Is that—?*'

'*A makeshift fermentation jar, yes.*'

Abbey turns to the guy sat with the vast bank of monitors in front of him.

'You!' Abbey marches over to him. 'Get on their fucking faces, man. Now!'

The man flinches and attempts to do as he's told, but he's flustered and keeps cutting to wider feeds, and even cameras that aren't anywhere near the crew.

'You fucking imbecile!' Abbey screams.

Finally, the man manages to find the right camera, and the main feed on the huge screen closes in on the crew.

Abbey storms off, seemingly satisfied for the moment.

Jacob's body leans away from mine, towards Alyssa. He's wincing – they must have been even more rough with him than they were with me.

'Lyss,' he whispers. 'What do we do now?'

Alyssa shakes her head, totally absorbed in the scene playing out on the screen, her hands clenched into fists in her cuffs. All we can do is watch as the crew's drama unfolds in front of us. It looks like a movie set. The light is so artificial, the lines of their environment so clean-cut, you could almost believe they are just next door, able to step out of the frame any moment and pop outside for a sneaky cigarette while the next shot is set up.

'*You're with Terra Revolution . . .*'

The Control staff gasp and whisper among themselves. Alyssa's shoulders sag.

'Fuck,' Jacob chokes.

Then a woman wearing a coat over her pyjamas is clambering over the ruined barricade, carrying a tablet and grinning manically. Abbey darts over to her, looks at the tablet and steps back, astonished.

'Are you serious?' he barks.

'Yes!' the woman cries. 'With it being around noon across most of the States, we're pulling in record numbers. Some news outlets have even linked up to our feed.'

Then an old man rushes in, escorted by Abbey's errand boy.

'Abbey!' he yells, pushing past the woman with a look of contempt. 'You need to stand down. You have no right to give orders to the Control staff.'

'Back off, Bob. Tell your Control team to get back to their stations and to do as I tell them. This is all about framing now. Shaping the narrative. Letting it all play out.'

'What the fuck are you talking about?' Bob cries. 'They're breaking down up there! We need to get someone on CAPCOM and shut down the feed. They can't be seen like this. The whole mission is in jeopardy.'

'Yeah, your fucking ex-commander and boss have seen to that.' Abbey gestures to us. Bob turns and reels at the sight of us all trussed up, Anders slumped, unconscious. He tries to move towards us, but a security guard advances, his hand on the butt of his gun.

Bob halts, alarmed.

'Have you lost your mind, George?'

'No. But apparently everyone else has. And the ratings have just gone stratospheric.'

Rubio

THE PEACE OF THE STARS THROUGH THE CUPOLA'S WINdows is in complete contrast to the chaos within.

'We can't trust him to roam the ship!' Lee cries.

'But we also can't afford to be a crew member down,' Ana says, voice strained.

'Put him in the damn storm shelter and leave him there!'

'Be reasonable, Lee,' Okeowo pleads.

'How can we trust anything that comes out of his mouth ever again?'

Look what he's done to us.

'Rubio,' Morin breaks through. I turn to look at her, and the others fall quiet. She looks utterly broken. 'Why didn't you tell me?'

I almost wish the yelling would start up again. At least I could sit back and hide in the mayhem.

'I – I was scared . . .' is all I can offer. 'That you'd all think less of me, or worse, not believe me.' God, so fucking pathetic. I'm disgusted by myself.

None of them speak. I search within me for something, anything I can say to make this better.

'I'm . . .' my voice is weak, just like my damn character. 'I'm so sorry.'

But then a tone sounds around the ship, making us jump. It's the emergency announcement system. My stomach drops.

'*Argo*, this is Control. Control to *Argo*.'

Alyssa!

Sébastien

ALYSSA'S VOICE REACHES ME THROUGH A HAZE OF PAIN AS I float free in the hab, the tablet spinning next to me.

What is she saying?

The ship has been hacked? Someone can compromise it from elsewhere?

The fog in my mind begins to clear, allowing me to process the meaning of her message.

The doors are compromised. All of them? But that would mean the pressurized doors, the airlock, the hatch. We'd be completely exposed . . .

And in that briefest of nanoseconds, as my life narrows down to this moment, I realize something that I never allowed myself to think before now: I've put all our lives in the hands of someone I've never met and have no idea if I can trust.

I look towards the tablet. My lifeline, the one thing that has been connecting me to my handlers. To home. The device that I just typed my distress call into.

Only then does it occur to me that Ultra contacted *me*. After months of communication with Terra Revolution, another representative reached out to me. More militant, with connections far beyond anything I'd seen before . . .

I was tasked with grounding space exploration for this generation. But what if I failed? Would Ultra ever let us land on Mars? Or did they have a backup plan?

What was it Anders said to us on launch day?

There is no greater mission than this.

Of course, Terra Revolution were not the only people who wanted this mission to fail.

We're talking about Mars here. An entire new world.

Nations have gone to war for far less . . .

I look back to the tablet, floating innocently in the micro-g. The code that I just typed in, burned into its pixels.

Have I just doomed us all?

Rubio

I DON'T THINK ANY OF US HAVE TAKEN A BREATH SINCE the end of Alyssa's transmission.

'*Any moment?*' Ana breathes. 'Did she say "any moment"?'

This snaps Morin out of her stupor.

'Lee!' she cries. 'Where is Brun's tablet?'

Horror spreads over Lee's face. 'The hab.'

Surely they can't be thinking . . .

But they're already flying out of the cupola, dragging and pushing themselves through the air. I follow them, Ana close behind me.

Lee gets to the hab first, and when he sees Brun floating free of his cuffs, he screams in rage and throws his whole body into him, sending Brun spinning off into the wall.

Brun cries out in agony.

Morin grabs at the tablet, her breathing heavy.

'I sent it!' Brun moans from the corner of the room, as Ana and Okeowo arrive.

'Sent what?' Morin snaps.

'The SOS code!' Brun wails. It's as though he's regressed to a childlike state.

Okeowo zooms out of nowhere and grabs hold of Brun, sending the two of them into a spiral. With one hand, she holds his body close. With the other, she grasps his face and pulls it to hers. When she speaks, her voice is cold, sharp, devastating.

'Tell us what you sent, Brun, or I swear to God I'll—'

'A message . . .' he gulps. 'They said . . . if I was discovered, I should send them a code and they'd release the truth. But now I think . . . Oh God!' He begins to weep uncontrollably.

'Lee,' Morin snaps. 'When did he send that message?'

'Confirmation of transmission is from thirty-two seconds ago.'

'Shit!' Morin yells, burying her face in her hands.

'Commander,' I start. 'Do you think Brun's contact will trigger—'

'Yes, Rubio, I do,' she mutters. Then she's moving to a console on the wall, typing in commands. 'Lee, pull up any protocols Alyssa has sent. Get them on all our devices.' He's already on it.

'*Argo* to Control, activating emergency lighting and life support on standby,' she recites.

'Listen,' Lee calls, his eyes whizzing back and forth across his tablet. 'We need to take every single door off the automatic system. Take them offline, and revert to manual operation only.'

'And if we don't?' Morin asks.

Lee shakes his head. 'If someone does trip the flaw, the whole system will fail. Best case, every door shuts and locks, and we're trapped wherever we are. Entombed. Worst case, every locking mechanism opens—'

'And the entire ship is breached to the vacuum of space,' Morin says, and the words ring out like a death knell. She shuts her eyes for the briefest of moments, then they open again, steely now.

'What's our time lag?'

'One minute, fifty-one seconds,' Ana states. I'm ashamed I'm still surprised she knows these things.

Morin looks to her watch. 'Brun's message will be reaching Earth any moment now. If Brun's friends pull the trigger, we have just under two minutes until the system could fail.'

Lee kicks off the wall, shooting down the hab.

'I'll take the hatch and airlock,' he calls out. I'm relieved; that's the most complex system.

'I'll help you,' Ana calls, strangely serene, and moves off after him, like a dandelion in the breeze.

'I'll take the landing module. We can't lose that. It's our life raft if the worst happens,' Morin says.

Okeowo looks to me.

'Looks like we're on internal pressurized doors?'

I nod, skimming over the instructions and trying to recall the manuals we spent months studying.

Then I remember Brun, who's staring at the two of us through his bloodied and swollen face.

'What about him?' I ask.

Okeowo looks back at him, her face darkening. 'One crisis at a time, Rubio. I'll take aft, you take forward,' she calls, pulling herself into the corridor.

I follow suit.

Each of us dispatched to save the others' lives.

Ana

I CATCH UP WITH LEE AS WE SOAR DOWN THE SHIP, TOWARDS the airlock. He's holding his right hand awkwardly from where he punched Brun, clearly in pain.

'*Pridurok*,' I hiss. 'You didn't need to hit him. Especially so much that you hurt yourself.'

'I'm fine,' Lee growls. But he winces when he opens the control panel of the door to the airlock. At least two of his fingers look broken.

I push him aside and type in the command codes to access the system. I tear Alyssa's instructions from him. The tablet quavers in my hand as adrenaline surges through me.

'Wait!' he cries. 'You need to open the door!'

'If we open this door, and the system fails, we're fucked,' I cry. 'The airlock will be fine until someone on the ground can solve the glitch in the code. We'll have no means of doing an EVA, but it is better than exposing the entire ship to—'

'There's an access point on the other side of this door that overrides this one. We have to disable the door on *both* sides to take it fully off the system.'

'Why would the ship allow someone to override the airlock door mechanisms from the outside?'

'In case someone ever needs to make it back inside!' he cries, as if it's obvious.

'But that's not the procedure. It would only be needed if—'

'If no one was around on the inside to open it,' Lee says quietly.

I almost laugh. 'But that's absurd. You'd have to have someone on the outside, working their way through an EVA when everyone on board just, what, drops down dead? That would never happen.'

'Ana,' he says more urgently again now. 'It did. The *Mayflower*.'

'But . . .' I was twenty-five when the *Mayflower* crew died. I followed it on the news, knew every detail of the disaster. 'They all died within minutes of each other. Rutherford's suit was shredded by micro meteoroids.'

Lee shakes his head. 'He was on a spacewalk. The ship was breached, but he survived, and when he tried to get back in, he was locked out. He ran out of oxygen. So they changed the design, put in an override on both the hatch and the airlock door so they can be opened from both sides. That's why I have to go in there and shut it down.'

Lee takes the instructions out of my limp hand.

'How long was he out there?' My voice quivers.

Lee grimaces. 'Six hours.'

I reel as though punched in the stomach.

'How do you know this?' I breathe. 'NASA can't have told you?'

Lee takes advantage of my astonishment to nudge me out of the way, and begins tapping at the door control panel.

'Alyssa,' he says over his shoulder. 'She was CAPCOM that night. She stayed on with him the whole time, until his oxygen ran out.'

It feels like I've been punched all over again. Of course, I knew Alyssa had worked at NASA – and I thought I'd heard her calm, measured tones before – but I'd never realized it was *her* voice on the footage I watched of the *Mayflower* mission. She'd stayed on the line with a man for six whole hours, as he worked to accept that he would be left to die, to suffocate out there, all by himself.

And now I understand it all. Not only Alyssa's mistrust of me, but her anger, her fury, her mad determination to protect the crew no matter what. But also, I finally understand the feeling deep within me that has been there since I took her spot and that I haven't wanted to speak of:

I'm not one of them.

The truth is, no amount of backup training or cramming of simulation runs or forced bonding exercises was ever going to make up for the years they have spent together, the incalculable amount of intimate knowledge they all hold about each other and the mission. Even looking at Lee now, I can see how deftly he handles the machinery of this ship. How vital he is for its very survival. How intrinsic every single member of this crew is for the fate of this mission. And just how much they have lost already.

I look at a comms screen on the wall, where the clock is ticking.

It's been nearly two minutes.

We only have seconds to take this airlock door offline on both sides before the hatch could blow.

So when the door to the airlock finally slides open, in the moment Lee takes to check behind him and to see if I'm all right, I slide through and punch it shut.

His face is a mask of shock, the breath snatched right out of him. I snap on the intercom.

'Don't you dare risk opening this door until we both know the system is offline. You hear me?' I say, my voice strangely calm.

He moves to the panel.

'Don't!' I cry out. 'We've already wasted too much time, and that was on me. If anything goes wrong, and that hatch opens behind me, it's better this way. You're more valuable than me. So shut up and tell me what to do, so we can fix this and I can get back on the right side of the door.'

Lee

THIS IS A WAKING NIGHTMARE, BUT ANA LOOKS AS THOUGH she was made for this moment, her face resolute as she takes in my instructions and initiates them flawlessly.

'Now hit confirm and it's offline,' I call.

'Confirmed,' she clips back.

'Lee, do you copy?' Morin calls over the comms system. Before I can reply, red lights flash and the alarm begins to blare.

'What the fuck?' Ana cries, looking up at the light pulsating behind her.

I pull up the alarm system, my eyes flying back and forth across the screen. But there's nothing, no fault, no failure. The alarm's been triggered by the ground.

I punch the wall, then turn on the comms.

'It's the ground,' I explain. 'No failure. No fault. Just generic alarms.'

'They're setting the scene,' Ana says quietly through the airlock intercom. 'A dramatic tone.'

My gaze locks on to hers, those breathtaking ice-blue eyes in striking contrast with the burning scarlet surrounding her. In another life, she could have been a screen star. Only this mission has turned us all into them, anyway.

I snap myself out of it and look at the clock.

We're well past two minutes. If the people on the ground have triggered the doors, they could open at any moment.

'We need to focus, Ana. Turn that lever and get back over here.'
She's already on it, her hand grasping and yanking. But then the mechanisms lock in. *What the hell?*

'Good job, Lee.' She smiles, then turns to the space suits hanging on the wall. She pulls one off its hook. My stomach flips.

'What are you doing?!' I cry.

'If I open that door and those bastards pull the trigger, the hatch blows and you're all dead. So while I'm here, I have to secure the hatch, too,' she says, fast and serious, as she slips her legs into the suit, then shrugs her arms into the top half.

'Ana, no!' I bang on the door again, but of course I can't open it. That's the whole point.

'We need a functioning airlock, Lee. We cannot continue without the ability to do an EVA, you know that.' She says all this while locking the joints of the suit in place. 'I suit up. I tether. Then I have all the time in the world to take the outer hatch offline too and secure it. I can do this, Lee. I can save the mission.'

'The mission is fucked, Ana!' I cry out. Tears well in my eyes, but they stick to my eyeballs, obscuring my vision. I frantically rub at them.

'Are all the other doors offline and secured?' she asks.

I fumble for the comms system, calling out to the others.

'Lee to *Argo* crew, can you confirm, all egress and ingress points are now offline and manually secured?'

'Confirmed,' Morin barks over the din.

'Confirmed.' Okeowo.

'Confirmed.' Rubio.

Ana nods, satisfied. 'See, Lee. We did it.' She smiles, reaching up for her helmet and taking it under her arm.

She raises a gloved hand up to the airlock door window and puts her palm against it. I follow with my own, and she smiles at me, her beautiful blonde hair tucked into the rubberized neck of the suit. Her confidence, her assuredness, calms me. I can barely hear the alarm, see the red glare. Despite everything, she has beaten them. They can lie to us, they can manipulate us, they can scare us, they can divide us, but look what she has done. Despite everything, she's risking herself for a crew that until ten minutes ago was ostracizing her. Maybe this can work. Maybe we can survive. Hell, maybe we can even thrive.

I look to the timer. It's been almost four minutes since Brun sent the message. But the hatch is still in place. Nothing has happened.

Maybe Brun's contact hasn't triggered the fault.

Maybe Ana is safe to come back through the door.

'Ana—' I start, but she cuts me off.

'I know.' She smiles brightly. She lifts the helmet over her head and winks at me. 'I'll be done in a moment.'

We both hear it before we see it.

That unmistakable click and hiss.

The pressure pops.

'Ana!' I cry, and I see the look of surprise on her face. Her hand clenched to tighten the seal on her helmet.

BOOM-VWIP.

The outer hatch door blasts open and Ana's body is sucked out into the vacuum.

A dull, low rumble begins.

But I can barely hear it through my own screams. Everything within me pours out through my lungs as, through globules of tears and the hellish glare of the alarms, I watch her disappear out into the nothingness, along with everything else not tied down in the airlock.

And then it's over. Everything is still.

The pressure equalized.

The rest of the ship safe. Secure.

The airlock exposed to the void.

And Ana is a dot, on a canvas of black.

Alyssa

HERE I AM AGAIN, STUCK WATCHING ANOTHER CREW THAT I feel responsible for fighting for survival, without any way of helping them. I watch them all sprint off to take their allocated doors offline.

But this was two minutes ago. Who knows what's happened since.

Abbey is frozen in front of the screen, enraptured by what is playing out on it, as are the two production team members, and the Control staff.

Bob breaks the silence first.

'Abbey.' His voice wavers. I've never seen him like this: the NASA stalwart, shaken to his very core. 'Is this true? There's an error in the code, and you knew?'

Above us, the screen flits between the panicked movements of the crew as they attempt to take all the doors offline. I count them down in my head. But Lee and Ana are taking too long. They're talking. No, arguing. What the hell are they doing?

'Abbey! Did you know about this?' Bob bellows.

'No.' Abbey's voice is small. He's a man totally out of his depth. 'No,' he says again, almost to himself. 'I knew there were glitches, but . . . it was drama, it was stakes. It was never supposed to be . . .'

Bob darts towards Abbey. The guards move as one, which seems to shake Abbey from his reverie. He turns to see them holding Bob at gunpoint, and everyone else in the room frozen in time.

'George, call your guard dogs off, please,' Bob says through gritted teeth. 'My team need to save our goddamn ship.'

The seconds tick away.

'If this mission – and your company – is to survive in any way, you need me, Abbey,' growls Bob. 'Step aside and let my team back at the controls.'

The two men exchange looks, Abbey's frantic mind whirring right in front of our eyes. When the answer comes, it's almost anticlimactic.

'Fine.'

Bob sags with relief and Abbey nods at his security men, who let him go.

Bob gestures to the Control crew, who all begin moving around the security guards and back to their posts. Bob darts to the CAPCOM desk.

'Now, George,' he says, beginning to work the controls. 'Take the live feed off and we can—'

'No,' Abbey says, his voice clear and strong again. 'You can work on the ship, but we're not going off air.'

Bob looks up. 'What are you talking about? They're fighting for their lives up there.'

Abbey gestures to the screen, to the tablet. 'We can't go off air now. This is a television show. No matter what, we keep the stream running. All this is only possible because people are watching.'

'All *this* is possible because you knew someone had hacked the damn code and you didn't tell anyone!' Bob bellows.

'Do you think Valdivian and all the stakeholders just signed up to this with a blind eye and threw money at it?' Abbey snaps. 'While you lot were pissing money up the wall developing faulty code and training nutjobs, I was taking out insurance, scrutinizing our investment. And it's a good thing I did, because we found a ticking time bomb, along with a bunch of other errors. Maybe we should have told you, but I couldn't risk anything shutting this down. And we had time, and a fucking criminal coder who could fix it for us. He didn't say anything about a trigger, though!' He rounds on Kai, who looks like he wants to kill him.

'Because he wouldn't fucking see me—' Kai's guard kicks him into silence.

Abbey continues, unblinking. 'Besides, if people started to switch off, at least we'd have something to draw them back in. And people *did* start switching off! Do you know how close we were to losing everything? How close I was to losing everything? But now . . . This is Apollo 13, this is the moon landing! It's 9/11! This is the most monumental moment in television history. And I am contractually obliged to keep rolling.'

Abbey breathes hard into the silence that follows.

Any doubt, any guilt, any fear is gone from him. He's got too much to lose by doing the right thing.

Suddenly, the red lights of the alarm system start pulsating on the *Argo*, and the room is filled with the sound of the siren.

'What the fuck?!' Abbey cries. His head snapping back to the screen.

'I triggered the alarms, sir, just a couple of minutes ago,' the weasel man calls out from his desk.

Abbey absorbs the scene in front of him.

'Brilliant.' He strides to the woman at the comms desk. 'Turn it up.'

'Sir, there's no point, they know—'

'Not for them. For us! For the audience!' Abbey yells, a look of fury and something else on his face. My stomach turns as I realize what it is – exhilaration.

'I can, sir,' the weasel man calls out from his desk, tapping at his keyboard, and the room is deafened by the wail of the alarm.

'Airlock!' cries Abbey. His arms raised up, like he's conducting a fucking symphony.

But the editor is way ahead of Abbey, cutting to the airlock, then to Lee outside of it, banging on the door at Ana, to Brun sobbing in his bloodied state in the hab, the clock ticking.

They're out of time.

And Ana's still in the airlock.

She's not going to make it.

'No!' I scream, launching myself towards the screen. But my cuffed wrists snap me back.

On the other side of the room, Bob looks back up at the screen, eyes wide. 'Abbey. Turn off the feed!'

'No!' Abbey yells back, intent on the lights, the sirens, the blood, the stakes. It's perfect drama. Perfect television.

I take in the scene. Ana in the airlock. Lee sobbing at her through the closed door. The rest of the crew rushing through the ship.

'Save them!' I yell. 'Please!' But this is all in the past. It's already happened. It's already lost.

Suddenly, Bob launches himself at Abbey, who flies through the air.

'Shut down the feed! Shut it down!' Bob yells.

A crash.

Screaming.

The guards launch themselves on the bundle that is Bob and Abbey.

Then our own alarms are blaring and lights on the screens surrounding the Control room turn orange, red.

My screams are snatched away from my throat as on the screen, for the entire world to see, the hatch blows and Ana Petrova is sucked out into the darkness.

I feel my body take a huge gulp of air, its own survival instinct kicking in, as I crouch on my knees, my wrists red raw behind my back, watching poor Lee's face sink down behind the airlock window, the unbearable weight of loss overpowering him.

The feed switches to the camera in the corridor outside the airlock, where Lee floats, curled up in the foetal position. Okeowo zooms towards him, looking out in horror at what's beyond the door.

Then Rubio is there, and Okeowo is screaming at him, before turning to Lee, trying to speak to him, trying to hold him. As Rubio stares out at the airlock, at the place where the hatch should be, he shrinks back from it, but can't seem to look away. Morin arrives and joins Okeowo in trying to grapple with Lee, who is now writhing, trying to tear away from their embraces.

A shadow passes below the camera, and Brun slowly pulls himself into shot. Morin, Okeowo and Lee are unaware, too entangled in each other in the corner, their mouths moving rapidly, clearly trying to calm Lee down. But Rubio sees him, and watches as Brun drags his broken body to the window in the airlock door and stares out at the nightmare he has created. He freezes, a look of astonishment on his face, of disbelief. He places his hand against the glass.

All this plays out in utter silence, apart from the incessant drone of the *Argo*'s alarm system.

On and on it goes. Just like the agony playing out before us.

Suddenly, Lee breaks loose from Okeowo and Morin. He kicks off, out of the room and shoots down the tunnel towards the hab. Okeowo and Morin follow, but Rubio lingers, watching Brun stare out into space a few seconds longer, before leaving him to his own torment.

The cameras track the crew as they move through the ship, to the flight deck, where Lee pulls himself up to one of the monitors and taps the displays.

I realize what he's trying to do immediately: he wants to pull up the *Argo*'s outer cameras, to seek her out in the nothingness.

Morin, Okeowo, and Rubio don't stop him.

Nothing can be done now.

Rubio turns aside from the others, and he looks straight down the lens of the camera we're all peering through. He considers us for a moment, his face blank. Then he turns to the door and floats out towards the hab. The movement sensors in the cameras track him to the table in the middle of the room, where Ana placed Anders' moon rock, all those months ago.

Rubio pulls it off the Velcro tab that's holding it in place. He turns it in his hands, slowly, just as he's seen his friend Anders do so many times, before looking back towards the nearest camera.

Abbey finally stirs. He's spread across a desk with Bob, both of them half pinned by the guards. In any other circumstance, it would look comical, but everything is imbued with the tragedy of what is unfurling in front of us.

'Turn it off,' croaks the producer, finally finding his voice again. Rubio floats slowly towards the camera, his eyes boring into us. 'Shut down the stream!'

But Bob keeps him pinned down, as we watch Rubio reach out for a handhold above the camera's lens, and position himself dead in front of it, the fake moon rock in his palm.

Rubio's mouth moves to form one word: 'Murderers.'

He pulls his arm back and smashes the rock right into the lens of the camera with all his might.

The feed crackles.

Blackness.

Then another angle from a different camera pops up. But this time it shows Okeowo, and we see her grim determination as she yanks hard at what must be the wires, because that camera goes dead too.

Next, it's Morin, smashing a camera in with what appears to be a storage container.

We watch as, one by one, all the cameras in the hab go down.

They make their way through the ship, snuffing them out until, eventually, there's only one left: the one outside the airlock, where Brun floats, weeping.

It's as if the crew purposely let that image sit with us. The alarm within the *Argo* is finally silenced, the red lights stop flashing, and the sounds of Brun's cries can be heard faintly above the background hum of the *Argo*'s life support.

A life-support system, originally built for six, now working for five.

I can't believe it.

She's gone.

My shocked stupor shatters when Jia begins to shout loudly in Cantonese, blurting out who the fuck knows what at the top of her lungs. It seems to break everyone in Control from their reverie. The guards pinning down Bob haul him off Abbey, who attempts to get back to his feet.

'Shut up,' Abbey bellows at her.

A guard strides past me and hits Jia hard around the face. Kai tries to kick out at him, but he can't reach.

Jia pauses for breath, then starts up again, screeching in a seemingly panicked and incomprehensible stream.

'She's fucking hysterical! Gag her!' someone yells. The guard pulls out his belt, looming over her.

Then quick as a flash, her face transforms from panicked little girl to a woman with fire in her eyes. Her face scrunches up with fury, and suddenly her foot is in the guard's groin and he's down. Within the blink of an eye, her boot finds contact with his head, too.

The guard nearest to us leaps into action, drawing his gun. But Jacob launches himself towards him, throwing his entire weight into tackling the burly man, taking him by surprise. I bet they wish they'd bound him, now.

Seeing their chance, Sophie from medical and an engineer rush forward. Sophie bashes the gun out of the guard's hand.

The two other men holding Bob drop him to grab their own guns, but Bob manages to pull the legs of one of them out from underneath him, sending him flying. He picks up a screen from one of the desks and smashes it into the other.

Soon, everyone in Mission Control is swarming the guards, gathering up the guns. Others return to their monitors, thrusting on their headsets and frantically pulling up data, trying to assess the damage and contact the *Argo*.

'*Argo*, this is Mission Control. Do you copy?'

Abbey watches, stunned and powerless, as everything unfolds around him.

Strong hands pull at my shoulders, and my eyes focus in on Bob, bloodied and breathless.

'Alyssa,' he pants. 'Are you all right?'

I nod dazedly.

He uses a pair of scissors to cut my cuffs free of the desk, and I follow as he moves to the heap that is the Mars One founder.

Bob feels for a pulse. There's so much blood.

'He's alive, but he needs the med bay,' Bob says.

'Hold on,' I mutter in his ear. 'Please, just hold on.'

And then someone cries out in the Control room and all heads snap back to the screens in front of us at the only shot we now have of the *Argo*. An anonymous hand, holding a fraudulent rock of lies and false hope, appears from below. It hovers a moment, a bold image within the frame, before it crashes into the remaining lens.

Leaving our screen finally . . .

Blessedly . . .

Blank.

MARS ONE – WHAT WE KNOW ON DAY 10 OF THE SILENCE

USA Today
By Samantha Stuart
April 8 2031

Ten days ago, a reported audience of 4.8 billion around the world was stunned to witness the breakdown of the Mars One mission live on television. Since then, the *Argo* has maintained a state of silence and no images of the crew or the ship have been received.

In an unprecedented move, NASA and the European Space Agency have struck an agreement with the Kazakh government to take over the facilities where Mars One is based, along with management of the mission. Criminal investigations into Mars One and the production company that funded it, Valdivian, are well under way and are beginning to expose not only how financial pressures and mismanagement led to the tragic events aboard the *Argo*, but how an allegedly state-sponsored hacker may have sabotaged the ship's code, leading some to question whether this doomed privatized mission is now part of a much wider geopolitical struggle for the control of space and the future of our species.

Speculation Over Mars Landing

The *Argo* was just 70 days into its 180-day voyage when the crisis unfolded aboard. While communications have not been forthcoming, flight controllers at the mission centre in Baikonur maintain that the life-support systems within the *Argo* are fully functioning and 'are being utilized'. Reports suggest that Baikonur has sent detailed instructions as to how to change the course of the *Argo* to bypass Mars and return to Earth in just over 6 months' time. However, there has been no indication that the crew are following these procedures. This has led to a vast amount of speculation as to what might happen if the crew decide to proceed with the mission objective to land on Mars, as was originally planned, on June 17 this year.

An Independent Colony?
As experts attempt to predict and pre-empt the *Argo* crew's actions, many in legal and political circles are beginning to question what – if the landing is successful – a silent Mars colony might mean and how they might survive in the long-term. 'No one knows,' explains John Postle, a specialist in space policy and law at London School of Economics. 'Technically, they would be a rogue, independent colony. They would be free to do as they like, and that would include seeking logistical support from whomever they choose, whether that be private companies or space-faring nations.'

Political Conflict and Mass Protests
Here on Earth, the tragedy has reignited a long-running debate about whether time and finances should be spent on high-risk space exploration projects such as Mars One, with the ultimate hope of making it humanity's next home planet, or whether these precious resources should instead be utilized in fighting ecological disaster here on Earth. Greenpeace, Friends of the Earth, and many other global environmental organizations have been organizing mass protests against NASA and the European Space Agency's escalating involvement in the Mars One mission, with coordinated marches planned across eleven capital cities next week. However, a major player in the environmental activism movement, the organization known as Terra Revolution, has also come under fire after a mission specialist on the *Argo*, Sébastien Brun, self-identified as a member of the

extremist ecoterrorist group during the dramatic events on March 29. Terra Revolution have since stated that while Brun was a former member of their organization, they lost contact with him one month before the mission's launch and have joined the widespread speculation that other 'malignant and powerful forces' are responsible.

The political fallout of the Mars One disaster is also being strongly felt across the globe. Following accusations of state-backed hacking and espionage, the People's Republic of China have denied any knowledge of or connection to the events surrounding the *Argo*'s failure and, just two days ago, made the shock announcement that they will be withdrawing from the Outer Space Treaty. A multilateral agreement that forms the basis of space law, the treaty maintains space as a neutral entity, banning nations from claiming sovereignty on celestial bodies and using them for military purposes. With China crashing out of the agreement, and tensions fraught between those still bound by it, some fear that a second space race may soon be upon us, with the likes of China, Russia, and the USA battling to control any future off-world colonies, including Mars One.

What Next?
As the weeks pass, the whole world – and especially the families of the remaining *Argo* crew members – will be waiting to see whether these five men and women will become the first to attempt to land on another planet, or whether they will choose to return to an even more complicated and troubled world than the one they left behind, all those months ago.

For more updates and information on the ongoing Mars One Crisis and legal cases, click here to see our live feed.

THREE WEEKS LATER

THE GRAVE IS TINY, INSIGNIFICANT IN SUCH A VAST LANDscape, in comparison to structures of epic proportions, reaching up to an infinite universe.

But it matters.

It matters to them.

Kai finishes shovelling the final mound of dirt, sweating in the light of the dying sun. He steps back, satisfied.

Jia places a single rose on the freshly turned earth, its delicate petals softly undulating in the desert breeze. Tears slip down her cheeks as her brother puts his arm around her.

'You know, for someone who always used to say how much she hated my cat,' Kai says softly, 'you seem awfully upset.'

'He wasn't your cat,' Jia sniffs, resting her head on Kai's shoulder. 'He was ours.'

The two of them stand arm in arm in the shadow of Gagarin's Start, the memorial to one of the greatest achievements in human spaceflight, and now also a resting place for one of its most unexpected heroes.

The sound of a car engine interrupts the silence, and the two siblings turn to see a pickup truck approaching fast across the Kazakh steppe. It pulls up a respectful distance away, and the doors open. The driver unfolds a wheelchair and lowers himself down, while a woman helps another man out of the back, supporting him gently under the arm.

'You didn't have to come out here,' Jia calls, as the three of them draw near.

'We wanted to.' Jake smiles, propelling his wheelchair across the barren ground. He reaches Jia first and embraces her in a huge hug, before doing the same to Kai, who hesitates a moment before returning it.

'May we join you?' a voice croaks, and Jia turns to see Anders and Alyssa approaching. Anders looks frail, his head still bandaged. He's definitely in need of the extra support that Alyssa is providing, despite his walking stick.

'Of course,' Jia says.

He stands beside her and looks down at the grave, then looks up at Gagarin's Start.

'Very fitting,' he says.

'Thank you,' Jia replies, and links her arm in his.

Alyssa wordlessly places a bag down beside them and pulls out a small metal plaque on a stake.

'I hope you don't mind,' she says, moving to the head of the grave and pushing the stake into the hard ground. 'But we had this made.'

She takes a step back and all five of them take a moment.

IN MEMORY OF ORION
LOYAL COMPANION

'That's very kind,' Kai says, his voice cracking.

Alyssa reaches back down to her bag and produces another plaque, and a small silk bag.

'May I put something next to him?' she asks.

Jia and Kai nod. Alyssa uses the second stake to burrow out a small hole in the ground. Out of the silk bag, she pulls out a small, gold badge, shaped like wings. She pauses for a moment, allowing enough time for the rest of the group to see the United States Air Force astronaut's badge.

'My dad pulled some strings and got this sent over, in her honour,' Alyssa says solemnly.

Jake smiles. 'It's beautiful, Lyss.'

He squeezes Alyssa's arm as she places the badge back in the bag and rests it delicately in the hole. With her bare hands, she scoops the earth back over it then installs the plaque above it, which simply reads: FOR ANA.

Anders sighs. 'Her father has commissioned a huge memorial, back in St Petersburg.'

'This would mean more to her,' says Alyssa. 'I know it would.'

'Abbey confessed, you know,' Anders says. 'He and Ana's father had an agreement. A place for Ana on the crew in exchange for her stirring up a bit of tension, to help with the ratings, and later on giving Mother Russia inside information on the new colony.'

'And what did Ana get out of it?' Alyssa asks.

'Money for her ailing mother's medical treatment.'

Alyssa huffs.

'She stopped responding to their requests,' Anders says, squinting into the distance. 'Abbey told us that after the stunt with the make-up, she refused to do anything that would jeopardize the crew.'

The wind blows some of the disturbed earth off the two mounds.

'What happened to Ana's mom?' Jia asks.

Anders shifts uncomfortably. 'She doesn't have much longer. Ana's father kept sending her updates, about her decline. Like he was saying it was her fault. But Ana still refused to play their game.'

Alyssa walks away, her hands over her ears. She can't bear to hear any more. She looks out to the Mars One launchpad, now dormant.

The silence is broken by the drone of a helicopter. The group watch as it approaches from the horizon, heading towards the Mars One campus.

Anders glances at his watch. 'I better get back.'

Jia looks up at him. 'Where are you going?'

'California.' Anders grimaces. 'There are some . . . charges . . . being made against me. It's time to face the music.' He looks up at the sky, towards the heavens. 'If they make it, it will have been worth it.'

Jia hugs him. 'Good luck.'

'You too.' Anders looks between Kai and Jia. 'Look after each other.'

'Come on, Lars,' Jake says. 'I'll drive you back.'

Alyssa goes to assist Anders, but he waves her off.

'I'm good, I'm good.'

Alyssa and Jake share a look. He smiles and nods to her, as if to say *go on*, then draws up beside Anders, who places his hand on Jake's shoulder as they make their slow way back to the truck.

Alyssa watches them a moment, then turns back to Jia and Kai. 'I'm sorry I haven't been around much,' she says, sheepish. 'With the fallout and the investigation, NASA wanted me on CAPCOM. Not that they're responding to me . . .'

'We totally understand,' Jia says.

Alyssa moves back towards the graves, her hands in her pockets. 'Gwynne said you're heading to the UK?' she says to the siblings.

'We have some distant family there and the government have offered us asylum. All of us.'

'Have you told her?' Kai nudges Jia, pride filling his face.

'Told me what?' Alyssa's head snaps up.

Jia rolls her eyes.

'Jia's been offered a place, at a London university,' Kai jumps in, grabbing Jia's shoulders and shaking her. 'To study International, Environmental and Space Law.'

Alyssa goggles. 'Seriously?'

Jia shrugs, bashful. 'I've seen a lot of stuff I can't ignore in the past four months. Might as well try and do something about it.'

Alyssa grins and Jia wonders if this is the first time she's smiled since that awful day.

'That's amazing,' Alyssa says. 'When you graduate, you should come back here.' She gestures towards the campus, then chokes out a bitter laugh. 'Hell knows we're going to need all the legal help we can get. Especially once they land.'

Jia cocks her head.

'You think they'll do it, then?'

'I think all this,' she says, waving her arms, 'has proven that we need to do everything we can to build a better world. Even if it isn't on Earth. And I think they'll agree with me.'

Alyssa looks back towards the pickup truck, where Jake and Anders are patiently waiting.

'What about Jake?' Jia asks.

'What about him?' Alyssa says, a little guarded. Jia levels a pointed look at her.

Alyssa rolls her eyes, but there's a hint of a smile on her face. 'He's staying here, too. There's a lot of handover for him to do with the NASA coders.' She raises her hand towards the truck, to signal she won't be long. 'Plus, he said he doesn't think he can leave me here by myself.'

'I'm glad you have each other.'

'I'm glad you have each other, too,' she replies, and they both smile. 'I better go. Anders has an extradition to catch. Keep in touch, yeah?'

Jia observes Alyssa, standing awkwardly on the Kazakh steppe. Her split lip is gone, the bruises have faded, she's even lost the support boot for her leg. She's healed . . . almost.

Jia surges towards Alyssa and throws her arms around her. Alyssa stiffens in surprise at first, but after a moment, she too wraps her arms around Jia and rests her head on hers.

'Thank you,' Alyssa says, the sincerity of her words resonating through every part of her. 'To you, your brother, your cat. Thank you.'

Once again, tears fill Jia's eyes.

'And you,' she says into Alyssa's chest. 'They'll answer you, you know,' Jia says softly, pulling back. 'They just need time.'

Alyssa wipes her eye.

'Yeah,' she sniffs, then takes a deep breath. 'Kai.' She nods in farewell.

'See you, Lyss.' Kai waves.

Alyssa gives him a sharp look, and he laughs. Only one person can get away with calling her that.

With a final look down at Ana and Orion's memorials, Alyssa turns and heads back towards the truck.

Jia and Kai watch as the doors slam and the wheels kick up the dusty steppe, until the truck is just a speck lost to the desert.

Jia's new phone pings, and she glances down. Relief washes over her face.

'They've landed,' she tells Kai.

'Great.'

'They're being escorted to fill out the paperwork.'

But Kai has turned back to the plaques, his face dark.

Jia drops her phone to her side and reaches for him. 'We'll get Agnes out of there, too. I promise.'

Kai lets out a sigh and places his hand on top of Jia's. 'I hope so.'

'Let's head back, then,' Jia says, gently turning him towards the campus.

Her phone rings and her eyes widen at the name on the screen. She fumbles to answer it.

'Erica?'

Kai smirks.

'Thank God. How is she? . . . That's great. Yes, he's here now. Hold on.' Jia lowers the phone.

'It's Mom. Erica says she's asking for you.'

Kai freezes.

'You ready?' Jia asks softly, kindly.

He looks at his sister and seems to draw strength from her.

'Yeah,' he says. 'Yeah, sure.'

He takes the phone.

'Ma?'

And the two of them walk on, across the vast steppe, the wind kicking the dust up around them as the sky reveals the very first evening stars, and a tiny red planet just peeking over the horizon.

Acknowledgements

THIS BOOK, JUST LIKE ANY SPACE MISSION, WOULD NOT exist if it weren't for the hard work and support of many people. So, let's begin with mission control. First thanks go to my agent, Sam Copeland, who took a punt on an overly ambitious book and a wide-eyed new writer. I hate to admit it, but you were right about everything. Speaking of essential people, I also have to thank Will Peterson, my TV agent. Thank you for not rolling your eyes when I said I'd written a novel and for becoming my first champion. But no spacecraft would launch or function without a flight director and I have been gifted with the best one in my editor, Thorne Ryan. I have never known someone so dedicated and brilliant at what they do, and I am honoured that you took me, and this novel, under your wing. We wouldn't have survived without you. Further thanks are also due to the entire team at Transworld – including the lovely Finn Cotton, my CAPCOM – as well as my international publishers Heyne and Longanesi. You all truly made *Mars One* fly.

Next, I'd like to thank the engineers, aka my proto-readers. Thank you to the first: Phoebe Okeowo. Your insights and encouragement kept me going in those early days. And to the friends who followed: John Rawkins, Joe Postle, David Hoy, Kris Richer, Harriet Lynch, Kate Lewis – you read A LOT of words and asked all the right questions. To Jeremy Webb – the ultimate science advisor – thank you for attempting to correct my A-Level Physics.

Any errors in here are completely mine. Thanks also to Kristie Ko and Paula Hämäläinen, who provided some well-needed cultural advice. Speaking of advisors, a special mention must be made to all my cats: Merry, Pippin and the late Angelos, who provided me with great insight into the life of Orion.

But despite all the technical expertise, every astronaut also needs emotional support: people to talk to when you're out in the dark vacuum of space, searching for meaning. So, to all my friends both at home and at work, who kept me (relatively) sane and inspired me – you know who you are – thank you from the bottom of my heart. And a special thank you to the Kindred family. You welcomed me into your world and constantly remind me how wonderful a place it is.

Of course, this book, nor I, wouldn't have existed without my parents. Thank you to my mum and dad, who always encouraged me to pursue my dreams, including this one. I'm gutted that my dad couldn't be here to witness this, but I know this would have blown his mind. And to my beautiful mum: your love and strength empowers me every day. I probably don't say it enough, but I love you.

And nearly last, but by no means least, I have to thank my husband, who has been with me every step of the way. James: your kindness, your patience, and your love knows no bounds. I am so blessed to have you as a partner, and as a best friend. This book is yours.

And finally, a mission would not be complete without my fellow astronauts: that's you, the readers. Thank you for putting your faith in *Mars One*. In this crazy world, that's becoming more complex by the minute, it means so much that you took the time to go on this journey with me. I hope you enjoyed the ride as much as I did. Who knows where we're all headed . . . but the most important thing is that we care for each other, and this beautiful planet we call home.

About the Author

Charlotte Robinson is a writer and television producer. After graduating from Exeter University with a degree in English, Charlotte started working as a runner in the television industry, before becoming a script editor and story producer on multiple shows including Amazon Prime's adaptation of Naomi Alderman's best-selling novel *The Power*. More recently, Charlotte has started working as a producer for broadcasters such as Sky and Disney+. Her latest role will be series producer on David Nicholls' upcoming adaption of *The Secret Diary of Adrian Mole Aged 13¾* for BBC One.

When she is not producing or working on her own writing, Charlotte is found devouring novels, or playing darts with a pint in hand. She lives in her home county of Essex with her husband, two cats – Merry and Pippin – and Dolly the bearded collie.